DESTINED FOR
TROUBLE

DESTINED FOR TROUBLE

A Jules Cannon Mystery

CLAUDIA LEFEVE

THOMAS & MERCER

Published by Thomas & Mercer, Seattle

www.apub.com

Amazon, the Amazon logo, and Thomas & Mercer are trademarks of Amazon.com, Inc., or its affiliates.

ISBN-13: 9781477829837
ISBN-10: 1477829830

Cover design by David Drummond

Printed in the United States of America

For my husband

CHAPTER ONE

I'm pretty sure it came out more like a choked squawk, but in my mind, it was a bloodcurdling scream—like the kind you'd hear in some bad B-rated horror movie.

There, between the wooden fence and the air-conditioning unit, lay Mr. Boyette.

Having been employed with the Federal Bureau of Investigation for the last five years, I'd seen my fair share of crime scene photos. No one had to tell me what had happened.

Harvey Boyette was dead.

But first, let me backtrack. This was neither the beginning nor the end of my story.

It all started the day my folks threw me a welcome-home party in the sweltering midsummer Texas heat. The entire island of Trouble was invited.

I'd spent the last hour fixing up the backyard and arranging patio furniture in order to accommodate the overwhelming guest list. I could already feel the tingling sensation of the sun's heat on my shoulders and the first drops of perspiration on my forehead. Even in June, the sun could turn your first layer of skin into a burnt crisp by eleven in the morning. My once perpetually tanned complexion—courtesy of years of island living—had since turned pale after being hidden under business suits and sitting under bad fluorescent office lighting. I rarely, if ever, saw the sun during my time living in Virginia.

So here's a tip: when you're running from the law, don't forget your sunscreen.

OK, I wasn't necessarily running from the law. Just one particular member of law enforcement's finest. When your FBI agent boyfriend of two years dumps you, and you find yourself surrounded by his presence twenty-four-seven because you both work for the same agency, the only thing a girl can do is head for the hills.

Or, in my case, the dunes on Trouble Island.

Ten years after flying the coop, I still considered the quiet island town of Trouble home. Which was exactly why I decided to take a long, overdue vacation from the bureau—using up almost all of my two months' saved vacation time in the process.

I used to visit my family often when I was away at college; then I moved out of state for graduate school, and my visits trickled to the occasional obligatory holiday visit. After that, I focused on building my career as a crime analyst and got lost in my relationship with James. My visits had become almost nonexistent. I hadn't been home in almost five years.

Someone (I forget who) once said, "You can't go home again," but in my case, I actually could. It's an age-old adage, but it's no more of a cliché than the "It's not you, it's me" speech I heard when my ex-boyfriend stopped by to pick up his belongings at my apartment a week after dumping me.

If you want to get technical, I guess this is really the point where my story begins and why I ended up in Trouble.

"I heard you're taking some time off," James said when he arrived at my doorstep, duffel bag in hand. The bag was empty, which meant he was picking up, not dropping off.

I shouldn't have been too surprised that the news of my sudden request for time off had already reached James. Even a stiff, conservative working environment like the bureau was a breeding ground for gossip. "Good news travels fast," I said, reluctantly opening the door for him.

James was so nonchalant upon entering the apartment; he was lucky I hadn't answered the door with the spare Bureau-issued Glock he kept over at my place. I made a mental note not to remind him I still had it.

His face pinched up, as if he were trying to find the right words to say to me. Not that there was anything he could say at this point to placate me. "Don't be that way, Jules. I still want us to be friends. We still have to work together, you know. I don't want any hard feelings between us."

After two years of dating and hints of marriage, I was—with good reason—offended by his attitude over the whole affair. We'd pretty much lived together, for crying out loud.

I held my hand to his face like a shield to prevent me from hearing any more of his crap. If he said anything more insulting, I really would use his gun. "Don't go there, James. Just get your things, and get out."

He sighed. "Look, I'm sorry about the way things ended, but you know how it is. It just wasn't going to work out between us. It's the job," he said, as if it explained everything. "It's better that we ended things now before someone really got hurt, don't you think?"

The more excuses he gave, the angrier I got.

Was he actually serious? We'd only been separated a week. Definitely not enough time for me to get over our breakup. He'd taken me to my favorite restaurant, under the guise of celebrating a major case he'd closed, only to blindside me by announcing he wanted to end our relationship. And to top it all off, he did it in between dessert (forever ruining crème brûlée for me) and grabbing the check. What a jerk.

The job. It was a bullshit excuse, and we both knew it. *I work for the bureau, too,* I wanted to remind him. Now, had he used the line on some other poor, unsuspecting female, I'm sure she would have believed him hook, line, and sinker. But I knew better. There were plenty of FBI agents that managed to maintain long-term relationships that included marriage, kids, a white picket fence, and the requisite Volvo.

"Don't worry, I'll be out of your hair for the next two months," I said. "Guess that works out peachy for you. Out of sight, out of mind."

James shoved the last of his personal belongings into his bag. "It's not that I don't want to be with you. I just don't think I can be with anyone right now."

A likely story. After years of working in a male-dominated field, I was able to translate what he really meant: it's not you, it's me.

I pressed my finger gently on my shoulder, feeling the heat radiate off my skin like a hot skillet. Whatever possessed me to come back to a place that could only be described as having yearlong blistering heat was beyond me. But I already knew the answer to that one—I had nowhere else to run.

The island itself was nestled in the northern portion of the Gulf of Mexico, a little over an hour's drive from Houston and about an hour from the Louisiana state line in the opposite direction. Due to its close proximity to both Texas and Louisiana, the island's original settlers couldn't decide which state would ultimately keep the land. In the end, Texas won ownership of the small coastal island. According to local lore, one of the original founders said the island was "nothing but trouble." It was, and the name stuck.

There were still a few descendants of the Louisiana settlers residing on Trouble Island, and after all this time they still hadn't let go of their claim to the land.

I wiped the beads of perspiration that trickled off my forehead with the back of my hand. Once again, I cursed myself for choosing the hottest time of the year for my little sabbatical. No, I take that back. I cursed both James and the blistering sun as I helped my mom finish decorating the backyard for the shindig that would be held in my honor later that afternoon.

The backyard picnic tables were already draped with linens in a red checkered pattern—not the plastic recyclable kind, mind you, but real 100 percent cotton. Never mind that they would ultimately be drenched in crab juice and heaven only knows what else by the end of the evening, Mom insisted on using real tablecloths as opposed to the cheap plastic or vinyl ones you could purchase at the supermarket for under two bucks.

I was somewhat embarrassed at having a welcome-home party thrown for me, but my mom had insisted. "What would people think if we didn't welcome you home properly?" she had inquired when I told her that a party was unnecessary. Only I knew better. It had nothing to do with welcoming me home but more to do with keeping up appearances. The party was her attempt to camouflage any displeasure on her part. In her mind, if my folks threw me a party, they were announcing to everyone that everything was just hunky-dory and that they were happy to have me home for the summer—though my mom was anything but. She wasn't thrilled with the idea of me taking the entire summer off, even if it meant spending time with my family.

So I continued to help Mom prepare the side dishes, played along with the charade, and didn't ask too many questions. I didn't even bother to ask who was on the guest list. But knowing my parents, the entire island of Trouble would be crammed into their backyard, which boasted a full Gulf Coast view.

As I continued to stew about my breakup with James, I added another heavy dollop of mayonnaise to the potato salad in an attempt to get it to the right consistency. Mom would simply be beside herself if I didn't get it just right. It wasn't even worth bringing up that with all the free beer they were serving, no one would remember the potato salad.

For the occasion, I went with one of my best Lilly Pulitzer shifts, knowing my aunt Lula would approve of my choice in attire, even if my skin was too pasty at the moment to do it any justice. It was one of the few things I shared with my aunt—a penchant for brightly colored clothes. It was an obsession I had reluctantly given up when I began working for the FBI. Black, navy, and slate—the unofficial colors of the largest federal law enforcement agency, in case you didn't already know—just weren't my colors. But now that I was back on the island, I'd reclaimed my old island wardrobe. You could take the girl out of the beach, but you couldn't take the sand out of her hair.

Speaking of Aunt Lula, I wondered if Mom remembered to invite her.

There was no love lost between Aunt Lula and my mom. If you asked my mom, my aunt Lula never did anything without a hidden agenda. Personally, I think my aunt did half of what she did just to spite my mom.

Satisfied with the potato salad and coleslaw—the only dishes Mom allowed me to prepare—I headed outside to greet our guests.

CHAPTER TWO

An hour later, the party was in full swing, and I still had yet to lay eyes on Aunt Lula. She was either late or hadn't been invited. Knowing both my mom and aunt, I wouldn't have been surprised either way. In the meantime, I did my best to keep up with the local island gossip and the obligatory small talk one had to endure during these types of gatherings. There were only so many times I could say to inquiring minds, "I'm just here for the summer," you know?

Just when I thought I had exchanged enough pleasantries with the entire town, offering one lame excuse after another as to why I was back in town, a familiar voice called out from behind me. "I was told the party was for you, but I didn't actually believe it till I saw it with my very own eyes."

I'd recognize that voice anywhere. It was Abby Lee, my best friend from high school. She yanked me out of my seat—literally—and embraced me in a hug.

"You haven't been around these parts in a good while," she said, obviously pleased I was home.

"Abby Lee! I didn't know you'd be here," I said, hugging her back. *Of course I didn't know*, I chided myself. I hadn't been in Trouble in ages and had been a piss-poor friend in the process. Hell, I hadn't even known she was still living here after all these years. I instantly felt guilty for not staying in touch over the years, but not enough to dampen the moment.

Bubbly, bright Abby Lee was the captain of the cheerleading team to my role as captain of the debate team. Her bright blond locks—bleached from years in the island sun—contrasted against my dull chestnut hair. She was short and curvy, whereas I was tall and lanky at almost five nine. Abby Lee always spotted the silver lining, while I only saw dark, stormy clouds. In any other world our personalities would have clashed, but here in Trouble, opposites made for the oddest pair of friends.

We had lost touch after I graduated college, went on to graduate school, and then ultimately moved to the suburbs of Virginia to start my career with the FBI in DC. A few visits home here and there during the summer weren't sufficient to sustain a childhood friendship, although most of it could be attributed to my lack of trying. But it was a friendship I had missed dearly. It was hard making friends when I spent most of my free time commuting to and from work.

"Your folks are obviously happy to have you back home," she said, finally releasing me from her grip. "This is quite a shindig."

"That it is," I said, neglecting to mention that my mom almost had herself a small coronary when I told her I was spending the next two months at home.

I could still hear the protests ringing in my ear from when I'd told her I was coming down for the summer. "You don't just take two months off from your job," Mom had insisted. "What if they give your job to someone else?"

Even after several failed attempts to convince my mother that they couldn't fire me, she was still wary about my taking vacation time. No matter how hard I tried to explain it to her, even when I told her it was time off with pay, she couldn't grasp the concept of accrued leave.

"How's your mom?" I asked, turning the tables. Abby Lee's mother had been diagnosed with cancer when Abby Lee was a junior in college. She had quit school and moved back to Trouble in order to take care of her. From what little tidbits of information I'd managed to gather over the years, her mother was doing better.

That was seven years ago. Abby Lee never went back to finish school, even after her mother went into remission. I don't know why I had foolishly assumed she'd moved off the island once her mother was better.

"Oh, she's doing fine, thanks for askin'," she said. "How long do we have you for?"

"I'll be here for the summer," I said.

Abby Lee grinned and clapped her hands in excitement. "Plenty of time to get all caught up. And your timing couldn't have been better," she said.

"Why's that?"

She shot me a wicked smile. I may have been absent for the last five years or so, but I knew that smile all too well—I wasn't going to like what she was about to say. "It's our ten-year reunion! Didn't you get the invite?"

What? My instincts were right—I didn't like what she had to say. Suddenly I felt old. Ten years had whizzed right by me, and I had hardly noticed. Where had the time gone?

I lied and shook my head. I distinctly remembered receiving something in the mail a few months ago with the school's return address. I'd thrown it out without even looking at it. I'd just assumed the school was asking for donations. "It must have gotten lost in the mail," I lied.

"No worries. Now that you're here, there's no excuse for you not to go. We can go together."

Did I really want to attend my ten-year high school reunion? "I guess it would look weird if I didn't, especially since everyone knows I'm in town," I finally said, silently cursing my folks for hosting my welcome-home bash. I wondered why Mom didn't mention the reunion. She's usually on top of things like social engagements. Plus, she would have insisted I attend. In her book, everything boiled down to appearances.

"Once you've settled in, we have to get together before the reunion," Abby Lee said. "I want to catch up before everyone vies for your attention."

"Oh, I don't know about that," I said, shrugging off her comment. She seemed to have forgotten she was one of the few friends I had back in school. I knew for a fact no one would care about me one way or another, even if I did have what some might consider a badass job. Unfortunately, most folks were only acquainted with the FBI as portrayed in television or movies, not the real agency, complete with its never-ending bureaucratic roll of red tape. In short, it wasn't as glamorous as fiction made it out to be.

Abby Lee could sense my hesitation. "Aren't you dying to know how everyone turned out?"

I smiled for the first time since I arrived back in Trouble, grateful Abby Lee had come to my party. Maybe it hadn't been such a bad idea after all. "I'll be there," I said. I wasn't so sure about the high school reunion, but I was happy to reunite with my oldest and dearest friend.

Just as I was promising Abby Lee we would catch up later, I froze. The fried catfish I had consumed earlier began to churn in my stomach at the sight of him. I knew I couldn't avoid him, Trouble being such a small island and all, but I had at least hoped it would be a few more days before I crossed paths with Deputy Chief Harper. I honestly didn't expect him to be here.

You could just add him to the short list of law enforcement professionals I wanted to run away from.

But there he was, standing right beside Daddy near the keg line, looking fine in a pair of crisp, pristine khakis and a white polo shirt. It was what the locals liked to call the unofficial uniform of the Trouble Island Police Department. He was making small talk with some of the guests who had lined up to pump more beer into their empty red Solo cups—it was the only concession my mom made in regard to disposable tableware.

With the short distance between me and the keg line, our past seemed like it was only yesterday. I watched with curiosity as I thought of what might have been had we stayed together. Of course, I knew I was simply suffering from posttraumatic breakup disorder, but I couldn't help myself.

Simply put, Justin Harper was the guy who got away.

We dated our junior and senior years of high school and ultimately went our separate ways when we went to college. Justin had gotten a scholarship to Sam Houston State, while I headed off to TCU. Justin pleaded with me to go to Sam Houston with him, with the idea that we'd graduate, get married, and return to Trouble to start a family. But at eighteen, I didn't want to be the kind of woman who settled down with her high school sweetheart. I wanted to see the world, live in the big city, and not be saddled with babies at twentysomething.

So far, I was two for three—I still hadn't seen the world.

Father Time was definitely Justin's friend. He looked just as good, if not better, as he had back in high school. The Texas Board of Tourism should consider placing him on their ad campaigns. The man was a walking advertisement of the Lone Star State's rugged good looks that women from other states could only dream of.

I had hoped he wouldn't spot me, but he did, just as I was about to head back into the house to hide. Call me chicken, but I wasn't ready to face the past. Though I was kidding myself thinking I could get away without seeing him. This was a party held in my honor—of course he was going to make an effort to stop by and say hello.

And just as I was making up my mind whether to stay put or go indoors, Justin made his way over to where I was gawking from afar.

"Jules," he slowly drawled.

Damn. Had his voice always been this sexy? I shook the notion right out of my head. This was my ex—from ten years ago, I reminded myself. I gave him another once-over and almost kicked myself for being a foolish teen back then. Almost. Obviously, he'd kept his end of the bargain and moved back to the island after graduating college. But did I really want that kind of life for myself? I was happy living in the DC metro area. How great of a catch could he actually be if he was still living in Trouble?

As I tried to talk myself out of the coulda-shoulda-woulda blues, I reminded myself that he was the one with a career, albeit in a small town, while I was currently running away from the big, bad city, licking my wounds after being dumped. If anyone was keeping score, he was ahead by a mile.

"Long time," he said when I didn't respond to his initial greeting.

"You still seeing Heather?" I didn't waste any time. I couldn't help myself—inquiring minds want to know. According to Mom, Heather Clegg leeched herself onto Justin right after he moved back to Trouble and joined the force. She'd been after him ever since high school, following him around everywhere he went, even when he and I were an item. The girl had no shame.

The smile didn't reach his eyes. "No. Didn't really work out between us."

"I see," I said. "The way I heard it, it sounded like you two were destined for marriage."

He laughed, showing off his bright pearly whites. "You of all people know how the gossip mill works around here. Half of what you hear is false. The other half are all lies." Despite laughing at his own joke, it was obviously a touchy subject, so he steered the conversation back to me. "So what brings you back? The way I heard it, you're in town for a couple of months. Things not working out with the feds?"

I ignored the jab. Local cops didn't like the feds and vice versa. I got it. Though I couldn't shake the feeling there was a double meaning behind his words. As if he knew the real reason I came back—to mend a broken heart. But I wasn't going to give him the satisfaction. I stuck with the same story I gave everyone else that inquired. "Just taking a much-needed vacation."

"I see," he said, not entirely convinced. "You know about the reunion, right?"

"So I heard," I said. "Are you going?"

"How could I not?"

Of course he'd be there. He was the town's star football player. The crown jewel of Trouble Island. Yes, even an island town the size of a crumb on a map had a football team—it would have been a sacrilege not to, living in a state entirely devoted to the sport.

"It'll be interesting, that's for sure," I said, wondering how well the others in our class had fared.

A throat cleared next to us. It was one of those forced guttural sounds—the kind that lets you know someone is intentionally trying to get your attention.

"Well, if it isn't Jules Cannon."

With the amount of contempt and venom in her voice, you'd think I had crashed her party.

"Hey, Heather," I said, turning slightly to face the devil herself. Now, my mom was the kind of woman that would be sneaky enough to invite my former high school sweetheart, but I knew she wouldn't have invited Heather.

"Heather," Justin said, equally surprised to see her. It wasn't hard to spot the tension in his eyes as he addressed her. Something told me their relationship didn't end on a good note.

"You two look awfully chummy. Just like old times, right?" She played every bit the part of the scorned woman, and I could tell she was doing her best not to claw my eyes out. What gives? By Justin's own admission, they weren't seeing each other anymore. I chalked it up to simple jealousy.

"Uh, thanks for stopping by—I think," I said, muttering the last part.

Justin laughed at my poor attempt to break the tension. "Now if you two ladies will excuse me, I have to head back to the station." I could be wrong, but it was as if he were doing his best to deliberately avoid Heather. Not that I blamed him. "Good to see you again, Jules—welcome home," he said to me as he made a beeline toward the side entrance of the backyard.

Heather gave me the once-over, similar to the one I'd given Justin a few moments before. Only, she didn't seem to approve of what she saw. "Are you sick or something? You look a bit pale," she said, noting my lack of color.

Knowing I hadn't seen the island sun in a good while, I wasn't going to allow her to make me feel bad about my appearance, so I ignored the comment. "Glad you could make the party, Heather," I said. "Although I have to say, I didn't know you were invited."

CHAPTER THREE

"Now, tell me the real reason you came back to Trouble." No one could pull the wool over on Aunt Lula.

I turned to face my favorite aunt. Seemed she'd been invited after all. Or maybe she was a party crasher. Either way, I was happy she made it—even if she was two hours late. I truly believe she was the inspiration behind the concept of being "fashionably late." She'd arrived well after the other guests, donned in all white—for a backyard fish fry. I stifled a giggle thinking she'd somehow gotten lost along the way, intending to be at an all-white Labor Day soirée in the Hamptons, not a get-together in my parents' backyard. Her platinum-blond bob was tucked behind her ears, showcasing pearl earrings the size of Whoppers.

If I was the prodigal daughter, then Aunt Lula was the black sheep of the family. Although for the life of me, I still couldn't understand the wedge between my mom and my aunt. She was my great-aunt actually, my maw-maw's sister. Once upon a time, the Bolling daughters, Lula and Marie, were considered the crème de la crème of Beaumont society and, by extension, Trouble Island. If the island had a royal court, Aunt Lula would be its reigning queen. And while our island wasn't nearly as Southern as, let's say, Charlotte or Savannah, my aunt Lula played the part of an aging Southern belle in a manner worthy of an Academy Award. She spent her time much like the rest of the silver-haired women in the antebellum South: playing bridge, going to church, spending one too many cocktail hours on the front porch, and provoking family members for sport.

Aunt Lula set her untouched plate down on the patio table and got straight to business. She posed the same question, only in a different way—just in case I hadn't heard her the first time. "Tell me why you left Virginia? Your mother didn't get into any of the details when she said you decided to move back home."

Leave it to Mom to fail to mention the finer points of my return. Although in this instance I couldn't blame her entirely. I surely didn't want her blabbing about the real reason I left, and frankly, I didn't want to rehash the details of my failed relationship with James. "It's good to see you, too, Aunt Lula," I said, embracing her in a hug before I explained myself. "And just so you know, I didn't leave Virginia. I was in need of a long vacation is all."

"Hogwash." She took a sip of her bloody mary.

Wait—where in the world did she find herself a bloody mary? We were only serving beer and wine as far as I knew, though I knew my dad had a few bottles of whiskey stashed around some-where. Then I remembered that Aunt Lula liked to travel with her own booze. And only my aunt would be brave enough to drink a bloody mary while wearing all white. If it had been me, I would've already looked like a gunshot victim.

"You have such a great job with the FBI," she went on. "Why are you taking a leave of absence? You're only twenty-eight years old. You're way too young to be burnt out already."

I chewed the inside of my cheek. Her statement wasn't too far off the mark. I loved my job as a crime analyst, and I cried when I packed for my two-month hiatus, knowing I would miss it. OK, maybe that was a bit of a stretch. Truth is, I cried because I felt like such a failure, running away the second things got rough.

And while I loved my job, I hated my supervisor. I know, who doesn't hate their immediate boss, right? But in my case it was justified. For example, I was an extremely organized person, teetering on the brink of obsessiveness (I'm always making to-do lists, reminders to myself, etc.), while my supervisor, Wendy, was a disorganized mess, always misplacing my files, blaming me for never turning them in—as if. Personally, I think she did it on purpose to sabotage my career. Plus, ever since she went on Weight Watchers and lost thirty pounds, she'd been a bigger bitch than usual. You'd think she'd be happy losing all that weight. I didn't know how much more I could take of watching her count jelly beans and calories while I did all the legwork. We'd already had one crime analyst transfer to another field office and lost two interns, all because the damn woman didn't eat.

So coming home was kind of a mixed blessing—I could escape the humiliation of any postbreakup gossip, as well as Weight Watcher Wendy.

"I was homesick, that's all," I finally said and left it at that. It wasn't much of an explanation, but it wasn't exactly a lie. I did miss home. Trouble Island was like no other place in Texas—or Louisiana for that matter, depending on which island descendant you bothered to ask.

Explaining any more on the matter was useless on my part, as my aunt questioned the sense of urgency in my need for a sabbatical. "I see. Well, now that you're home, I think it would be nice to have some brunch and catch up. And . . . ," Aunt Lula drawled a little longer than necessary, "I thought maybe you could help me out with something."

And there it was.

As much as I wanted to ignore that last statement, my curiosity was piqued. I knew I would regret asking, just like I had when Abby Lee informed me about the reunion, but I asked anyway. "What exactly do you need help with?"

"One of my girls just up and quit unexpectedly yesterday," she said. "Since you're home for a few months, I thought you could be a dear and help out at the store."

"You want me to work at Palmetto Pink?" I hadn't intended for my voice to go an octave higher, but I was caught off guard. I'd only been in town one day, and already I was regretting my decision to come back to the island. The last thing I had in mind was working part-time for my aunt.

Palmetto Pink was a specialty store my aunt owned that carried high-end, chic resort wear. Think Palm Beach–resort type clothing. It was definitely a niche market, which suited her customers just fine—we lived on a coastal island, after all. Aunt Lula was very proud of her store, or, rather, proud to be able to call herself a business owner. After my great-uncle Jep passed away, she decided she needed something to occupy her time, so she bought the building and opened up shop. Even though she came from an era when women didn't work, much less own their own businesses, she decided that selling clothes and accessories to fashion-savvy women was an acceptable employment option for a woman of her social status.

"Just until I find a suitable replacement," Aunt Lula said hurriedly, knowing full well I was about to decline her offer.

I groaned at the prospect of working at her store. I came here to relax, work on my tan, and forget about my troubles for a while—not to spend my vacation helping customers pick the right beach ensemble.

Don't get me wrong; I loved wearing island apparel. I just didn't want to sell it.

Aunt Lula kept going on and on about the store, and I wasn't paying much attention, until I heard her say, "So it's settled then."

It was easy to lose track when Aunt Lula was talking a mile a minute. That was her MO—talk really fast until the other party lost track of the conversation and she got what she wanted.

"What's settled?" I asked.

"You'll work part-time for me at Palmetto Pink."

"What?"

"Isn't that what we've been discussing?"

Her gift of gab had lost me somewhere around the new summer collection, but I distinctly remembered not giving her a definitive answer on working at the store. As much as I hated to admit it, sometimes Mom was right.

"But I've never worked retail before," I began to protest.

"Nonsense," she said, waving her hand in the air as if my wants were irrelevant. "All you have to do is smile at the customers and ring them up. If they need assistance finding something, you help them."

My dear aunt Lula seemed to have forgotten one minor detail. "I'm horrible with people," I said. *Where did Daddy hide the whiskey*? I needed a shot right about now.

"You work for the FBI. Isn't it your mission to help folks? How could you hate working with people?" she asked. "You'll do just fine."

Just what exactly did I get myself into? There was just no winning with Aunt Lula once she had an idea in her head. But it didn't stop me from trying.

"I sit behind a desk and analyze intel. And I didn't say I hated working with people," I mumbled. It was simply a matter of not being a people person when it came to handing out service with a smile. It was my opinion that people became annoying when demanding assistance. Which was exactly why I never worked in food service, either.

With Aunt Lula considering the matter closed, we spent the rest of the party talking about everything I'd missed while I'd been gone, which I refer to as "the gossip according to Aunt Lula," purposely avoiding the issue I knew was on both our minds: I was going to be a horrible sales associate.

After I reluctantly promised Aunt Lula I would start work bright and early Monday morning, I politely excused myself to mingle with the other guests, hoping I could avoid committing myself to any more engagements, like high school reunions or summer retail jobs.

❀

Once the last of the guests had left, I brought up the subject of the reunion. "Mom, why didn't you say anything about my high school reunion?"

She looked at me with surprise. "Why, I thought you already knew."

"No. Abby Lee brought it up at the party. A little heads-up would've been nice." If I had known about the reunion, I would have packed nicer clothes before coming home. Nothing says success more than a killer wardrobe.

Mom frowned. "They mailed out the invitations. Plus, it was all up on that Friends Space site, I'm told. Aren't you linked on or chained in—whatever it is you kids say these days?"

"That's LinkedIn," I said. "And that's a different networking website." As much as my job required me to be on the Internet doing research, I hardly had time to check social media sites for my own personal enjoyment. It was kind of frowned upon at work. Unless, of course, it was for research on a case.

"If you want, I can go with you to pick out something suitable for the reunion," Mom offered. "There's still time." There was nothing you couldn't cure or disguise with a new dress or a tube of lipstick, according to her. In this instance I was sure she wanted to camouflage the fact that I was dumped and ran home to lick my wounds.

"That's OK. I'll pick up something at Palmetto Pink. Maybe I'll get a discount."

That stopped Mom cold in her tracks. Any mention of Aunt Lula or her store put her on high alert.

"Now why would you get a discount?"

Even though my aunt owned the place, it wasn't like she went around handing out family discounts. Aunt Lula always presented us with gifts from her store, sure, but she would never allow any of us to purchase anything at below retail. It would mess with her profit margins, she was fond of saying.

Damn. I still hadn't told her about working at Palmetto Pink. She was going to flip a lid for sure once I told her. "Uh, because I'll be working there for the summer," I finally said, waiting for the inevitable you-know-what to hit the fan.

"You're going to be doing what?" Mom exclaimed on cue, her arms suddenly stuck on pause from drying the last of the serving platters.

My dad, on the other hand, found it somewhat amusing. I swear the man only commented on things that he considered funny or downright ludicrous. "That's wonderful, Butter Bean. You could learn a lot from the old gal."

"Like what?" Mom echoed my sentiments exactly, her body back in motion as she resumed drying the platters, scrubbing them to the point I thought the intricate floral patterns would rub off. I, too, wondered what exactly I could learn from working retail.

He glared at the two of us. "Learning the value of a dollar for one thing. Seeing the inner workings of a business from the inside," he explained. Daddy made it sound as if I were twenty-one again and fresh out of college.

"She already has a job. A good one," Mom protested. She quickly turned her attention back to me. "One that I sincerely hope you go back to. Sooner rather than later." I avoided the glare in her eyes as she offered her two cents.

I almost laughed at her defense of my career. When I first started at the bureau five years ago, she'd cried for weeks, thinking

I was going to put myself in danger, despite my insistence that I was a civilian employee and sat behind a desk all day. For months she urged me to come home and forget about working for the FBI. Never mind that I lived in the burbs, a good fifteen-minute drive—if there was no traffic—from Washington, DC, just out of reach of what she considered to be the plight of the nation.

It wasn't like my mother and I were always at odds with each other. We just had very different viewpoints on the ways of the world. She was strictly old school, having grown up in Louisiana before marrying my dad and settling here in Trouble, while I, on the other hand, spent more than half my life living as a carefree island local. My poor father often served as the intermediary during many heated arguments over the years, but for the first time in years, Mom and I were on the same page—half the time we weren't even reading the same book.

"I tried to tell her I wasn't cut out for retail, but you know Aunt Lula . . . ," I said.

"I have half a mind to call her myself," Mom said.

Daddy sat there and listened to me and Mom agree that working at Palmetto Pink was a bad idea. "Both of you need to stop complaining long enough to look at the advantages of the situation," he finally said. "Jules needs to do something while she's here. She can't very well stay cooped up in the house the entire summer. And Lula obviously needs help, or she wouldn't have asked."

I felt like it was a bad time to mention my plans for getting a tan this summer, so I kept quiet. Nobody, not even Mom, could argue with Daddy's logic—at least not right away. Somehow she always managed to get her way with Daddy. Eventually, he'd come around to her way of thinking, but I was stuck for the time being. I sighed as I helped my mom put away the last of the serving pieces.

So thanks to the girl who unexpectedly quit and Daddy's infinite wisdom, it was beginning to look like I was stuck having to work at Palmetto Pink.

"It's going to storm," my dad said, looking out the window above the kitchen sink, breaking me from my thoughts. "I better make sure we brought everything inside."

I stopped him from getting up. He'd done enough already throughout the day, grilling and frying enough fish to feed the entire island. "Don't worry about it, Daddy. I'll go out back and see if we left anything important outside."

I did a quick sweep around the deck, looking for anything we might have left outside that we didn't want ruined during the storm, and checked for any items misplaced by our guests.

As I approached the side of the house, near the gated exit, I noticed a brightly colored object flapping against the Gulf wind behind the air-conditioning unit. Even with the massive cloud coverage from the impending storm, there was still enough light from the moon to see there was something wedged between the unit and the gate.

I walked closer to investigate further and screamed.

And that was when I found Harvey Boyette's body.

CHAPTER FOUR

To say my mother was beside herself upon learning a dead body was on her property was an understatement. She was beyond inconsolable—but not for the reasons one might think.

"What will the neighbors think?" Mom asked no one in particular. "No one will ever want to be entertained at our home again."

"Now, Livy dear, we don't know what happened," Daddy said, doing his best to calm his wife. "From the looks of it, it seems Harvey had himself a heart attack."

"I told you not to double fry the catfish," Mom chastised my dad. "Everyone will think all that fried, greasy food we served killed him!"

It was my turn to try to console her. "Take it easy, Mom. I don't think anyone's gonna blame the food for Harvey's death," I said. "It's probably like Daddy said, a heart attack. He owned a restaurant for Pete's sake."

Harvey's restaurant, The Poop Deck, was considered an institution on Trouble Island and everyone's favorite restaurant in town. Normally, a seafood menu is considered healthy, but half the items on the menu at The Poop Deck were either stuffed or fried. It was more akin to a crab shack than a fine-dining establishment, but he'd put his heart and soul into the place. He had even gone so far as to name his restaurant after the countless seagull droppings that gave the outside deck a permanently stained white-wash appearance.

Mom shot me a look that could have killed, which would have made me the second dead body of the evening, so I stayed quiet after that.

It seemed everything Daddy and I said only made my mom feel worse about the entire ordeal. She didn't even wait for the ambulance and cops to arrive before retiring to her room to tend to her migraine. Mom always fell victim to migraines when confronted with something unpleasant.

Justin arrived at the house shortly after the responding officers and EMT unit. I don't know why I was surprised to see Justin back at the house. He worked for the department; it was part of his job. Even if Harvey had dropped dead of a heart attack, police presence was standard protocol.

"We gotta stop meeting like this," he said, trying to lighten the mood.

I nodded. "Poor Harvey," I finally said. "We think it might have been a heart attack."

Justin scratched his chin in thought. "Possibly, though it's still too soon to tell."

"Maybe all the restaurant food finally did him in," I said. As soon as the words tumbled out of my mouth, I felt bad for talking about Harvey like that when he was still lying in our backyard.

"It's anyone's guess at this point," Justin said.

I stopped by The Poop Deck the next day, despite the recent tragedy. Even with Harvey's death, it was still business as usual at the restaurant. According to the town's gossip—arriving right on schedule, just before breakfast—the newly widowed Mrs. Boyette had insisted it stay open. "Harvey would have wanted it that way,"

she had said. As much as the town disliked Harvey's wife—again, according to town gossip—I'm pretty positive she was right on that count.

My eyes roamed for an available seat. I didn't want to sit in the main dining area, so I scouted for a seat at the bar, although the restaurant didn't have much of one. If you wanted a solid margarita, you had to go over to The Crooked Gator. But a nice glass of wine was just what the internal psychologist ordered. I also wanted to check in on Abby Lee, who worked at the restaurant. She couldn't have been taking the news of Harvey's death well. I hadn't even known she was working there until my mom mentioned it in passing the night of the party.

Abby Lee's grim smile upon seeing me stroll over to the bar only confirmed what I already knew. She was saddened by the loss of her friend and boss. "That didn't take long," she said, pretending to look at her watch. "I gave it at least another day before your parents got on your nerves and you found your way here."

I had only been in town two full days before seeking solace somewhere other than my parents' house. "That was being generous," I said. "How are you holding up?"

"As good as can be expected under the circumstances. I really loved ol' Harvey, ya know? I just can't believe he's gone. None of us can." Her face pinched up, as if she were about to cry, and I bet it wouldn't have been the first time since she heard the news.

My heart went out to her. Not only had she lost her boss, but quite possibly a good friend. I'd been gone a long time, but even I could tell, from her demeanor alone, just how much of an impact his death had on her.

"I'm so sorry," I said.

Abby Lee wiped a single tear that had rolled down her cheek, but feigned a smile to let me know she was OK. "So what'll it be?"

"Just a glass of house wine," I said. Maybe this hadn't been the best time to call on my friend, but since I was already here, I might as well have a drink.

"Coming right up." She pulled a bottle from behind the bar and poured me a generous glass of red. "How long do you have? I'm off in about thirty."

I took a sip of the house red and allowed it to linger. It wasn't great wine, but I wasn't picky. It cured what ailed me. "I've got time. Just come over when you're done with your shift," I said. "Hey, is that pecan pie I see Mrs. Wysong devouring over there?"

Her face brightened. The first genuine smile I'd seen on her face since I arrived. "Sure is. Just made it this afternoon."

"That pairs well with wine, right?" I asked, not caring in the least. I loved pecan pie just as much as I loved most desserts, crème brûlée notwithstanding.

Abby Lee chuckled. She knew I really didn't expect an answer to my question. "I'll go grab you a slice."

While I waited for my pie and for Abby Lee to get off her shift, I checked my phone for any important e-mails and texts from the office. Even though I was technically on vacation and wasn't supposed to respond to work e-mails, it still didn't stop people from trying to contact me—one of the downsides of working for the federal government.

As I perused the unopened e-mails, Abby Lee managed to slide a fresh piece of pie my way before heading back to attend to the customers seated in the main dining area. Out of the corner of my eye, I spotted Heather Clegg having dinner with her family. I internally groaned in annoyance. I had nothing against her family, but two Heather sightings in the span of two days was two too many. I didn't want a repeat confrontation with her, so I went back to my e-mails before she eventually caught me staring at their table.

My attempt to go unnoticed was in vain. "Well, look who it is," Heather said, walking up to where I was seated at the bar. She cast her eyes down at me hard enough to make me squirm. This was exactly why I was only a civilian employee with the FBI. I wasn't very good with confrontation. I liked to think of myself as the behind-the-scenes type; I wrote reports, made lists, and kept the agents organized, all things that were strictly task oriented.

"Nothing gets past you, does it, Heather?" I said. I didn't like her, and she clearly detested me, so why did she purposely go out of her way to make conversation? No, scratch that. I knew the answer to that one. Her sole purpose in life was to annoy me. Just like back in high school.

"Do you plan on seeing Justin while you're here?" Heather asked. "Because he's taken."

"Good for him." It wasn't worth the energy to explain the jig was up. Justin had already told me they were no longer an item, so she could cut the act. Or maybe she hadn't received the memo. I knew she was only trying to rile me up, but I wasn't biting. No sense getting into a jealousy match over someone I dated back in high school.

With limited options, since I was waiting for Abby Lee and couldn't very well leave, I had to figure out a way to get rid of Heather, and fast. "Hey, it's been great catching up, but I gotta run to the ladies," I finally said. In an attempt to ditch her for the second time in two days, I left a speechless Heather alone at the bar as I went to the bathroom to wait her out.

I waited a solid five minutes before heading back to my spot at the bar. I could have stayed in the bathroom an additional five minutes, but there was only so much primping I could do in a public restroom that boasted a small mirror situated much too low for my height and with only a tube of lip gloss in my purse.

After mentally counting to ten, I headed back to my seat. I breathed a sigh of relief as I slid back onto my stool and did a quick survey of the dining room. Heather and her parents had left the restaurant. Crisis averted for the time being. My gut told me I was going to be doing a lot of dodging over the next two months.

Still waiting for Abby Lee to clock out, I nursed my wine and went back to my unread e-mails. I responded to the few friends who wanted to make sure I was OK post breakup with James. I assured them in harried e-mails that I was fine, more than fine, in fact, better than fine—all lies, of course.

No sooner had I finished shooting off the last message than I glanced up to find Abby Lee sliding onto an empty bar stool next to me.

"That was fast," I said, glancing at my watch. I still had half a glass of wine. I'm no lush, but I generally drink faster than that. Had thirty minutes already gone by? I knew I hadn't spent that much time checking my e-mails and texts—I didn't have that many friends to get back to.

"There's only two tables left, and Pete said he'd cover for me and close up," she said. "Was that Heather I saw you talking to a second ago?"

Even the mention of Heather's name irked me. "Yeah. Seems she was peeved I was talking to Justin at my welcome-home bash yesterday."

Abby Lee's eyes got big. "You know, I wondered about that."

"What, Justin?"

"No, Heather. I saw her mingling at the party. Was she even invited?"

I shook my head. "Not even my mom is that polite. I think Heather knew Justin would be there, took a chance, and showed up. Guess she figured that while she wasn't officially on the guest list, with that many folks around no one would have the nerve to ask her to leave."

"You're probably right," she said. "So what about Justin? What did he say to you? Doesn't he look good?" Abby Lee didn't waste a second to let her slew of questions start flying. She knew all too well about our high school romance, having been placed on the back burner one too many times to count when he and I got hot and heavy. "But more importantly, what did she have to say when she saw y'all talking?"

"Not much. Justin ran off pretty quickly, and I excused myself and left her standing there. It was almost as if he couldn't wait to escape her."

"That sounds about par for the course. He's been dodging her the last couple of weeks." She laughed, then got serious. "That girl harasses just about anyone she thinks is making a move on Justin. I'd watch your back while you're here."

I didn't take Abby Lee's warning seriously. I mean, we were talking about Heather Clegg. As far as I was concerned, she was an inconvenience at best and an insignificant person in my life. The woman was hardly someone I would waste my time worrying about.

"When did they break up, anyway?" I asked. "She seems to think they're still an item."

Abby Lee flashed me a mischievous grin. "Trying to rekindle old flames while you're in town?"

"Of course not! That was ages ago," I said. "Call me curious."

"It's been off and on. After Justin came back from college, she staked her claim on him, but it didn't last long. Then they went out a few more times this past spring. I guess they decided to give it another go, but that didn't last long either. Justin seems to back off just as soon as they get together," she said. "But again, I'd watch out for her. She's like a vulture circling her prey."

I laughed at the imagery. If memory served, Heather was exactly that. A vulture. "Thanks for the warning, but I can take care of myself."

I downed what was left of my wine and stared longingly at the pecan pie I hadn't had a chance to eat. Reluctantly, I left the uneaten pie on the counter for the server to clear away. I would have taken it home, but Mom would throw a fit if I brought back a dessert that she hadn't personally baked herself.

Abby Lee grabbed her purse, and together we walked out into the thick island Gulf air. I took a big whiff, instantly becoming intoxicated by the salty air. The humidity wreaked havoc on my hair, making it so frizzy no amount of hair product could tame it, but I soaked in the heavy layer of dampness, grateful to be home again.

The island was roughly ten miles long, and while you still needed a car to get from one end to another, almost everyone took advantage of the cool Gulf Coast breeze and walked pretty much everywhere within the half-mile radius of the town center or drove around in a golf cart (if you were a member of the AARP) or dune buggy (if you were under twenty).

"How are you doing, really?" I asked. Now that it was just the two of us, I wanted to offer her my shoulder. The news of Harvey's death must have devastated her.

Abby Lee seemed to know what I was getting at. "I'm still in shock. Harvey took me under his wing when I moved back and gave me a lot of responsibility at the restaurant. I was thinking I might even go back to school and get my culinary degree."

"That's great," I said, genuinely happy for my friend.

"Yeah, my time at the restaurant will count as experience on my application to the CIA. Harvey was even going to write me a letter of recommendation."

"Where?" I wondered if the CIA, headquartered in Langley, Virginia, had a setup similar to the bureau's. Our building housed a full-service cafeteria, and it wasn't great food, but at least I never had to leave the building. It took me two years, but I'd finally convinced the chef to serve rare roast beef sandwiches.

Now I really felt sorry for Abby Lee. Here was her chance to leave Trouble, and the man who had mentored her was now gone. "You were going to move to Virginia?" I didn't know much about cooking—aside from the occasional side dish—so I wasn't one to judge, but I knew she deserved better than slaving away in a cafeteria.

"Huh?" She seemed as baffled as I was. "Why would I move to Virginia?"

"You said CIA, right? The Central Intelligence Agency?"

My confusion was rewarded with hysterical laughter. "No, silly. The Culinary Institute of America. They have a campus in San Antonio that has a program in baking and pastry arts."

Duh. Why didn't I know that? I managed to feel like an idiot while being impressed at the same time. "Seems like you have it all planned out," I said. I loved the island just as much as she did, but it was good to hear Abby Lee talk about her future away from Trouble. "Do you think you'll still apply?"

Abby Lee grimaced. "Probably. I just need to figure out how to break the news to my mother."

"I'm sure she'll understand," I assured her. "And again, I'm sorry about what happened to Harvey."

From what I remembered about Harvey Boyette, he had always been a gracious person. He had owned The Poop Deck since a time before I could even remember. Everyone in town loved him, and he would be sorely missed. I shivered in the damp, warm air just thinking about him, my most recent memory being his lifeless body lying in my parents' backyard.

Talking about Harvey was a solemn subject, but it didn't stop me from prying. "What do you think of Harvey's wife?" I remembered my mom mentioning something about Harvey getting hitched to some woman from Florida. According to her, it was all the town could talk about for weeks. Personally, I thought it was kind of romantic meeting someone at his age and getting married after only a few days—a whirlwind romance they called it.

"Sheila," Abby Lee said, with just a hint of bitterness in her tone. "She doesn't come around much, but when she does, she thinks she owns the place."

I thought about that for a moment. "She was Harvey's wife," I pointed out. "I'm sure she considers The Poop Deck partly hers."

"Maybe," she said. "The staff can't stand her, though. Harvey always tried to intervene when she was around, but she undermines everyone. Including Harvey."

"Interesting," I said.

We walked the rest of the way to our respective homes in silence, enjoying each other's company. I made myself a vow to spend more time with Abby Lee while I was in town.

CHAPTER FIVE

Right on schedule, the daily gossip arrived earlier than the morning newspaper. Mom broke the silence during breakfast with a full report surrounding the circumstances of Harvey's death. "The police don't think Harvey Boyette died of a heart attack."

Thick maple syrup got stuck to the roof of my mouth. I was halfway through eating Mom's famed blueberry pancakes when she reiterated the early morning news coverage.

"What? You're kidding!" I sputtered.

She was aghast at me even suggesting such a thing. "Why, Julia Bernard Cannon, I would never joke about something like that."

Sheesh. "I know, Mom. It's just an expression."

"According to Edith Clemmons, the police department is looking into leads. They're even going to be interviewing all the employees over at the restaurant," she said. Even after all these years, Mom still refused to call the restaurant by its name. She thought the name was vulgar.

I silently wondered why the town bothered to publish a newspaper at all. Or better still, why my folks even bothered subscribing. Between Mom, Aunt Lula, and half the meddling women in Trouble, news managed to circulate just fine without one. "How do you know all this"—I stopped to look at my watch—"at eight thirty in the morning?"

She shrugged. "Edith's son works for the department. And while I may not approve of some of Harvey's marketing decisions, he was a nice man," she said. "Please be a dear and call the florist. I'd like to send some flowers from the family."

Contrary to popular belief, things could move very quickly in small Southern towns, even those programmed on island time. After the immediate news of Harvey's death, plans for the funeral arrangements quickly spread throughout the island. The service was to be held only two days after he'd been discovered in my parents' backyard. According to my sources—the rumor mill—Widow Boyette had said there was no reason to delay the inevitable. It seemed a reasonable enough request.

I really hadn't planned on attending the service, but my mom insisted as soon as she caught wind of me trying to skip out. "It wouldn't look right if you didn't pay your respects," she said.

Of course it wouldn't.

It's not that I didn't want to go; I loved Harvey just like everyone else around the island. I just felt awkward about attending. Funerals always unnerved me for some reason. Mainly because I never knew what to say. I had only ever been to two funerals—Uncle Jep's and Maw-Maw Marie's—and all I remembered about both of them was the adults fighting over land, property, and jewelry. Fortunately, I was too young when my other grandparents had passed, and I was excused from attending their funerals.

Aunt Lula, on the other hand, was just as persuasive on the matter but for different reasons than my mom. She thought I should go if only to offer my friend Abby Lee moral support. "Poor lamb, it's almost like she's lost a father," she said. "Again."

This was true. Abby Lee's own father had died when she was five, leaving her with only her mother to raise her. And from all she'd told me last night, from the very day she started work at The Poop Deck, Harvey was like a surrogate father to her. It was only right that I attend the funeral service to support my friend.

I wanted to pay my respects to Harvey, of course, but I was really going for Abby Lee. It was time I earned our friendship back.

When I'd hastily packed my bags for my trip back to Trouble, I hadn't planned on attending a funeral. Hell, for that matter, I hadn't expected to find Harvey Boyette dead in my parents' backyard, either. Heaven knew I had enough dark suits for work to suffice for several funerals and then some, but those were back at my apartment. With limited options—I didn't really want to spend money on yet another drab suit to add to my collection—I rummaged through my childhood closet for something decent to wear. Bingo. Behind half a closetful of Lilly shifts, I found an old navy dress hidden in the back. It was as close to black as I was going to get, and even better still, it fit.

It seemed the whole island came out for Harvey's funeral and ultimately the gathering at Sheila's house after the service. I can't say I was too surprised. He was a stand-up guy, and everyone loved eating at his seafood joint. It looked like everyone, most of whom had only a few days before eaten their weight in crab and fried catfish at my parents' house, was packed in and around Sheila Boyette's living room like a can of sardines.

The Poop Deck handled the catering at Sheila's. Just a light fare consisting of crab dip, fried oysters, and half-portion shrimp po'boys on a platter. Personally, I thought it was kind of tacky having the kitchen staff from The Poop Deck work on the day of his funeral, but in the last few hours I'd gotten the distinct impression that was the kind of woman Sheila was—cheap and tacky. I'm sure she figured she could save a few bucks on catering if the food came from her deceased husband's restaurant. But then why wasn't it a potluck? I was sure the women of Trouble would have gladly brought over enough casseroles to feed the entire town.

As if reading my thoughts, Aunt Lula whispered in my ear, "We offered to bring over food so she didn't have to lift a finger, but the woman wouldn't accept. Said she had food allergies or some such nonsense. As if we'd try to poison her."

Unless you were over sixty and part of the centuries-old Texas/Louisiana turf wars, everyone was pretty much civil toward each other—it's the Southern way. But Sheila Boyette, on the other hand, was a newcomer to the island, and she didn't leave a good first impression. To hear my mom tell it, Harvey had met her about four years ago on a fishing trip to Florida and surprised nearly everyone when he announced they'd been married by, and I quote, "a bona fide boat captain." Sheila didn't necessarily warrant the standard Yankee reception, being from Florida and all, but there was speculation about her true nature just the same.

You would have needed a defective hearing aid to miss the whispered chatter among the mourners.

". . . gold digger."

"Not a nice bone in her body . . ."

". . . woulda keeled over too if she was my wife."

"Sure played him the fool . . ."

If Sheila overheard what the others were whispering behind her back, she didn't mention it. For that matter, I doubted that she even noticed what people were saying directly to her. She spent the entire time drinking bourbon and Coke, draping herself on the arm of a man I didn't recognize.

If the stars weren't already aligned so badly, I would have been surprised to see Justin again. But there he stood by the buffet, talking to Mr. Irsik, in his unofficial police garb.

Shifting his eyes away from Mr. Irsik, he caught me staring and shot off a nod of recognition. He excused himself from the conversation—which was no small feat when talking to Stanley Irsik. The man could talk your ear off about offshore fishing whether you cared to listen or not.

There was no way to politely slip away from where I was standing. Justin had already spotted me. I don't know why my first instinct was to run anytime he was within a ten-yard radius. "Hey there," I said.

"Hey, yourself," he said. "Going to take some getting used to . . . seeing you around, that is."

There. That was why my first instinct was to flee whenever he was around. I wasn't going to allow him to make me feel guilty about being absent the last five years. Mom did that plenty enough already.

"I'm here for the summer, so you might as well get used to it." I didn't mean for it to come out snarky, but it did.

"No need to get defensive. I meant it as a good thing," he said.

I certainly wasn't expecting him to say that. I still imagined him holding a grudge after I dumped him before we left for college. "How so?"

"Maybe we could get together sometime. I don't know, dinner, or something."

That had me speechless for a moment. The way I remembered things, we broke up, he was hurt, and I moved on. I thought he had, too. The few occasions I had managed to come home over the years, we'd pretty much avoided each other. It was easy, since I never came home for more than a weekend or so. Mom always kept me busy at home, and he focused on police work. Now I was here for the whole summer.

"Gee, I don't—"

He wasn't going to let me come up with an excuse. "Come on, Jules. All that was years ago. What is it they say? Water under the bridge? What's dinner between old friends?" He looked so eager and hopeful, and I hated to turn him down when he put it that way.

"I'll think about it, OK? I have to spend some time with my folks first," I said. It wasn't completely true, but I knew he couldn't argue about that. "And I'll be working at Palmetto Pink."

"What? That I'd like to see." He laughed, knowing full well how much I hated interacting with people. "How'd Lula get you to work there?"

"Don't ask. Anyway, looks like I might have a full schedule." What was wrong with me? Why was I being so stubborn? If he was willing to be friends again, the least I could do was meet him halfway.

He seemed disappointed. "Sure," he said, like it was no big deal either way. "So what are you doing here, anyway?"

"I didn't realize I needed an engraved invitation." My defenses were up again. "I'm here for moral support," I said. "And in case you've forgotten, I've known Harvey my whole life, same as you. Just because I left town doesn't mean I stopped caring."

"I see," he said, rubbing his chin. It was a nervous habit he had developed over the years. He only did it when he thought too hard about something. For all I knew, he was on the defensive as well. I'd just turned down his dinner invitation.

"And while we're on the subject," I continued, "why are you here? Surely you have better things to do—like solve crimes. I heard through the grapevine you guys don't think it was a heart attack."

"Touché. Actually, I'm here on official business."

I hadn't put much stock in what my mom or the rest of the gossip hounds had spread all over town, but if he was here on official business, perhaps there was some truth to the rumors.

"Do you really think it was foul play?" It was one thing to suspect Harvey died from mysterious circumstances, but Mom would bust a gut if she knew someone was actually murdered in her own backyard.

Justin's mood shifted again. "I didn't say—"

He didn't have to spell it out. "Do you think he was murdered?" I pressed.

Justin took a step back. "Whoa, hold on there a second. I said no such thing. And keep your voice down, will you?" He glanced around to see if anyone had heard me. "I'm just here to talk with his nephew."

"Harvey had a nephew?" This was news to me. Until the day Harvey married Sheila, he'd lived the bachelor life with no other family to speak of. In all the years I'd lived in Trouble, there was certainly never any mention of a nephew.

Justin seemed pleased to know something I didn't. "You seem surprised. Then again, you haven't been around these parts in a while. Why do you care whether Harvey had a nephew or not?"

Another jab. His comment stung as guilt set in again. *Damn*, I told myself. I wasn't going to let him or anyone else guilt-trip me. I was home now, wasn't I? "Yeah, well I like to stay informed."

Justin took his eyes off me for a moment to scan the room, looking for the mysterious nephew. "Nephew's from Lufkin," he continued, eyes glued to the crowd. "Took us a while to track down Harvey's next of kin. After we notified him of his uncle's death, he said he'd make the drive down for the funeral."

I glanced around the living room, where most of the entertaining was going on, and didn't see anyone that fit the description of an estranged nephew. Despite the large crowd, it wouldn't be hard to spot a stranger, as I recognized everyone in the room. I thought back to the strange man that had been consoling Widow Boyette earlier on the couch. Maybe he was the mysterious nephew. "I don't see him here, but I did notice a guy sitting with Sheila earlier," I said. "And you're here to talk with him why again?"

"I never said," Justin replied. "We just want to ask him a few questions about Harvey."

It was what he wasn't saying that made my head go into over-drive. A theory slowly began to formulate. Harvey didn't look the picture of a heart attack waiting to happen the day of the party. In fact, he looked pretty healthy for a man his age. So if his sudden death wasn't due to a heart attack, Justin was indeed working an open case.

"Are you here to question him?" I insisted, fishing for more information.

His eyes narrowed down at me. Clearly he was getting annoyed with my questions. "For what? He's not a suspect, Jules. Get that thought right out of your head. I thought it would be nice to personally give my condolences while asking him a few questions about Harvey. That's all."

OK, maybe I was jumping to conclusions. But then, why would he ask an absentee nephew of all people questions about Harvey? Plus, he said he was here on official business.

"I guess that makes sense," I said, even though it didn't.

"Now if you'll excuse me, I gotta pay my respects so I can get back to doing my job."

Ouch. Did I detect a hint of sarcasm there? "Sure."

Justin spun back around before leaving. "And hey . . ."

"Yeah?" It was wishful thinking on my part, but for a second there, I thought he was going to ask me out to dinner again. This time I'd say yes, to make up for being rude earlier.

"For what it's worth, it's good to have you back."

It was a start.

CHAPTER SIX

Normally, the reading of the will is done in private, with only immediate family present, presumably in some stuffy lawyer's office, but according to the family probate attorney, it was Harvey's wish that the will be read immediately following the funeral.

Not surprisingly, everybody present was anxious to hear Harvey's last will and testament, even though most of the people in the room didn't stand to inherit anything. I had a sneaking suspicion half the town wanted the early scoop so it could be included in the early morning addition of the daily gossip, while the other half secretly hoped Harvey left them some sort of gift or token. It was kind of like the lottery—the odds were bad, but everyone played to win.

The probate attorney seemed out of place as he loosened his pale-blue necktie and looked uncomfortable with all the attention focused on him. I guess he wasn't used to making house calls. As far as I knew, there were only two practicing attorneys in Trouble, and he wasn't one of them. Like I said, it was easy to spot a stranger in this crowd. He must have been from the city. Houston, maybe Galveston.

"Uh, I know these are unfortunate circumstances," he began. "But it is time for the reading of the will. As I explained earlier, it was Harvey's wish to have everybody present to hear his last wishes."

Since I didn't know Harvey well enough for him to have left me anything, and I certainly wasn't family, I tuned out most of what the attorney was saying in favor of observing the room. Even though I wasn't what you'd call a "people person," I still loved to people watch. It was amazing what you could tell about a person just by observing their habits and mannerisms.

The attorney droned on and on, and I continued to ignore most of what he was saying until he got to, ". . . and to my wife, Sheila Boyette, I leave the remainder of my estate, after all debts, expenses, taxes, and other bequests are made."

Everyone turned in the direction of Harvey's widow, including me. I'm not sure if it was my imagination, but Sheila certainly appeared smug at her sudden windfall. She didn't look to be the grieving widow who'd just lost her husband. I felt bad—for Harvey. He would have been considered quite a catch to any woman over the age of fifty, had he never married Sheila. Certainly he deserved a wife who would mourn him properly.

The probate guy continued. "To Abby Lee Kleburg, who I often thought of as the daughter I never had, I bequeath my most prized possession—The Poop Deck. I know you will continue to run it the same way I would have."

Gasps were heard throughout the room. Sheila turned angry in a second flat as the news sunk in. She was off the couch in a flash. No time was wasted as she marched right up to Abby Lee and slapped her. "You whore! Were you two having an affair? Is that why he left you the restaurant?"

The idea that Abby Lee was sleeping with Harvey was preposterous. Hopefully everyone in the room thought so, too. He had easily been thirty years her senior, if not older. But it didn't surprise me in the least that Sheila would think of something as trashy as a girl sleeping her way to an inheritance.

Abby Lee, to her credit, was in a complete state of shock. Either from the news of inheriting the restaurant or from being slapped by Harvey's widow. "I . . . I don't know what you're talking about," she stammered. "I had no idea he was leaving me anything."

From the second we all learned Abby Lee was to inherit the restaurant and she got slapped, everything seemed to happen in slow motion. Thankfully, some of the men snapped out of it and restrained Sheila from assaulting Abby Lee again.

"You'll be hearing from my lawyer," Sheila screeched as she was led back to the couch.

With Sheila restrained, I ran over to Abby Lee and searched the room for Justin. Surely he wasn't going to let Sheila get away with assaulting Abby Lee, but he wasn't anywhere in the room. Go figure. When I actually wanted him around, he was gone. He must have found Harvey's nephew and left before the reading of the will.

The attorney cleared his throat. "Uh, shall I continue?"

Since no one else was speaking, everyone still unsettled over what just happened, I took the liberty of responding on behalf of the large gathering and nodded in his direction.

". . . in the event Abby Lee Kleburg fails to survive me, the gift shall become part of the estate. In addition, if Abby Lee does not wish to operate the restaurant, or if she later wishes to sell, my wife, Sheila Boyette, will have first opportunity to purchase it."

"You mean I have to buy back what's rightfully mine?" Sheila sobbed, as if the offer was already on the table. I had to give the woman credit. She was now giving a star-studded performance as the poor, grieving widow, not the gold digger she'd appeared to be a few minutes before. The woman certainly hadn't acted like a victim; she'd seemed pleased to have inherited all his money and, quite possibly, a huge life insurance payout.

All eyes reverted back to Abby Lee, a faint red mark marring her cheek where Sheila slapped her. "I don't know what to say . . ."

Again, I didn't know if she meant the slap or the generous gift from Harvey.

"You don't have to say anything right now," I said, hugging her. "Come on, let's go. We can get the details later."

I turned to the attorney. I bet he'd never witnessed a show quite like this. Welcome to Trouble. "Is it OK if I take her home now?"

He looked nervously over to Sheila, not knowing if she was going to cause another scene. "That might be a good idea," he said, hoping to avoid any further dramatics from Sheila. He dug into his pocket and handed me his business card. "Please have her call me so we can discuss this matter at a later time."

Abby Lee didn't say a word as she allowed me to take her home. The crowd was still stunned, so no one argued as I quickly whisked my friend out of Sheila's house.

It was another nice evening, so we decided to walk home. Abby Lee didn't say anything for the first two blocks. It was another block before we finally reached her house. I had to say something.

"I can't believe Harvey left you The Poop Deck," I finally said. "What are you going to do? Keep it—sell it to Sheila?"

"I don't know. I mean, I'd love to take over the restaurant, but I don't want to cause any trouble," she said. That caught me by surprise. Unlike yours truly, who avoided conflict on any level, Abby Lee was known to rock the boat from time to time.

But she had a point. I didn't know Sheila very well, despite her brilliant performance back at her house. I had already moved away by the time Harvey married her, but judging from her reaction to the news of Abby Lee's inheritance, the woman spelled t-r-o-u-b-l-e. And boy, did she come to the right place to cause it.

"Why don't you sit on it for a while?" I suggested. "I'm sure Sheila will realize it's not worth the effort to keep up a restaurant and decide it's in better hands with you."

I caught the hint of a smile. "She'd have to be a reasonable person in order to come up with that conclusion," Abby Lee said.

"Maybe I should just sell it to her. I don't know if I'm comfortable running it with Sheila attacking me every chance she gets."

Another good point. "You're right. The woman doesn't seem capable of rational thought." I knew if Abby Lee kept the restaurant, Sheila wouldn't give it up without a fight.

I wasn't sure if this was the right time to ask, but I was dying to know. "Why do you think he left you the restaurant?"

Abby Lee sighed. "I don't know. I swear I had no idea. I guess it's like he said in his will, he always said I was like the daughter he never had. He felt bad when I had to move back to Trouble and take care of my mother when she got sick. Said I was destined for better things than to be stuck here on the island. Guess this was his way of making sure I'd be taken care of. Aside from Sheila, he didn't have any other kin or anyone else that cared about his restaurant."

I guessed she hadn't heard about Harvey's nephew. But what she said made sense. Harvey knew exactly what he was doing when he left the restaurant to her. But what of the estranged nephew who'd miraculously appeared after all this time? The pessimist in me didn't believe in coincidences.

"When did he tell you all this?"

"I don't know. A couple months ago?"

Then naming Abby Lee as a beneficiary might have been recent. Which meant either Harvey hadn't gotten around to creating a will until recently or he'd changed it. If it was the latter, I wondered who'd gotten bumped in favor of Abby Lee. Sheila? His nephew? Maybe it wasn't too far-fetched for me to believe that Harvey's own nephew could be involved somehow. I decided to keep the estranged nephew and my thoughts about his possible involvement quiet. For now.

"Do you think I'll have to hand over the restaurant to Sheila?"

"No. Harvey was pretty direct with his wishes, and I'm sure his attorney will make sure you aren't bullied into handing it over. Why? Are you thinking maybe you don't want it?"

Abby Lee shook her head. "It's not that. I want it. I can't believe he left it to me. It's like a dream. But I don't want any problems."

Understood. If what I saw back at the Boyette house was any indication of what Sheila was like when she didn't get her way, I would worry, too.

CHAPTER SEVEN

With the excitement of coming home, the party, and Harvey Boyette's death, I had almost forgotten about promising to work at Aunt Lula's store—almost. Oh right, I hadn't promised her anything. I'd been hoodwinked. Just how did I get roped into working at Palmetto Pink? I had a small reprieve, as my first official day was delayed due to everything that happened, but damned if I still didn't have to work there.

After a fitful night's sleep, the preset alarm on my phone woke me up, annoyingly alerting me of the time. Waking up before eight in the morning was certainly not my idea of being on vacation.

Since it was my first day, Aunt Lula wanted to give me the nickel tour and show me the ropes—despite the fact I practically grew up in her store—before opening the doors to the public. With the recent resignation of my predecessor, my aunt only had two other employees to assist at the store.

"This is where we keep all the clothes in back stock," Aunt Lula informed me, pointing to rolling racks of dresses and designer tops draped on hangers. "If a customer can't find their size in the store, you can look for it back here."

We quickly moved on to the other back room that occupied the store, which served as her office. There was even a small bathroom to the left side of the office. Prior to Aunt Lula purchasing the space for her clothing boutique, it had been home to a struggling real estate office. Anyone could have, and probably had, told the realty company that our island hardly ever saw any newcomers looking for residential real estate. It didn't take long for the company to go belly-up after a few years. Smart business woman that my aunt was, she snatched up the building for a steal.

"And over here," she said, pointing to a clear plastic bin under her massive oak desk, "is where you'll find basic office supplies."

She was showing me everything I already knew or could figure out on my own, but in the hour I'd been at the store, she'd neglected to teach me the most important thing. It was the one thing that'd kept me up almost all night worrying I'd screw it up—the reason I still had dark circles under my eyes. "Uh, how do I work the register?"

To say I was nervous about running the register was an understatement. I had spent the entire night worrying I would annoy customers because I couldn't figure out how to ring their purchases correctly. I made my living working with high-tech computer software programs, but a cash register? Even a girl with a master's degree could get freaked out by the mere notion of running a cash register. It's the little things that scare us.

"Oh, my heavens, how could I forget?"

It took another half hour to teach me how to work the antiquated register—an old DOS computer rigged to work with a cash drawer—but much to my relief, I managed to figure it out after a few practice runs. And just in time for the store's first customer of the day.

The customer strolled in, or rather, waddled in. The woman was heavyset, but still managed to look good with her designer duds, complete with diamond earrings the size of nickels. Unless you were an expert, you just never knew if diamonds were fake or real, but I'd bet my first paycheck they were the real deal. This was Texas after all. When it came to trucks, hair, and jewels, we literally took the phrase "go big or go home" to heart. I didn't recognize the woman, so I assumed she was from one of the bigger cities on the mainland, spending the day shopping on the island.

The woman walked straight up to the sales counter with a purpose. Even though she was staring right at me, she waited for me to address her first. I wasn't sure of the proper etiquette in dealing with retail customers. Should I ask if she needs help? Or should I wait until she asks for assistance? Judging from her expression, she was waiting for me to make the first move.

"Hi, can I help you with something?" I put on my best smile.

Already the woman looked impatient. "Yes. I was here last Saturday, and I ordered a denim shirt to pick up."

If she already looked put out, she was about to be even more annoyed with me. "We don't sell any denim here," I said. Even though it was my first day on the job, I had a pretty good idea of what my aunt carried in stock. Her inventory hadn't changed much in the twenty years she's been in business—Lilly Pulitzer, Tommy Bahama, St. John, and a few other luxury resort brands. Every year I received colorful Lilly shifts for my birthday, Easter, and Christmas. But never denim. So I was pretty confident she didn't carry any.

"Yes, you do," she insisted. "I ordered it. Perhaps it was chambray then."

"Um, we don't have anything in chambray either, but OK. What's your name so I can look up your order?" If the woman had ordered something, it would be in the customer-information file. Thankfully, Aunt Lula gave me a quick tutorial on how to look up past purchases.

"Trudy Baker."

"Do you remember who assisted you?" Not that it mattered. I was prepared to look into the computer system to locate the woman's purchase the way Aunt Lula had showed me earlier. I was just stalling until I found my way around the system to find her transaction.

"I think her name was Heidi," she said, clearly annoyed.

I was only half listening to her by this point, trying to figure out how to pull her name until I finally found it. Then I realized why it took me so long to find the purchase history—there were no sales transactions in the system for a denim shirt. "I'm sorry, ma'am, but we don't have a record of your purchase. Uh, are you sure you're in the right store?"

The woman stopped scowling at me long enough to observe her surroundings. "No. I guess I'm not."

Yeah, like I said, we didn't sell denim here. Maybe I should have been the one annoyed. My first customer of the day and I felt like I was already giving quality customer service a bad name. And it wasn't even my fault.

The woman waddled out the same way she waddled in, not even bothering to browse what we had in the store. It was a shame—my aunt carried some awesome pieces that would have looked great on her.

"See? That wasn't so hard now, was it?" Aunt Lula said, coming up from behind me. I hadn't realized she'd been standing right next to the counter during the entire exchange.

Dealing with rude customers wasn't part of the job description as far as I was concerned. "I guess not," I lied. It was only an hour into my shift, and I already felt like throwing in the towel.

"Though it wouldn't kill you to be nice to the customers, even if they are wrong. Denim," she said, shaking her head in disapproval. "At her age!"

Six hours later, my feet were sore from standing all day and my back hurt from hanging items back on the racks. I was in desperate need of some downtime. I wasn't ready to go home, so I decided a glass of cheap house red was in order. Conveniently, the store was only a block down from The Poop Deck. It couldn't hurt to have a glass of wine before I headed back to my parents' house.

"Hey! How was your first day?" Abby Lee asked as soon as I parked on a stool at the bar. I was surprised to find her back at the restaurant after the whole incident at Harvey's funeral. I had expected her to take a few days off, even if she technically owned the place now, but knowing my friend, she wouldn't hear of it.

"I didn't think you'd be working today," I said, secretly pleased she'd stuck to her guns.

"You know, I thought about taking a day off—you know, to give Sheila time to cool off, but the more I thought about it, the more I realized it's my restaurant now. It's my responsibility."

"Good for you," I said and meant it. I might avoid confrontations, but I totally believed in standing up for yourself.

I took a quick glance at the menu, left on the counter from the previous customer, but I already knew what I wanted. "So—what does a girl have to do around here to get a glass of wine with her whine?" I was still thinking of my sore feet.

"That bad, huh?" She sounded like a true bartender, pouring my wine and listening to my tales of retail woes. I was sure I wasn't the first one to come in and complain about a job.

"I don't know how you do it. How do you deal with rude customers all day?" I asked, imagining food service was even worse than retail.

She shrugged. "I don't. Most folks are generally nice, and I love serving people."

"Maybe it's just me then. Am I that horrible to be around?" Maybe I projected negative energy to those I came in contact with. That would explain a lot. It was probably why James left me.

"Jules, if you were a bad person, we wouldn't be friends," she said. "You're just a tough cookie to crack is all."

"I think you mean 'nut' . . . a tough nut to crack." I laughed at her attempt to make me feel better. Abby Lee was one of the most positive people I knew. If we could get along, maybe I wasn't as negative as I believed myself to be—maybe.

"In any event," I continued, "consider me overbaked then. And speaking of people not liking me—do I have to go to the reunion?"

"Oh my God, Jules! Is that what you think?" Abby Lee asked. "No one disliked you in high school."

I shrugged, wishing I hadn't said anything. Now I was going to get a lecture on how ridiculous I sounded. "Could have fooled me."

Abby Lee poured herself a glass of wine. I raised my eyebrows. She shot back a look that said, "I'm the owner now, I can drink on the job if I want."

After taking a long sip, she sighed. "You know, you would have been much more popular if you were—how should I put this—more outgoing."

She was right, again. It wasn't like I was a social outcast or anything. I had at least one friend in each of the different cliques in school: the athletes, the nerds, even the agriculture kids, but I was kind of invisible in a way. They were more acquaintances than real friends. There was never a time I wanted to go all Carrie at the homecoming dance, but I certainly would have been the last person picked for Most Popular, even though all my friends were strong contenders.

If Abby Lee hadn't taken me under her wing, I probably would've spent my Friday nights alone at home reading the latest thriller. And if I hadn't been dating Justin our junior and senior years, I most likely would have spent my Saturday nights alone at home watching old syndicated television sitcoms.

"I can't help it," I finally said. "I don't intentionally push people away."

Her face softened. "I know you don't, sweetie. But you gotta admit, when you're gorgeous, smart, and always appear as if your time is better spent doing something else, it's a wonder you had any friends at all."

I thought about that for a moment. What she said was so not true—I wasn't gorgeous. Smart, possibly, but not gorgeous. That distinction, in my opinion, was reserved for Abby Lee. She was the one voted Most Beautiful (she'd lost Most Popular by one vote).

"Basically what you're telling me is, everyone was jealous. Is that it?"

She took another swig of her wine. "Hmm, probably."

I wasn't convinced. "It's a nice thought," I said, a little surprised she thought of me that way, even if it was a white lie to make me feel better. "But doubtful."

The door of the restaurant slammed, breaking me from my thoughts. Which was probably a good idea considering the topic of conversation—I didn't want to take a walk down memory lane. It was bad enough I had to go to the reunion.

My reflexes kicked in as soon as I discovered the source of the slam. This wasn't going to be good.

"You!" Sheila stormed toward the bar, heading right for Abby Lee. "This is my restaurant, and I want it back."

Like I said before, I always tried to stay in the background when it came to a fight, especially when it involved psycho, menopausal women, but I had to do something. You could walk all over me, but no one messed with my friends.

I wedged myself between the counter and Sheila, purposely obscuring her view of Abby Lee. "This isn't the time or the place for this, Sheila. Go talk to your lawyer," I said, knowing full well there was nothing her lawyer could do. As far as I could tell, Harvey's will was ironclad.

I could tell by the sour look on her face she'd already consulted a lawyer and had reached a similar conclusion. Why else would she be here throwing a tantrum?

"This place is mine," she yelled over my shoulder, trying to get a better view of Abby Lee.

"You're making a scene," I said. "Stop and think for a moment, Sheila."

"And just who the hell are you?" Sheila yelled over the restaurant's background music. "This isn't any of your business."

"I'm a customer," I said. "A customer with enough friends and family members to steer them away from this place if you keep this up." I even raised the ante for good measure. "I'm sure you know my aunt Lula."

Just the mere mention of my aunt brought fear to her eyes and calmed her down a bit. Everyone in Trouble, even someone like Sheila, had reservations about going against my aunt.

"Enjoy it while you can," Sheila sneered over my shoulder in the direction of Abby Lee. "This isn't over yet." On her way out she plastered on a fake smile in an attempt to appease the customers whose dinners had been interrupted by the scene she'd just caused.

Abby Lee slapped her hands over her face. "I knew this was a bad idea. I should just hand over the restaurant. Sheila's never going to stop." Her words came out jumbled behind her hands.

"Harvey gave you this place for a reason," I said, soothing her concerns. "You know as well as I do that Sheila would either run this place into the ground or sell it."

We both knew it was true. If this was how Sheila dealt with problems, there was no telling what could happen to The Poop Deck. If she ever got her hands on the restaurant, I'd give the woman one month before the place either went out of business or sold to the highest bidder. The latter made the most sense. According to Abby Lee, the staff couldn't stand Sheila. There was no way Sheila could possibly be interested in being a restaurant owner—she only wanted to make a fast profit. Hell, I wouldn't put it past her to set fire to the place to collect an insurance claim.

I might just be crazy, or maybe the wine had something to do with it, but I now had a vested interest in keeping Sheila as far away from The Poop Deck as possible. The restaurant was considered a local treasure, and there was no way the town would allow Sheila to run it, burn it, or sell it.

"She'd probably burn the place down for the insurance money," Abby Lee said, echoing my exact thoughts.

I laughed. "That's exactly what I was thinking," I said. "So you see? You need to stand your ground and take ownership of what's rightfully yours." My words came out with a little more bravado than necessary.

CHAPTER EIGHT

I looked deeply into the reflection that was staring right back at me. Call me vain or whatever, but I looked pretty damn good in a dark-blue version of a little black dress Aunt Lula had helped me pick out from her store. "I don't know," I said to myself in the mirror as I twirled one last time. "Too much for a high school reunion?"

Mom must have heard me talking to myself from the hallway and popped her head in the doorway to check on me. "I'd say you look just about right," she said. "Don't forget to put on lipstick."

How could I forget lipstick? Growing up, my mom never let me leave the house without lipstick or, at the very least, tinted lip gloss. Even if I was only going as far as the driveway to get the mail. "You never know who you'll run into," she always said. She was also fond of saying, "Dress as if you were going to meet your future husband." It was her version of "dress to impress." Ha! Like that gem of advice had gotten me far. Not that I was looking.

"I won't," I said. "Are you sure the dress isn't a bit too much?" The clingy wrap dress was actually Aunt Lula's idea. One of the rare instances where she didn't insist I wear a bright tropical print.

Mom inspected my dress. "Well, personally, I don't know if I would have chosen something so low cut, but it does seem to suit you," she said, nodding in approval. The dress's deep navy hue accented my light-blue eyes and dark hair, and it wasn't cut so low it screamed "streetwalker."

I gave another little twirl for her benefit and decided she and Aunt Lula were right. What's a little cleavage? It was my ten-year reunion. And weren't reunions all about showing off? I didn't believe Abby Lee one bit when she said everyone was jealous of me back in high school, but I wouldn't mind them being a little envious now.

"Just don't let your daddy see you in that," Mom added. "He might not let you leave the house."

Thirty minutes later, I walked into the building that was my alma mater. Go Tarpons! I was immediately greeted by a sign-in table where I scanned the rows of name tags for my name. They were aligned in alphabetical order, so I was able to find mine easily enough. I peeled the back of the self-adhesive tag and stuck it on my chest, drawing even more attention toward my plunging neckline.

"Here goes nothing," I said under my breath.

"Excuse me?" The girl manning the table looked at me expectantly. Her name tag read "Kate Myers." I didn't recognize her, but no surprises there. Aside from Abby Lee and Justin, I didn't really give myself a chance to get to know many of my classmates. My brother, Scott, on the other hand, was two years older and had been the proverbial popular kid in school. I loved him, but I was glad when he finally moved away to Dallas and I stopped living under his shadow.

"Nothing," I said, making my way toward the music. I gave myself exactly five minutes to locate Abby Lee. If she wasn't here by then, I was going back home. The bravado I felt prior to arriving was all but gone. I didn't want to be here all by myself, sexy dress or not.

Once inside the school gymnasium, I cringed at the tacky seaside theme the decorating committee came up with. How original.

They might as well have just stuck up a banner announcing, "We Live on an Island!" As if we didn't already know. Every school dance I'd attended in high school had the same unoriginal theme. I wondered if they just recycled the decorations.

I made my way toward the sea-foam-colored draped tables in search of Abby Lee. I wasn't sure if I could survive the night without her. Aside from dating Justin, she was one of the reasons I'd made it through high school unscathed without any permanent psychological damage.

Ready to throw in the towel, I finally spotted her near the bleachers. One minute later and I would have bolted. She was dressed in a bright kelly green sundress that showed off her tan. Even at twenty-eight, she looked exactly the same—still stunning. Despite my earlier appraisal of myself, I wished I looked half as good as she did. But no envy on my part, she was the best friend I'd ever had.

"There you are," she said, rushing up to me. "I was afraid you weren't going to show up."

"For a moment there, I wasn't so sure either. I was just about ready to bail. But hey," I said, pointing across the room, "at least they're serving booze."

"Let's hope it's not a cash bar," she said. "All I have on me is a five."

"Doubtful. How else are they going to pay for all the lovely decorations for our twenty-year reunion?" I laughed as we made our way over to the refreshment table.

Abby Lee giggled, catching the sarcasm in my statement.

"Don't worry, I'll spot you."

"Look, there's Justin over there by the bar. Let's go over and say hi," Abby Lee said.

I tugged at her elbow. "But look who he's with," I said. Heather was standing right next to him. She was very animated in whatever she was saying. Justin looked like a rabbit cornered by a rabid coyote.

"Aww, let's go save the poor guy. Maybe he'll buy us a drink," she said. "You know, I think he still has the hots for you."

"I doubt it," I said. Why would she even think that? I'd only been home a few days. Certainly not long enough for her to form an opinion on the matter. Sure, he had asked me out to dinner, but a decade was a long time between exes. A lot of change and growth happens between eighteen and twenty-eight. Besides, since I'd been home we'd only run into each other a few times.

"Stranger things have happened," she said, nudging me toward the two of them.

I gave her a cross look as we walked over to the table to join them. Justin looked happy to see us. Heather, on the other hand, scowled as she saw us approach.

"Jules . . . Abby Lee. I didn't think y'all were going to make it tonight," Justin said, genuinely surprised to see us.

"That makes three of us," I said.

Abby Lee gently punched me in the ribs with her elbow. "Wouldn't miss it," she said.

"Yeah, what are you doing here? I thought you'd be bored by all this," Heather said, looking directly at me.

Even though I didn't want to be here in the first place, I'd be damned if I gave Heather the satisfaction of hearing me admit she was right. "Why would I miss this? I did graduate from here, same as you," I said.

Heather just shrugged and turned her attention back to Justin.

"Come on, Abby Lee. Let's go dance," I said, pulling her out to the dance floor just as the DJ blasted Gretchen Wilson's "Redneck Woman." I remembered when the song came out. It was such a hit every girl in town went and bought her lingerie from Walmart.

For a brief moment, I was transported back in time, circa 2004. It was our high school prom, and it was the last dance I attended here in this very gymnasium. I remembered my light-pink crepe dress Mom had ordered from Neiman Marcus and how grown-up Justin had looked in his tuxedo.

Now I'm sure you're probably wondering, if I was such a social loser in high school, how'd I end up dating a catch like Justin Harper? Well, you got me (and, I'm sure, everyone else who wondered the same thing). But I never looked a gift horse in the mouth. I always felt a little like Molly Ringwald's character in *Sixteen Candles*, who got Jake Ryan at the end of the movie.

I was brought back to the present the instant I heard Abby Lee yell, "Hell yeah!" at the top of her lungs along with the song and the rest of the crowd on the dance floor. We continued to laugh and danced like fools, not caring what anyone thought of us. *This is more fun than I thought it would be,* I thought. It was just like old times. I'd forgotten how great it was hanging out with Abby Lee. I hoped we wouldn't lose touch again after I went back home.

Abby Lee and I stayed on the dance floor as "Soak Up the Sun" by Sheryl Crow came on over the speakers. We squealed as we danced to the unofficial anthem of our youth. I couldn't remember the last time I had so much fun dancing. Wait, I knew the answer to that. It was before I became a workaholic and forgot how to have a good time.

The moment was short-lived as I spotted a uniformed officer headed in our direction. What was a cop doing at a high school reunion? *He probably needed the overtime and volunteered to work security,* I decided.

I expected the officer to make the rounds, but instead, he walked straight toward the dance floor and locked eyes on his intended target. He intercepted Abby Lee and me on the dance floor.

"I'm sorry to have to do this, Abby Lee, but I'm going to have to bring you back to the station for questioning."

Abby Lee seemed to know the officer, but I didn't. He looked young, early twenties at best. He probably was a few years behind us in school, or I would have recognized him. Abby Lee probably served him all the time at The Poop Deck and was on a first-name basis with him.

"For what?" I said.

At the same time Abby Lee asked, "I'm sorry? Why am I needed for questioning? All of us at the restaurant already gave our statements."

"Chief Poteet asked me to bring you in to answer a few more follow-up questions. If you don't mind, I won't keep you long."

"But Justin's here," I pointed out, still confused. "We were just talking to him. If he wanted to ask Abby Lee a question, he would have done so."

The officer looked nervous, like he had been caught doing something wrong. "I, uh, was supposed to bring her into the station earlier, but she wasn't at home. Your mom said I could find you here," he said to Abby Lee. "I'm sorry for the intrusion, but I have my orders."

I cleared my head and approached the officer, whose name tag read "Officer Clemmons." "I repeat, questioning for what?"

Officer Clemmons just shrugged. "Chief's orders," he said. "Sorry, Abby Lee, if you don't come with me willingly, I'll have to take you in with cuffs."

Abby Lee just stood there without saying a word, but I was standing my ground. Maybe it was the salty Gulf air, but I was beginning to find my voice. "What? On what charge? You can't just handcuff someone without arresting them first."

Abby Lee placed a hand on my shoulder to reassure me. "It's OK, Jules. I'll go with Randy." So she was on a first-name basis with him.

We'd been standing close to the bar, so I quickly grabbed our purses from where we'd left them and followed right behind Abby

Lee and the officer. "I'll meet you at the station," I said. "When they're done, I'll take you home. There's no sense in worrying your mother."

She gave me a small smile. "Thanks, Jules. I'm sure it's just a misunderstanding. I probably forgot to pay a parking ticket or something."

Or something. The police didn't just haul you away from a high school reunion for a couple of measly unpaid parking tickets. This was definitely not routine procedure.

A crowd began to form around us, wondering what all the commotion was about. I wanted to yell at them to go away, but I knew it would just make matters worse. So I let them gawk.

"Don't say anything without an attorney, OK?" I continued to follow right behind them and said it loud enough for her to hear me as she was being escorted out of the gymnasium.

I frantically looked around for Justin and finally spotted him standing near the front entrance as Abby Lee was being taken away. He looked upset over the whole situation, as if it pained him to see Abby Lee escorted out like a common criminal right in the middle of our reunion. And he should have felt bad. She was his friend, too. If anything, he'd be able to tell me what was going on.

I marched right over to Justin as he stood there, allowing Officer Randy to escort our friend out of the gym, not doing anything to stop him. It took all the restraint I had not to shove him against the cinder block wall.

"What the hell, Justin? What's going on?"

Justin looked guilty. He knew something bad was going down, and I'm sure the last thing he wanted to do was give me bad news, but tough shit—he had some explaining to do.

Before I could say another word, he said, "I can't go into it now. It's official business, Jules. I'm sorry."

"You've got to be kidding me. This is Abby Lee we're talking about." I could tell how much he hated having this conversation, but I didn't care. He was the deputy chief of police, and there was certainly something he could do about it.

"I'm sorry, Jules, I can't go into the details."

"Why not? You obviously know what's going on."

"Jules, you of all people know how investigations are run. I can't tell you anything. At least not right now," he said.

"But why is that officer dragging Abby Lee to the station?" I asked. Then it hit me. "Do you really think she had something to do with Harvey's death?"

Justin wouldn't commit to an answer, but I already knew what was happening without him spelling it out.

Knowing there was nothing else he could say to ease my mind, he said his good-byes and left the gym, leaving me a seething, hot mess. The deputy chief knew better than to stick around when I got angry.

Even though Justin was being tight-lipped, it didn't take a genius to put two and two together. If Abby Lee was being taken in for additional questioning, it wasn't as a formality, because she was an employee of The Poop Deck, but as a suspect.

As I stood there fuming, former classmates approached me to ask questions about Abby Lee, and I shrugged them off. This wasn't the kind of attention I wanted at my ten-year reunion, so I brushed past them and stormed out of the building. As promised, I was going to wait at the police station until they released Abby Lee.

I knew something was wrong the second I approached my truck. It was my most prized possession—Daddy's classic 1970s Ford Bronco that had been passed down to me when I graduated high school. My mom had told me about a billion times to get rid of the clunker, but aside from some rust in the undercarriage, courtesy of the salty island air, it was still in good condition. I had left it behind after college, and Daddy never had the heart to junk it. The Bronco was the quintessential island mobile.

And someone had taken a baseball bat to it.

I stared at the shards of broken glass on the hood of my vintage Bronco. My insurance was going to love this—someone had gone and broken my windshield. I circled my car, trying to see if whoever did this vandalized any of the other windows. I was relieved to find only the windshield was damaged. It was the worst window to have smashed in, but at least it was the only one that needed to be replaced.

Even though he was the last person in the world I wanted to see right now, I turned around to see if Justin's cruiser was still in the lot. I needed an official police report for my insurance carrier, but he had already taken off.

Guess I'll just have to take care of it myself. It was just broken glass after all. It was probably just some drunken classmate who'd mistaken my windshield for someone else's. Or maybe my low-cut halter dress turned some heads after all and made some female classmate jealous. Who knows? Tempers always run high when there's a reunion going on.

The weather forecast was calling for clear skies over the next couple of days, but still, I was now stuck driving around without a windshield until I could take it to the shop. I brushed the glass off the hood as best I could, and as I tried to remove stray pieces of glass from the interior, I found a note on the driver's side seat:

I'm watching you.

CHAPTER NINE

We didn't want to upset Abby Lee's mother, especially in her frail condition, so after I picked Abby Lee up from the police station, we headed straight to The Poop Deck so she could give me a rundown of what had happened. The restaurant had been closed for hours by this point, but as the new owner, Abby Lee had a set of keys.

She'd just spent several hours with the police, and I felt bad for what I was about to do, but if I was going to help my friend, I wanted to get a feel for what the police were thinking. Sitting behind a desk as a crime analyst didn't exactly make me a subject matter expert on police interrogations, but I figured I had a leg up over your average Joe.

The two of us resumed our normal positions at the restaurant: Abby Lee behind the bar, pouring me a glass of red wine, and me in front of the bar, waiting to take a long sip.

Abby Lee looked like hell. If no one had known she had been picked up by the police and questioned over the death of her former friend and employer, just one look at her would have given it away. She'd only been in their custody a few hours, but she looked like she'd spent the night there.

She'd barely placed the glass of wine in front of me before I started to barrage her with my own line of questioning—the part I hated having to do.

"What happened? Do they really suspect you killed him? What evidence do they have? You didn't tell them anything, did you?"

The idea that Abby Lee had murdered Harvey was ridiculous. She didn't have a mean bone in her body, much less the capacity to kill someone. I mentally cursed Deputy Chief Douche Bag for allowing this to happen.

Abby Lee shook her head. "They didn't tell me very much other than the coroner's report came back, and they don't think it was a heart attack like they originally thought. They seem to think he was poisoned."

I nodded. I'd imagined they had already determined Harvey's death wasn't due to natural causes. A fact confirmed earlier by Mom's gossip circle. But the fact that he was poisoned was certainly new information to me.

In Texas, unless the deceased was under a doctor's care or had a known, documented illness like cancer or heart disease, the medical examiner always ran an autopsy to confirm cause of death, even when natural causes were suspected. But I was a little surprised they'd actually had sufficient time to rule out natural causes.

I didn't want to lose momentum, so I continued. "What about Sheila?" I thought back to the day of the funeral. Apart from losing the restaurant, Sheila had looked rather pleased about receiving the house and whatever money Harvey had left in his accounts. Could she have murdered Harvey? That theory sure as hell made a lot more sense than Abby Lee. If you believed Abby Lee—and I did—she wasn't aware of the contents in Harvey's will until the reading, so what motive could she possibly have to murder him? That should have been enough to prove there was no premeditation on her part.

And no one knew much about Sheila's life before she moved to Trouble. If you asked me, she should be the one in the hot seat. It was basic Criminology 101: it's almost always the spouse.

"Oh, they questioned her, too. I bumped into her at the station as she was leaving, but since I was the one who inherited The Poop Deck, I guess I'm just as much a prime suspect as she is."

"Unbelievable," I said. What were the police thinking? I had a mind to go over to the station myself and have a few choice words with Justin. Heaven help me, I was beginning to sound like Aunt Lula and Mom.

"Oh, no," Abby Lee said. "I know that look. Don't get involved on my account. I'm sure the police will figure it out and find the person responsible."

She was putting up a brave front, but I could see the tearstained streaks on her cheeks. She'd obviously cried during the interview, which led me to believe it was more of an interrogation than a few simple questions. But they did release her, which also told me they didn't have enough evidence to charge her with anything—yet.

"You've been in Trouble too long," I said, taking a long swig of my wine. "This is a small island. They don't handle cases like they do in the big cities." I didn't think for one second this investigation would be handled like the feds or even larger police departments would handle it. It wasn't that I didn't trust the local cops to do their jobs, but I knew they didn't have the resources, not to mention the experience, to handle a murder investigation. I couldn't even remember the last time Trouble had a homicide. And trust me, even in my absence, my mom would have told me if there had been one.

"I don't have a choice, do I?" Abby Lee asked.

Abby Lee was right, but there had to be a way to help her.

"I hate to have you repeat everything you just told the police, which by the way, I still can't believe you told them anything at all without an attorney present, but tell me exactly what happened the last time you saw Harvey. And don't leave anything out." With any luck we could try to piece together what happened that night and clear her off the suspect list.

She let out a sigh and started from the beginning. "I think I might have been the last person to see Harvey alive."

I sat there stunned for a moment. First off, he was killed the night of my welcome-home party—a party attended by most of the island. Second, how would anyone really determine the last person to see Harvey alive with a guest list that large? Normally, being the last person to see the victim alive wasn't good news, but I knew my friend was innocent. I really wanted to prompt her along and ask more questions, but I knew it was best to let her ease into her story. I'd try to stay quiet until after she finished.

"According to the witnesses—the police wouldn't say who—they said they saw me talking to Harvey right before he left. They didn't see him talk to anyone else after that."

Says who? It was enough to make my mind spin (although by this time maybe the wine was to blame). Who's to say Harvey didn't talk to one more person before he dropped to his death on the side of my parents' backyard?

"Did he say anything to you before you left?" There had to be something we were missing.

Abby Lee shook her head. "Not really. Harvey was on his way home. He said Sheila hadn't been feeling well, so he was ducking out early to check in on her. Then he said good night and that he'd see me in the morning."

It was a stupid question, but I had to ask. "Did you tell any of this to the police?" Everything Abby Lee had said sounded innocent enough to me. Did the police honestly think she was a suspect? So far, the case was circumstantial at best. And that was a far stretch.

Her eyes welled up again. "I tried, but they kept asking the same questions."

I nodded. That was standard in police interrogations—repeat the same questions over and over hoping to get a different response. The idea was that suspects would crack under pressure and change their story. "I see. What else did they ask?"

"The usual, I suppose. When did I leave the party . . . did Harvey and I leave together . . . was there anyone who could back up my story . . . I tried to tell them that all we said was good-bye, but they stuck to the same questions," she said.

"What about the restaurant? Did they ask you anything about that?" By now, everyone knew about Harvey leaving the restaurant to Abby Lee. If the will had been read in the privacy of the lawyer's office, instead of in front of the whole population of Trouble, news of her inheritance might have taken a few more days to get around town. But since it was public knowledge, it only stood to reason the police would have heard and questioned her about it. Especially if they were looking for motive.

"They asked if I knew anything about his will prior to his death," she said, fresh tears springing from her eyes. "Honestly, Jules, I had no idea he was leaving me the restaurant. I told them that, but they didn't seem to believe me."

A huge knot formed in the pit of my stomach—my best friend was about to get railroaded. I had been trained to believe that the system always worked. Hell, I was employed by the system. Damn it, I believed in the system. But I had to remind myself again that this wasn't DC. We were dealing with a small-town police department that didn't have the experience or manpower to investigate a murder. For them, it would be easier to play the odds and hope that the last person to see Harvey alive was the killer, who coincidentally also stood to gain from his death.

"Did they tell you anything else? Did they actually say you were a suspect?"

"No, but they said I was a person of interest and not to leave the island."

The good news was she hadn't been arrested yet. "You have options," I said. I wasn't entirely sure what those options were at the moment, but surely there had to be something we could do.

"Like what?"

An idea struck me. "We're going to find Harvey's killer and clear your name." Of course I said this with more confidence than I actually felt. I might work for the bureau, but I knew absolutely squat about investigative techniques aside from the basics I'd managed to pick up from the agents I worked with.

"What? You'd do that for me?" Abby Lee asked.

"Of course. I can't let my best friend go to jail for something she didn't do. Plus, we can't let his killer get away with murder. We owe it to Harvey." The more I spoke, the more I slowly started to convince myself that we could actually pull this off. This time it had to be the wine talking, but it sounded like a solid plan.

"Can't we get in trouble for interfering?"

"Let me worry about that," I said. "What do we know so far?" If we put our heads together, maybe we could figure out a motive or suspect.

"Like what?"

Like a smoking gun, I thought. But that would be easier said than done. "Anything that could help steer the investigation away from you. Think, Abby Lee. What do we know about Harvey that could possibly get him killed?"

Abby Lee thought about it as I polished off the last of my wine. She quickly refilled my glass without me having to ask. God bless her. "Sheila. She seems obsessed with taking over the restaurant."

"OK, that's a start. We'll add her to the list of possible suspects."

"He obviously made the provisions in his will a secret," she went on. "So how would anyone know what he had planned? I mean, I had no idea he was leaving me the restaurant . . ."

"And that's why the cops are looking in the wrong direction." At some point he must have changed his will in order to add Abby Lee as the sole beneficiary of his restaurant. And if it was that recent, there was a high probability that someone else thought they were inheriting The Poop Deck, not Abby Lee. Which meant thoughtful planning and premeditation on the part of the killer.

"What else?" I asked.

"Ugh, I don't know! I just can't imagine anyone killing Harvey."

"Me neither, but someone did," I pointed out.

My gut was telling me The Poop Deck was key to the investigation. And my instincts were never wrong. Except when it came to men.

I thought back to the reading of the will. It just seemed unlikely that there would have been another motive for someone to murder him. Harvey didn't have any enemies, he wasn't a philanderer (or it would have been all over the *Daily Gossip*), and although his restaurant did fairly well, it wasn't like he was a wealthy restaurateur. But despite his lack of great wealth, I still couldn't shake the feeling that someone had high hopes for the restaurant and was now a disappointed killer.

"Jules, I'm tired. I think maybe I should get home. Mother's probably worried about me."

I glanced at my watch. I hadn't realized it had gotten so late. The reunion would have ended hours ago. "You're probably right," I said. "You need to get some sleep after what you've just been through. We can brainstorm some more tomorrow."

She looked hopeful. Or at least like she was comforted by the fact that someone was in her corner. "Do you really think we can figure out who did this to Harvey?"

My heart broke. I knew how the system worked, and the way things were going, it didn't look good for Abby Lee. I was determined, more now than ever, to help my friend.

"Absolutely," I assured her. "But we're going to need some help." As soon as the words were out of my mouth, I hoped I could back up my promise.

"Who, Justin? I don't think—"

I snorted. "No, I have someone else in mind."

It was akin to making a pact with the devil, but the way I saw it, she owed me one.

CHAPTER TEN

True to my word, I ventured out first thing in the morning to gather intel. Since I didn't have much confidence that the local police would be pounding the pavement for new leads, I went in search of the one person who could help me gather enough information on Harvey and his widow—Aunt Lula.

Once, I assisted on a RICO case against some notorious family with mob connections in New Jersey. All I have to say is, these guys had nothing on Aunt Lula. Come to think of it, even the FBI could learn a thing or two from her. My aunt had a network of associates and underground informants that went beyond the island. Mob bosses used fear and intimidation, while Aunt Lula killed people with kindness. She even had folks from the tristate area who owed her favors. Simply put, my aunt traded in secrets. Any organized-crime syndicate would envy her cache of informants and spies, and the finesse with which she garnered such information. Aunt Lula didn't have to resort to violence to be feared. In her world, people didn't fear death, they feared being ostracized.

So it was on this bright, sunny morning I came to ask Doña Lula for a favor.

Aunt Lula captured the true essence of women in the South— she was the embodiment of the Texas frontier spirit. She could feel at home at the ballet or be comfortable hanging out with the menfolk for a day of dove hunting. I swear the woman would wear blue jeans with her pearls—if she actually owned a pair of denim. So it wasn't so unusual that she and her friends were members of the Trouble Island Ladies Trap & Skeet Club.

Being a hunter myself—having been taught by my dad how to shoot by the time I was ten—I respected the women's marksmanship and skill, but as I met the women early Saturday morning, I began to truly understand the club's appeal. Spread out across the wooden platform, I found the aging quartet, donned in pristine khaki hunting garb, each taking turns shooting skeet while sipping cocktails in between rounds. To them, it was like playing a round of golf, only with ammo. Per town ordinance, they practiced over on the far end of the island, far away from the center of town.

"Pull!" yelled one of the women.

A shotgun blast rang out, followed by, "Damn." The clay pigeon was still intact, getting smaller as it flew over the dunes into the brush.

"You're getting rusty in your old age, Ginny," commented one of the women.

"Hell, she's getting tipsy," Aunt Lula said in response.

I approached the women with caution, not relying on their aging eyesight. They were actually champion marksmen, but just the same, I didn't want to risk a stay in the hospital due to an accidental gunshot wound—then again, it would get me out of working at Palmetto Pink.

"I thought I'd find you here," I said, approaching my aunt.

"Jules! To what do we owe this lovely surprise? Care to join us?" Aunt Lula asked.

I eyed the gallon of premixed bloody marys by her side. Drinking this early in the day with my aunt and her cronies, with shotguns no less, was not how I'd planned to spend my day, but if I wanted the skinny on Sheila, this was the place to be.

"Actually, I'm here to ask you for a favor this time."

Her eyes were full of curiosity. "Speaking of favors, aren't you supposed to be at the store?" Aunt Lula questioned.

I'd wondered how long it would take her to notice. "Not till one," I said. Without her permission, I'd switched schedules with one of the other girls for this particular outing. "Do you have a moment?"

Aunt Lula gently propped her shotgun against the railing. "Why, of course, dear. Let's move farther down the deck, I'm afraid Ginny's had one too many cocktails this morning. No telling where her shots are going to fly."

I knew Aunt Lula was teasing, knowing full well the members of the Trouble Island Ladies Trap & Skeet Club held numerous trophies for their marksmanship skills. They even held celebrity status around town. Imagine, a group of little old ladies over the age of sixty being honored for the sole purpose of being good shots—only in Texas.

"Abby Lee's in trouble," I said, getting right to the point. "The police hauled her in for questioning. I suspect they think she killed Harvey."

Aunt Lula let the information sink in. When she finally spoke, she was furious. "Why, that's preposterous! Poor lamb couldn't hurt a fly. I have half a mind to go over to the station and give them a piece of my mind."

I cringed. That was exactly what I'd said to myself the night before.

"Poor Abby Lee. Those fools wouldn't know a cow patty from manure."

"I don't think they'd appreciate you telling them how to do their job, but we do need your help."

"And what could I possibly do to help?" Aunt Lula asked.

How could I phrase this delicately without completely offending her? "Um, well, it's well known you are always the first to know about the comings and goings around town." It was as nice as I could get without outright accusing my aunt of being the main instigator of all gossip on the island. Truth be told, I was actually surprised she didn't already know about Abby Lee being questioned last night. Her network of informants must have been sleeping on the job. "I thought maybe you could tell me a little more about Sheila."

Her eyes narrowed in on mine. "I see. And you think perhaps Sheila had a hand in killing her husband. Well I wouldn't be surprised. That woman has been nothing but trouble since she set foot in this town," she said, not noting the irony in her statement.

"What are y'all cackling about over there?" Jackie came over, losing interest in the clay pigeons in favor of our conversation. Following her lead, the other women lost interest as well and came over to where Aunt Lula and I were huddled.

"It's Abby Lee," Aunt Lula said. "Seems our town's finest think she murdered Harvey."

Gasps of surprise befell the women all at once. If you thought they loved guns, they loved gossip even more.

"What?"

". . . that poor girl."

"How do you know?"

". . . couldn't possibly!"

"Are you sure?"

A few of them cast raised eyebrows at Aunt Lula. No one had to tell me what they were thinking. They were wondering, like I had, why they hadn't already heard about Abby Lee being hauled in for questioning. If my aunt had known about it, it would have been the first item on the agenda.

"Now, ladies, hush for a second. I gotta think," Aunt Lula ordered.

The women simply stood there in silence and nodded. No one dared interrupt my aunt while she was in deep thought.

Upon further reflection, maybe asking Aunt Lula for advice wasn't one of my better ideas. I could have just as easily gone to Mom for information. No, scratch that . . . if I had gone to my mom, any information she gave would have accompanied an earful from her about not getting involved in a police investigation, blah, blah, blah.

After a moment of contemplation, Aunt Lula finally addressed the group. "Well, we all know that Abby Lee isn't capable of murder. So the solution is simple—we try to find Harvey's killer ourselves."

It was exactly the conclusion I had come up with the previous night, but it wasn't exactly what I had in mind when I'd asked Aunt Lula for help. All I wanted was some information that could help cast suspicion on someone other than my friend. The justice system called it "reasonable doubt." I called it saving my friend.

"I don't think—" I started to say before the old women started talking all at once again.

"Brilliant!" Ginny remarked.

"Where do we start?" Jackie wanted to know.

Carol didn't seem so sure. "Oh my . . ." Of the group, she was always the last on board when it came to my aunt's schemes. She only went along with Aunt Lula for fear of losing her social standing in the town. Although I suspected most of them went along with whatever my aunt said for the same reason.

"Ladies, quiet down. Really. How can anyone get a word in with all your cackling?" Aunt Lula said. "I suggest we all take a rain check for the day and go home and try to think of any suspicious activity that's occurred over the last few weeks. If you remember anything, call me immediately."

I was in shell shock—no pun intended—as I watched the women gather their shotguns and coolers, speaking eagerly among themselves, clearly excited about the prospect of solving a murder, as they made their way to their cars.

"Aunt Lula, do you think that was wise?" I asked. "Now they're just going to go around town letting everyone know what we're up to." I didn't have to mention that they weren't as discreet as my aunt when it came to idle gossip. I had hoped we could keep this on the down low. Especially from Justin.

"Nonsense," she assured me. "We'll keep it among ourselves. The gals know how to keep a secret."

Right. For them, not spreading rumors was like asking someone not to breathe. Somehow I knew this was going to bite me in the rump, but I kept my mouth shut, realizing I had just made the biggest mistake ever.

I finally arrived at Palmetto Pink for the afternoon shift. Aunt Lula wasn't supposed to be in today—Saturday mornings were reserved for shooting skeet with the gals and the afternoons for recovering from all the booze—but since I'd disrupted their shooting practice earlier that morning, she was still sober and too wound up to stay home.

"So? Where do we start?" Aunt Lula asked as soon as she walked in. I could tell she was trying to appear casual, but it had only been a couple hours since I last saw her. She could hardly contain her excitement about possibly solving a murder case. I didn't have the heart to tell her it was a long shot. We weren't police detectives. Hell, we weren't even private investigators.

I'd kept myself occupied by replenishing the floor with merchandise we'd sold out of during the last couple of days. While clearing Abby Lee's name was constantly on my mind, I had momentarily put it on hold to finish the task at hand. Now here was Aunt Lula ready to play Nancy Drew.

"On what?" I played dumb, knowing exactly what she was getting at. After I left Aunt Lula and her cronies, I'd decided right then and there not to get them involved. Maybe if I didn't bring it up again, they'd forget about my stupid idea of trying to outwit the police.

"What have you come up with so far? Any potential suspects?" It seemed my aunt had about as much patience as a kid in need of Ritalin. Though, I can't say I blamed her for her enthusiasm. This was the most excitement Trouble Island had seen in a while.

I didn't remind my aunt I came straight to the store after seeing her this morning. "It's too soon to tell."

Then I thought of something. Damn. It looked like I was going to need her help after all.

"Hey, did you know Harvey had a nephew?" I rehashed the conversation I had with Justin about the estranged nephew from Lufkin. Even though I had my sights on Sheila as suspect *numero uno*, it wouldn't hurt to take a look at Harvey's nephew. I thought any family member would be just as likely to kill someone over an inheritance.

She nodded. At least this time I wasn't giving her new information. Her reputation was secure. "Surprised me for a spell when I found out," she said. "In all the years I'd known Harvey, he never mentioned any sort of family. Then one day a few months back, his nephew strolls into town. I guess we all have our secrets."

"I wonder why he never mentioned him."

"Maybe the nephew's a convicted felon," she pondered out loud. "If that's the case and he were my kin, I wouldn't be bragging about him either," she said.

Here we go. "We don't know he's a convicted felon." Boy, how my aunt loved to speculate about people.

"No, I don't think that's it," I went on. There had to be another reason Harvey never mentioned having family. Maybe they just didn't get along. Lots of families didn't. Why should the Boyette clan be any different?

"You'd be surprised what people are capable of once they take their masks off. Why just the other day, at the diner, I heard Stanley Irsik bragging to Carol that he only bathed once a week. As if he were proud of it! Said taking a morning dip in the Gulf made him clean enough. Imagine!"

I ignored her commentary on personal hygiene. "Still, it seems odd that Harvey never spoke of his family before. I heard his nephew was going to stick around a few days and sort out some of his affairs. Maybe I'll pay him a visit and find out what his story is."

Aunt Lula's face broke out into a smile. "You see? You're already thinking like a real private eye."

I didn't want to burst her bubble of excitement by reminding her I wasn't a private investigator. Far from it. Sure, I had a graduate degree in criminology, but that didn't equate to a license. I was simply a friend helping out another friend.

Her eyes gleamed. "In fact, why don't you take the afternoon off so you can go talk to him?"

It was only two hours into my shift, but I wasn't going to refuse her offer. I'd do anything to be able to cut off work early. Even if it meant locating the estranged nephew of a murder victim so I could ask him questions. But first, I had to lay down some ground rules.

"Before I go off to do anything, I want you to promise me you aren't going to get your friends involved in all this," I said.

Aunt Lula eyed me before answering. "Fine. I'll keep them out of it, but you'll at least let me help, right?"

I couldn't see any way around it. "OK. But no snooping on your own, got it?"

She smiled, satisfied by our compromise. "Deal."

CHAPTER ELEVEN

There were only two places to stay on Trouble Island, aside from condo and beach-house rentals. Somehow I doubted Harvey's nephew was staying at Sheila's, so finding him wouldn't be too difficult in a town this size.

Just as I left the store, I realized I didn't know his name. What if he had a different family name, not Boyette? I couldn't very well call around asking for a guest without a name.

I quickly pulled out my cell phone. Aunt Lula was only too pleased to be able to offer the information. His name was Donald Walker. Maybe it wasn't such a bad idea to keep her on call after all.

I called the Trouble Inn, and fortunately for me, Teresa Brown was working reception at the inn. She'd had a major crush on my brother back in high school and had always been nice to me as a result. Teresa was all too happy to tell me what I wanted to know.

"Oh, sorry, Jules. We don't have a Walker listed on the registry. Why don't you try the Trouble Island Hotel? If he's not staying here, he probably checked in there," she said. "And how's Scott doing?"

"He's good. Still in Dallas. Thanks, Teresa." I quickly hung up before she asked what his relationship status was.

I didn't bother to call the hotel. Like Teresa said, if he wasn't staying at the Trouble Inn, he was staying there. With the hotel being on the other end of the island, I opted to take my truck—it had only taken a few hours to get my windshield replaced.

I found Donald seated at the bar, just where the hotel receptionist said he'd be. This was easier than I'd thought. It was a bit early in the day for happy hour, but who was I to judge? Earlier that morning, I'd left five gracefully aging widows drinking bloody marys out of a Tupperware thermos while in the possession of firearms.

Finding him was easy, but at this point I didn't know where to start. I'd never questioned anyone in connection to a murder. Sure, I worked for the FBI, but it was kind of like being a car salesman and not having a clue how to fix what's under the hood. I knew the particulars, but I had no experience in actually investigating crimes.

I hovered near the entrance to the bar and watched as he sipped his drink. I decided he seemed harmless enough, so I put on my big-girl pants and mustered up the courage to approach him at the bar before I got cold feet. My plan was to wing it, hoping I'd find my stride. The guys back at the bureau made it seem so easy.

Here goes nothing, I said to myself as I slid onto the bar stool next to his. "Hey, I recognize you from Harvey's funeral," I said. "I'm sorry for your loss."

Donald must have been deep in thought, staring into his half-empty glass. He jumped at the sound of my voice. "Oh, um, thanks."

"Were y'all close?" I already knew they weren't, but I was interested in his take on the relationship he had with his uncle.

He seemed more interested in getting a refill for his drink than the conversation. "Not really. I just came down to pay my respects," he said.

"You drove all the way down to say good-bye to an uncle you hardly knew? That's awfully good of you," I said.

"Not really," he said absently as he signaled to the bartender for another round. "Been down here before, actually."

A fact already confirmed by Aunt Lula. "Really?"

He finally turned his attention to me and gave me the full once-over treatment. I must have passed muster, because he went on to elaborate. "Up until a couple months ago, I had no idea I had an uncle, until my mother told me about him, so I finally came by for a visit."

"When was that exactly?"

Donald narrowed his eyes. He was getting suspicious. "You're awfully curious. Is there something you want?" he asked, not answering my question.

Looked like I'd have to brush up on my investigative techniques in the future. I waved off his suspicions. "You know how it is in small towns, we're always poking our noses in other people's business."

"Yeah, I guess," he said and downed the rest of his drink. "It was nice talking to you, but I'd better head out. I'm supposed to help Harvey's wife, and I'm already running late. What was your name again?"

"Jules."

"Well, it was nice meeting you, Jules, but I gotta run." Donald signaled for the check. "Just charge it to my room," he said to the bartender as he left the bar.

The man behind the bar looked expectantly at me. As much as I wanted to down a glass of wine to calm my nerves, I passed. "Oh, nothing for me. I was just leaving."

I learned absolutely zilch from talking to Harvey's nephew, but at least he confirmed he had visited Trouble Island before. Perhaps it was nothing, but it was still odd that a nephew Harvey never mentioned would randomly come for a visit.

I wondered what exactly he was helping Sheila with.

CHAPTER TWELVE

Thank God it was my day off at the store. Even after only a few days, I wasn't sure how much more working at Palmetto Pink I could take. If the sole purpose of my being there wasn't to help my aunt out, I would have quit already. Then again, I wouldn't have taken the job in the first place.

Since we were all free for the day, Aunt Lula invited me and Abby Lee over to her house for her famous ceviche. It was famous only because it was the only thing she knew how to make, and fortunately, for everyone involved, it was delicious.

Aunt Lula lived on the opposite end of the island from my folks, so I had to drive to her place. Going over to my aunt's brought back fond memories. I always loved going over to Aunt Lula's as a kid. The house that she and my uncle Jep built together was right on the water, her enclosed sleeping porch overlooking the Gulf. Every weekend I was allowed to stay over, much to my mom's annoyance. It was during those times Aunt Lula let me play dress up, taught me how to set a formal dinner table, and taught me how to play poker with a straight face.

When Aunt Lula realized both Abby Lee and I had a day off, it was her idea to meet at her house. She thought it wise to conduct what she considered business in private. She of all people knew that talking in public would only ignite the already-fueled gossip surrounding Harvey's murder.

We decided to hold off discussing the case until Abby Lee arrived, which wasn't long as we finally heard Abby Lee pull up onto the drive. My aunt and I each greeted her with a hug the moment she entered the house. She didn't have to say it, but I could tell the investigation was taking its toll on her. The dark circles under her eyes were a dead giveaway. I wondered how many sleepless hours she'd clocked in.

Once the pleasantries were over, Abby Lee and I settled into the living room and waited for my aunt to come back out of the kitchen with the food. I couldn't help but notice Abby Lee looked a bit more withdrawn than I'd last seen her. My friend's once bright and optimistic disposition had turned sullen.

I had no new information to lift Abby Lee's spirits, so we sat in silence as we waited for Aunt Lula to put together the finishing touches on lunch. To occupy the dead silence in the air, I was flipping through the pages of a *Garden & Gun* magazine my aunt had left on the sofa, when something caught my attention. Right there, on the bottom left corner of the page, was a brief write-up on Trouble Island.

Holy crap! I looked at the circulation date—it was the March/April issue. The piece mentioned our quiet "hidden gem" of an island town, showcasing its hometown feel and regional Southern cuisine.

There was a sudden sense of pride that surfaced from within, seeing our small island written up, but at the same time I felt it was the cause of all our troubles here in Trouble. The magazine was most certainly regional, catering mostly to Southern subscribers, but it was large enough that it would draw attention to our town.

"Hey, Aunt Lula—did you happen to read your latest issue of *Garden and Gun*?"

She came out from the kitchen holding a tray of tostadas and ceviche. "Of course I have. Why?"

"Did you see this?" I asked, pointing to the magazine article. "Trouble Island is mentioned."

Abby Lee came over to where I was seated on the couch to take a closer look. "Oh yeah. I remember that. After the article came out, we had tons of restaurant people coming by The Poop Deck asking if Harvey was willing to sell."

"Did he entertain any offers?" I asked.

"No. He said he'd never sell," Abby Lee said. "Pissed off a lot of folks. But Harvey was adamant. He said he would never let anyone get their hands on his place. No matter how much they offered."

"Let me see that." Aunt Lula grabbed the issue from my hand as I helped myself to a tostada chip from the tray and dipped it in the ceviche—delish. I was ravenous, and no one made ceviche like my aunt, not even my mom, complete with extra lime and chile pepper for that extra kick.

I shoved another overflowing chip in my mouth as Aunt Lula perused the article. I couldn't help but notice she had to squint in order to read the small piece on our island. She was too proud to wear glasses. "I guess I must have missed this. I only ever look at the pictures."

A likely story. "Why don't you get your eyes checked?" I asked, already knowing the answer.

"Once you admit to losing your eyesight, next thing you know, people will think you're losing your marbles, too."

Aunt Lula must have been losing a little bit of both. How could she have missed the attention given to The Poop Deck as a result of the write-up? Maybe the news wasn't juicy enough for her to give it a second thought. Who cared about folks eating their weight in crab cakes and fried shrimp? Right?

"What are you thinking, Jules?" Abby Lee asked, bringing me back to the present. "Do you think it has something to do with the case?"

"I'm thinking that all the unwanted attention on the restaurant could have gotten Harvey killed," I said.

"Oh my God! Do you really think someone would kill him for The Poop Deck?" Abby Lee asked.

"Dear, I hate to remind you, but the police already think you killed Harvey for the restaurant," Aunt Lula pointed out.

The thought of unwanted publicity certainly broadened the pool of suspects. The only question was, who else besides Abby Lee, Sheila, or Donald had motive to kill Harvey over a small seafood shack?

Or what if Sheila had gotten wind that Harvey stood to gain some major bucks by selling his restaurant? What if some greedy restaurateur got angry at Harvey's refusal to sell and wouldn't take no for an answer? I began to get excited at the possibilities. I wanted to find out exactly when Donald came to visit Harvey. If we added him to the list of suspects, maybe we could cast some doubt on Abby Lee.

Donald said he had visited Harvey a few months ago. What if it was right around the time the article surfaced? I wondered if he or his mother found out about his uncle's restaurant from this issue of *Garden & Gun*. If they had, I wondered if his previous visit to the island was for the purpose of buying the place from Harvey. What if Donald had demanded money, thinking Harvey was rolling in it? One look at the place would tell you it was nothing more than a modest restaurant, but maybe he figured it was worth much more, thanks to all the attention.

"Hey, did you ever meet Harvey's nephew?" I asked Abby Lee.

She shook her head. "I didn't even know he had family."

"Well, he did, and when I spoke to his nephew at his hotel earlier today, he told me he had met Harvey once before. I'm guessing it was right around the time the issue came out. I'm curious if his visit had anything to do with The Poop Deck."

"Harvey didn't say anything about it," Abby Lee said. "But that doesn't mean anything. Why? Do you think he did it? His nephew wasn't even at your welcome-home party. At least, not that I know of. If it was him, when would he have slipped Harvey the poison?"

Damn. Abby Lee was right. Donald hadn't been at my party. As far as we knew, he arrived right before the funeral. Still, it was a lead worth pursuing. At the very least, as Harvey's blood relative, he could try to stake a claim on Abby Lee's inheritance. Besides, how did we know Harvey's nephew wasn't already in Trouble with the intention to kill him? Donald could have easily laid low until the funeral. We just had to figure out how and when he'd slipped Harvey the poison.

The toxicology report. It would tell us exactly what kind of poison was used—and once we knew that, the police could determine a time frame.

I took a page from Aunt Lula's playbook and set out to have another look at Harvey's nephew. This time, I planned to do my homework first, instead of approaching a suspect totally blind.

If anyone thought I relied only on my aunt and the local gossip mill to dole out valuable information, they'd be wrong. I had a friend on the inside that I knew would be willing to help.

One of my colleagues, Charisse Berree, a crime analyst like myself, was another Weight Watcher Wendy casualty. When the opportunity for a transfer came up at the Boston Field Office, she vied for the opportunity to get out from under Wendy's reign of terror. I would have jumped at the opportunity myself, but I was involved with James and I didn't want to move. She knew that with me not competing against her, she was a shoo-in. In the end, she got the transfer. Charisse was so happy to get out of there she said she owed me big-time.

It was time to collect.

"I need you to do me a huge favor," I said. "Can you look up a Donald Walker and let me know what you find? I'm looking for the usual. Debt, liens—anything that raises any red flags."

"Screening a prospective boyfriend?" Charisse laughed. She knew about my breakup with James, so it was no surprise she'd jumped to that conclusion, even though I knew she was kidding. She didn't say it, but I was sure she was happy he and I broke up after the transfer opportunity came up, or I might have been the one sitting pretty in Boston right about now.

"No. Just a potential suspect."

"Causing trouble in Trouble already, Jules?"

"Hardly."

I gave her the lowdown and what I knew of Donald: age, birth date, place of birth—everything I was able to glean from the Internet. Hopefully she would be able to get some dirt on Harvey's nephew, the info I couldn't get with just a simple online search, anything that could put him on the suspect list.

"Oh, and can you also check his credit card transactions within the last week or so?" That would tell me the exact date he arrived in Trouble. "I'm interested in any charges made to the Trouble Island Hotel."

"You got it, Jules."

Two hours later I had my answer. Charisse never disappointed.

"The guy is clean. No judgments, liens, pays his taxes on time," she said. "It was hard to sort through the credit card transactions for specific dates, but it looks like he arrived in Trouble on the seventh."

The day of my welcome-home party.

We had a timeline, but I was hoping she'd find something else that could give Donald some kind of motive. Or at least cast some reasonable doubt on Abby Lee. If he was in debt or owed money to someone, it wouldn't be a stretch to imagine him wanting to get rid of his uncle for the restaurant.

"Thanks, Charisse. I owe you one," I said.

"I'll just put it on your tab," she said and hung up.

I settled in to review the facts of the case. I pulled out my agenda to take some notes. With all the advances in technology, I still preferred to write things down. I was sure I was one of the few people left on the planet that still used a notebook agenda instead of an electronic calendar. There was something satisfying about writing things down and being able to scratch them off a list—a sense of accomplishment. That, and I was always afraid that if I deleted something permanently, I would need the information again later and it'd be gone. So it was pen and paper for me.

I started with a fresh page and began to write down all the facts:

1. Harvey was poisoned.
2. Harvey left The Poop Deck to Abby Lee.
3. Sheila is contesting the will.
4. Abby Lee is a suspect in Harvey's murder.
5. Sheila is also a suspect.
6. Magazine did a write-up on The Poop Deck.
7. Harvey's nephew arrived the day he was killed.

The last item certainly made Donald Walker a suspect in my book. Something about his presence in town the day of the murder nagged at me. Was there a failed reconciliation between the family members during his last visit, and had he come back to finish what he started?

I continued to glare at the list, hoping I would see something I'd overlooked. So far, most of the items on my list seemed to tie directly to The Poop Deck.

Jotting down notes and staring at my short list made me more frustrated than before. Even if Harvey didn't have much money, the real estate value on his restaurant or future earnings from the place alone could be enough for an estranged nephew—or anyone for that matter—to kill over. As next of kin, Donald certainly had a right to contest whatever Harvey left in his estate. Then I realized the same held true for Sheila.

And Abby Lee—the person who ended up inheriting it.

CHAPTER THIRTEEN

As much as Aunt Lula supported me investigating Harvey's murder, she still demanded much of my time at Palmetto Pink. She didn't budge an inch on her insistence that I help around the store. I had hoped that once she was on board with our plan to help clear Abby Lee's name, she would find someone else to take over my responsibilities at the store, but no such luck.

I was stuck in perpetual retail hell.

This particular morning made me once again regret my decision to work for Aunt Lula at Palmetto Pink, even though I didn't remember agreeing to be a part-time associate in the first place. For in walked the kind of customers every retail sales associate dreaded—children.

There were five kids total, all under the age of ten—I think—running around the shop, picking up items, imprinting their ice cream–slathered hands on the mirrors, and leaving droplets of Big Red, resembling a trail of blood, on the pristine white tile behind them.

I watched in horror as the little hellions continued to wreak havoc around the store like a tornado. I cringed every time one of them handled a scarf, touched a bikini bottom, or picked up a pair of sunglasses. I had no choice but to follow behind them, straightening every item they managed to put out of place. Where in the hell was their mom?

"And Mom thinks this is what I need in my life? No thanks," I said out loud to no one in particular and certainly out of earshot from the kids. At least, I didn't think they heard me. Who was I kidding? I didn't really care if they did.

Judging from their clothes, the kids were definitely tourists. Plus, no Trouble Island mom would allow her kids to storm into Aunt Lula's shop without supervision. They knew better. I was still searching for their mother when Aunt Lula came out from the back room.

"Oh, dear," she said upon seeing the running children. She had to step back in order to avoid one of the boys running past her.

I glanced up, grateful we were both on the same page. "You have insurance, right?"

At that precise moment, a frazzled-looking woman ran into the store. "There they are! I was window-shopping, and somehow they managed to get away from me," she said breathlessly, rounding up her spawn. "I hope they weren't any trouble."

"None at all," Aunt Lula said.

I had to bite my tongue to keep from suggesting she invest in leashes, but somehow I didn't think she wanted my opinion on the matter. It was an unspoken rule that if you didn't have children of your own, you couldn't criticize someone else's.

She quickly rounded them up, and they left the store—amazingly leaving the store in one piece—with the mother again apologizing for the inconvenience.

"This is exactly why I don't want kids," I said to Aunt Lula. "Much less five of them."

"Oh, I bet you'll think differently when they're your own."

That's what they all say. "You don't have any," I pointed out.

"No. Your Great-Uncle Jep and I never did," she said. "Wasn't in the cards."

From her tone, I couldn't figure out if she was regretful or grateful.

There was a lot about Aunt Lula I didn't know, but it wasn't for lack of trying. Every time I asked about anything too personal, she would shut down, and the matter was closed. I even tried asking my dad about Aunt Lula's past, and true to form, he also remained mum on the subject. "If she wants you to know about her past, it's her story to tell," he told me.

With no other customers to corral or clean up after, I straightened up the store for the second time that morning. The task was mundane and beyond boring. I wondered to myself for the billionth time why Aunt Lula insisted she needed the extra help. It was obvious she didn't need another sales associate.

With all the ruckus from the kids and the redundancy of folding T-shirts every hour on the hour for lack of something else to do, I almost forgot to eat. My stomach fortunately reminded me of the time.

And who should show up right as I was about to take my lunch break?

Justin.

"Care to join me for lunch?"

Aunt Lula didn't even give me a second to turn him down or wonder what he was doing at the store before answering for me. "She'd love to go to lunch."

As a properly raised Southerner, I couldn't very well decline after that. My mom, not to mention Aunt Lula, would tan my hide. I shrugged my shoulders and grabbed my purse. "Sure, why not?"

The two of us walked in silence as we made our way over to the diner across the street. It was owned and operated by Carol Breault, one of Aunt Lula's best friends. Since Carol was also a member of the Trouble Island Ladies Trap & Skeet Club, the diner boasted pictures of their championship trap team along the far wall of the restaurant. Only open for breakfast and lunch, it was another favored landmark on the island. Her pies were legendary—if you could make it there before three.

"Glad you finally decided to take me up on my offer," Justin said, sliding into the booth across from where I had already seated myself.

I didn't remind him that it was Aunt Lula who accepted on my behalf. "This is lunch, not dinner."

"So it is," he said, oblivious to my indifference. "Either way, I'm glad you accepted my invitation. I know you're still mad at me, and I don't blame you, really I don't. But you of all people know I'm just doing my job."

Yeah, I'd heard that one before. Why did every male member of the law enforcement community use "the job" as an excuse for everything? Little did he know I'd only reluctantly agreed for fear of Aunt Lula's wrath and to find out what he knew about the case. If I played nice, maybe he'd offer up something. He had to know I would try to pry information out of him sooner or later. He probably already had a defense strategy in place. But it wasn't going to stop me from trying.

I shrugged. "Sure, why not? It's only lunch."

"Come on, Jules. I know you're still pissed that we took Abby Lee in for questioning. Believe me, it was the last thing I wanted to do. At least, not the way it went down," he said. "If you want to be mad at anyone, be mad at Chief Poteet. It was his call."

"Sure."

He sounded sincere. I knew he hadn't intentionally treated Abby Lee that way, but I kept telling myself he was still the deputy chief. He could have intervened.

We placed our order with the waitress and spent the remainder of the time while we waited for our food staring at each other. As we sat there in silence, I realized that no matter how angry I was at him, I would always have a soft spot when it came to Justin. I wondered again what would have happened if we had gone to college together and gotten married. It was a moment of wishful thinking on my part—with my track record it probably wouldn't have ended up well.

The silence between us was palpable, and the tension didn't go unnoticed by Justin. "Jules, this is ridiculous," he finally said after ten minutes—yeah, I was keeping track. "You can't keep blaming me. We're just doing our job."

There was that word again—his job.

"I know, OK? But just because I understand doesn't make it any easier," I said. "Abby Lee is my oldest friend. And your friend, too, I might add. I can't just let her go down and take the rap for someone else. She's being railroaded, and you know it."

"No one's getting railroaded. She's just a person of interest, that's all."

"If you say so."

His gorgeous chocolate browns narrowed, as if he were going to say something in response, but he quickly changed his mind. "So how's the bureau? You like it there?" Justin asked, changing the subject.

"It's all right." No need to mention that my boyfriend left me and my half-starved supervisor made the fifty-plus hours per week I worked a living nightmare. It wasn't as bad as working at Palmetto Pink, but it was a close second.

"Is this how it's going to be?"

"Pretty much." I felt bad about my behavior, but I was still mad at him.

I gave Justin credit, though; he wouldn't let up. He seemed bound and determined to have a normal conversation. "You seeing anyone?"

That was a question I wasn't expecting. I certainly didn't want to rehash my failed relationship, least of all with Justin. "Nope. Still single."

"I see."

Eventually he gave up on having a decent conversation, and we spent the remainder of our lunch eating our sandwiches and staring at everything but each other. So much for getting the inside scoop on his investigation. It was wishful thinking on my part to think he would willingly let me in on the case, considering my behavior and how I'd basically told him what a crappy job he was doing. It certainly wasn't how I had imagined spending time with my former high school sweetheart, but that was the story of my life—nothing in real life happened the way it did in my fantasies.

"How was lunch?" Aunt Lula asked the second I entered the store.

"Fine, but I imagine Justin is regretting his choice in lunch dates right about now."

"Jules! You didn't antagonize the poor man, did you?"

I already felt bad enough about how Justin and I left things at the diner; I didn't need to be reminded again by Aunt Lula, but I still felt justified. "I hadn't planned on it. And why do you care? He's not doing anything to stop Chief Poteet from placing Abby Lee as their number-one suspect or searching for the real killer."

Sometimes my aunt made me feel like she was constantly losing her patience with me. Today was no exception. "Yes, dear, but he is still a man," she chided. "You can't go around making them feel any less."

I snorted in response. "He had it coming."

"When this is all over, you are going to regret treating him that way, you mark my words."

I didn't bother to remind her that by the time all this blew over I would be back at headquarters helping agents solve other crimes.

Since arriving in Trouble, I'd gotten to the point where I stopped obsessing about my breakup with James. My heartache had dulled enough that I only thought of him right before settling in for the night. That was bad enough by my estimation, but, hey, a girl had to take her victories when she could, no matter how small.

My thoughts were replaced by another member of the male persuasion—Justin. Sure, I talked a good game in front of him, and I felt justified in my reaction over the way the police were handling the case, but I couldn't help but wonder "what if?" I could be mad and still lust after him, right?

Was a fling even worth having, knowing full well I was only here for a couple of months? Hell, was it worth dealing with Heather once she found out? And believe me, she'd figure it out fast on her own. No need to involve the gossip circle.

No, I ultimately decided as I tossed and turned in my sleep. I would keep my relationship with Justin strictly platonic—no matter how much his gorgeous smile invaded my dreams.

It was a fitful night's sleep to say the least, but I was pleased to have come to a decision.

CHAPTER FOURTEEN

If I thought being employed by the FBI would give me a leg up in tracking down Harvey's killer, I was sorely mistaken. I had gotten no closer to getting some solid leads, even after meeting with Harvey's nephew. This was going to be a long summer if I didn't come up with something soon. Working at Palmetto Pink wasn't the kind of summer hiatus I had envisioned.

Same routine, different day. I had another shift at Palmetto Pink, and I was getting restless. No sooner had I imagined having to work the rest of the summer for my aunt than another customer walked into the store with her daughter in tow. The customer carried one of the store's signature shopping bags. I groaned—she was here to make a return.

"I'd like to make a return," she said, holding a dress without the tag.

Gee, really? I smiled at my deductive-reasoning skills. Maybe I shouldn't discount a career in private investigation after all. "Sure, do you have the receipt?"

The lady's face puckered up like she'd just sucked on a lemon. I was all too familiar with that look. She didn't have a receipt and was going to try to talk her way out of it.

"My husband bought it for me, but he threw away the receipt. He's standing right outside the store," she explained, as if his mere presence could be substituted for a sales receipt.

I knew it! "I'm sorry, but without a receipt you can only get store credit or make an exchange." I didn't even bother to point out that even if she had the receipt, the dress was missing the price tag.

"But he just bought it last week! My daughter was with him. Right, Mary?"

The little girl, who couldn't have been more than ten, nodded vigorously at this. It didn't take a genius—or an experienced mom—to realize that the little girl would agree to just about anything her mother said.

"Do you know if you're in our system?" I asked. Aunt Lula had a system that captured all customer purchases, including their contact information, so she could send out mailers for promotional events.

She pretended to think. "My husband said he was, right, Mary?"

Again, the daughter nodded.

My fingers rested on the keyboard, ready to type. "OK, what's the name?"

"Michael Harris," the woman said slowly, pronouncing every syllable as if I were daft. Clearly she didn't appreciate me calling her out on the return.

My sixth sense told me I wouldn't find his name in the system, but I typed in the name anyway. And just as I expected, nothing popped up. "Well, it looks like he isn't in the system."

"But he gave his name. My daughter was there." She continued to argue as Little Darling Snowflake continued to nod.

I really wanted to ask the lady how her daughter could possibly remember a sales transaction from a week ago, but instead I said, "Ma'am, we ask all our customers their name. If they don't appear in our system, they are then asked if they'd like to be entered.

Since his name isn't listed, your husband probably declined. Unfortunately, because he did, I can't pull up his purchase history."

She dropped the hostility and went the sympathetic route. "He was so sure I would love the dress he threw away the receipt."

Seriously? What man buys a gift for his wife and throws out the receipt? Better yet, who buys a gift and doesn't ask for a gift receipt?

There was also the issue of the missing price tag. My bet was she wore the dress, then decided to return it.

"I'm sorry, ma'am, but the best I can do is store credit or an exchange. If you don't like the dress, you're welcome to try on a different style or size for an exchange."

"Oh, forget it," she said, finally giving up. She made a big show of snatching the dress and shopping bag from the counter and pulled Little Darling Snowflake along as they abruptly made their way out of the store.

This was yet another reminder of why I wasn't cut out for retail. I just had to tell myself that this job was only temporary until I went back to Virginia.

After a stressful day at the store, I was in dire need of a drink. I immediately thought of Abby Lee. She was spending all her time at the restaurant lately. Personally, I think she spent all her waking hours there to avoid being alone. Not that I blamed her. Fortunately, the restaurant patrons didn't let a minor thing like her being a suspect in a homicide investigation get in the way of their two-for-one crab special. Everyone, except for the Trouble Island Police Department, knew she was innocent.

I looked up the main number for The Poop Deck and gave her a call.

"You read my mind," she said after I asked her to meet me for drinks after work. "We're a little swamped, but nothing Pete can't handle, so I'm game. Meet you at the Gator in ten?"

"I'll grab us a table," I said, pleased she was able to take off at a moment's notice. *That*, I reminded myself, *is the marking of a true friend. Someone who'll drop everything for happy hour.* I had to make it a point not to let our friendship fall through the cracks again after I left.

While most of the island believed in Abby Lee's innocence, she wasn't exactly the most favored person in Trouble—she was still a murder suspect after all—and could probably stand to stay away from the limelight until her good name was restored. I knew the folks over at The Crooked Gator wouldn't give her any grief, though. It was the closest thing we had to a dive bar on the island. They had an open-door policy, which even extended to murder suspects. Their unofficial motto was, "Everybody gets service, unless you can't pay." Plus, it would be good for her to get out, away from the restaurant.

She found me at the corner table by the bar ten minutes later, waving excitedly as she approached. "I'm so glad you called. I could use a drink myself."

"I bet."

"So, what are we having?" Abby Lee asked.

I didn't have to think twice. "A Gatorita," I said. "On the rocks, salt." Ever since I came back to Trouble, I'd been craving one of the Gator's legendary margaritas. They were legendary because they were so good you didn't realize how much tequila you'd actually consumed until the next morning.

"Two Gatoritas coming right up," Abby Lee said as she made her way to the bar to place our drink order.

Five minutes later, we were both savoring our margaritas. I had yet to find a bar anywhere in the DC metro area that could make tequila taste so good.

"Now spill—what's the real reason you're here?" Abby Lee asked.

I marveled at her ability to forget about her troubles for a while and focus on someone other than herself. I could read between the lines. I knew what she was really asking—why, after all these years, did I decide to come back home for almost the entire summer?

"I got dumped," I finally admitted. After what Abby Lee had been through the last week, she deserved to know the truth, even if the truth paled in comparison to her own problems.

She offered me an apologetic smile and raised her glass. "Nothing like a few margaritas to mend a broken heart."

Or being unofficially accused of murder.

"You got that right," I said.

"So what happened? Was he cheating on you?"

I sighed into my almost-empty margarita glass. I watched as Abby Lee signaled to the bartender for another round. "Nothing as dramatic as that. Although I almost wish that were the case. No, he just decided I wasn't the one."

"Ouch. That had to hurt."

"No kidding. I think I could handle another woman, just not a woman that doesn't exist," I said.

Abby Lee sat, thoughtful for a moment. "What about Justin?"

"What about him?"

"Any interest now that you're back?"

I was taken aback by her question. "Seriously? You're talking about the guy who's basically accusing you of murder. How much tequila did they put in these?" I asked, pointing to our mugs.

"He's just doing his job, Jules."

Ugh. The job. There was that ugly three-letter word again.

I was always amazed at Abby Lee's forgiving disposition. Here she was worried she'd be formally charged any day now, yet she was cutting the future arresting officer some slack.

"There'll always be something between us, but I don't think that's enough to build a new relationship on, especially since I'll be going back home soon," I said, thinking the margarita was making me more open and honest about the subject.

"Too bad. You two were a great couple," she mused.

"Hmm . . . way back when perhaps," I said. "In case you haven't noticed, we're all grown up now, with big, real-world problems, not hot and heavy teens."

She shrugged and polished off the rest of her margarita as the bartender placed a new one in her direction. Abby Lee raised up her fresh margarita for a toast. "To Harvey."

"To Harvey," I said.

"So really, no old sparks?"

She couldn't let sleeping dogs lie. It was about time to put the kibosh on the tequila. What more could I say about a relationship that ended a decade ago? Sure, every time I ran into Justin I wanted to hit him. But I wouldn't necessarily call it sparks.

"None," I lied.

She nodded. "Probably for the best. 'Cuz look who's making her way over."

I turned around and saw Heather Clegg heading straight in our direction. Didn't she have better things to do?

Heather didn't waste time exchanging pleasantries. "They say you can tell a lot about the company you keep," she said, pointing her head toward Abby Lee, the implication clear. She was now standing right next to me and bent down low enough to whisper in my ear. Her damp breath made me squirm, and I could smell the beer on her breath. "Just remember, you had your chance—he's mine now."

Abby Lee couldn't help herself, especially not after the jab at her expense. "You know, I've always wondered, was it Justin who dumped you, or the other way around?"

I giggled in my margarita.

Heather's face turned ten shades of red. "We're still dating," Heather insisted. She stood up from her crouched position and looked down over me. "Just see to it that you stay out of the way."

Justin had said they were over, but Heather seemed so convinced they were still together it was hard not to believe that there was some truth to it. Maybe he was embarrassed to admit he was still dating her. Though how he could stand to be with her this long was a mystery to me. The ratio of eligible women to men may have dwindled over the years, but I still refused to believe Justin was so hard up that he had to settle for someone like Heather.

Abby Lee laughed. "You just keep telling yourself that."

Just as Heather sashayed back to her seat at the bar, her hip bumped our table, spilling my margarita onto my lap. I tried to tell myself that it was an accident, but something told me it wasn't. Thankfully, the glass was only half full.

"She did that on purpose," Abby Lee said, almost half out of her seat, ready to confront her. It was nice to see the semblance of her old self, but we both knew it was a waste of energy to go after Heather.

"It's OK, Abby Lee. The last thing you need is to get into a bar brawl with Heather. You know as well as I do she doesn't fight fair."

"You're right. She's more slippery than a pocketful of pudding," she agreed. "Did you know she got that dispatcher job at the department just so she could be closer to Justin?"

Good employment opportunities were slim on an island this small, so most folks commuted to work over on the mainland. I was sure Heather working as a dispatcher was just a coincidence. I didn't condone dipping her pen in the company ink, a lesson I'd learned firsthand, but to each her own. "I'm sure she doesn't have many job prospects."

Abby Lee shook her head. "No way. She got that job to keep tabs on him."

"As much as I hate to admit it, I almost feel sorry for her," I said. Heather was either insecure or crazy. Either way, it was sad.

My best friend lifted her margarita, signaling another toast. I followed her lead. "To renewed friendships, psychotic girlfriends, and Gatoritas," she said, clinking her glass to my now-empty glass.

"To tequila!" I added and quickly ordered another round.

By the next morning, I was cursing Jose Cuervo.

CHAPTER FIFTEEN

The fact that I was hungover was compounded by the ringing doorbell. It rang once, then twice, and then, when I thought the obnoxious sound had finally stopped, it chimed again.

Where in the world were my parents? It wasn't like my mom to keep a guest waiting on the front porch. Furthermore, who in the hell came calling at such a god-awful time? My eyes were still shut, so I didn't know the actual time, but my aching head told me it was too early to receive visitors.

A thunderous pounding on the stairs, followed by a loud voice yelling, "Jules!" gave me my answer.

"Jules, wake up!" Aunt Lula cried again, almost out of breath.

"Whaaa . . . ?" I rubbed the crust out of my eyes and focused on my aunt. My always graceful and elegant aunt looked like she had just run a half marathon. "What?"

"I just came from church. It's Abby Lee," she said.

Either I hadn't had my morning jolt of caffeine and was truly hungover, or Aunt Lula wasn't making any sense. I opted for the latter. "What are you talking about? You saw Abby Lee at church?"

So that's why no one answered the door. My folks were at church. The whole town went to church on Sundays—except for yours truly. I didn't live in Trouble anymore, so in my mind that absolved me from having to attend.

"No. I heard they were going to arrest Abby Lee soon!"

I sprung out of bed faster than you could say "hot skillet" and went into full-blown panic mode. "What? How do you know?"

They couldn't already be making an arrest. It had only been a little over a week since Harvey was killed. And I hadn't done anything to help Abby Lee. All I'd done so far was speculate about motives and possible suspects.

"Edith Clemmons. She told me and the gals after the service that the police said they got a search warrant for Abby Lee's house and The Poop Deck." Edith was the one whose son worked for the police. Now why did that name ring a bell? The officer at the reunion who took Abby Lee in for questioning! He must be the one feeding his mom information.

I had to calm down in order to think straight. I let the questions fly. "What? Does Abby Lee know?"

Aunt Lula shook her head. "My sources didn't say when the police were going to make their way over, but they're doing it sometime today. I tried to go over to Abby Lee's after the service, but she wasn't home. I suspect she was at church as well." Abby Lee and her mother were Episcopalian, so they didn't attend the Catholic mass over at Our Lady of the Sea. "When I couldn't find her, I came straight over here to tell you. What are we going to do?"

My mind went in a million directions. I had hoped that by now I'd have something to offer the police in terms of evidence, or at least be able to offer another theory or alternate motive. If the police were going to search Abby Lee's house and place of business, they were looking for something specific. And if they found whatever they were looking for, she could be arrested.

I snapped out of my tequila hangover and went over to The Poop Deck. It was after eleven, and the early churchgoers were already headed to spread the local town gossip over bloody marys and crab legs. I figured Abby Lee would be at the restaurant after church, prepared to meet the morning brunch rush.

Just as I suspected, Abby Lee was prepping for brunch. I didn't exactly intend to start the day by being the bearer of bad news, but hey, that's what best friends were for, right?

"I skipped mass today, but still managed to catch the gospel according to Aunt Lula," I said, half dragging her into the small office.

"What?"

"According to her sources, the police obtained search warrants for here and your house."

Abby Lee slumped into the office chair. "What?"

I told her everything my aunt had managed to gather from Edith Clemmons. Which didn't amount to much. "I don't even know what it is they're looking for. As far as I know, they don't even know what kind of poison killed Harvey. This doesn't look good."

I knew I could trust Justin not to do something dishonest and plant evidence, but I didn't trust the others. Especially Chief Poteet. As idealistic as our island beach town appeared, our police chief was as crooked as the criminals he pretended to protect the town from.

"At this point, it doesn't seem like the odds are in my favor no matter what happens." Abby Lee seemed resigned to the fact that all leads pointed to her. It was heartbreaking to watch the once bubbly former high school prom queen's world fall apart.

"Is your mother at home?" I asked. I was sure the last thing Abby Lee wanted was to have to alert her mother that the police were about to search their home. Somehow, Abby Lee had managed to keep the issue of her being a prime suspect from her mother. It was now only a matter of time before her mother figured out just how much trouble Abby Lee was in.

Abby Lee shook her head. "It's Sunday. She went over to her sister's, Aunt Jean's, in Port Arthur. She won't be back until tomorrow."

"Good. Hopefully they plan to execute the search today, before she gets back."

"What are you going to do?" she asked as I pulled out my cell.

"I'm calling Justin. The least he could do is tell us where they're searching first."

After what seemed like a one-sided conversation, with me doing most of the yelling, I finally got Justin to tell me they were going to start with the house first. "I can't keep you two from being there, but I really wish you'd just let us do our job," he said over the phone.

Abby Lee and I arrived at her place just as Justin and the officers got there to begin their search.

"You can stay, but I will not have you interfering or asking questions," Justin said the second we pulled up.

"Fine. But can you at least tell us what you're looking for?" I asked.

"No interfering, Jules," he warned.

We didn't want to be asked to leave, so Abby Lee and I camped out in the kitchen while the officers conducted their search.

"What do you think they're looking for?" Abby Lee asked.

I took the warrant Justin had handed her before searching the house and glanced at it. It was a blanket search warrant, which meant the police could search her home without specifying what they were looking for. I was shocked that a judge would sign off on something like that.

"I have no idea," I answered. "Is there anything in the house that would implicate you in any way?"

"No. We got some old firearms from Daddy, but Harvey wasn't shot, so I guess they're not looking for those."

A couple hours later, the officers left empty-handed. I breathed a sigh of relief. Now they were headed over to The Poop Deck to conduct a similar search.

"I'll have to close the restaurant early," Abby Lee said. "This is all so humiliating."

"Don't worry. They didn't find anything here, and they certainly won't find anything at the restaurant," I said as we made our way out of the house.

Before we could make it to my truck, Justin pulled me aside. "I appreciate you wanting to help, but you need to trust me. I don't like this any more than you do."

"Then why are you doing this? You know she didn't do it."

"I wasn't the one who made the call, but I still have to do my job."

I shrugged, climbing into the driver's seat of the Bronco. Abby Lee was already waiting in the passenger seat. "I'll see you over at the restaurant."

Like we had at her house, Abby Lee and I waited quietly as the officers took the restaurant apart, looking for anything that would directly link her to the murder. Only this time, we poured ourselves a glass of wine as we watched them go over the place with a fine-tooth comb.

Another two hours later, after an exhaustive search, the officers hadn't found anything to connect Abby Lee to Harvey's murder. Neither of us said a word to Justin as the police left the restaurant. And, to his credit, he didn't bother to insult us with any lame apologies.

"I don't know if I should be grateful or worried they didn't find anything," Abby Lee said after they left.

"Don't think that way. The way I see it, you haven't been arrested yet, so that's good news. But just because they didn't find what they were looking for doesn't mean they'll stop trying. We still have time to figure out who did this."

She wiped the tears from her eyes and for a brief second looked hopeful. "What do you have in mind? We've tried everything with no luck."

No, we hadn't. "Sweetie, we've barely scratched the surface. Look, I have an idea. I just need to make some calls." The wheels in my head were already in motion, and no sooner were the words out of my mouth than I had another idea.

A few phone calls later, I had my answer. With a little help from my friends in the Houston Field Office, I was able to find out the name of the assistant district attorney assigned to the Harvey Boyette case. Though, as it turned out, had I waited to watch the evening news like everyone else, I would have figured it out all on my own without the help of the feds. It seemed our little island hamlet was big news. Normally, prosecutors weren't assigned cases until an actual arrest was made, but a case like this was a career builder. Sure, it wasn't enough of a high-profile case to warrant national coverage on Fox News, but any murder trial could help jump-start a young ADA's career.

"Julia, honey, turn that off. All that talk about the murder here in Trouble boils down to sensationalism. Our town does not need this kind of publicity," Mom said. "You'd think with all those bombings and wars going on around the world they'd find something more newsworthy to report."

No one ever dared argue with my mom when she was in one of her moods, so I turned off the television and headed upstairs to see what the online news sources were reporting.

I did a quick search, and according to the online news article, Hartley Crawford had been assigned the case. At this stage, he had elected not to respond to questions from reporters, but the network provided a nice head shot of the up-and-coming assistant district attorney. If he wasn't prosecuting a case in which my best friend could very well be the defendant, I would have drooled—he was that good-looking. He was what Aunt Lula would call a prized stud.

So this is the guy who could ultimately be in charge of my friend's fate, I thought. Now that I had more to go on, what was I going to do next?

I'd begun to daydream about the handsome attorney when Mom called up from downstairs. "Jules, you got a package! I think it's flowers!" Under any normal circumstances, my mom would never yell—it wasn't ladylike—but receiving flowers was cause for excitement. In her mind, flowers equated to a man—and a man equated to grandchildren.

Were they from James, pleading for me to come back home? Or maybe they were from Justin, as some sort of peace offering showing he realized I only had my friend's best interest at heart, although I doubted it. During the time we dated, he never once splurged on flowers.

I ran down the stairs and took the rectangular box from my mother's outstretched hands. I think she was more excited than I was.

"Well, open it," she urged, anxiously waiting to see what my admirer sent.

I opened the box and moved the delicate tissue paper, only to reveal a box of black roses. I'd heard of black flowers before, a custom novelty variety that only goth chicks and serial killers would order, but who would send me these?

Mom frowned in confusion. "Is that a new trend? Black roses? I'll never understand you young kids."

Once the climactic letdown sunk in, she finally walked away, leaving me alone with the flowers, disinterested now that they weren't the customary roses of the red variety. I dug around the box, mindful of the thorns, to look for a card. There, wedged between the tissue and the bottom of the box, was a small note, similar to the one I got when my Bronco's windshield was bashed in:

Watch out.

With all the drama going on with Abby Lee, I had forgotten about the first note I'd received. And now here I was, standing in front of the kitchen counter with a box full of black roses—the proud recipient of a second warning. But who sent them? And more importantly, why? Was I getting close to finding the killer? No, that couldn't be it. I wasn't anywhere near figuring out who'd killed Harvey. That only left one other conclusion—the threats had nothing to do with the case. Then again, maybe I was close and didn't know it yet.

It had to be about the murder, I ultimately decided. I had been in town less than two weeks; I hadn't lived in Trouble long enough to have enemies. So if I were a logical person, which I liked to think I was, the simplest explanation made the most sense. The warnings had to be from Harvey's killer.

There had to be something I was missing. Why else would a killer send me threats? Was there a clue I'd overlooked?

I immediately hopped into the Bronco and drove over to Aunt Lula's to tell her about the threats. I told her about the broken windshield and the first note. Then I told her about the flowers and the warning I'd received.

"The killer sent you what?" Aunt Lula asked.

"We don't know if it was the killer," I said, even though I had already resigned myself to the fact that it probably was. "But I'm afraid you might be right."

"Who else could it be? He knows we're onto him, and he's trying to scare you. That means we're getting close!"

Even though I had already decided the person behind the threats had to be the killer, something about the threats nagged at me. The acts seemed so benign and juvenile—breaking a windshield, sending black flowers, leaving notes—but could Aunt Lula be right? I tried to ignore the obvious excitement in her voice, but were we really getting closer to figuring out who did it?

"How do we know it's a he? It could be a woman," I pointed out. I'd helped agents with many cases involving female offenders. I may have been brought up to be a fine, proper Southern lady, but I was still somewhat of a feminist—crime was an equal opportunity employer in my book.

Aunt Lula snickered. "You're right. I'm not too old to believe women can't do just about anything men can do." In Aunt Lula's world, women did most things better than men.

I frowned. If someone was trying to send me a warning, I needed to at least inform the police. In my experience, criminals could escalate from committing petty acts, like sending a box of dead roses, to more violent acts of aggression, like murder. I certainly didn't want to be on the bad end of that continuum.

"Maybe I should call Justin," I said, even though I was reluctant to rely on him for anything at this point.

Aunt Lula scoffed. "Then the deputy chief will know for sure we've been snooping around," she said. "He'll want to know why you're receiving those ominous notes."

For once, we were in agreement with each other. Approaching Justin with the threatening notes and flowers was out for the time being. In the end, we decided to hold off on reporting it until I received another one. If we got more evidence, I would turn everything in to Justin then.

"What did you do with the flowers?" Aunt Lula asked.

"I kept them just in case we needed them as evidence. The notes, too."

Aunt Lula nodded. "Good thinking."

I wasn't entirely sure if she actually knew why it was a good idea, but she played along as if she were actively involved in a homicide investigation every other week.

As for me, I had full intentions of carrying out the plan I'd mentioned to Abby Lee earlier, but not before I paid a visit to Justin.

CHAPTER SIXTEEN

"What the hell was all that about?" I said, referring to the search warrants, as I stormed into Justin's office at the station the next day. I had waited to cool off before confronting him, but it turned out I was still steaming.

"Shut the door," he said.

I complied and slammed it for good measure. Yesterday, I had nothing to say to him regarding the search warrants for Abby Lee's property, but today, I was more than happy to give him a piece of my mind.

"A blanket search warrant, really? Is that what this case has come down to?"

Justin avoided eye contact. "I told you already. I'm not the one who made the call on the search warrants. It was Chief Poteet. I may not agree with his methods, but I still had to do my job."

It was pretty much what I had expected, but I was still mad at Justin. He could have given Abby Lee a heads-up. We didn't have to hear it secondhand from Officer Clemmons's mother via Aunt Lula.

"Did he even know what he expected to find?" I demanded.

"Look, I'm not even supposed to be discussing this with you, but you're right. It was a wild-goose chase, and I warned the chief he was getting ahead of himself."

"Why is he so determined that it's her?"

Justin shifted in his seat. "I don't know."

I slumped into the chair across from his desk. "So what are you saying? He's going to keep trying until eventually he convinces the entire department and this town that Abby Lee is guilty? What's he going to do, plant evidence next time?"

He looked hurt, like I'd accused him of dishonorable conduct instead of the chief. "I'm taking care of it," he said.

"It doesn't look like it from here."

"You're going to have to trust me."

"You keep saying that, yet I feel like I can't," I said. "Am I wrong to think that?"

"I don't know what else to say, Jules. You think this is easy for me? You think I come to work every day loving what I do? I'd be lying if I said I did. Sometimes I have to deal with the shit parts of the job, and right now, this is one of them."

I rose from my chair, the matter obviously closed. I went in like a lion and out like a lamb, closing the door softly behind me.

The previous night, I had spent the entire evening racking my brain to figure out a way to gain access to the district attorney's office. If I could somehow finagle a meeting with the ADA, perhaps I could persuade him to urge the Trouble Island Police Department to look for more leads before getting an arrest warrant. After the show they'd put on the day before, I was now more worried than ever about how they were handling the case.

The district attorney's office was located right in the heart of the county seat. I knew it went against my better judgment to go to the district attorney's office, but with Abby Lee's livelihood at stake, I had nothing to lose. It was over an hour's drive, but it was worth it if there was even a chance I'd get an audience with the hot ADA.

There had to be a way to reach him without marching into his office, unannounced, demanding to see him. There was a thing called professional courtesy within the criminal justice profession, but since I was investigating the crime on my own and not in an official capacity, I'd be laughed out of the office—or worse, it would get back to the bureau.

It was time to get creative.

I did what any girl would do to screen a potential date in this day and age. I went directly to Facebook—I had plenty of time for social media now—to see if Hartley Crawford had a page. And as luck would have it, he did. I quickly scanned his page for any information that could be useful: age, hobbies, relationships, and friends.

Hartley was thirty-five, Episcopalian, and a Republican. No surprises there. I already knew he was good-looking, but his photos reinforced his handsome features. He went to Yale Law School—impressive—and most importantly, he was single. That last fact was essential if I wanted my plan to work.

And then I hit pay dirt.

After reading a few of his updates and comments, I found out he planned to attend a retirement party for a colleague the following evening. Conveniently, for them, the bar was located right across the street from the courthouse. Crashing the party seemed like a better idea than just storming into his office at the county government building. This was where his being single would work to my advantage.

The only question left remaining was, what should I wear?

Before I executed my plan, I filled Abby Lee in on my little scheme. She came right over with a bottle of red wine and helped me pick something suitable to wear for undercover work.

"Are you sure you don't want me to come with you tomorrow?" Abby Lee asked as I debated what outfit was appropriate for infiltrating a bar full of drunken prosecutors.

"No way! If you so much as set foot in the general vicinity of the ADA, you'll be alligator bait. You're a murder suspect," I reminded her. "It's better you stay here."

"Still, I don't think you should go alone."

I laughed. "Abby Lee, I'm not meeting a serial killer for a night of dinner and dancing. I'm seeking out an officer of the court. I'll be safe."

She didn't look convinced. "Yeah, but if he finds out you're on a fishing expedition, you're the one who's going to be bait."

"I have a plan," I said.

"Using your feminine wiles to get a guy to talk doesn't sound like much of a plan," she said.

"You don't know men very well," I said. "You forget I work primarily with men. Overworked, stiff, uptight men who still cave to a pretty woman. I know how they think." Not that I considered myself a pretty woman, but it was worth a shot. "Especially if they've been drinking."

It was Abby Lee's turn to giggle. "If you say so."

In the end, I settled for a pair of white denim capris—a cursory glance on the bar's website told me the place was casual—and a sleeveless navy light-silk top. Something told me Hartley Crawford didn't go for the trashy look. I glanced at myself in the mirror and decided that I looked good enough to pass for a conservative, girl-next-door type.

The next evening I slid the Bronco into the parking lot of the bar just after six. The event details on Facebook said the retirement party had started at five, but the timing was perfect. Plenty of time for Hartley Crawford to have a few beers and get his buzz on.

I walked in and looked for a group having a retirement party. It wasn't hard to spot the lawyers. Cheap but well-cut suits—they were on the state's payroll not Wall Street's—and a lot of laughter between swigs of beer. All I had to do now was look for Hartley and play my part.

Bingo. I finally spotted him at the bar, buying another pitcher of beer for his colleagues. This was my opportunity. It was now or never.

I made my way over to the bar and bumped into my target, spilling his beer in the process. I didn't mean to do that, but it was as good an introduction as any.

"I'm so sorry," I said.

At first he was annoyed at being drenched with cheap beer, but he quickly softened when he saw my horrified expression. "It's OK. I'm sure my dry cleaner can get it out."

"You have to let me buy you another pitcher," I said.

"Thanks for the offer, but not necessary," Hartley said.

"No, really, I insist."

"Well, if you insist. Who am I to argue when a lady offers me a drink?"

As we waited for the bartender to pour him another pitcher, I got into character. In person, the ADA seemed like a nice guy, and was much better looking than his photo. I felt crummy about spilling beer on him, but not bad enough to stop my undercover mission altogether.

"So, what do you do?" I asked.

He looked at me curiously. He was probably not used to being asked this question by a woman who'd just dumped beer on his best suit. "I work for the district attorney's office."

"You're a lawyer?" I asked in feigned wonder.

Hartley seemed amused. "Does this surprise you?"

"No, I just took you for a banker," I said, "or something having to do with business."

Hartley chuckled, and I had to admit hearing him laugh brought tingles down my spine—the good kind. Flirting in order to get the info I wanted wasn't going to be a problem. But I had to be careful not to blow my cover.

"I'm an assistant DA."

"You look too young to be an ADA," I said.

"I'm thirty-five," he said.

"I didn't mean to insult you or anything. I just meant that government lawyers tend to be old and stuffy. You don't seem like that at all," I said.

Hartley relaxed and smiled. "And what do you do for a living?" he asked.

Fortunately, thanks to Aunt Lula, I had the perfect cover and didn't have to lie—at least not entirely. "Oh, I work for a clothing boutique on Trouble Island," I said.

The bartender finally came back with a Shiner Bock for me and a replacement pitcher of Bud for Hartley. I handed the bartender a ten and told him to keep the change.

"You live in Trouble?" Hartley asked.

"Born and raised," I said proudly.

"Small world. I have a case from there."

I pretended to be in total shock. "You don't mean Harvey Boyette's murder, do you?"

His cocked his eyebrows. "Did you know him?"

"Well, yeah. Everyone on the island knew Harvey. Wow, I can't believe you're working that case," I said. "The whole island is on alert since they haven't caught the killer yet."

"I can imagine a small town like Trouble being worried, but we're actually close on getting a warrant for an arrest," he said.

"Really? Who? Maybe I know them?" *Please don't say Abby Lee.*

"And that's exactly why I can't tell you. It's still an open investigation, and we can't let information like that leak out."

Damn. I was afraid he was going to say that, no matter how much I flirted. But it didn't keep me from trying again.

"Don't the police already have a suspect? I heard they think it was one of Harvey's employees. Is that true?"

"You heard that, huh?" he asked, evading my question.

I shrugged. "It's a small town. Everybody loved Harvey."

"So tell me, who do I have the pleasure of thanking for the beer? You never did tell me your name."

"Julia," I said, once again not answering in full truths and feeling guilty about it. Even though technically it was my given name, I doubted anyone outside my immediate family knew what my actual first name was—everyone on the island knew me as Jules. I found it hard to lie to this guy. Despite my first impressions from looking at his Facebook profile, he was very easy to talk to.

"Hartley Crawford," he offered, not giving me the chance to ask first.

"What kind of a name is Hartley?"

"I know, ambiguous, right? It's my mother's maiden name. She wanted to make sure the name stayed in the family."

"Me, too. I mean, my middle name is my mom's maiden name."

Wait. Was he was one of *the* Hartleys? They were well-known throughout the state. The Hartley family had dealings in oil, cattle, and even dabbled in technology. I'm sure they were even involved in business dealings that went above my pay grade. They were like the Bushes, only with more money. I'm talking major oil money.

"I can tell from your expression you've heard of my family."

I recovered quickly, but there was no way I could deny knowing who his family was. I tried not to be too impressed. "Who hasn't?"

"And I'm sure you're wondering what I'm doing working in public service, huh?"

Actually I was, but it didn't really matter. I could tell just from our brief conversation that there was real depth to this guy—more than just dollars and cents.

"Because you want to help people," I said.

He laughed. Damn. Even his laugh was intoxicating. "From your lips to my parents' ears."

"I take it they don't approve," I said. I was sure his parents expected him to take over and run the family empire, not spend his time enjoying happy hour with friends over five-dollar pitchers.

"They tolerate my career choice now, but they didn't at first. Now they seem to think they can parlay this experience into a career in politics."

"And I take it you don't approve," I joked.

Hartley gave me a small smile and sighed. "I can't say that I'm not intrigued by the prospect of running for office one day. But I'd feel so removed from the people I'm trying to help. I like to get my hands dirty."

You and I both, I thought. Going undercover to help my best friend definitely counted in the get-your-hands-dirty department.

"And what about you?" he asked. "Any ambitions besides working retail?"

I was momentarily taken aback. Would a guy like Hartley be interested in someone who just worked in a clothing boutique? In a way, I felt a little embarrassed that he only saw me as a retail sales associate. I wanted to tell him that I had a master's degree and worked for the FBI, but I couldn't. The question lingered in the air like the stench of stale beer.

"To be honest, I'm not sure what I want to do with my life. I'm not really happy where I am at the moment," I said, thinking of my current situation at work with Weight Watcher Wendy. As soon as I uttered the words, I knew I wasn't just feeding Hartley a line. I wanted to help people directly, like him, not by sitting in front of a computer screen all day.

A voice yelled above the music. "Hey, Hart, you coming back? You're missing the roast!"

"In a moment," Hartley yelled back to the guy seated at the four top before turning his attention back to me. "Sorry about that. They've been drinking awhile."

"That's OK," I said. I really wanted to tell him to go back to his party, but I couldn't until I got what I came for. And I felt like a total heel for doing it. "Anyway, you were saying the police were ready to make an arrest?"

"I hope so. The police seem to have narrowed down the suspects, so we should have an arrest warrant soon."

This was all I was going to get out of him. It was time to head back to Trouble.

"I must have lost track of time," I said, looking at my watch. "And from the looks of it, you need to get back to your friends."

"It was nice meeting you, Julia," he said, rising from the bar stool as I rose. "You can bump into me anytime."

"Maybe I'll see you around." *Not likely.* I had to remind myself that this was the man that could ultimately prosecute my best friend.

In another time or place, I would have considered myself lucky to meet someone like Hartley Crawford.

CHAPTER SEVENTEEN

The only good thing that came out of working at Palmetto Pink was that it temporarily kept my mind off the investigation. Though one could hardly consider what the Trouble Island PD was doing an investigation. Every time I folded a shirt, hung up a dress, or assisted a customer, it diverted my attention away from the problems facing Abby Lee. For a few hours every day I went into denial mode—I didn't want to face the reality that if my best friend was arrested, tried, and convicted, I would never forgive myself.

A customer called out from one of the dressing rooms. I groaned as I made my way over to assist her. She walked out of the room and stood in front of the floor-length mirror. It was obvious she had picked the outfit out herself without any direction from me; I wouldn't have chosen something so tight.

"So what can I do about this?" She pointed to her bulging abdomen. The dress she was trying on did nothing to complement her figure. I had pulled out several dresses that would have been more flattering, but she'd insisted on trying on the red halter dress—that was also a size too small.

Uh, wear Spanx? Hell, even I was known to wear control-top underwear from time to time. Quickly approaching my thirties, my body didn't metabolize the way it used to.

"Do you want me to get the size ten?" *Like I suggested in the first place?*

"No. I'm a size eight," she insisted.

Why did women always obsess about numbers? If something fit, it fit. Who cared if the dress was a size eight or a ten? But now that I'd entered the world of retail fashion, I'd come to realize that many women came into the store expecting miracles—clothes that would transform their bodies into figures they simply did not possess. Sure, there were some fabrics and cuts that could make you look slimmer, but that was not always the case. Then there were others that came in our store complaining that our clothing exposed their flaws. This might very well be true, but it wasn't our fault.

I quickly rushed over to one of the racks near the dressing room—the sooner I could get her out of the store, the better—and picked out a nice, loose cotton tunic that would flatter her figure. "Here, why don't you try this one on?"

The woman gave the dress I was holding the once-over. "Hmm, I don't know. It looks like something Mrs. Roper would wear, don't you think? Oh, you probably don't even know who that is."

I knew exactly who Mrs. Roper was. Anyone who'd ever watched an episode of *Three's Company* was familiar with the sexually frustrated, muumuu-loving landlady of Jack, Chrissy, and Janet. She had great taste for a lady her age if you asked me. Besides, the customer was well into her sixties; where did she think she was going to wear a red spandex dress?

But I had to keep my opinions to myself if I wanted to make a sale. "I bet if you try it on, you'll see how flattering it is," I said.

"No, that's OK. I'll just try another store."

And good luck with that, I wanted to say. I was so not in the mood to argue with her. It was a good thing I didn't work off commission. Not the way I was functioning today, anyway.

"Sorry the dress didn't work out for you," I called after her.

I'd had enough of customers for the day, and I'd only been at work for two hours. A pint of beer and a hearty sandwich were just what I needed to get out of my funk. I waved to Aunt Lula as I headed out to lunch.

Engrossed in my oyster po'boy and Shiner, I didn't hear Justin sneak up behind me.

"Mind if I join you?"

I glanced up to see Justin hovering over my table. I wasn't exactly in the mood for company, especially Justin, but I reluctantly offered him the seat opposite mine. I still wasn't sure how I felt about being around him—I wasn't one to let sleeping dogs lie—but I couldn't show him I was uncomfortable, especially since he wasn't doing anything to help steer the investigation away from Abby Lee.

"Sure."

"So—fancy seeing you here."

He was up to something. I could tell by the way he had accidentally bumped into me here at the diner.

"Not really. Considering it's one of the few places open for lunch around here," I said. "Are you following me around town? Keeping tabs on me?"

"No, but while we're on the subject, had myself a nice little chat today with the ADA in charge of Harvey's case," he said. "Seems you've been keeping your eye on someone yourself."

"Oh yeah?" I asked, not giving anything away.

"Yeah. He wouldn't stop talking about someone named Julia from Trouble Island. The question I'm dying to know is, why were you there asking about the case?"

Damn. I'd been made. "Why do you automatically assume it was me?"

"You're the only one on the island that fits the description. And the only one named Julia." He stressed the syllables of my given name.

He had me there. I thought hard before answering. There was nothing he could really do if he found out I had spoken with Hartley about the case, but I decided to play it safe just in case.

"Yeah, well, if you must know, I just happened to bump into him," I said. "Literally. I accidentally spilled his beer."

Justin did that thing he always did with his chin. If he rubbed it any harder, he'd leave a permanent mark. "Now why don't I believe that?"

"I don't know, Justin. It's the truth. I knocked his beer, and we chatted for a bit. I didn't know there was anything wrong with that."

"See," he said, leaning over the table. "That's the problem, Jules. There is no such thing as just chatting with you. I know damn well you were fishing."

I shrugged. "I can't help it if he offered information about Harvey's case. Anybody would have been interested in what he had to say. There's a murderer on the loose, you know."

This set him off. "Damn it, Jules," he said, slamming his hand on the table. "You are not working this case, and furthermore, you aren't a federal agent. You can't go around town pretending that you are."

"Now you're just getting technical," I said. "And I wasn't impersonating an agent. I acted just like any other concerned citizen of Trouble."

"You know, you could get into some serious trouble if you keep digging."

"Why whatever do you mean?"

"Cut the coy crap, Jules. You and Lula need to stop interfering in police matters. I happen to know for a fact the feds wouldn't stand for you meddling in their cases, even if you are technically one of their own, and I sure as hell don't intend for you to do the same here."

"You don't even know who killed Harvey!" I accused. "I know you don't actually believe Abby Lee did it. Admit it! You have no more of an idea than I do. So why is Hartley saying you guys are close to making an arrest? Do you have another suspect that's good for the murder, or have y'all just given up looking?"

Justin shifted uncomfortably, not because I'd called him out but because I wasn't going to let the matter drop—no matter how many years had passed, he still knew me well enough to know how stubborn I could be.

"It's still an active investigation. I assume, being a big shot from the bureau, you're aware of how these things work. You can't just walk into the ADA's office demanding answers."

"But I'm not just anyone. And I didn't storm into the ADA's office. I already told you, there was beer involved."

"That's the thing, Jules, you are 'just anyone.' At least around these parts."

That stung. I'd pushed his buttons too far. Even Justin had his breaking point. I didn't want to completely ruin what relationship we had left, so I adopted a gentler approach.

"I can help, Justin. I'm not just some average citizen that doesn't know criminal procedure. My best friend is being accused of something she didn't do, and you know it. I promised I'd help her, and I'm going to keep that promise." I was more determined than ever to help Abby Lee.

"Would it make you feel better knowing I'm working on it? I know Abby Lee isn't involved in all this, but unfortunately, the chief has a different agenda. I'm doing my best to gather more evidence to the contrary, but it's going to take some time."

"Why are they so insistent that Abby Lee killed him? They have to have a reason."

"Well, for starters, she inherited his restaurant, which gives her motive. And he was poisoned. Which naturally makes them suspect a woman committed the murder."

"That's ridiculous. If she was named in Harvey's will, why kill him if she was going to get the place anyway? And really? They're basing their entire case solely on the killer's MO? If that's the case, why not focus on Sheila?"

"I'm not arguing with you, Jules. I'm just telling you what the chief is thinking. Believe me, I'd like nothing more than to find out who killed Harvey."

"And I can help," I insisted.

His face scrunched up in the cute way I remembered it doing whenever he got frustrated. "No way. There's a murderer out there, and I'll be damned if he or she figures out what you're up to. The island is only so big—it won't be long before they realize it's still an ongoing investigation. Right now, the best thing for everyone, including Abby Lee, is to let the killer think otherwise."

"I'm not afraid. Especially not of someone who commits murder via poison."

"Damn it, Jules. I don't want to have to tell you again, stay out of it."

"Look, if you want me to stay out of trouble, then help me out here. I'll let you know if I turn up anything, if you'll do the same."

A sigh as big as the great state of Texas escaped from him. "And there's no way I can change your mind?"

"Nope."

"You're a loose cannon, Jules. Always have been."

"Funny," I said, not amused by his attempt at humor.

He tried another tactic. "You know I can have you arrested for interfering with an active investigation."

I smiled. "You could try, but you said it yourself, 'The island is only so big,'" I pointed out. "Word gets around. You arrest me, you not only let the killer know why I was arrested but that you're still looking for a suspect."

CHAPTER EIGHTEEN

It was almost closing time at Palmetto Pink, and I was looking forward to heading home and taking a long, hot bath. There was only twenty minutes left before I could lock the doors, and I prayed no one would come in.

Maybe I didn't pray hard enough. Maybe I had been a rotten person in another life and karma had it in for me. At the last minute, Heather Clegg walked into the store. I hoped she hadn't come by just to harass me again. All I knew was, whatever her reason for being here, she'd better make it quick.

"I need a dress," she demanded.

"OK. What did you have in mind?" Even though I hated Heather, this was still my aunt's store. I could only refuse service for not wearing shoes or shirts, not for being a thorn in my side. So I would be polite and smile when dealing with a customer, even if it was Heather. I plastered on a fake smile as I guided her over to the dresses.

"Something hot. I have a date with Justin tonight," she said.

You do? Since when were they seeing each other again? Or was this part of a delusion she insisted on telling herself? Then again, what did I know? Maybe they really did have a date. For a second there I felt a pang of jealousy. Even if I didn't want to admit it, I still believed there was something there between me and Justin.

My fake smile remained glued on my face. If this was all for show on Heather's part, the least I could do was get in a good sale. Even though I hated working here, I still cared about my aunt's business. "Let me show you what we have."

While she browsed around, I picked out a few dresses—one was a $500 St. John dress that I knew she couldn't afford on her salary—and started a dressing room for her. The faster I could speed things along and get her out of the store, the better.

After several attempts to squeeze into the dresses I had chosen, she was starting to get annoyed. "Don't you have any dresses in this store that actually look good?"

"I can get you a size eight, like I suggested earlier," I started to say.

She may very well have been able to squeeze herself into a size six, but the girl was all boobs and backside. There was no way she'd be able to sit down in the size six dresses she insisted on trying on without busting the seams.

"I am not a size eight! I'm a six," Heather insisted.

I rolled my eyes. *Here we go again.* What did it matter as long as you looked good?

Personally, I'm not that vain when it comes to women's fashion—or sizing—but I couldn't resist a jab at her expense. "Well, I'm a size four in this style, and I'm a bit smaller than you, so I'm thinking an eight would fit you best."

"Ugh! Do you even know anything about fashion?" she cried, flinging the dress over the closed door. "The dress fits, OK? It's just a crappy dress." She came out of the dressing room, back in her own clothes, and proceeded to stomp toward the door. "It doesn't matter anyway. Justin likes me in anything."

"Have a good time," I managed to yell out before she slammed the door behind her.

What exactly did Justin see in her?

My aunt came out from the back office. "Problems?"

"No. Heather came in to find a dress for a big date with Justin. She didn't seem to like my suggestions."

"I've always thought there was something off about that Clegg girl," she said. "If you hadn't left the way you did, you'd be the one having dinner with Deputy Chief Harper, not her."

It wasn't worth reminding her that Justin and I hadn't dated in over a decade. "She can have him," I said, even though I didn't really mean it. Something told me Heather was lying about her date, though. It was as if she was just putting on a show at my expense.

Aunt Lula gave me her "I know better than you" smile. "If you say so, dear."

※

A little while later it was finally closing time. "Just remember to lock the doors after you leave," Aunt Lula called out before walking out of the store.

Ugh. She didn't have to remind me. Part of my closing duties—before I could even think about leaving—was to restock merchandise that had been sold during the day, so I spent the last half hour replenishing merchandise, pulling dresses and shorts from the stockroom to the front floor. On my third trip back from the stockroom, I asked myself for the millionth time why I had agreed to work at Palmetto Pink. After my fourth trip back, I came to the conclusion that I was a sucker.

Back in the stockroom, as I pulled a pair of white jeans from one of the bins on the top shelf, the lights flickered a few times before the room finally turned pitch black.

The power had gone out.

Damn! If I had been on the top rung of the ladder, I would've totally fallen from the start it gave me. Thankfully, I was only half-way up and recovered quickly. I climbed down the ladder and went to see about the lights. I walked slowly, using my outstretched arms as my guide, and felt around for the doorknob. *Double damn!* The door was locked. And unfortunately for me, the door locked from the outside. Whoever came up with that brilliant idea was a moron.

Did Aunt Lula return to the store while I was in the back and forget I was still here?

"Aunt Lula, I'm still in here!" I yelled through the closed door, hoping she hadn't left the store altogether. I pounded on the door a few more times for good measure.

No answer from my aunt. That left only one other alternative. The kind that sent shivers up my spine.

Someone had cut off the power and locked me in the stockroom.

But why? How?

I panicked for a second before I realized I wasn't completely stranded in the dark. Whoever did this obviously hadn't thought things through. I felt my way around to the desk where I always left my purse. I dug around and reached for my cell phone, glad I still had enough juice to make a call, and called my aunt.

"Is there a problem at the store, dear? I'm in the middle of watching *CSI*. It's a good one, too. Did you know there are people that get all dressed up in animal costumes to get their jollies on?"

I'd seen that episode a few years back. She must have been watching a rerun. "Yeah. They call themselves furries," I said, my words a little too rushed. "Uh, were you just here? I got locked in the stockroom."

"No, I just said I'm at home watching *CSI*. For research," she said, sounding proud of herself. "Wait, did you say you got locked in the stockroom? Impossible. It locks from the outside."

"I know. I think someone cut the power and locked me in here. I was thinking maybe you turned off the lights, forgetting I was still here."

"No, I . . . it could be the killer! I'll be right over." Aunt Lula's fictional foray into the world of paraphilias was just going to have to wait.

There wasn't much I could do sitting in the dark, waiting for Aunt Lula to arrive, so I made a mental list of all the customers that had come into the store during the last hour we were open. Any one of them could have easily stayed hidden after I locked the front doors and waited until I was in the stockroom to lock me in.

Jackie Wysong, one of Aunt Lula's best friends, had come in around eight just to say hi—I ruled her out immediately. Then there was Sheila, Harvey's widow. Aunt Lula had mentioned Sheila had stopped by earlier that morning to purchase a few items for her upcoming cruise. The fact that she was already planning a vacation so soon after her husband's death was suspicious. I kept her on the list.

That left Heather. I didn't buy her excuse that she needed a dress for a date with Justin. Could she have made the story up in order to stick around to scare me? I wouldn't put it past her. And she was the only one in town who hated me enough to lock me in the stockroom.

I had two possible suspects, but no concrete motive. On one hand, the person responsible could very well be Harvey's killer, who wanted to scare me off the case. But on the other hand, I was dealing with someone stupid enough to leave me locked in a room with my cell phone. Heather was looking pretty good. I decided to keep my eye on her just in case.

Ten minutes and a short list of suspects later, my aunt had me out of the stockroom. "Are you all right?" She hugged me close to her bosom. "You certainly gave this old woman a fright!"

"I'm OK. Just glad I had my cell on me to call, or I'd have been here overnight."

Aunt Lula grimaced. "And I'm sure your mother would've given me an earful if you had."

"It wasn't your fault," I assured her.

"Isn't it? It was my idea to have you work here at the store. I don't know what I would do if something happened to you."

"I'm OK, really. If it wasn't at the store, whoever it was would have cornered me somewhere else." The thought was unsettling.

"Just the same, I will have one of the other girls work closing from now on."

I can't say I wasn't a little unnerved by the incident, but I still said a silent thanks to whoever locked me in. They'd just done me a huge favor—I didn't have to close anymore.

CHAPTER NINETEEN

"Excuse me, miss? I was hoping you could help me pick out something for my mother," a voice called out from behind me.

I knew that voice.

I turned around to find Hartley Crawford standing right in front of me. My heart literally skipped a beat. He was the last person I expected to walk into the store. "What are you doing here?"

He looked amused, obviously pleased the element of surprise had worked in his favor. "Oh, I have a meeting with the Trouble Island PD this afternoon concerning the Boyette case."

"No, I mean, what are you doing *here*?" God, I hope he hadn't figured out the real reason I bumped into him at the bar. He didn't say whether he was spoken for when I bumped into him at the bar, and his Facebook page made no mention of a girlfriend, so I secretly hoped he was single.

"Honest truth? I couldn't get you out of my head after we met, so when the chief asked to hold a meeting to talk about our case, I insisted on holding the meeting here. I just had to look you up," he said. "You know, I had to go to three other shops before I finally found you here."

I was flattered; most guys wouldn't have bothered. I knew there was something different about him the first time we met. And it was something I definitely liked.

What was I doing? He was the ADA, not just some random guy I'd met at a bar. I couldn't let him find out that I'd purposely staged our chance encounter. If he was here, it meant he didn't know. I wondered what my chances were that it would stay that way.

"Did you already meet with the police?" It was only a matter of time before he spoke to Justin and my cover was blown.

"Not yet. I wanted to find you first. Would you like to go to dinner with me this evening?"

The butterflies in my stomach fluttered into overdrive. "You mean like a date?"

"Yeah, I guess so. But you don't have to. I thought maybe—"

"I'd love to," I said, maybe a little too quickly. What was I doing? I was taking a big risk by accepting. If he found out from Justin who I really was and why I was so interested in his case, he might not seem so excited about our date. I was taking a huge chance that my name wouldn't come up at their meeting.

"Where would you like to go? I don't know the island very well."

Most families around the Gulf Coast have spent at least one summer vacation on Trouble Island. It wasn't much of a family destination, like South Padre Island, but we still got tourists from time to time. Though I imagine that a family like the Crawfords vacationed in more exotic locales, like Turks and Caicos, or perhaps Fiji.

"The Poop Deck," I said without hesitation. "The food is great, and I know the owner." I didn't add that the owner was his prime murder suspect. Don't ask me why I was suggesting we go straight into the lion's den. It seemed my mind was working faster than my mouth.

"Sounds great. Always trust a local," he said. "What time?"

"What time does your meeting end?" I still couldn't believe I was doing this.

"I'm not sure. We have a lot to review before we can get an arrest warrant. But I'm sure I can end it with plenty of time to meet you for dinner."

"Great. How about seven?"

"Should I pick you up?"

I weighed the options. If I allowed Hartley to pick me up at my folks', my mother would insist on giving him the third degree (and, boy, would she be shocked to learn who his family was) and the rumor mill would be clocking in overtime. On the other hand, if I met him at the restaurant, it would lower the odds of him finding out who I really was, but then he might take offense. I wasn't sure how dating worked in other areas, but around these parts, chivalry wasn't dead.

I decided to play it safe. "Why don't we meet at the restaurant? It's only a couple blocks away, and I can just walk over after my shift." I was actually scheduled to work until eight, but Aunt Lula wouldn't care if I ditched once she found out I had a date.

"Great. See you then," he said.

What in the world am I getting myself into? I thought to myself. Did I really just get asked out by one of the hottest, most eligible bachelors in the whole state? He was probably the biggest catch in the entire South. Was I ready to be wined and dined by Southern royalty?

Then, once the daydream divorced itself from reality, the bubble burst. I was able to see the big picture. Holy crap! I'd just accepted a dinner invitation from the one man that could possibly destroy Abby Lee!

Most people assumed it was the cops that called all the shots in a case, but it was actually the prosecutors. They were the ones who decided whether or not a case had enough merit to prosecute, and they were the ones that had authority over plea bargains and reduced charges. So yeah, Hartley was the one man that could seal Abby Lee's fate.

I heard a shuffle in the back and knew it could only be Aunt Lula. She'd probably overheard the entire exchange. I couldn't be sure, but I thought I'd seen her reflection in the mirror when I was talking with Hartley. No doubt she'd have an opinion on the subject.

"I know you're hiding. You can come out now," I yelled toward the back of the store.

"Why, I have no idea what you're talking about," Aunt Lula said, looking all innocent. "I just came out of my office."

I laughed. "Uh-huh. How much did you catch?"

"Enough to know you need a new dress if you're meeting that handsome young man for dinner after you leave here," she said. "And really, you should have insisted he pick you up at home."

"Do you know who that was?" I asked, not sure if she understood the severity of the situation I'd just gotten myself into. "That was the assistant district attorney. He's the one assigned to Harvey's case."

"Oh, dear. Are you sure it's a good idea to meet him for dinner? And at The Poop Deck? He'll recognize Abby Lee for sure. Or her name, at the very least."

I could understand her initial concern. But I was hoping to turn this dinner into an advantage. Perhaps if he actually met Abby Lee, he would realize she couldn't possibly be guilty of murder, despite what the local police here thought. It was wishful thinking on my part, but it was something worth considering. Plus, if he did manage to meet Abby Lee, I wanted to gauge his reaction.

"Yeah, the thought did cross my mind, but maybe it won't be so bad," I said. "Plus, I thought I could get some more information out of him. He's meeting with Chief Poteet and Justin before our date."

She instantly got excited. "Good idea. More undercover work."

"Something like that." There was no way I was telling her the real reason I accepted his dinner invitation. The man made my insides feel like Jell-O. Sure, I was going to try to find out what happened at the meeting, but I couldn't help but be intrigued by him.

Aunt Lula clapped her hands. "I've got it!"

I eyed her warily. "Got what?" I asked slowly, not sure I wanted to hear the answer.

"You need to entice him. And I've got the perfect dress."

I assisted the few customers in the store and tidied up the storefront while Aunt Lula busied herself with choosing my outfit for my date with Hartley. When she finally beckoned me to the dressing room, I was horrified.

One look at the ensemble Aunt Lula picked out and I immediately balked. "Oh, hell no." It was a tight emerald-green dress that was cut low enough to show my belly button. How could she possibly insist I wear such a dress? It was something a cast member from *Jersey Shore* would wear, certainly not a piece one would wear to a beachside crab shack. A better question was, why in the world did she carry something like that in her store? It wasn't resort wear, and it certainly wasn't what she—or anyone with a lick of fashion sense—would consider classy. Had she been hiding it in one of the bins in the unlikely event a slutty customer came in?

Aunt Lula frowned and looked at the dress she had picked out. "What? Not enough cleavage? And don't use that tone with me."

"Sorry," I mumbled. "But I'm not trying to give the man a heart attack, Aunt Lula." Even I had my standards.

In the end, we decided on a cute flowered shift dress. It was short enough to showcase my newly tanned legs, yet tasteful enough to not give Hartley a massive coronary upon entering the room.

Hartley met me outside The Poop Deck at seven on the dot. He even thought to pick up flowers before meeting me. Real flowers this time—carnations and mums—not the black-rose variety I had received a few days before from my lethal secret admirer. I was pleased to find out my earlier assessment was correct—chivalry was still alive and well in the Lone Star State.

"Thank you," I gushed as Hartley presented me with the modest bouquet. It wasn't a dozen long-stem roses, but what he gave me spoke volumes. Here was a man who was rolling in dough, yet appreciated understated gestures. The guy had class.

"You're welcome," he said, pleased his gesture went over well.

"So how did your meeting with the chief go?" I asked as the waiter showed us to our table. "I hope the police are close to figuring out who killed Harvey so you can make that arrest." *Just as long as it's not Abby Lee*, I prayed silently.

Hartley pulled out my chair. "I can't say much about the case, but I can say we're still at a crossroads. The local police are itching to make an arrest, but I'm hoping they'll hold off until we can get more evidence."

I was relieved to hear him say he wasn't ready to sign off on obtaining an arrest warrant just yet. That meant there was still time to clear Abby Lee's name. Then again, if the Trouble Island Police Department was that anxious to make an arrest, Abby Lee could very well turn out to be its scapegoat if it didn't get any other leads.

Even if he didn't know it, Hartley was on our side. There were some prosecutors out there who would've rushed to obtain an arrest warrant just to speed things up and bolster their careers. He was smart to wait. If the police arrested the wrong person, it could not only jeopardize Hartley's career, but a killer would go free and an innocent person would end up in jail.

"Well, I'm glad you're making some sense," I replied. "As much as the island would love for the killer to be caught, we'd hate for them to arrest the wrong person. This is a small town," I reminded him. "It would be more devastating if the wrong person were arrested than it would be to let a killer roam free." I finally began to relax, having said my piece on the matter, knowing Abby Lee was still safe. For the time being, at least.

Then the proverbial shit hit the fan.

A chair scooted directly behind us, interrupting our conversation. I turned to face the source of my annoyance.

It was Justin.

Holy hell! What was he doing here? Yikes!

"Hartley. Jules. Fancy seeing y'all here," he said, addressing us in mock surprise.

I did my best to suppress a groan but failed. I had to play it cool. Maybe he wouldn't rat me out. If he told Hartley who I really was, I was toast.

"Oh, hey, Justin. We were just having dinner."

"I can see that," Justin said. I couldn't tell if he was irritated that I was having dinner with Hartley on a date or that I was having dinner with the ADA—undercover. Either way, his expression didn't look good from where I was sitting.

"We were just about to order. Why don't you join us for a drink?" Hartley said, oblivious to the tension between me and Justin.

"Well, if you're sure y'all don't mind," Justin drawled, knowing full well just how much I did mind.

Justin scooted his chair closer to us so that he formed a wedge between us, then signaled to the waiter that he'd switched tables.

"So . . . ," Justin started, looking at the two of us. "I didn't know you two knew each other."

Justin knew damn well we knew each other. Didn't he just read me the riot act the other day for bumping into Hartley?

Hartley beamed. "She's the one I was telling you about, remember? We met a few days ago, and I was fortunate enough to track her down. How do you two know each other?"

Before Justin could utter a word, I jumped into the conversation. The less he said about our past, the better off I'd be. "We go way back," I said. "High school."

"Ah, yeah. I forget this is a small town. Everyone knows everyone, right?"

"We dated our junior and senior years," Justin added. I could've killed him. No, scratch that, reverse it—someone put me out of my misery.

My date wasn't very good at hiding his disappointment. "Really? I didn't think—"

"And that was ten years ago, Hartley," I pointed out, doing damage control. "We were basically kids."

This time, Hartley laughed and looked over to Justin. "Then I guess I don't have to tell you what a catch Jules is."

Justin's nostrils flared. He didn't waste any time selling me out. "Quite a catch. Beautiful and smart. Did she mention she works for the feds?"

Hartley looked confused. Once he realized what Justin was actually saying, he looked crushed. I knew he was a smart guy and could connect the dots. "You what?"

There was no way I could spin this. The damage had already been done. "I'm not a federal agent, if that's what you're thinking— just a crime analyst."

It might have been poor form for Justin to blow my cover like that, but he certainly knew when to make his exit. "I think I'll leave you two to talk this out." He excused himself from the table, leaving Hartley and me to defuse the bomb he'd set.

Hartley wouldn't even look me in the eye. "Why did you tell me you worked at a clothing store?"

My mind went blank. There wasn't a good excuse I could give him, so I told him the truth. "I do—it's my aunt Lula's store. I'm sorry I didn't tell you before. I didn't want you to think I was trying to interfere in your investigation."

"And were you?" Hartley didn't look convinced.

Again, I didn't have a good response. "Not really. OK, in the beginning, when we first met—"

"So was all this," he said, waving his hand toward the dinner set in front of us, "just a setup? Did you really just bump into me at the bar there the other day, or was that part of your agenda all along?"

It probably wasn't a good time to point out he was the one who'd sought me out at the store and asked me to dinner. "There was no agenda," I mumbled. "I thought I could find out what your office was doing about the case. Then, after we met, I realized you were a nice guy."

"I see."

This was turning out to be one of the worst dates ever. That included the time my friend fixed me up on a blind date with an albino tax adjuster who was so dull his personality paled in comparison to his alabaster skin, and it even topped the night James dumped me over dessert.

"I really wanted to have dinner with you tonight," I said quietly.

"Why?"

"Because I like spending time with you," I said.

It was the truth. I had started to think of him as an ally, and I couldn't deny that he made me weak in the knees. He was just the kind of distraction I needed to get over James. Too bad he'd never want to see me after this.

"No, I mean why did you go through the trouble?"

I sighed. I might as well tell him the whole truth. "My best friend, Abby Lee. I'm sure you're aware she's the prime suspect in the case. I can't let her take the rap for a crime she didn't commit. She didn't kill Harvey."

Hartley considered what I said, then threw his napkin on the table, signaling the end of the conversation. "I'm not sure what to believe at this point," he said as he stood up to leave. "Since we arrived separately, I'm sure you can find your own way back home."

"Hartley, I—"

"I'll see you around," he said, leaving enough bills on the table to cover the check.

Still classy.

With my head hung low, I left the restaurant. I was pretty sure everyone had overheard the entire scene, and it would be front-page news by morning. Mom was definitely going to have a few words with me.

And if I thought my night couldn't get any worse, Justin was waiting by the entrance.

Did he have a death wish?

"You!" I said to him, pissed he had conveniently kept his distance soon after he ratted me out. Why was he still here? Curiosity got the better of me as I waited for an explanation.

"He had to know the truth, Jules," he said without the slightest hint of apology in his voice. I had no idea if Justin had done it because he was truly worried I was getting too involved in his case or because I was having dinner with someone other than him. Either way, I was pissed off.

"Why? What in the world were you possibly thinking, telling Hartley who I was?" I demanded. "Are you jealous? Is that what this is about?"

He winced. "I'm just trying to keep you safe. I told you to back off, and you couldn't leave well enough alone."

Was he for real? Did he really think he could charm his way into my heart with that cockamamy excuse? By implying I couldn't take care of myself?

"Safe? From who, the ADA? He's one of the good guys. At least he isn't making rash judgments like your department. If it weren't for him, Abby Lee would be in jail right now."

"Jules—"

"Save it, Deputy. You could take a page from a guy like Hartley."

CHAPTER TWENTY

The next day, Justin came over to apologize. I refused to open the door when he knocked. He could stand there all night for all I cared. I wasn't going to let him in, even if it meant pulling out Daddy's shotgun and forcing him off the property. Law enforcement officer be damned. I was still peeved over the shit storm he'd created.

"Come on, Jules. Let me in."

His pleas for me to open the door got louder. Mom was within earshot in the kitchen; otherwise, I would have let loose a flurry of obscenities through the closed door, letting him know exactly where he could go.

After another minute or two of begging, he finally said the magic word. "Aconite."

Like flipping through a volume of *Encyclopedia Britannica*, my mind skimmed through all the useless knowledge I'd acquired over the years. I knew that word from working for the FBI.

Aconite was poison.

Justin knew my curiosity would overpower my stubbornness. I opened the door and allowed him to set foot into my parents' house—albeit reluctantly.

"Better known as wolfsbane," he continued, pleased he was able to get me to open the door.

"I know what it is," I said. "He was poisoned by aconite. You can determine a timeline now."

If the forensic folks knew what type of poison was used, they could figure out how long it took for it to go into effect and determine the approximate time of death. This was vital information if the police wanted to narrow down the individuals who'd been in contact with Harvey before his death.

Justin nodded. "It appears so. Aconite is a pretty fast-acting toxin. Death within hours."

"How'd you manage to get the toxicology report so fast?" It usually took weeks, even months to get results.

"It turns out the medical examiner knew Harvey and requested a rush job," Justin said.

"I didn't realize Harvey was so popular," I mused. Or the medical examiner, to have enough clout to get through all the red tape.

My mom chose that exact moment to poke her head out of the kitchen. "Will you be joining us for dinner, Justin?" I could tell from the frown she threw in my direction she was none too pleased that we were discussing topics like poison and medical examiners in her foyer.

Justin's face lit up at the invitation. "If you're sure it won't be a bother, ma'am."

"Of course not. It's been years since y'all have been together."

If this was Mom's way of matchmaking, she was a decade too late. She'd already gotten over the whole black-flowers incident and now had herself a new opportunity to find me a proper husband.

While my mom didn't think talk of murder was appropriate dinner conversation, my daddy, on the other hand, found it fascinating. Since his retirement a couple of years ago, he'd spent most of his time watching the crime channel. He claimed it was so he could learn more about what I did for a living, even though I'd told him about a million times that I didn't actually go out and solve crimes. Personally, I thought he'd missed his calling. He would have made a great detective.

"Poison, you say? Well, I'll be. And here we thought it was my fried catfish that done him in."

"Daddy—"

Justin had always been amused by Daddy's bluntness. "Now, Mr. Cannon, I'm not really supposed to divulge information like that, so you'll keep it on the down low, right?"

I almost choked on my dinner. If anyone was going to spill the beans, it was most certainly going to be Mom. There was a sense of pride and accomplishment in having the juiciest and most recent gossip for the women in town. And my mom was just handed the Hope Diamond of all gossip. I knew Daddy could be trusted. When he did get excited about a topic, it only ever involved hunting or fishing.

"Yeah, Mom," I said, glaring directly at her. "The police would hate for that kind of information to get out."

Wisely, she avoided my stare. "Why are you looking at me like that? I don't go around discussing things like murder. Those matters are best left for officers of the law, like Justin."

"We'll see," I muttered under my breath. Since the cat was already out of the bag and I couldn't make my mom take a vow of silence, I asked, "How'd the medical examiner know what poison to look for?" Unless the medical examiner was sure poison was involved, the ME only ran preliminary tests. Even then, the ME had to specifically know what to look for.

"Normally, I would have questioned that, too, but the good doc knew something was off based on the incident report. Vomiting right before you keel over from a heart attack isn't a common symptom—"

"Wait, he puked? How'd I miss that?"

"You were probably too shocked to find Harvey's dead body in your parents' backyard to notice. It happens."

Yet another subtle reminder that I wasn't cut out for investigative work.

"So, getting back to the ME," he continued, "he figured he would cross-reference poisons capable of causing cardiac arrest as well as inducing vomiting. Did you ever hear of the Curry Killer case?"

I shook my head. It sounded interesting, though.

Daddy thought so, too, and got all animated. "I just saw an episode about that on TV! You know, one of those true-life crime shows. Tell us more about it."

"Honestly, Boyd, I don't know why you spend your time watching those programs," Mom said.

Justin, pleased to have a captive audience, continued despite Mom's concern about appropriate dinner conversation. "It was about five years ago or so. Anyways, the case involved murder through the use of aconite. Seems some British woman got jilted by her boyfriend of sixteen years . . . traded her in for a younger model . . . and in a fit of rage, she laced his curry dinner with aconite she managed to acquire in India. There was a bit more to the story, but the gist of it was the poor guy died an hour after being rushed to the hospital."

"I don't care for curry myself. Leaves such a distinctive odor, it takes days to get rid of." Leave it to Mom to find some way to contribute to the conversation despite her aversion to the topic being discussed.

I made a mental note to look up the case after he left. "And the medical examiner got aconite poisoning from remembering that particular case?"

"Seems he has an affinity for studying up on odd murders involving poisons. At any rate, the symptoms were similar, so he had a pretty good idea of what to test for."

"Smart guy," I said.

Justin shrugged. "That's why he's in charge of the forensic center."

Hours after I'd reluctantly let Justin into the house, I was showing him out for the night. As annoyed as I was at having him over for dinner, it actually turned out to be not so bad. Aside from freaking out my mom with talk of murder and mayhem, it was fun having company over for a change. And, as an added bonus, he'd told me about the aconite poisoning. He didn't have to, but he did. I wondered why he suddenly did a one eighty.

"Why'd you tell me about the poison?" I asked as we said our good-byes. "I thought you didn't want me to get involved."

"I still don't, but since you insist on meddling, I thought maybe I could use it to my advantage."

I knew there had to be a catch. Any other person might be fooled, but not me. "I'm listening."

"You do research for the bureau, right?" Justin didn't wait for an answer. He knew exactly what I did as a crime analyst. Doing research and gathering intelligence made up a good portion of my job description. "Well, I need you to see if you can track down who might have recently come into the possession of aconite."

Before I could say anything in response, he added, "And by 'track down,' I mean on your computer. I don't need you running around asking folks in town or breaking and entering people's homes."

Right, as if I would break into someone's home. But he did make a good point. I could easily use my connections and resources to get the type of information that could take days, if not weeks, for a small police department from Trouble to acquire.

"You really want my help?"

Justin offered me a smug smile. "If it means satisfying your need to help Abby Lee and keeping you out of trouble, then, yes, I'd like your help."

He must have really felt bad for ruining my date with Hartley to come over and give me this information. I accepted the olive branch, but on my terms. If Justin thought he could keep me occupied with sitting in front of my laptop, he was seriously mistaken. I would definitely take him up on his offer, but that still wasn't going to stop me from snooping around. "Deal."

After I saw Justin out, I dodged questions from Mom about Justin and immediately ran up to my room. I flipped open my laptop to see what I could find on aconite poisoning. First, I did a preliminary search on aconite. While I had an idea of what kind of poison it was, I didn't know the specifics. Justin said it was a fast-acting toxin. But how did it work? Did it need to be ingested, or was contact through the skin sufficient for a lethal dose? Knowing this would tell me a lot about the person who acquired it and how it was administered. If I could find the answers to that, it might point me in the right direction and narrow down my scope.

Within seconds, I had everything I needed to know about the poison. Aconite, or wolfsbane, was highly toxic, with symptoms typically occurring within an hour, and death within several hours. The poison could be either ingested or absorbed through the skin.

Next, I had to find out where it was available. If the plant could be grown locally, it would broaden my suspect list. But if it only grew in remote locations, that could narrow it down. A few more quick keystrokes on Google, and I had my answer. Aconite could be used in planters as a filler, but with warnings to use extreme caution. It was grown in India, as well as various parts throughout the northern United States. But not in the South, I noted— especially not in the Gulf Coast region.

This told me two things: one, the killer had to purchase the plant, and two, it was premeditated, very much like the case Justin told me about earlier. I didn't think the killer had to go all the way to India to procure the plant, since it was widely available in most areas in North America.

I had to look for someone who either recently made a trip up north or ordered it.

Also, because the poison was fast acting, whoever poisoned Harvey did it the night of my welcome-home party.

CHAPTER TWENTY-ONE

Now that I knew what to look for, I had to enlist Aunt Lula's help once again, against my better judgment, in order for my plan to work.

"I need to gain entry into Sheila's house," I said the second I set foot in Palmetto Pink. It was my day off, but I knew she was working that day.

Aunt Lula stopped what she was doing and looked at me like I was a crazy person. "Good Lord, child. Why would we want to go visit Sheila Boyette?"

"Well, I don't really want to visit her, per se. I just need access into her home. Think you can get me in?"

My aunt lowered her eyes down at me. "You want to do some snooping. Do I have that right?"

"Yup." I smiled, not the least bit apologetic. "Is there a problem with that?"

She mirrored my wicked grin. "Not at all. The gals and I have always wanted to know the exact shade Sheila uses to dye her hair. Personally, I think it's a cross between banana parfait and banana pudding, but I could be wrong," she said. "Now, I don't think I can get us in without her being there, but I might have an idea."

"Us?" Did I inadvertently invite her along? "No way, Aunt Lula. I can't let you get involved. I'm willing to risk getting caught, but I can't let you get in trouble, too."

"Nonsense! Besides, I have an idea, and it won't even involve us getting arrested for breaking and entering."

I eyed her suspiciously. Even some of her better ideas had a way of backfiring. Like the time I was ten years old and she had the brilliant idea that she could teach me how to shoot skeet and operate a boat at the same time. She ended up accidentally shooting a hole in the boat, and Daddy had to come rescue us. Aunt Lula had me promise not to tell Daddy or Uncle Jep she'd been drinking while operating heavy machinery.

"What did you have in mind?" I asked.

"We're going to bring her a casserole."

"I don't see how—"

"Her husband just died. She probably hasn't gotten around to doing any cooking or baking. Not that she was much of a homemaker." She said the last part under her breath.

"Ah, the old Trojan horse trick."

"Exactly."

We plotted, planned, and cooked all afternoon. It was decided that the best way to approach Sheila was by using the element of surprise. There was a lesser chance of her turning us away if we went over unannounced instead of calling in advance—it was easy to come up with an excuse over the phone.

Nervous, I rang the doorbell to Sheila's small beach bungalow. Even though I desperately wanted to have a look around, I almost prayed she wasn't home. I didn't think I was cut out for detective work.

An annoyed Sheila finally came to the door after the third ring. "What's this?" she asked, eying the condolence casserole in Aunt Lula's outstretched hands.

"It's a King Ranch casserole," Aunt Lula gushed. "My niece and I figured you needed a good, homemade dinner after everything you've been through the last two weeks."

"A what?" Hailing from Florida, Sheila probably hadn't sampled all the regional culinary cuisine Texas was known for. This particular casserole was, in a nutshell, an unsightly, hot mess consisting of chilies, cheese, and chicken, with a can of Ro-Tel thrown in for good measure—oh, and the requisite cream of chicken and mushroom soup.

A sigh escaped Aunt Lula's lips. She didn't like repeating herself. "A King Ranch casserole, dear. It's a Texas staple," she explained, horrified that Sheila had never heard of the dish.

Sheila was so preoccupied, staring at the foil-covered Pyrex dish my aunt held, she didn't recognize me from the incident with Abby Lee back at The Poop Deck. I was sure if she had, she would have thrown us off the premises.

She held her arms out to accept the offering. "Thanks. I'll just put it in the freezer with the others." Guess we weren't the first ones to bring over a dish.

"Oh, goodness me! I totally forgot to write down the instructions," Aunt Lula said, handing her the casserole. "If you're going to freeze it, you're going to need to know how to reheat it."

"What instructions? Isn't it already baked?" Sheila asked.

"Yes, but you have to set the temps correctly. Bake it too low and you got yourself an icy center, bake it too high and it'll just turn into a big glob of hot goo. If you've never had this casserole before, I insist on showing you the proper way to reheat it."

"That's OK, I think—"

"Nonsense! Now, this will only take a minute or two to jot it all down for you, right, Jules?"

Aunt Lula poked me in the ribs. I'd been peeking over Sheila's shoulder to get a better look at the inside of the house. "Oh, right. It won't take long at all."

Sheila totally didn't want to invite us in, but she was stuck. No one refused Aunt Lula. "Uh, yeah, sure. Do you two want to come in?"

Satisfied, Aunt Lula marched straight into the kitchen to show Sheila how to reheat the casserole. Personally, I didn't think my aunt knew what she was doing, but it got Sheila's attention away from me.

I loitered in the living room, while the two of them remained in the kitchen. I could hear Aunt Lula reciting bogus heating instructions. I took a quick inventory of the room. Nothing much had changed since we were here the day of the funeral. Though it looked like Sheila hadn't done any housekeeping since then.

There was no way I was going to get access to any other part of the house without getting busted, so I called out to the kitchen. "Sheila, do you mind if I use your restroom?"

Ideally, I was going to need more than a few minutes to toss Sheila's house for anything incriminating. But that meant breaking into her home, and I wasn't sure if I was ready to add breaking and entering to my repertoire, so I had to work with what I had.

Sheila popped her head into the hallway that separated the kitchen from the living room and narrowed her eyes at me. If she didn't want us in her home in the first place, she certainly didn't want me in the bathroom. "I guess," she finally said. "It's the last door on your left."

I passed the hallway guest bathroom and went directly toward the master bedroom. If she was hiding something—like poison, for example—it wouldn't be in the guest bathroom. Hopefully Aunt Lula would stall long enough for me to have time to check her medicine cabinet.

First impressions? The woman was a slob. It seemed her lack of housekeeping in the living room extended to her bedroom—and the bathroom. She must have had three months' worth of mildew buildup in her tub, and her toilet wasn't much better. Gross. It was a good thing I didn't really have to go to the bathroom.

The mildew Chia Pet growing out of her tub was the least of my concerns. I headed straight for the medicine cabinet. Since her place was as close as you could get to a pigsty, I doubted she'd notice if I left something out of place.

I quickly realized this mission was a bust. There was nothing in here to implicate Sheila of any wrongdoing. A half-empty tube of toothpaste and a roll of Tums were all she had lying around. She didn't even have a bottle of Tylenol. This wasn't going to be as easy as I thought.

Knowing my time had run out, I scurried out of the bedroom and into the hallway.

And bumped right into Sheila.

"Find what you were looking for?" she asked.

"Uh, yeah," I said. "Thanks for letting me use the toilet."

Aunt Lula grabbed me by the arm before Sheila demanded to know what I was doing in her bedroom. "There you are. I was getting worried," Aunt Lula said. She turned to Sheila. "My niece has irritable bowel. Sometimes she can't control herself."

Ew! "I—"

Even that stopped Sheila from demanding an explanation. "I think you two better be on your way."

"Yes, of course." Aunt Lula pulled me toward the front door. "Now, don't forget," she called out to Sheila. "Thirty minutes at three fifty."

Aunt Lula couldn't even wait until we crossed Sheila's front yard. "Did you find anything?"

"Sh . . . she'll hear you," I said, looking over my shoulder to make sure Sheila didn't have a window open or something. I knew it was a bad idea to get Aunt Lula involved. On the bright side, at least no one got hurt—or arrested for trespassing.

"Well?"

"Not a thing. It was weird. You'd think someone who's been living in the same house for several years would have more than just toothpaste in her medicine cabinet."

"Maybe she's a naturalist," my aunt offered.

"A what?"

"You know, those folks who don't rely on modern medicine."

"Oh, you mean holistic."

"Yeah, one of those."

"Nah. She doesn't seem the type." Sheila was artificial from head to toe—fake hair, fake nails, and fake tan. Which made it all the more confusing. Why would a woman like Sheila—who obviously favored the fake look—not even have a bottle of nail polish?

"Did you by any chance get a peek at what color hair dye she uses?" Aunt Lula asked.

"Nope. It's like the woman was only visiting."

CHAPTER TWENTY-TWO

I stopped by to check on Abby Lee before my shift at Palmetto Pink. The temperature had already reached record-breaking highs. It was like an open sauna outside. Even if you managed to run to the nearest building with central air, the steam from the outside would eventually penetrate through the cracks.

Abby Lee had been prepping all morning for the lunch crowd. She was pleased to have the company before she got too busy dealing with customers.

"God, it's like that song," I said, fanning myself with one of the menus. The oppressive heat had put a damper on my mood. All I could think about was spending an hour in her walk-in freezer.

"Jules," Abby Lee said, snapping her fingers. "You're not making any sense. What song?"

"You know the one . . ." I proceeded to sing off-key, mixing up the words as I sang. "I think it was Tanya Tucker who sang it—where she hopes to go to Texas if she doesn't get into Heaven. Only she had it all wrong."

"I think the humidity is seeping into your brain. Had what wrong?"

"Texas—being like Heaven. She had it wrong in the song. It's more like hell. Lord knows it's just as hot here as it is down there."

She laughed. "Nothing we can do about it, unless you want to go for a swim after we get off work," Abby Lee said.

That reminded me of how we used to spend our summers here on the island. Every weekend, Abby Lee and I would go down to the beach and catch some rays. Sometimes Justin and his friends would join us for some beach volleyball or football, often extending our time well into the evening, complete with a bonfire on the beach. I missed that.

And now, I'd been home for two weeks, and I still hadn't found the time to go swimming or get a decent tan. The only reason my legs had gotten any sun at all was due to walking to and from Palmetto Pink for work.

"Can't I just spend five minutes in your walk-in?"

She giggled. "No. What if I forgot you back there? I'd be accused of two murders."

"Good point." I shuddered. It made me think of being locked in the stockroom at Palmetto Pink. I certainly didn't want to relive that. But I was glad Abby Lee still had her sense of humor.

Since none of the other staff members had arrived yet, I filled her in on what happened at Sheila's house the night before.

Abby Lee doubled over, laughing at my expense. "Irritable bowel? Did Lula really say that? Classic! Where does she come up with that stuff?"

"Wasn't that funny," I mumbled under my breath.

She wiped the tears from her eyes. "Seriously, Jules," she said, placing her hand over mine. "I can't tell you how much I appreciate you and Lula going out on a limb to help me."

"You're my best friend," I said. "I know I haven't been around the last few years and we haven't really spoken in ages, but—"

"Stop. I know how much you hate talking about your feelings," she said. "You're my best friend, too."

❀

Aside from my heart-to-heart with Abby Lee that morning, it was definitely not a good day for me to be working at Palmetto Pink. It was an unusually busy day at the store, and we were short staffed.

This pretty much summed up my day at the store:

"What you need is a padded bra if you want to fill out the bust of that dress," I told one customer who was so flat chested nothing in the store fit.

"Have you considered using duct tape to bind your boobs down?" I asked another customer whose chest was too big to fit into anything we carried.

And the lady who inquired about the Lycra-spandex blend in a pair of capris wasn't pleased when I suggested she consider supportive undergarments. "You know, everyone wears Spanx these days."

After running back and forth around the store, hanging up clothes no one bothered to purchase, I went back to the dressing room area to make sure everyone was doing OK.

"Excuse me," a woman said, tapping her perfectly manicured foot on the tile floor. I hadn't noticed her earlier. She must have come in while I was assisting the other customers.

"Yes?"

"How long do I have to wait for a dressing room?"

How could I even begin to respond to a question like that? For starters, Palmetto Pink wasn't that big of a store; it only had two dressing rooms. Normally this wasn't a problem, as we didn't have customers come in all at one time, but apparently this customer was above waiting like everyone else.

"As soon as one becomes open," I said, trying my best to sound polite. I mean, what did she want me to do? Kick someone out of the dressing room?

She huffed. "I am a valued customer here, and this is exactly the kind of treatment that will keep me from coming back."

And what the hell could I say to that? It was not my fault the other two customers got there first. "I'm sorry you feel that way, ma'am," I said, once again controlling what Aunt Lula called my "attitude." "But I assure you, it won't be long." I prayed the other women trying on clothes overheard the exchange and took their sweet time.

"Well, your manager will be getting a complaint from me."

Clearly she wasn't local, or she would have known who Aunt Lula was. So much for being a "valued customer." I knew this was her first time setting foot in the store. Because if she had known my aunt, she wouldn't dare complain about having to wait her turn. Aunt Lula was a wealthy woman in her own right, but she couldn't stand the pompous nouveau riche that trickled onto the island from time to time. Aunt Lula always said it was easy to spot the true affluent from the phonies. And this was a perfectly good example.

I'd had enough of pretentious customers from across the causeway. I took a chance that this woman didn't know my aunt. "And tell her what exactly? That you don't have the proper manners to wait your turn?"

The woman's face turned beet red at being called out like a five-year-old. "Well, I never!" She dumped the clothing on the floor and stomped off.

"You're fired," Aunt Lula said after hearing about the scene.

"What?" I couldn't believe my ears. She was firing me? I thought she'd be pleased when she found out I'd put that lady in her place. I knew damn well she would have done the same thing. Don't get me wrong, I was elated at the news, but at the same time I was disappointed in myself. I couldn't even hack it in retail.

"You heard me, dear. I do not like being wrong, and the good Lord knows I hate admitting defeat, but I know when to cut my losses."

"I'm that bad, huh?" I should've been upset at being fired for the first time in my life, but I was delighted. "What will you do without the extra help?" As much as I was doing mental cartwheels at my sudden termination, I didn't want to let my aunt down.

"Don't you worry about that," she said, a little too brightly for having just canned me. "I have a girl interviewing tomorrow morning. You remember the Duck girl, don't you?"

I flipped through my internal Rolodex to match a face with the name. "I used to babysit her." Little Sarah Duck had to be about sixteen or seventeen by now.

"She's trying to save some money for college. Seems she's interested in fall recruitment, and her parents have already flat-out refused to pay sorority dues," Aunt Lula said. "Poor lamb."

Of course Aunt Lula would believe joining a sorority was the cornerstone of a proper college experience. I should have been so lucky to have my parents balk at sorority dues. When I headed off to college that was one of the ongoing battles I'd unfortunately lost to Mom and Aunt Lula. It was one of the few times they agreed on anything, insisting I not only go through sorority recruitment but join ADPi like they had; I was considered a legacy. And to be honest, it actually wasn't so bad. I made a lot of great friends, and it forced me to be more outgoing than I had been in high school.

"I'll write her a letter of rec," I said.

My aunt beamed. "That would be wonderful, dear. She's very excited and determined to save enough money."

"I hope she works out better at the store than I did," I said.

Wait. Did she say the Duck girl already had an interview lined up for tomorrow? That meant Aunt Lula had been planning my replacement for a while. Now I felt like an even bigger failure.

Aunt Lula stroked my arm. "There now, you weren't the worst sales associate I've ever employed," she said. I knew she was lying for my benefit. "And now that you have more free time on your hands, you can concentrate on your investigation."

I smiled. My aunt could be so transparent at times. I now understood the real reason behind my termination. It had more to do with finding Harvey's killer than my lack of skills in retail— although they were pretty pathetic. Aunt Lula had just given me an out.

While I was relieved to be done with my tenure at Palmetto Pink, I couldn't help but feel humbled by the experience. There should be a rule that everybody has to work retail, or even food service, at least once in their life. Those workers now had my utmost respect. Having to deal with rude customers on a daily basis was bound to have an effect on the human psyche. I'm not saying all retail clientele or restaurant customers are inconsiderate—they're not—but even if you had to serve just one obnoxious customer, you'd probably think twice before being rude ever again.

I made a solemn vow right then and there to never rumple a shirt I didn't intend to purchase, leave clothes in a heap on the dressing room floor, or waltz into a store five minutes before closing. In fact, I would continue to do my shopping online (and never make a return).

CHAPTER TWENTY-THREE

For the first time since coming back to Trouble, I finally had an opportunity to sleep in. Not having to work at Palmetto Pink gave me an extra hour of pressing snooze on my alarm. I can't tell you how much satisfaction I got from pressing the snooze button on my phone.

I had just fallen back asleep—for ten minutes, until my alarm beeped again—when I heard a different ring on my phone. A quick glance told me it was Abby Lee. If she was calling me this early in the morning, it couldn't be good news.

"Someone broke into the restaurant last night," Abby Lee said in a hurried panic.

I shot straight out of bed. "Oh my God! Did they take anything?"

"No. Well, at least I don't think so. They trashed the office, though."

Since Abby Lee had taken over The Poop Deck, I had been privy to the back office. While I'd hardly call the small broom closet an office, it was large enough to accommodate a desk and a chair. That was where she did all the ordering for the restaurant. I wasn't sure what all they could have damaged.

"They were looking for something," I said, confident in my estimation of the situation.

Abby Lee, however, wasn't convinced. "I don't know. Whoever did it also left a big mess at the bar," she said. "Who'd want to vandalize my restaurant?"

I could think of only one person: Sheila. "I think the mess they made was to steer you off track. I've seen your office, and my bet is that they were looking for something."

"Like what?"

"I don't know. Does your office have a safe? Do you keep cash around?"

"All deposits are done nightly. We only leave cash overnight in the safe in an emergency, and then it's deposited first thing in the morning."

I let out a long breath. "OK, let's think about this for a second. Do you think it's possible someone like Sheila would ransack the place just for spite?" I knew the answer to that one without even having to ask—yeah, she would.

"Anything is possible, I guess. Do you really think she's the one responsible?"

"You said it yourself, anything is possible. The only thing left to do is comb through the office ourselves and see if we can find whatever it is they were looking for," I suggested. "I'll be over there in a few."

I scrambled to put myself together in a hurry. I didn't want to leave Abby Lee to sort out the mess alone. There was a killer on the loose and now a burglar. They could be one and the same, but I wasn't taking any chances. It wasn't safe for her to be there by herself.

I'd almost made it out the door when Daddy called out from the kitchen. "Jules, you're up late today."

I still hadn't told my parents about being fired from Palmetto Pink. Even though Mom wasn't happy about me working there to begin with, she'd worry everyone would think I was incapable of selling overpriced resort wear.

"Yeah, about that. I'm not working for Lula anymore."

He raised his eyebrows but didn't bother to ask. I watched as he continued to man the skillet. "Have a seat. I'm making breakfast tacos."

Yum. I was starving, and his breakfast tacos were the best. "I'd love to join you, but I really have to get over to The Poop Deck." I didn't want to worry him, so I neglected to mention the break-in.

"Not before you have breakfast. I don't know what all the rush is with you kids. And don't think for one moment I don't know what y'all are up to—getting involved in Harvey's murder. You even managed to get Lula all wrapped up in this," he said, pointing a wooden spatula in my direction. "Make your old man happy, and eat something before leaving the house."

My daddy, the voice of reason. Before he'd retired from his position as an oil executive, he would be gone for weeks, overseeing oil rigs, often leaving me and Mom alone to fend for ourselves. It was there on those trips that he learned how to make the best chorizo and eggs from Benito, a cook on one of the rigs, who, in turn, had learned from his mother, who was originally from Guatemala. Or was it Guadalajara?

"How about we split the difference? I'll eat breakfast if I can take it to go," I said.

"Deal," he said. I watched him crack the eggs into a bowl while the chorizo simmered in the pan. "Now why don't you tell me what's troubling you?"

"You mean Abby Lee?"

"No. I already know about that. Is there something going on between you and a certain young man?"

Was I that obvious? Damn, now I wished I had turned down breakfast. There's nothing worse than talking to your dad about your love life, or lack thereof.

"How did you know?"

He gave me a wink. "I had the same pathetic look when I was trying to date your mama." He was never one to mince words.

"Nothing to get all worked up about, Daddy. It's nothing," I said.

He gave me a knowing smile. "I'm sure Deputy Chief Harper doesn't think it's nothing."

What? My dad caught me totally off guard.

"I wasn't talking about Justin." I had been thinking about Hartley. I had hoped that he would call or come back to the island to talk, but no such luck. Not that I blamed him. I had basically humiliated him.

My dad wrapped my breakfast taco in foil and passed it over to me. "Then I guess you ought to figure out whatever needs figuring out."

Gee, thanks, Daddy. "I'll do my best. Thanks for the advice."

I devoured my taco on the way to The Poop Deck. Oil from the chorizo dribbled down my arm as I walked the quarter mile to the restaurant. Thankfully, it was still early in the morning and no one was milling about yet.

Once I arrived, Abby Lee handed me a paper towel to clean my orange-streaked forearm. "You look a mess," she said.

"Daddy wouldn't let me leave the house until I was properly fed."

"And speaking of messes, we have our work cut out for us," she said, allowing me to survey the damage.

"You weren't kidding." The place hadn't just been broken into; it'd been ransacked. Dishes lay broken and discarded around the main dining room floor. Wineglasses and beer mugs had been smashed, and bits and pieces covered the perimeter of the bar. Burglars who broke into businesses went straight for the cash register or back office to look for quick cash. Whoever did this either tossed the place looking for something of value or was trying to send a message. Maybe it was a little bit of both in this case.

"Did you call the police?"

"I was afraid to. You're the first person I called."

I sighed. "Look, I know how you don't want them to get involved, especially since you're a suspect in their investigation, but we can't get to the bottom of this unless you call them. It can't hurt. Besides, there's enough damage done you'll need a report to file with your insurance."

She looked doubtful. "I suppose," she said. "But what if they think I did it?"

"What? That you trashed your own place to cast suspicion on someone else? That only happens on TV—and really bad crime novels," I said. "I'm sure if you report it, they'll believe you." I knew this was a small island town, but the police weren't that dense.

I was wrong. Chief Poteet himself made an appearance after Abby Lee reluctantly made the call. Every time I ran into him, I had flashbacks from when I was a kid watching *The Dukes of Hazzard* reruns with Daddy. The chief reminded me of Boss Hogg, minus the white suit and cowboy hat.

"Did you really think we'd buy into the whole 'someone broke into my restaurant' routine?" Chief Poteet asked the second he walked into The Poop Deck. "You're still a person of interest in the Boyette case. No break-in is going to change our minds."

The beefy chief of police loitered around the restaurant for a few minutes, mumbling to himself about wasting his time, but out of courtesy—there'd be hell to pay if it actually did turn out to be a burglary—had his boys take a formal statement.

"I'm sorry. I didn't realize how pigheaded he was," I said after they left us to clean up the mess. "I mean, does he really think you made all this up just to throw suspicion off yourself?" If Abby Lee wasn't already in enough trouble, I would have told him where to shove it; I was that pissed off. No sense in getting her into deeper waters with the head of the police department.

Abby Lee's disposition was grim. "Oh, he's a jerk, all right. I know from experience. He's married to my aunt Gail's cousin on her daddy's side."

I'd gotten to know her aunt Gail well while we were growing up and had always considered her a nice lady. It was hard for me to imagine a cousin of hers being married to an oaf like Poteet.

"And he's gone out of his way to treat family this way?" I thought of how he had one of his officers haul her in for questioning for a crime she didn't commit and conducted a bogus search on her home and business, and now this. I'd worked in law enforcement long enough to know that officers couldn't go easy on a murder suspect, even if they were somehow related, but still. A little tact between family members would have been understandable.

"Oh, Aunt Gail and her cousin can't stand each other. It's been a feud going on twenty years now. Something about my grand-mother's china."

"Ah." Despite our relaxed island atmosphere, the town still held traditional, old Southern customs, like the passing down of the heirloom china and crystal. I'd be inheriting Aunt Lula's one day—if I ever got married. "I'm sure this whole situation makes for some interesting dinner conversations," I said, trying to liven up the situation.

"You're telling me," Abby Lee said. "Mother won't even take Sally Poteet's calls anymore."

"Come on, let me help you clean up this mess before we search the office." It might not have looked like your garden-variety break-in, but I was sure there was something they were after, and my gut was telling me it was hidden in that back office.

"What are we even looking for?" Abby Lee asked after about an hour of pulling the office apart.

"I don't know, but this wasn't a random act of vandalism, that's for sure. Someone was looking for something."

"And you really think it's here?"

I shrugged. "Your office is just as good a place to hide something as any." Harvey didn't strike me as being the creative sort, so if he'd had something he wanted hidden, it would be in his office.

Despite the office being trashed, it still remained somewhat organized. In an office the size of a tin can, everything had a purpose and was arranged accordingly. Everything except the calendar above the desk, dated 2011, which should have been a huge tip-off to anyone looking. I pulled it off the nail that hung from the wall.

Perhaps I'd underestimated Harvey. They say that if you want something to be well hidden, hide it in plain sight. If that's true, then you'd think burglars would stop searching for hidden compartments and safes and take a look at what's right in front of their noses. I certainly didn't at first, yet there it was.

Pay dirt.

Taped behind the back of the old calendar was Harvey's will. From the looks of it, it appeared to be an older version. It certainly wasn't the one that was read at his funeral. This had to be what the burglar was looking for. How did the burglar know to even look for it here?

"Abby Lee, check this out," I said. "Did you know Harvey kept this in the office?"

"No. Where did you find it?"

"Taped to that old calendar over his desk."

"Clever, Harvey. I always wondered why he had an outdated calendar from 2011. But what does it matter now? We already know what it says," she said.

"Not exactly," I said, pointing to the document. "This looks like it was drawn up prior to the one that was read after his funeral. It names Sheila as sole beneficiary—for everything."

"You're kidding! Then why—"

I cut her off, knowing what she was thinking. "At this point we'll never know what Harvey was thinking when he changed it.

But this does put Sheila in a bad position. If she knew this existed, she could've been the one to break in, hoping she could use it against you if she decided to contest the will."

"But it's dated. They both are. Surely a judge would consider this one void," Abby Lee said.

"One would think, but even if a judge still dismissed her claim, it could certainly delay or halt the process of you officially taking over the restaurant in the meantime." I looked at Abby Lee's confused gaze. "Which means it could give Sheila the opportunity to drag the court process for as long as it takes to get you to give up and sign the restaurant over to her." Even though we were talking about civil court, I'd seen this type of thing happen so many times in criminal court. Defendants would file countless motions or extend trial dates so that ultimately the injured parties would eventually give up and drop the charges.

Abby Lee let it all sink in. "Oh my God, do you think Sheila killed Harvey knowing this will existed?"

At this point I wasn't sure of anything, but it was a pretty good argument for motive. "I wouldn't put it past her. If that's what really happened, I'm sure she got the shock of her life when she found out he changed his will and left you The Poop Deck."

"I can't believe the police missed it when they tossed the place the other day."

"Because they're idiots," I said, perhaps a bit too harshly. "They didn't even know what they were looking for."

"What about the nephew? Do you think he had any idea about the will?"

"Seeing that neither he nor his family were included in either version, I doubt it." I thought back to the conversation I'd had with Donald. "Besides, both were written well before the magazine write-up and his visit to the island." There was no need to mention I had also conducted a somewhat illegal search on Harvey's nephew.

"I wonder why Harvey hid it?"

"I don't know. Maybe he didn't like to throw things out. For his records."

"I guess. So what do we do now? Take it to Justin?"

I shook my head. "No. There's really nothing to show him. Yeah, we have Harvey's original will, but I know Justin's going to say it's not sufficient evidence to charge Sheila. What we have is circumstantial at best. But it's enough for me to keep digging further."

CHAPTER TWENTY-FOUR

After what happened back at the restaurant, I wasn't going to let Abby Lee out of my sight. With her mother at her weekly knitting group for the evening, I invited her to come over to my parents' house for an early dinner.

If I thought a pleasant evening at home with the folks was in the cards, I thought wrong. I didn't dwell on the fact that I'd been wrong a lot lately.

We saw it as soon as we approached the front of the house. Or rather, we smelled it.

Lying right on the front porch, on top of my mom's welcome mat, was a dead black cat. I wasn't superstitious or anything, but just the sight of that poor dead animal gave me a case of the heebie-jeebies. Now, I'd seen plenty of crime scene photos and had even been witness to a dead body or two within my time at the FBI, but this went beyond someone's idea of a sick joke.

"What the hell?" I asked out loud.

"Is that a dead cat?" Abby Lee took a step back.

"Yeah. Looks like someone left me a gift."

"How do you know it's intended for you?"

"Call it a hunch," I said. After everything she'd been through, I still hadn't told her about the threats I'd received. She would only end up blaming herself for putting me in harm's way.

Abby Lee just kept staring at the dead cat. "Hey, there's something underneath it."

I knew Abby Lee wasn't going to go anywhere near the lifeless feline body, so the task fell to me. I gently tugged at the white slip of paper that lay underneath the cat.

The message was quite clear:

Mind your own business!

"Your gut was right," she said. "It was definitely meant for you. Why would someone send you something like that?"

I had hoped to avoid telling her altogether, but it was time to fill her in on the other warnings. What if whoever vandalized The Poop Deck was the same person sending me the threats? And now that the cat was out of the bag—literally—I didn't have a choice.

"It's not the first message I've received," I said.

"What do you mean?"

"The night of the reunion, someone bashed in my windshield and left a note. Then, a few days ago, I got a box of black roses with another warning. This one makes three."

It was obvious my confession upset Abby Lee. "Why didn't you tell me?"

"I didn't want you to tell me to stop investigating Harvey's murder."

She pointed at the dead cat on my mom's mat. "This is serious, Jules."

The matter was closed as far as I was concerned. I had too much invested to back out now. "I know, trust me. But I'm not going to stop until we find out who killed Harvey."

I just hoped Mom didn't see the body before I had a chance to dispose of it.

Over sweet tea, spiked with a little splash of vodka, Abby Lee convinced me to report the threats. The incidents were escalating, so I didn't put up much of a fight. Call me foolish, but it took more than a broken windshield and ugly flowers to scare me—like a dead cat on my parents' front porch.

"Uh, it's not the first message I've received," I admitted to Justin. Filling him in on what had been going on, much like the conversation I'd had with Abby Lee, was a little bit like déjà vu.

I braced myself for the hell he was no doubt going to raise. I thought he'd probably be pissed over the fact that I'd been threatened or that I'd been keeping the information from him.

"Goddamn it, Jules! And you're telling me this now?" he asked. "This is exactly why I didn't want you to get involved. I'm not sure you realize how serious this is."

OK, maybe it was a little bit of both.

This time, I deserved it. If I were in his shoes, I'd be just as upset. How was he supposed to do his job if I kept things from him? I might not agree with how he was handling the Boyette case, but I could trust him to get to the bottom of the threats I'd received.

But what did he want me to say? Of course I knew there was a risk in investigating a murder on my own, but there was an even bigger risk at stake. I refused to believe that the system could fail. And right now, it seemed like my faith in the system was failing me.

"Trust me, I know, Justin. There was a dead cat on my mother's front porch. I get it. I'm in way over my head."

"When did all this start?"

"The night of the reunion. That's when my windshield was smashed. You had already left, so I didn't report it. And Bill over at the garage owed Daddy a favor, so he fixed it for free, so I never got around to filing one for the insurance claim.

"Then someone sent me a box full of black roses and another note," I added. "Boy, you should've seen my mom's face when she saw they weren't red. Oh, and after that, someone locked me in the stockroom at Palmetto Pink. They didn't leave a note that time. Then the dead cat I mentioned earlier. And that brings us up to date."

Justin's face got redder the longer I spoke. "Since you don't seem to care about your personal safety, I'm placing someone to keep an eye on you. I'll have an officer patrol park outside your house to make sure you're safe."

Oh, crap. "I really don't think that's necessary, Justin."

He put his hand up to stop me from talking any further. "This is not up for discussion. Either you promise to stay indoors or I'll put you in lockup myself."

"On what grounds?" I demanded. "You can't just incarcerate me for no reason."

"You want to bet? How about meddling in an investigation for starters? God help me, Jules, if that's what it takes to keep you safe—"

"OK, fine," I said, cutting him off. I wasn't going to win this round, but I didn't have to like it. "I'll try to keep a low profile."

"That's just not good enough," he said.

Officer Clemmons—the same officer that took Abby Lee for questioning the night of the reunion—showed up at my parents' house and reported for duty later that evening. I didn't think Justin was actually going to send someone out on security detail, but there he was.

"Uh," he said nervously, looking uncomfortable as I stared him down, "the deputy chief said I was to keep an eye on you."

"Who is that outside, Jules?" I heard Mom yell from the living room.

I ignored her as I continued to give Officer Clemmons the stink eye. "Fine. Just see that you keep your distance. I don't need my parents worrying, got it?"

"Uh, yeah." He quickly ran back to his cruiser, doing his best to stay as clear of me as possible. Justin could put him on babysitting detail, but it didn't mean I had to follow orders. I wasn't about to let Justin's threats of jail get in the way of finding out the truth. Having an officer watch my house had more to do with keeping tabs on me than my protection. Officer Clemmons could sit in his patrol car and drink coffee from a thermos all night for all I cared. And if he thought I was going to bring him cookies and milk, he was seriously mistaken.

In the end, however, it looked like I needn't worry about being put under twenty-four-hour surveillance. Not even an hour had gone by when I heard a frantic knock on the door. It was Officer Clemmons again.

What could he possibly want now? It better not be because he has to use the bathroom.

"Yes?" I asked, allowing only a crack between me and the officer. Mom still hadn't noticed the cruiser parked across the street, and I wanted to keep it that way. If she found out about the threats and the fact that I had security detail on me, she'd flip. Heaven forbid the neighbors find out.

"Uh, do you think you could tell that lady to stand down?"

"What lady?" I glanced past his shoulder and saw the source of his discomfort.

Aunt Lula was standing at the far end of the porch with her 20-gauge shotgun. I wanted to laugh at the sight, but I could tell Officer Clemmons was mortified.

"No, I don't think I can. Is there some sort of problem, Officer? You see, that's my aunt Lula, and she doesn't seem to be doing anything wrong. This is my property and, by extension, hers. As far as I know, there's no law that says she can't be armed on personal property."

"Well, uh, she told me I had to get the hell off your property or she'd tell my mother."

I looked over at my aunt and saw the corners of her mouth twitch. She hadn't said a word during the entire exchange, content to stand there and intimidate the poor officer instead. If Officer Clemmons had anything to fear, it wasn't my aunt's shotgun, it was his mama.

For a moment there, I almost felt sorry for the guy. I was sure he was struggling with the potential fallout of disobeying direct orders from Justin, my shotgun-wielding aunt, or his mother. No matter how it turned out, none of those scenarios worked in Officer Clemmons's favor. In any other place, this would have been a no-brainer, but this was Texas. You obeyed law enforcement, you stayed clear of old ladies with guns, and you most certainly minded your mama.

As the officer and I argued about the merits of home protection, I saw a truck pull up behind the cruiser. The cavalry had indeed arrived. I wasn't surprised to see Justin hop out of the pickup and make his way toward the house. I was pretty sure the neighbors had gotten the jump on Mom and called in the standoff between Officer Clemmons and Aunt Lula. They were probably having a field day—it would provide enough fodder to fuel their gossip for an entire week. Maybe two.

"What seems to be the problem?" Justin asked, making his way up the walk to the front porch. He ignored Aunt Lula and looked my way. "It's only been an hour, and you're causing trouble already?"

Aunt Lula immediately chimed in with her two cents, before Officer Clemmons and I could offer our version of events. "Deputy, I'm sure Chief Poteet wouldn't think too highly of you authorizing spending taxpayer money to have one of your officers keep an eye on my niece."

"Well—" He knew as well as Aunt Lula that the chief would be none too pleased he'd approved overtime so one of his men could sit outside in the middle of the night protecting their prime suspect's best friend.

"And if Jules is in danger, which I have no doubt she is, I am quite capable of seeing that she remains safe."

"Lula—"

"In fact, I've even called for backup," Aunt Lula said with a grin.

"Lord help us," he said, shaking his head in defeat. Deputy Chief Harper knew when he was beat. At least when it came to Aunt Lula.

CHAPTER TWENTY-FIVE

It took something major for my dad to get involved in anything. Whether it be a heated discussion or a friendly argument, he always preferred to stay quiet and interject only when someone was likely to get injured. But this time he put his foot down.

Between the break-in at The Poop Deck and my mysterious lethal admirer, it was decided the following day that Abby Lee and I were the killer's next targets and needed protection. No daughter of his—or Abby Lee by extension—was going to be threatened on his watch.

After the whole Mexican standoff between Aunt Lula and Officer Clemmons last night, I had to tell my parents everything that had been going on these last few weeks, and as a result, they insisted Abby Lee stay over until things blew over. Needless to say, Mom was furious when she found out I'd been playing detective. I also neglected to mention Aunt Lula's role. That would have sent her over the edge.

I was not sure if one could consider five old women suitable bodyguards in any situation, but they felt they were up to the task of protecting us. And who was I to judge? They were excellent shots. I felt more protected with them around than I would have with five of the bureau's best agents.

"Do you really think it's a good idea for them to stand guard like that?" Abby Lee asked. We'd been confined to the house—Daddy's orders—and were watching as Mom made her famous blueberry pancakes. "I feel kinda silly—having armed protection, especially given that they're all old enough to be my granny."

I laughed, picturing the women that made up the Trouble Island Ladies Trap & Skeet Club. The idea itself was preposterous—five little old ladies perched on their rocking chairs on the front porch with loaded shotguns—but it gave them a sense of purpose, being needed. They had arrived earlier that morning at the request of Aunt Lula, dressed in their Sunday best, each one in a coordinating bright green dress. I think it was their version of camouflage.

"Have you ever seen them shoot?" I asked.

"No," she said.

"Let's just put it this way, if a killer's after you, he or she better hope they're a better shot than they are," I said.

My mom, on the other hand, was not amused. "What in the world do they think they're doing? Do they not understand the severity of the situation?"

"They're doing their civic duty, Livy," Daddy said.

"Their civic duty?" Mom asked, an octave higher than her usual shrill tone. "What does that have to do with anything?"

Daddy held his ground. "They're protecting the good citizens of Trouble Island," he said, pointing to me and Abby Lee. "It seems to me these girls need a little bit of protection, so I reckon the old gals are just doing what they need to do."

"This is ridiculous. What are the neighbors going to think?"

"Those old gals haven't seen this much action since they burned their bras in the sixties," Daddy said. Abby Lee and I muffled our giggles so as not to antagonize my mom any more than she already was.

"Really, Boyd."

I was sure her concern about the neighbors was the reason she stayed within the sanctuary of her kitchen, distancing herself as much as she possibly could from the scene playing out on her front porch. If we were lucky, we'd come out ahead with some freshly baked pies by afternoon.

Truth be told, I halfheartedly agreed with Mom, but for different reasons. I didn't exactly protest the display of firearms by my respected elders, but the principle of the matter.

"Daddy, really. Can't you tell them to go home or something? I don't think anyone is going to come after us here," I said. Besides, I didn't want the killer to think we were hiding behind five old ladies and my daddy.

He chuckled. "Oh, let them have their fun, Butter Bean. It makes them feel needed, and if it means they accidentally shoot a hole in my porch, well, so be it." Even though the women were champion marksmen, it hadn't escaped Daddy's attention that they'd also come armed with enough bloody mary mix and vodka to serve the entire neighborhood. It was kind of like *The Golden Girls*, only hyped up on booze and too much testosterone.

I sighed. There was no arguing once he made up his mind about something. "If you say so."

But I had something up my sleeve. Here's a poker tip—if you're gonna cheat, don't get caught with cards up your sleeve.

Don't ask me why, but Mom didn't say a word when Abby Lee and I decided to sneak out the kitchen's back door. The kitchen was situated at the other side of the house, so with the peanut gallery out on the front porch, and Daddy snoozing in the den, they couldn't hear the squeak of the screen door.

"Thanks, Mom," I said through the screen. "We'll be back soon."

Mom kept kneading her dough, doing her best to ignore the circus going on in her home. Secretly, I was pleased she was taking everything in stride—I had high hopes for a peach pie. "Just be careful," she said.

"We will, Mrs. Cannon," Abby Lee said.

Once we were out in the backyard, we crossed through the gate that faced the Gulf. We couldn't go around the house, or the armed women of Trouble would insist we march ourselves right back inside. We took off our flip-flops and walked along the sand, taking advantage of the dunes for coverage. As soon as my parents' house was a good distance away, we took the public access walkway onto Gulf Boulevard, walking in the direction of The Poop Deck.

It was time to brainstorm.

"I have to talk to Donald again, if he hasn't already checked out of his hotel room," I said once we got to the restaurant. I'd kind of lost track of his comings and goings once I started to focus my attention on Sheila. Time wasn't on our side, so we had to move quickly. If Aunt Lula or the other armed grannies knew we'd flown the coop, this would be the first place they'd check. They took their security duties seriously.

Abby Lee wasn't so sure of my plan. "Do you think that's a good idea? I mean, what if he's the killer? Imagine, killing your own uncle over a piece of property."

If he was guilty of murdering Harvey, prying more information out of him probably wasn't one of my better ideas. I just had to make sure to tread very carefully. "Don't worry. I'll be careful."

Lucky for me, I found him exactly where I hoped he'd be. Donald was back at the hotel bar. Then again, maybe it wasn't luck. Whenever I had to go to a conference for work, I always managed to find myself seated at the very last stool at the bar, making awkward conversations with complete strangers. Because who wants to be away from home and sit all alone in a hotel room?

"Hey," I said, taking the seat next to him. "I didn't think you'd still be here in town."

"Oh, hi," Donald said, slightly confused by my attempt at idle conversation. "Sorry, who are you again?"

"Just a local. I met you at your uncle's funeral, remember, and here at the bar," I said. "I didn't think you'd still be here. I mean, I'm sorry for your loss and all, but rumor has it you and your uncle weren't exactly close." There. I said it.

He eyed me with suspicion before answering. "This really is a small town," he finally said. "Yeah. I guess you can say we had our differences. Mostly him and my mom. But they finally managed to patch things up. Too bad it was short-lived."

"Why? Did your mom and Harvey have issues?" It was hard for me to imagine holding any type of grudge with a sibling. I had my own issues with my brother, Scott, but they were nothing more than sibling rivalry. Each of us competing for our parents' love and affection. What siblings didn't? But to purposely alienate yourself from your own family?

I didn't really think he'd tell me, but he surprised me by saying, "Money."

"Money?"

Yup. That was a surefire way to ensure a feud, even among the best of families.

"When my mom's daddy died, he left my uncle Harvey the land here on Trouble Island," he said. "Back then, men believed that women weren't suitable enough to own land, so he left everything to his son, thinking Mom would marry a good provider."

I was intrigued. "And did she?"

Donald's face looked grim as I asked the question. "Doesn't appear that way. See, my dad didn't amount to much and left us when I was about seven. By then, Mom had already given birth to two other kids."

I was beginning to get the picture. I imagined they struggled, while their uncle Harvey had himself a decent business and life here on Trouble Island. "And Harvey never stepped in to help?"

He shook his head. "Honestly, I don't think my mom ever really told him how bad it was. She struggled to provide for us, working two jobs, and never said a word. Guess he assumed we were all right."

"But how—"

"She resented the fact that her brother was doing well, but was too stubborn to ask for help. I think half of the reason she resented him was misdirected anger. My mom was unhappy with how her life had turned out."

A falling-out between brother and sister could have been avoided if only she had asked for her brother's help. I told Donald as much.

"She was a proud woman. But when that article came out in that magazine and I showed her, she finally snapped. Drove all the way from Lufkin to confront Harvey. Actually, I think she visited him to finally make peace with him—and herself."

"Why's that? What happened?"

Donald's grim demeanor changed into a sad smile. "My uncle ended up being a very generous man. He made some good investments over the years and made sure his little sister was well provided for in the end."

That seemed to coincide with the man I had grown up knowing. "That was awfully generous. But I meant, what made your mom finally confront him?"

"Cancer."

The admission left me speechless. I knew the appropriate words to convey sympathy; they just never seemed to come out right when I said them aloud. Perhaps it was because I wasn't much of a people person. So I went with how I felt at the moment. "I'm sorry."

"Thanks."

There was a moment of uncomfortable silence. Should I keep the conversation going? It felt inappropriate to ask him about

Harvey now, especially after he'd just told me about his mother having cancer. I probably didn't need to inconvenience him any more than I already had. But I was still curious about his mom's relationship with her brother.

"So Harvey found out about your mom's illness and decided to help out?"

"In a nutshell. My mom was finally able to get better health care."

I kept thinking back to the will I'd found in Harvey's office, which was the whole reason for seeking him out in the first place.

"There's just one thing I don't understand. If they made amends, why didn't Harvey leave the land and restaurant to you or your mom?"

"She didn't want it. And frankly, neither did I. I've got a great job already. Besides, I don't know the first thing about running a restaurant. And my mom, well, she's getting on in years and set in her ways. She's pretty optimistic about beating the cancer, but she doesn't want to spend her life sweating in a hot kitchen."

Everything he said made sense and tied up quite a few loose ends. But I still wasn't any closer to finding Harvey's killer and clearing Abby Lee's name.

Now I was just curious. I was beginning to like Donald and felt sorry that he'd had such a rough childhood. "Why didn't your mom or the rest of the family come down for the funeral?"

"Mom was finally able to schedule her chemotherapy treatments. She didn't feel she was well enough to make another trip down, so she sent me to represent the family. My sisters are with her now. They didn't think they should leave her. It's not like they really knew him or anything, so we figured it would be OK if I came alone."

Harvey pretty much saved his sister's life. I felt like such a heel for intruding on Donald during his stay here. He'd simply come here to pay his respects to a man he hardly knew, but loved.

"And in answer to your previous question, I stuck around to look at some rental properties. I think my wife and kids would really like spending their summers here."

I smiled. Trouble Island was a pretty good family getaway. As Harvey's nephew, he'd have no problems fitting right into the island fold. It was too bad Sheila had been left Harvey's house. I was sure the Walker family would have enjoyed it. But I kept that thought to myself.

※

After a long internal debate with myself, I decided there was no way around it. I was going to have to pay Justin a visit and show him the will Abby Lee and I discovered back at the restaurant. I hadn't technically done any intentional snooping; I'd simply helped Abby Lee clean up after the break-in.

"And you want me to do what with this, exactly?" Justin asked, waving the document in the air.

Even when the answer was right in front of them, some men still needed a good poke with a cattle prod. It was up to me to spell it out for him.

"Doesn't it seem odd to you that Sheila was supposed to inherit everything until Harvey suddenly had a change of heart? Isn't that enough to investigate her instead of Abby Lee?"

He rubbed his chin. "Sure, it's odd, but changing a will is not unheard of, Jules. Hell, my mee-maw changes her last will every six months, when one of her grandkids falls out of favor. It doesn't mean Sheila killed him."

"Well, the current will doesn't mean Abby Lee killed him, either," I shot back.

CHAPTER TWENTY-SIX

I kicked the sand hard enough to get caught in a mini sandstorm. I had to blow off some steam after my chat with Justin and took a walk. A good stroll along the Gulf had always been cathartic for me. I was also avoiding going home. I was sure Aunt Lula and her friends had already discovered by now that Abby Lee and I had snuck off. They probably already had a search party going.

Coming up with no new answers to my problems, I cut through the beach's public access sidewalk, the same route Abby Lee and I took earlier, and headed back down on Gulf Boulevard. I planned on checking back in on Abby Lee. She'd stayed back at the restaurant when I went in search of Donald.

I was almost to the restaurant when I saw the last person I wanted to run into coming from the opposite direction.

The island simply wasn't big enough for me and Heather Clegg. I tried to turn the corner to avoid having to talk to her, but she'd already spotted me.

"Jules, wait up," Heather said, running across the street to catch up with me.

"Oh, hey, Heather," I said, pretending I hadn't tried to lose her. "I'm on my way over to my aunt Lula's, so I don't have much time for whatever it is you have to say to me."

"I deserve that," she said. "I haven't been very welcoming since you came back to town, have I? So, um, that's why I was wondering if you'd like to come over to my place for coffee or something."

I think I stood there with my mouth open in shock. To her credit, Heather pretended not to notice. Though I imagine she must have anticipated some kind of reaction from me, given our history.

Heather stood there, waiting for my response. She looked sincere in her invitation, but I was still wary. Then again, if I accepted, maybe she'd stop antagonizing me everywhere I went. As I debated the pros and cons of her invitation for coffee, I could tell she was anxious for an answer. Perhaps she really did want to call a truce. I was still a bit hesitant, but I figured it couldn't hurt. "OK. When?"

"Are you free later this afternoon? Today's my day off at the station."

I'd forgotten she worked at the station as a dispatcher. "Sure. How about four o'clock?" I asked. "I'm not needed at the store anymore." She might have been extending a peace offering, but there was no way I was telling Heather I got canned by my own aunt.

If I was surprised by her offer to have me over for coffee, what Heather did next was unthinkable—she actually hugged me, making me feel even worse for hedging on whether or not to go over to her house. "Thanks so much for giving me a second chance, Jules."

Why not? Coming back to Trouble was about second chances, right? Reconnecting with my family, solidifying my friendship with Abby Lee, and who knew? Maybe rekindling old flames with Justin.

She didn't leave me much choice but to hug her right back. It was a halfhearted hug at best, but I didn't want her to think I felt weird about the exchange. My defenses were still up, but what the hell? I knew it would never lead to becoming best friends, but what was the worst that could happen? We'd make our peace and put the past behind us.

Spending the last couple of hours with Heather wasn't as bad as I had first imagined. If you had asked me earlier that morning, I would have said I'd prefer to be at the dentist's having a root canal rather than at Heather's, but after spending a little time with her, it was kind of fun. We talked about old times, friends we remembered back in high school—I allowed her to do most of the reminiscing, as I didn't have much to contribute on the subject matter. I even toyed with the idea of inviting her to join me and Abby Lee one night at The Crooked Gator for some wicked Gatoritas.

"Hey, Heather, where's your restroom?" We'd switched it up, going from coffee to wine, and it was time to break the seal.

"Through the hallway, first door on your right."

I felt a little light-headed from the wine as I got up from the couch. *Which door did she say again?* I stumbled along until I found a room with the door closed. *This has to be it,* I thought to myself.

I fumbled with the light switch and blinked. I gasped in horror, my buzz quickly fading into shock.

This definitely wasn't the bathroom.

The spare bedroom had no furniture or decorations—with the exception of the walls.

Oh my God, the walls.

Every square inch of her walls had been covered with photos of me. You couldn't even tell if there was wallpaper or paint hidden underneath.

I hesitated at the door, wondering what to do next. My somewhat inebriated state made it hard for me to concentrate. Heather still thought I was in the bathroom, so I gathered the courage to approach one of the decorated walls. Some of the photos were as old as a decade ago. I gingerly swept my hands over the pictures, trying to convince myself they weren't real.

I took a step back to get a full view of the obsessive pictorial. It was then I realized not all the walls were adorned with pictures of me. The wall behind me was entirely devoted to Justin. Another wall boasted photos of me and Justin together—older pictures taken of us at the prom, hanging out at Carol's diner after football games, and at the beach. Newer photos were taped over older ones—faraway shots taken of Justin and me talking at my welcome-home party, at Harvey's funeral, and some of me working at Palmetto Pink.

What the hell?

The pieces all began to fit together: being locked in the stockroom, the black roses, the dead cat, the smashed windshield. It was Heather the entire time. While I had been tracking down a killer, I was being followed by a stalker.

I heard movement behind me, but it didn't stop me from staring at the mad wallpaper collage. I was transfixed by what was in front of me. Heather was behind me now, but I still couldn't peel my eyes away.

"Do you like what I've done with the room? I figured you might, since it's all about you. It's my tribute," she said.

Tribute? There were no words to convey how I felt about seeing my picture plastered on her walls. No, I take that back. I knew exactly how I felt—I was scared. Her hatred toward me ran deep. It wasn't about simple jealousy; it had snowballed somehow into a crazed obsession. I could have dealt with your garden-variety murderer, but not an obsessive, psychotic stalker.

"It was you the whole time, wasn't it? Locking me in the stockroom, the flowers, my windshield, the dead cat . . ." I heard her shuffling around the room without saying another word. I still couldn't turn around to look her in the eye. "Heather, did you do those things and leave those notes?"

Heather stopped pacing the room. "I thought that if I scared you bad enough, you'd run back to Virginia."

Oh, I was plenty freaked out. I was about ready to pee my pants—I never did make it to the bathroom.

Turning slowly, I managed to face her directly. "So you admit it."

"Guilty," she said. Her bright smile made me shudder—she looked like she was proud of herself. "But I didn't lock you in any stockroom." She laughed as she walked closer to me. "Looks like I'm not the only one that has a problem with you being here."

Even with her admission, it was still hard for me to imagine that someone could go to that much trouble for a man. Then again, maybe I wasn't so different. I'd taken two months' leave and high-tailed it to Trouble just to get away from my ex-boyfriend. The irony didn't escape me.

"Why?" I finally asked, although I already knew the answer.

Eyes wild, a sardonic grin appeared on her face. "Did you really think I was going to let you waltz back into town and take Justin away from me?" Heather screeched. "Do you know how much time I've invested in him?"

"How long have you been planning this?" Judging by the photos, she'd been obsessed with both of us for quite some time.

"Long enough to know you're a problem," she snapped. "When I heard you were coming back to town, I decided it was time to finally do something about it."

It was a snap decision to come to Trouble after my breakup with James. She couldn't possibly have had enough time to plot and plan. But that was the nature of someone like Heather. If she had begun her fixation well over a decade ago, she'd been prepared, waiting for the right opportunity, waiting patiently for me to come home.

"Honestly, Heather, I have no interest in Justin." As I said this, I didn't know if that was a lie I was telling Heather or myself. The past few days had certainly made me feel something, but I had no intention of acting on it. Whatever I'd had with Justin was ancient history.

"Don't think I don't see the way he looks at you. It was only a matter of time before you two got together again."

"Heather, I swear—"

"Save it. It doesn't matter now, does it? Now that you know what I did, you're going to go running to Justin to tell him what I've done." Her smile spread across her face, creeping me out even more. "And I can't let that happen."

Seeing her there, eyes ablaze, made me feel sorry for her. Almost. My sympathy ran along the lines of, *Gee, I'm sorry you're suffering from a severe psychological pathology.* It wasn't my fault if she'd misread something between Justin and me that wasn't there to begin with. Or was she right—did Justin still harbor feelings for me, and I just hadn't noticed?

"Look, I promise not to say anything to him, OK?" Then I remembered stopping by the station earlier to report the threats I'd received. Even if I didn't go back and tell him it had been Heather all along, I had a feeling he would figure it out soon enough on his own. He might work for a small-town police department, but I still gave him credit for being able to figure it out.

"Why couldn't you have stayed where you were?" Heather said, tears now streaming down her face. She'd shed the crazed, obsessive act. "Now you've ruined everything." It was like witnessing Dr. Jekyll and Mr. Hyde. Aunt Lula would say Heather was two sandwiches short of a picnic.

There was no point in reasoning with her. I knew she and Justin hadn't been in a relationship for a while, but in her mind, she thought she still had a chance with him.

"That's between you and Justin. Like I said, I haven't done or said anything to indicate I want to get back together with him."

"You lie," she accused. "You expect me to believe there's nothing going on between you two? I saw y'all at lunch. Several times, in fact. That doesn't sound like nothing to me."

Shivers ran down my spine. She'd been spying on us the whole time. I wondered what else she'd seen.

"It wasn't like that. We're just friends."

Heather inched her way closer to me. "Now why don't I believe that?"

"It's the truth. I'm only in town for a few more weeks. Why would I start something with Justin?" That was a question I'd been struggling with myself. "If you think I've crossed the line, it's all in your head." Probably a bad choice of words on my part.

Each time she took a step closer to me, I took a step back. Pretty soon, I'd be up against the wall. I had to figure out a way to get out of here, and fast.

"It should have been you who died that night," she cried.

What? What the hell was she talking about?

"Heather—"

We heard loud footsteps coming from the hallway.

"Jules, get out of here, now," Justin ordered.

This time, I didn't argue with him. I hightailed it out of there as fast as my size eights would take me.

CHAPTER TWENTY-SEVEN

For once, I wasn't at the police station waiting to get reprimanded for getting involved in Harvey's murder. After the incident at Heather's, Justin called to ask me to come down and give my statement. I still hadn't come to terms with what actually happened, but I was grateful Justin had figured it out and was able to get me out of her house in time. I wasn't sure what she had in store for me, but I was indebted to him just the same.

We sat in his office as I gave him the rundown on how I had ended up at Heather's house and what she had admitted to me. Justin didn't say a word as he wrote down everything I said. When I was done retelling my tale, I realized just how crazy Heather was and how close I had been to getting seriously hurt. If Justin hadn't shown up when he did, who knew what might have happened?

When I finished my statement, I asked, "How did you know I was at Heather's? More importantly, how'd you know I was in trouble?"

He shrugged. "I saw your car parked at Heather's. I knew you two weren't exactly friends, so I put two and two together. And to be honest, I've known for a while there was something not right about Heather," he said. "Seeing you there drew up a big red flag."

If anyone had an inkling toward Heather's mental state, it was Justin. He was being modest, but as far as cops went, he wasn't half bad. In fact, he was pretty damn good, even if he did work for a small-town police department. I felt guilty for doubting him. There was no telling what Heather would have done to me if I had stayed in her house much longer.

"What's going to happen to her?" There was still a small part of me that felt sorry for her. I only wished someone had caught on to her mental state well before she'd trapped me in her house.

"Oh, I imagine she'll be looking at life. Unless she finds herself a good defense attorney and pleads insanity."

"For stalking?" Stalking didn't warrant a life sentence. Depending on the state, it could take a second conviction for it to be considered a felony charge. Even then, it wouldn't be anything close to a life sentence.

Justin stared at me in disbelief. "You mean you don't know? I thought for sure Lula and her geriatric armed militia would have already spread the word by now."

"I've been sitting here at the station, waiting to make my statement, all morning," I reminded him. "What else is there to know? The woman was obsessed with the both of us."

"Jules," he said slowly, making sure he had my attention. "She confessed to killing Harvey."

I was momentarily stunned. "What?"

"The aconite was meant for you."

I was having problems thinking straight. "What? How?"

"According to Heather, she crashed your welcome-home party with the sole purpose of poisoning you. She said she knew you coming back would . . ." He paused as if he didn't want to continue. ". . . she said you being here would hurt her chances of being with me. She left the party thinking she had poisoned your food, only to find out later that Harvey accidentally ate it."

So that was what she'd meant when she said I should have been the one to die. Poor Harvey!

"He must have taken my plate by mistake," I said, instantly feeling horrible that his death was all my fault. "That's why she showed up at my parents' house uninvited. But none of this makes sense. That was only my first night back in town. There's no way she could've acted so quickly." But deep down I knew, just as I had known when I was stuck in that room, that she had been planning this for a long time, just waiting for the right moment to strike.

"It seems she's been waiting for an opportunity like this for years. News of your arrival spread pretty quickly, so she acted on it. Carried around enough poison on her to cause serious damage, hoping for just the right opportunity. When she found out she'd poisoned the wrong food, she waited to see if she'd be linked to Harvey's death before she tried again."

I shuddered, thinking about all the times I'd had run-ins with Heather since I arrived in Trouble. She certainly had plenty of opportunities. I wondered why she'd taken her time after the first attempt. There was really no evidence that would have linked her with Harvey's murder. The reality sunk in.

"She was going to try to kill me back at her place."

He nodded. "Heather had a casserole baking in the oven. I suspect she was going to try it again. When we asked her about it, she said she was going to claim you'd had too much wine and possibly food poisoning, hoping the paramedics would say it was alcohol poisoning."

"Oh my God, did she really think she'd get away with it? Surely she must have known the autopsy wouldn't have corroborated that."

"Heather was ill. She wasn't in the right frame of mind to consider anything beyond her plan."

As off-the-wall as he made it sound, what he said wasn't improbable. I had studied the typology of stalkers back in grad school, and there really were no boundaries when it came to the objects of their obsessions. There was a disconnect between reality and fantasy. Stalkers could fixate on their victims for years, even decades, and prepare themselves to take action when the opportunity presented itself. There was no rhyme or reason when it came to people like Heather.

"I feel so bad about Harvey. If I hadn't come home—"

"Jules, stop. If she hadn't tried to poison you then, she would have done something later on. And if it wasn't you, it would have been somebody else."

"There was someone else. Harvey . . . he died because of me."

Justin got out of his office chair and came over to where I sat opposite him. He placed his hand on my shoulder in an attempt to comfort me. "No, he died because of Heather."

Intellectually, I understood what Justin was saying, but I was having a hard time coming to terms with it. I sighed. "She was sick, I know."

"If anyone should feel sorry, it's me. I swear, I had no idea she had it out for you like that, but I should have seen the signs. I knew there was something wrong, but I just chalked it up to jealousy and possessiveness. Now that I look back, there were dozens of red flags I missed. It didn't register until I saw you were over at her house."

I shook my head in his defense. "You couldn't have known. I mean, no one knew I was coming back to Trouble. Who knew she was harboring those kinds of feelings toward me?"

"I should've, though. It's the reason we broke up."

I looked up at him.

He continued. "The thing about me and Heather was, we were never as serious as she made it out in her head. Sure, we went out on a few dates, but in her mind, we were in a committed relationship. I wasn't ready for it, and she wouldn't let up. That alone should have been the biggest indicator that something was off with her."

"Didn't you ever have a talk with her? Let her down easy?"

Not that it would have mattered. People like Heather were so far removed from what they heard and what they actually believed.

"I know how it looks . . . that I should have caught on sooner, but you want the truth?"

I nodded, though I wasn't sure if I really wanted to know.

"In the beginning, she made living here much more bearable."

"I don't understand. I thought you loved living here in Trouble. It's all you ever talked about when we were teens—moving back to the island and starting a family."

"And I still want those things, but it gets lonely around here. For a while, before Heather got too intense, it was nice getting all the attention. She'd come to work at the station with cookies, bring me dinner when I was too tired to cook after a long day. You of all people should know how it is around here. All the other women around our age are already married or spoken for. The options are limited."

That was no surprise. Of course the dating pool was limited; this was a small island. I didn't know how I felt hearing him say that, but I didn't feel bad about my decision to move away when I did. I could feel guilty about Harvey being killed because of me, but not Justin's lack of a love life.

"I'm sorry. I had no idea," I said.

"He wants to throw the book at her, you know," he said casually, changing the subject.

"He who?"

"The assistant DA. When he found out that the source of Heather's obsession was you, he seemed bound and determined to prosecute her to the hilt. He can't charge her with first-degree murder because Harvey wasn't the intended victim, but he's going for second-degree murder, felony stalking, and intent to commit," he explained. "You must have made quite an impression on him."

"Oh." Hearing that gave me the warm fuzzies. I instantly felt guilty about feeling good about Hartley when Justin was clearly going through his own relationship issues.

Like Justin, I quickly changed the subject. "Does this mean Abby Lee is in the clear?"

"Pending a confirmation on everything Heather said, yeah, she's cleared as a suspect."

At least there was a silver lining.

❀

One thing still bothered me. There was still a piece missing from the big picture. That night at Heather's house she had said that she hadn't locked me in the stockroom at Palmetto Pink. If it wasn't Heather, then it was someone else. But who? And for that matter, why?

Abby Lee and I were seated on my aunt's porch swing, drinking ice-cold sweet tea as I told my story again for the second time that day. I had called her with the news that she was no longer a suspect as soon as I left the station.

"That is sooo creepy!" Abby Lee said. "I can't believe she was that obsessed with both y'all."

"What's even scarier is her fixation with me before I even came back to the island. Apparently she'd been obsessed since before she started dating Justin." Just saying it out loud gave me a case of the creeps. "Probably since high school," I said, thinking of the old photos Heather had of us taped to the walls of her room.

"But I don't understand. You haven't lived here in like forever. Why was she so focused on you?"

I shrugged my shoulders. That was the million-dollar question. Who knew what motivated people to do things?

"Like I said, I think it started well before that. My guess? Justin never let the idea of me go, and it drove Heather to the extreme."

It was as if I was the sole obstacle in her attempt to get closer to Justin. "Or maybe it really had nothing to do with me at all. She had to blame someone other than herself for Justin never committing to a relationship with her."

The typology of stalkers alone generated a lot of questions as to her true intent. Some stalkers could go after a person for a real or imagined wrongdoing. Others did it for undying love and attention. At this point, it was anyone's guess. Even if Justin never mentioned my name the few times they went out, she clearly associated me as part of her failures with Justin. Heather either hated me that much, believing I was in the way, or loved Justin too much and didn't want competition.

"Damn . . . remind me to screen potential boyfriends," Abby Lee said.

"You and me both," I said.

"Speaking of, what are you going to do now?"

"I don't know," I said with a shrug. Trying to track down a killer wasn't part of my summer vacation plans, but now that it was over, I wasn't sure how I was going to spend the rest of my time here in Trouble. "I guess work on my tan."

Abby Lee shook her head. "No, silly. About the boyfriend situation. Who's it going to be? Justin or that hot prosecutor?"

I stared at my friend, my mouth agape. "What are you talking about? There's nothing going on between me and either of them," I insisted.

She raised an eyebrow. "Oh, I don't know . . . I feel a summer romance brewing in the horizon."

"I think what you're feeling is the humidity." My shirt was already sticking to my back. This was going to be a three-shower kind of day; I could already tell.

"There's nothing wrong with having a fling before you head back to Virginia."

"The last thing I need in my life is a man. Even if it is for a few weeks." I wasn't going to admit to Abby Lee that maybe I did need a little dalliance in my life—with either one of them. It'd been a while since I'd been intimate with anyone.

"Are you still sore about that loser back home?"

With working at Aunt Lula's store, trying to solve a murder, and being pursued by two men—possibly—and a stalker, I had almost forgotten about James and the way we left things.

"Honestly, no. I guess I didn't love him as much as I loved the idea of being with him."

"So what's the problem? You and I both know Justin still has a thing for you. But then again, that prosecutor is easy on the eyes," Abby Lee said. "I say go for it."

"With which one?" I asked, laughing. "No, scratch that. I'm leaving soon, remember? I don't think either one of them would appreciate a fling. Besides, I don't think Hartley wants to hear from me anytime soon."

I'd be lying if I said I wasn't disappointed about how he and I had left things.

CHAPTER TWENTY-EIGHT

The invitation came in the form of a rose-imprinted note card that arrived via postal service. At first, I thought it was a thank-you card from Abby Lee's mother for helping her daughter avoid prison (that's how we rolled in the South), but as I scanned the note, I was surprised to learn it was Sheila Boyette asking me to join her for coffee at her home. She wanted to thank me in person for identifying Harvey's killer.

After the whole incident with Heather, I was a bit hesitant about meeting Sheila for coffee, but I couldn't very well say no. She might be disliked around town, but how did you decline an invitation from a woman whose husband was murdered because of you? I was lucky she didn't hold me personally responsible.

On a conscious level, I knew there was nothing to be apprehensive about, seeing that Heather was the one responsible for Harvey's death, but my gut told me otherwise. From the little interaction I'd had with her, I knew I didn't like Sheila much. That alone was enough for me to want to say, "Thanks, but no thanks."

But still, the responsibilities (or burdens, depending who you asked) of being born in Texas included proper manners, and Mom would have herself a conniption if she knew I turned down an invitation for coffee—even if the offer did come from Sheila Boyette.

Sheila had tidied up since the last time I was over at her house. Gone were the empty glasses and plastic frozen-dinner containers that had littered her coffee table. Perhaps I'd misjudged her. The entire town thought she was a gold digger with bad fashion sense. Aside from wanting to get her hands on the restaurant, maybe she really had been broken up about losing Harvey in her own way. You could hardly fault someone for neglecting something as trivial as household chores when her husband was found murdered. Even I'd forget to wash a dish or two.

"First, I'd like to apologize for my behavior," Sheila started off, in an attempt to clear the air. "I know you're Abby Lee's friend, and I didn't mean to get carried away. It's just, Harvey's death struck me hard."

Understandable. But that still didn't excuse her from assaulting or harassing Abby Lee. I hadn't forgotten. It was best if I just let Sheila go through her apologies before I said anything I might regret. I was here for a civilized chat over coffee.

Sheila continued. "Could you please tell her that I've ceased trying to take ownership of The Poop Deck and that I won't bother her anymore? Harvey had his reasons, and I suppose the restaurant rightfully belongs to her." I couldn't help but notice she said the last part rather reluctantly.

"Well, I'm sure she'll appreciate it," I said. Hopefully this would calm the waters, allowing Abby Lee to run the restaurant stress-free, without having to worry about Sheila or the courts getting in the way.

"So there's no need to worry about me standing in the way."

"Sure." I wondered how long I had to stay here in her house. The faster I could leave, the better. There was a rule about accepting invitations, but I didn't think there was one regarding length of stay. I should just politely thank her for the coffee and go. Somehow, I didn't think she'd mind.

"How's your coffee?" Sheila asked.

I took a sip of the lukewarm coffee and offered her a fake smile. "It's great, thanks." Sheila hadn't even put out any cookies or pastries. Probably just as well. I doubted she even knew how to bake.

"It's a special blend."

Yeah, it's called instant. "Oh, really?"

I was having a hard time focusing on Sheila. My head started to feel a little woozy. Maybe Sheila had added a little kick to the coffee, but it didn't feel like the start of an alcoholic buzz.

"Did you put something in my drink?"

Sheila couldn't have. Could she? As I pondered whether or not Sheila had roofied my drink, I must have nodded off.

The next thing I remembered was waking up tied to the armchair. How much time had passed?

"What the hell?" I muttered to myself, still in a haze from the drugs.

"You're awake," Sheila said.

"Why?"

It was all I could manage to say. Thinking too much hurt my head. What the hell did she put in that coffee?

"You were going to ruin everything!" Sheila cried out.

Not this again. I'd already had my fair share of psychos to last me a lifetime.

"What are you talking about?" I struggled to say. Whatever she gave me certainly packed a punch. I was still seeing two of Sheila.

"You were getting in the way."

I was having trouble following her. Heather had already confessed to Harvey's murder. Was Sheila involved somehow? I felt like I was stuck in a bad Lifetime movie. My mind was foggy from the drugs, and I tried to focus on the situation.

"What do you mean 'ruin everything'? You said earlier you weren't going to go after the restaurant anymore."

Sheila sneered. "Do you really think I was going to let you two get in the way of my piece of the pie? It was bad enough trying to get rid of Harvey, but you two have become a major thorn in my side."

"What do you mean 'get rid of Harvey'? Heather confessed to killing him already." What the hell was she talking about? We caught his killer, and she confessed. Case closed.

"I know exactly what happened to him," she snapped. "I have to say, that girl did me a favor, but because of your meddling, I now have to tie up some loose ends."

I was afraid to ask. "What loose ends?"

Sheila paced around the room. I had a feeling she hadn't really thought things through, aside from luring me into a trap. What exactly did she plan on doing with me?

"Did you know I had plans to get rid of Harvey? Then, wouldn't you know it? That insipid girl comes along and does the job for me," she said. "Imagine my surprise when that old codger keeled over at your parents' house."

"But why?"

"Isn't it obvious? For the restaurant, of course."

My drug-induced haze was slowly lifting. I was beginning to understand.

"You thought you could cash in on The Poop Deck. Harvey wouldn't sell, so you decided to kill him for it. Only you didn't know he left it to Abby Lee," I said. "You'd only seen the first will Harvey had drawn up. Only he changed it without you knowing."

"I had no idea he was leaving it to that slut. I can only imagine what she had to do to get it."

"Abby Lee isn't like that. Harvey thought of her as a daughter."

Sheila snorted. "It doesn't matter now. The restaurant belongs to me. I earned it. Do you know what I had to go through? Living with that man? He was an old bore," she said. "Don't you think I deserved to get something for my troubles?"

"You didn't have to marry him," I said.

"You know what he told me when we first met? He said he owned a fabulous restaurant on an island just off the Texas coast. I couldn't believe my luck. I thought to myself, now, here's my chance to be the wife of someone so important. Then he brings me here to this dump of an island."

What? Did she think she was marrying Wolfgang Puck? I was sure she'd had a rude awakening when she moved to Trouble.

"Then the magazine article came out. And you thought you'd finally capitalize," I finished for her. The drugs were wearing off, and I was getting stronger by the minute. If I could keep her talking, maybe I could get out of this. "But Harvey didn't want to sell."

"You're a smart girl. Too smart. Which is a problem."

Where was she going with this?

"How? Technically you haven't done anything." *Aside from possibly attempted murder and drugging me*, I thought.

"True. But you have a knack for getting in the way. I can't let anyone know I had plans to get rid of Harvey. Don't think I don't know you were snooping around my house when you and your aunt stopped by to drop off that casserole."

Yeah, I needed to work on my stealth skills.

"That chicken dish was dreadful by the way," she added. "Had to run to the bathroom every ten minutes. Anyway . . . what was I saying? Oh, yes. My little problem. What should I do? You seem like the best person to ask. Always sticking your nose in other people's business."

"I don't understand. How would anyone even know? They already have Heather behind bars for killing Harvey. Why would they look at you?" The police weren't going to reopen the case now that they already had their killer. As far as the police were concerned, Sheila was off the hook.

"Why?" Sheila mimicked. "Isn't it obvious? What have I been talking about for the last ten minutes? For the restaurant, of course."

Abby Lee! She had plans to take out Abby Lee!

"You're going to kill her, aren't you?"

"I hadn't planned on it at first. When she was suspected of murdering Harvey, I just hoped they'd finally arrest her, so I could pull the restaurant from under her in civil court."

"You ransacked the restaurant hoping to find the original will, hoping to gain leverage in court. But now that Abby Lee's no longer a suspect, you still can't claim it," I said.

"A mere technicality I hope to rectify. Now that that other girl is in jail for killing my husband, I have to take care of Abby Lee," she said with a smile. "And that's why you have to go. I can't have you running around pointing the finger at me. With both of you out of the picture, I can sell the damned place and get the hell out of this godforsaken island."

Her cruise! I'd almost forgotten about her little shopping spree at Palmetto Pink. So that was the plan? Eliminate me and Abby Lee and set sail for the Bahamas. Nice.

"That day you came to the store to buy clothes for your cruise . . . you're the one who cut off the lights at the store and locked me in there."

She laughed. "I tried to give you a warning, but you just kept poking your nose where it didn't belong."

Call it stress from the last week, being abducted by a psychotic stalker and tied to a chair by a crazed widow, but I started laughing. "You'll never get away with any of this," I said, realizing how stupid I sounded the instant I said it. What was it with me and clichés?

It was Sheila's turn to laugh. "Oh, but I will. The restaurant is mine. You think I like living here on this godforsaken island? That place is my ticket out."

"So that's your plan? Finish me off and kill Abby Lee and take the restaurant?"

Her eyes flickered. "Something like that. If she had just given me what was rightfully mine, it wouldn't have had to come to that."

"You won't—"

"Get away with it?" she finished. "You said that already. And of course I will. I've gotten away with it so far."

Sheila had me tied to the chair that faced the patio doors. I sensed movement from behind one of the palm trees that adorned her backyard. She was facing me, so she didn't notice, but I could've sworn I saw someone moving out there.

"Yeah, but you're forgetting one thing," I told her.

"And what's that?"

I smiled as I spotted Aunt Lula crouching closer to the glass doors. "I have a family that cares."

Even though my aunt was as good a shot as any man, I ducked my head to my chest as the glass exploded all around us.

As happy as I was to see my aunt come to my rescue, I was relieved to see Justin trailing right behind her—she might be a tough old broad, but I couldn't risk her getting hurt on my account. I could tell from his expression that having my aunt shoot through the sliding glass door wasn't part of the rescue plan.

Justin restrained Sheila with handcuffs as Aunt Lula untied me from the chair. I never felt so happy to see anyone in my life.

Aunt Lula hugged me so hard I thought my face would be permanently imprinted into her chest. I caught a good whiff of her Coco Chanel.

"How'd you know I was in trouble?"

"Jackie called me. She lives a couple doors down from Sheila. Saw you entering the house, and when you never left, she got suspicious."

Thank God for nosy neighbors.

"When Lula realized something was wrong, she called me immediately, and we decided to check it out," Justin said.

Aunt Lula snorted in response. "He thought I was crazy to even suggest you were in any type of danger. The only reason he tagged along was to prove to me what silly old ladies we were."

"Now that's not how it happened, and you know it. And you," he said, pointing his finger in my direction, "I told you that you were putting yourself at risk."

"That was before we figured out who killed Harvey," I reminded him. "How was I supposed to know Sheila was planning to kill Abby Lee for the restaurant? But it all turned out OK. You guys came at just the right time, and I'm still alive."

"Jules—" Justin started to say.

"Leave the child alone," Aunt Lula cut him off. "Hasn't she been through enough?"

CHAPTER TWENTY-NINE

To make up for everything that happened the last few weeks, Aunt Lula said Abby Lee and I could pick anything we wanted from the store, her treat. It was like Christmas in July. We spent the entire afternoon trying on dresses and sipping champagne Aunt Lula had stashed in her back office. This was exactly how I'd planned to spend my vacation.

We were getting tipsy from the bubbly and twirling around, and I almost missed him. I caught his reflection in the dressing room mirror. He was standing near the opening of the dressing room with a bouquet of carnations and mums.

Hartley.

Abby Lee noticed, too. "I think I'll go up front and have Lula show me the new collection," she said, giving us some privacy.

"I'm sorry about my abrupt departure the other night," Hartley said, handing me the flowers. "I guess you can say I was taken by surprise."

"No apologies necessary." After the way we'd left things that night at the restaurant, I hadn't thought I'd ever see Hartley again. Granted I hardly knew him, but there was definitely a spark between us. A spark I wanted to explore.

"I made a few phone calls. The FBI, huh?" He still seemed befuddled at the notion that the woman he'd believed to be a retail salesclerk actually worked for the bureau.

I could feel my cheeks turning red. "It's not like I'm an agent or anything. Strictly civilian," I said, shrugging it off. It was not like my job was any less important, of course. Without crime analysts, agents would have a hell of a time staying on track. But I didn't want him to make a big deal out of it.

"Could've fooled me. You caught Harvey's killer. And the plot to kill Abby Lee. That's something not even Trouble's finest can say."

"Well I didn't exactly catch a murderer . . ."

No, Harvey's killer cornered me with the intent to kill me—so did his widow. But I wasn't going to say that out loud. I was happy to take whatever compliment he paid my way.

Hartley grinned at my poor attempt at being humble. "Close enough. The right person is behind bars, and that's because of you. In fact, two people are behind bars because of you. You should be proud."

My face had to be ten shades of red by now. "I'm just glad we can all get back to normal around here."

"So," he drawled, letting the last syllable drag just a second too long, stalling for what he was about to say next. "What are your plans now? Going back to Virginia? Or were those things you said that night part of your cover?"

"Like what?" I'd said a lot of things.

"About changing careers. You said that night at the bar you weren't happy. Were you serious?"

"Oh right. Yeah, that part was true."

"Does that mean you're not going back?"

"No, I've got a little over a month's vacation left before I go back."

"Oh, I see." I could tell he was disappointed.

"Oh—no! It's not what you think. I'm going to close up my apartment and get my things."

"You mean you're moving back to the island?" There was a glimmer of hope in his eyes. "You're really thinking of leaving the feds?"

I wasn't sure I'd made the right decision, but I had already e-mailed Weight Watcher Wendy my letter of resignation. I probably could have put in a request for a transfer and not quit entirely, but I wanted a fresh start. Once I returned to Virginia, I was going to spend the next two weeks organizing my case files and packing my belongings.

"I'm not sure if I was ever really happy there, you know? I think I was meant to do something else with my life."

"Think you'll have room for someone in this new life?"

I could daydream about Hartley all I wanted, but now that the question was out in the open, I hesitated. After my failed relationship with James—the reason I'd come back to Trouble Island in the first place—I wasn't sure if I was ready to get involved in a new one. That and I still had unresolved issues with Justin. There was certainly some residual chemistry between us. Was it worth going down that path again, or should I start with a clean slate with someone like Hartley?

In the end, we agreed I'd call him the second I returned to Trouble.

❀

"You still have over a month of vacation time left. What will you do with your time?" Aunt Lula asked over chilled ceviche and cold beer. Did I mention ceviche was the only thing she knew how to make, aside from her dreaded King Ranch casserole?

"I don't know. Spend it outdoors? Take some shooting lessons from a pro like you? Work on my tan?"

My aunt gave me the once-over. "Yes, a little bit of sunshine is just what you need after all that time you spent cooped up at that job of yours."

Thinking about my drab cubicle at the bureau made me shudder. I was relieved I didn't have to go back to work under the supervision of Weight Watcher Wendy. After I turned in my resignation, I felt like the weight of the world was off my shoulders. I began to really consider all the other opportunities I had in front of me.

"I think I want to go back to school," I blurted. Ever since I met Hartley, I'd been thinking about pursuing another career. There was something about him that made me think about the future and want to make the best out of it.

"And study what, dear?" Aunt Lula asked, genuinely interested. She'd always been the one to encourage my education. "You already have a graduate degree."

"Oh, I don't know. I can finish up the credits I need to get my PhD, or I could go to law school," I said.

"Does that mean you're moving back here permanently?" Aunt Lula asked, hopeful. Houston was home to several universities, and commuting from the island to the city wasn't nearly as bad as my daily commute in Virginia.

"I guess it does."

All my life I'd tried to escape the sleepy little island town in favor of the big city. It never occurred to me that the island needed me as much as I needed it.

"Even if I don't decide to go back to school right away, I think I belong here."

A big smile spread over my aunt's face. "Then it's all settled. You know that condo I rent out? You can live there while you decide on whatever it is you want to do."

I was momentarily speechless. Aunt Lula had a beachfront condo she'd inherited from Uncle Jep. She rented it out to families during the summer season to cover the real estate taxes.

It was a generous offer, but I reluctantly had to decline. "Thanks for the offer, Aunt Lula, but I won't be able to pay rent without a job. I have a little bit of savings, but not enough to last me through winter. I'll just stay at home until I find something."

I cringed at the thought of living with my folks, but I had to save some money before I could afford a nice-enough place. Plus, if I was going to go back to school, I needed to figure out how I was going to pay tuition.

"Nonsense. You're a grown woman. The last thing you need is to live under your parents' roof. Especially with your mother around. You'll stay at the condo rent-free."

"I couldn't do that," I said. Though the idea was appealing.

"Why not? You need a place to live, and I have a place to offer," she insisted. "Well?"

It took me only a moment to weigh the pros and cons and ultimately give in. I was sure I would regret taking her up on her offer at some point, but it was just too good a deal to pass up. She did insist after all—and one never refused Aunt Lula.

"Only if you're sure. I can start paying rent as soon as I get a job." I didn't want to take advantage of my aunt's generosity. Plus, I still had to support myself.

"Out of the question," she said. "I'm leaving you the place when I die, so I don't see any reason why you can't take ownership now. At least this way, I'm still alive to watch you enjoy it," she said. "Besides, there's a catch."

Of course there was a catch. There were always strings attached when it came to Aunt Lula. I only hoped working at her store again wasn't part of the deal.

She didn't keep me in suspense long. "I must insist that you have dinner with me at least once a week," she said.

After everything I'd been through—meeting my stalker face-to-face, being tied up by a calculating, greedy widow—spending time with Aunt Lula didn't sound like such a bad deal in the grand scheme of things. I would've agreed to dinner every night of the week if it got me my own beachfront condo. I grinned as I hugged my aunt. "You got a deal."

"Oh, and there's one more thing."

Damn. I knew it was too easy. Nothing was ever easy with Aunt Lula.

"You might want to make it a point to be a little nicer to the deputy chief," she said. "Seems that boy is still stuck on you."

"What?" I couldn't believe my ears. Aunt Lula was encouraging me to date Justin?

"He might have inquired about your relationship status, and I might have told him you'd recently broken up with your beau, but I drew the line on the issue of him taking you to a romantic dinner."

"Thanks, but I don't know what to do about Justin." I wasn't sure how I felt about that. Now he must be thinking he still had a chance with me. Did he? Was I ready to go traipsing down memory lane? There was too much history between us. Now more than ever, with the memory of Heather almost killing me because of our past. And what about Hartley? There was definitely something there, and I thought I wanted to pursue it.

"All I'm saying is that you could be nicer to the boy."

"You mean you didn't encourage him?" I was surprised Aunt Lula didn't run out that second and buy me new monogrammed stationary.

Aunt Lula laughed. "I may be an old crow according to your mother, but I like to think of myself as a modern kind of gal. Only you can decide when it's time to start a family or not start a family. Why, look at me now—I run a successful business all by myself."

Incredible. "Thanks, Aunt Lula."

I gave my aunt several more hugs to show my gratitude over her gift before leaving to tell my folks that I'd made a decision to stay in Trouble.

✿

Justin was waiting for me outside my parents' house.

"Word is you're sticking around for a while," he said.

"I guess good news really does travel fast. Let's just say my aunt made me an offer I couldn't refuse." And I supposed the possibility of rekindling old flames could be considered a small factor in my decision, although I wouldn't admit to it out loud. We still had a few issues to iron out, but perhaps in the meantime I could let him take me out to dinner, as friends. At least for now.

"I see. And what if I said I would've been willing to make my own offer?"

Was I ready to pick up where we'd left off all those years ago? No. Not yet. We had a lot of baggage to unpack before I could even consider the possibility of us seeing each other in a romantic way. There was also Hartley. He seemed excited about the prospect of me moving back to the island. How did I come to Trouble minus a boyfriend and end up with the possibility of dating two?

"Do you think that's a good idea?" I asked.

"We're different people now, Jules. Maybe it's the right time to start over, don't you think?"

We'd grown up over the last ten years, and I'd be lying if I said I wasn't interested in getting to know him better this second time around. A decade was a long time. I was a different person now—at least I'd like to think so—and I'm sure he was, too.

The question was, was I ready?

ACKNOWLEDGMENTS

This book was a long time in the making, and I wish to thank all the fabulous folks that made it possible. To my former colleagues at the Fairfax County Police Department and the Office of the Commonwealth's Attorney, all I can say is, "good times." We worked on some great cases together, and I am honored to have worked with some of the best law enforcement professionals in the field. To Karri Klawiter and Jeff Bryan, I wouldn't have gotten this far without you. Special thanks goes out to my friends and family members who loaned me the use of their names: Charisse Berree, Teresa Brown, Sara Duck, Ryan Irsik, Cannon Manatt, Carol Rheal-Breault, and Jackie Wysong. And to all the gals at Lilly Pulitzer Tysons, y'all will always continue to bring color into my life.

AUTHOR'S NOTE

I worked in the law enforcement field for many years, but I am also a writer. I make things up, I fudge things . . . in other words, I write fiction. While I have a good working knowledge of how the justice system works, I take full responsibility (but make no apologies) for taking creative liberties with my story.

I hope you enjoyed *Destined for Trouble* as much as I enjoyed writing it!

ABOUT THE AUTHOR

Claudia Lefeve was born and raised so far down the Texas Gulf Coast she has to pull out a map to show people it's nowhere near Houston. Now living in Northern Virginia, she is taking a temporary hiatus from a civilian career in law enforcement in order to write full time. She lives with her husband and three dogs. You can visit Claudia at www.claudialefeve.com, www.facebook.com/claudialefeve, and twitter.com/claudialefeve.

The Woman in the Red Dress

To Tammie
Best Wishes
for good Networking

Renate

Other Titles by Renate Zorn

Good Conversation is for Everyone:
Ten Steps to Better Conversations

Coming in 2005
There's a Hole in My Bucket:
Dissident Stories of Inspiration and Opportunity

The Woman in the Red Dress

and Nine Other Secrets of Networking Success

By RENATE ZORN

Published by Make Your Words Count

National Library of Canada Cataloguing in Publication

Zorn, Renate, 1957-
   The woman in the red dress : and nine other secrets to networking
success / Renate Zorn.

Includes bibliographical references and index.
ISBN 0-9732689-1-3

   1. Business Networks. I. Title.

HD69.S8Z67 2004   650.1'3   C2004-901922-8

Cover Design by MYWC with technical assistance by Chris Wood

Published by *Make Your Words Count!*
Mississauga, ON.

Limit of Liability / Disclaimer of Warranty

Dedication

To *Li,*
The Woman in the Red Dress.
Thank you for your inspiration and encouragement.

Acknowledgements

My special thanks go to the following people

Maureen Chorny, for taking care of those details at which I'm so bad.

Steve Chorny, who listened to me for hours and hours as I went on about the Woman in the Red Dress.

Azhar Qureshi and *Li Xue* for their ongoing encouragement.

Louise Howcroft for her continued faith and support.

To all my friends throughout the district for their unfailing patience with me and my endless "I was wondering what you think when..." questions.

Table of Contents

*Alone we can do so little; together
we can do so much.*

Helen Keller

Introduction

Networking has taken a bad rap over the last few years. As more and more people have recognized that alliances are critical to business and personal success, hundreds of "Networking Clubs" have sprung up all over the country. These include small informal groups that meet occasionally for coffee, large business networking groups that cost members several thousands of dollars a year, and just about everything in between. Some are one of a kind, others are part of a larger network. In theory, these clubs should help the members a great deal. After all, you have a group of like-minded individuals meeting together with common goals. But rarely do I run across someone who has anything really good to say about their own networking group(s), past or present. Most admit they belong because they feel they have to, after all, we know networking is important, right? But they also complain that they don't really feel they're accomplishing much. I hear the same complaints about the networking receptions at conferences and workshops. *"I didn't get a single new lead at that reception last night,"* is a common refrain. Many people tell me that they routinely avoid that part of conferences because *"it's a pretty big waste of time."*

So why aren't they (networking groups) working? After talking to hundreds of people, I've come to the conclusion that it's because many people still don't really understand networking. Why do I think that? I'm regularly invited to be a guest speaker for networking groups and receptions of all varieties and sizes. It never fails that while I'm there I see several people running around, handing out business cards as if they were Vegas dealers, never stopping to connect with anyone. One woman told me she gives out an average of twenty five cards a night. What do you think happens to most of those cards? They get lost, forgotten, tossed, or maybe filed, unlikely to be taken out again. Invariably at least one person will corner me and bombard me with an "intromercial" (short promotional self-introduction), followed by several brochures, a sales pitch and sometimes even a full press kit. Over the next week, I can virtually guarantee that I'll get calls and e-mails from many of the attendees, letting me know that they enjoyed the presentation and "...oh, by the way, I sell/do x, y and z so if you know of anyone who needs some..." At least two people will put me on the mailing list for their electronic newsletter, even though I've never expressed any interest in their topics. Many people still think it's a numbers game, meeting and calling on as many people as you can, hoping that there will be a payoff somewhere along the way. They've read some networking books and diligently keep files on everyone they meet, calling and e-mailing regularly and then puzzling over why their networks aren't as productive as they wish they could be. Others break out the address book only when they need a job, and then complain that no one seems willing to help them out.

In my view, this isn't networking. It's not even close.

Why would someone want to help you out with a job or a job lead if you haven't talked to them in three years or never really knew them well to begin with?

Why would you want to refer a client to someone if you don't know them well enough to be assured of the quality of their work?

In a room of two hundred people, what do you think the chance is that you'll meet up with the exact four or five people who are going to be needing your products or services in the near future?

But now turn that around and ask, if I meet and get to know two or three people really well, what is the likelihood that they will know one or more people who may need my products or services or that they will be able to help me out in some other meaningful way (and vice versa)? The key is finding those two or three people and "connecting" with them in such a way that you feel willing and able to do something for each other at some future point, whether that is referring, advising, introducing, explaining, or whatever help you can provide. Wherever and whenever you "network," it's a long-term process of building trust and respect. It's the quality of the relationship that matters, not the number of calls you make. First, you find people with whom you have something in common, and then you get to know them well enough so that you want to help them succeed and they want to help you.

In the 21st century, effective networking is critical to business success and professional advancement. Most of you have by now heard how we live in the age of information and in a global economy. Information rules. You're expected to know about what's going on in your company's other division on the far side of the country. You're supposed to be informed about that pending merger or the new strategic direction. The likelihood of you being affected by a consolidation, merger or downsizing is better than ever. If you're out looking for work, applicants from all over the country, not just local people, compete for jobs as we see more and more regional, national and even international electronic job boards. Being uninformed or unaware can be more career-limiting than ever.

The good news is that networking has never been easier. It's so simple to send off an e-mail just to keep in touch. It's not intrusive and you can easily forward a job opening, lead or just a piece of useful information. The downside is that many people see e-mail as a substitute for conversation. While you can accomplish a lot by e-mail, you still need to have "face time" if you're going to develop a really strong relationship. Over ninety percent of our communication is through body language and voice - both of which are absent in e-mail. You just can't get to know people well enough if your relationship is only electronic.

So why should you read this book? Because it's much more than just another "how to network" book. It's more of a *How to Make Your Networking Count* book. The basics of joining clubs, meeting people and organizing your contacts are covered well elsewhere. *My goal in writing this book was to show how each of us can go about improving our networking relationships, establishing them more quickly and making them last longer and work more effectively.* I wanted to help people understand how to build and nurture these very important networking relationships, from finding the *right* contacts and figuring out what to say, to learning more about them and being able to ask for or offer help when it's needed. I've tried to answer many of those questions people still have after reading other books - the ones they are embarrassed to ask their friends and colleagues - because they think that somehow they're supposed to know - questions such as:

"I know I'm supposed to follow up, but I haven't a clue what to say when I call."

"Do I really have to buy lunch for all these contacts?"

"But what do I have to offer anyone else? I'm just starting out in my career."

"I still feel awkward when I need help from someone. How do I come right out and ask?"

"Do I really have to send out all those thank you cards and other stuff I read about doing?"

I also wanted to address some of the new challenges and realities of networking in the 21st century, talk about e-mail, voice mail, electronic newsletters and how to make communication more personal over distances.

Finally, I wanted to share some of my own experiences with networking. Much of my career success would never have been possible without the encouragement and support of the people in my network. Even though I write and speak on the subject regularly, it never fails to amaze me how helpful and supportive people can be and just how long-term a process networking is. Sometimes, years after I've done something helpful for a friend or acquaintance, and I've long forgotten about it, I'll unexpectedly get a resulting lead, contract offer or a referral.

So, read on! I've tried to keep it all straightforward, easy-to-read and follow, and I've included as many useful tips and examples as I could. Best wishes for successful networking!

If you are planning for a year, plant grain.
If you are planning for a decade, plant trees.
If you are planning for a century, plant people

var. Chinese Proverb

Chapter 1

The Myths and the Magic
Networking Is Much More than Just Finding Work

"Demeaning, embarrassing, tedious, just for job hunting, mainly for salespeople..."

These are just a few of the popular misconceptions about networking. If the word "networking" conjures up visions of desperately begging friends for job leads, suffering in two hour "power lunches," and of standing through endless hours of boring cocktail parties, struggling in vain to make small talk, you aren't alone. Yes, networking can help you find work and yes, networking may involve lunch, parties and conversation, but it's much, much more than that and it doesn't need to be either desperate or boring. Finally, if it's done right, networking can be a mutually beneficial and enjoyable activity, not a one-sided and relentless pursuit of people with whom you have only a passing acquaintance. So let's look a little more closely at some of these fallacies.

The Many Myths of Networking

Networking is Just for People Looking for Work!

Absolutely not! In fact, if you only start networking when you do need a job, it's probably too late. Networking relationships take time to develop. If you start networking <u>before</u> you need to find a new job or change careers, you'll be ready when the time comes. You'll hear about openings before you need them and you'll know more about the quality of openings when they do come up. People will be comfortable passing on leads and willing to put in a good word for you.

Networking Is Humiliating - It's Like Begging!

Many people do have difficulty when it comes to asking for help, but that has more to do with their own background and personal inhibitions than with the realities of networking. If your timing is right and you've developed a good relationship, there is no need to feel bad about asking. Most people say that, under the right circumstances, they don't mind helping. In the course of my business, I provide many referrals, arrange contacts, give advice and suggestions, provide free seminars and supply leads. None of it causes me any significant personal hardship and most of it is done easily, naturally and without any inconvenience. Usually I'll offer before being asked and most other people I work with do the same for me. If asking is a big hangup with you, pay special attention Chapter 10, "If You Could Read My Mind."

It's Demeaning. You're Just Using People!

Networking is based on mutually beneficial relationships, not exploitation. In researching this book I interviewed dozens of senior executives, professionals and managers. Not one single person said they minded being asked. They believed they were giving, not being "used." By far the majority said they actually liked being able to help people, as long as the request was reasonable and appropriate. However, if you do a lot of taking and not much of your own giving, your network will soon fall apart. Similarly, if you do all the giving, and never ask for anything, you'll start to seem like a doormat. Soon people will start to feel uncomfortable around you. It's all about balance - as you'll see in Chapter 4 "Overdrawn at the Networking Bank."

You Have to "Do Lunch" All the Time!

To network effectively, you do have to meet with other people, one-on-one, in settings that are conducive to discussion and to getting to know one another. The place is usually mutually agreed upon. These days most people are far too busy for frequent long lunches. Respecting people's time is one of the cardinal rules of networking. When I meet with my contacts for whatever reason, more often than not we'll end up at a coffee shop. If you're meeting with several people throughout the day, it's also easier on the waistline and the wallet if you're not going to sit-down restaurants all the time.

I Don't Have the Time for Networking

To put it bluntly, if you want to succeed in business, <u>you don't have time not to network</u>! There is good news though - networking doesn't have to take a lot of "extra" time and in the long-run, it can help you accomplish more and reach goals more quickly. Much of networking just means paying attention to the opportunities and taking advantage of them. You do have to spend time building relationships, but if you are doing it with the right people, that is those with whom you have something in common or a "connection," then the time can be enjoyable and built into your daily routine. While some of the people with whom you network may end up being close friends whom you see regularly, many won't. Some will be occasional contacts, some you may see rarely. I have strong relationships with some people that I touch base with only once or twice a year. The key is making sure you maintain the quality of the relationship, not necessarily the quantity or length of the meetings.

But You Have to Be a Born Conversationalist!

Here's more good news and not so good news. Yes, to be effective at networking you do have to be able to talk to people. Through conversation we get to know each other and develop trust and respect. But the good news is that anyone can learn to converse well, and if you're networking with the right people - that is people with whom you have some connection or common interest - you'll find conversation much easier. In the Chapter 8, "The Big Deal About Small Talk," you'll find many useful tips for brushing up on your conversation skills.

Networking Is Just for Salespeople!

Sales people do need to meet new people and generate leads all the time, but networking is for everyone. Why do you need to network? Because it makes a tremendous difference, really! Study after study has proven it. The size and quality of your network affects your career success whether you are an executive, a salesman, a nurse, a lawyer, an accountant, a secretary, a student or a public employee. It affects the jobs you find, how much business you get, how quickly you are promoted, how well-known you become and how much money you earn. On the personal side, networking affects your access to top quality goods and services and your effectiveness in dealing with problems and bad service when they arise. It affects the people you meet, the friendships you make and even where your kids end up going to school.

Networking is a <u>long-term</u> and <u>incremental</u> approach to developing productive business and social relationships. Some relationships pay off very quickly, some years later, and to be honest, some never do. In the long-run though, networking IS effective if you do it well. Your goal in attending a networking event shouldn't be a short-term one, such as getting a new client, sale, job or contract. You don't have enough time in any single event to develop the kind of relationship that would allow you to accomplish any of these. You DO have the time to meet a few new people, arrange an introduction, find some common ground, and to lay the foundation for a future relationship. Each time you attend one of these events, you establish a specific goal that fits in with your overall networking strategy. For more information, read the Chapter 7 "Being There is Not Enough."

But I'm Doing Well in a Secure Job...I Don't Need Networking

No one has a secure job these days. Whether you've just been hired or have been with the same company for twenty years, you can't afford to be complacent. Industry consolidation, continued economic uncertainty, intense global competition and changing beliefs have altered the way we view employment. Staying with one employer for a lifetime is no longer a common expectation, nor a realistic one. For most people, the possibility of being laid off, downsized, right-sized, restructured, transferred, re-classified, or otherwise removed from their existing position, job description or employer is significant. In addition to changing employers and jobs more frequently than ever before, most people today will change careers three to five times throughout their lifetime.

Networking is part of a proactive and deliberate approach to managing your career. It can minimize career interruptions and help ensure that any career changes are planned and desirable, not unexpected and disruptive. Networking helps keep you informed of what's going on around you in your line of work, it makes you more marketable and attractive for new jobs and promotions, and it positions you well to take advantage of new opportunities.

It's Better to Keep Your Nose Down and Work Hard!

Sure your boss appreciates your hard work. He might even acknowledge it when it comes time for performance appraisal or raises. Networking is never a substitute for top quality work, but in terms of career planning, promotions and job security, your hard work does not speak for itself. Decisions around hiring, promotion and new opportunities are rarely made only on the basis of technical competence. They involve feelings, trust, opinions and sometimes just plain gut instinct - all of which mean that the decision makers need to get to know you better. YOU are responsible for seeing that your work gets noticed, appreciated and that come promotion time, your name comes to mind. See Chapter 3, "It's What You Show, Not What You Know."

But I Don't Work Out of a Traditional Office Setting

More and more people no longer work in traditional situations where they go to the company office every day and work in relatively close physical proximity to the boss and co-workers. Over the 1990's the greatest job growth was in the area of self-employment. Millions of others (close to 20 million, according to the U.S. Department of Labour) "telework." Teleworking refers to any job performed at someplace other than the main company office, with the assistance of technology. It includes working from home, working in a remote location (e.g. a hotel, automobile, client office, airport) or sharing an office space on an occasional or as-needed basis.

While there are many advantages to these situations, there's one huge disadvantage. People form relationships, both personal and professional, with those people who work in close proximity.

In *Making the Team*, Leigh Thompson reports a near perfect negative correlation between physical separation of employee offices and the frequency of communications and strength of interpersonal relationships. So imagine the impact of moving out of the office to a place where random meetings and casual interaction are non-existent - no hallway conversations, no coffee breaks together, no ad hoc brainstorming sessions, no daily updates from the office grapevine and no commiserating together over a drink after work. The risks are substantial. How do you ensure that you stay uppermost in your manager's mind come time for promotion? How do you stay up-to-date in your field? How do you keep informed on what's happening in your company?

Networking can keep you "on the radar screen" or "plugged in to the grapevine." Whichever metaphor applies to you, networking can help you strengthen your relationships and maintain a high profile when you are not in the mainstream of what's happening (and it can help you even if you are).

So Then What IS Networking?

Networking is the purposeful development and nurturing of relationships that help you advance in your business and personal life and in return, also let you help others. The more diverse your network, the greater the potential.

Networking is based on three fundamental and time-tested principles:

- We prefer to do business, work with, and socialize with those people we know and trust.

- We are willing to do more, to extend ourselves and to go out of our way, for people we know and trust.

- We can accomplish more with the connections and support of others than we can accomplish on our own.

As a general rule, the people in your network provide you with one or more of information, influence, guidance and/or support:

Information gathering keeps you "in the know" about what's happening in your company, industry, community and social sphere, and you can expand that information gathering to collect details about almost any specific area of interest. Developing your *information* network means you'll have a better chance of anticipating changes that might be coming in your organization. You'll hear about new projects, contracts, new openings, and promotional opportunities in a timely enough way to pursue them effectively if they interest you. When you're job hunting in the outside world, you can get inside information on the decision makers, company goals, previous incumbents and what kinds of people they really need.

Influence or advocacy can help when you need a little extra leverage. While *influence* isn't a substitute for doing your work well, it can give you a much needed edge in today's very competitive business world. If you have a great idea for your company, the right influence can get you a priceless ten minutes of the VP or CEO's listening time. If you have a great product or service, influence can get you an audience with a buyer or some coverage in the media. At times, other people speaking out on your behalf may add much needed credibility. While influence may not actually get you the contract, job or the sale, it may get you a lead, interview or introduction...and then the rest is up to you.

Guidance or education provides you with the collective knowledge, background and experience of others. While information (statistics, figures, news, abstract knowledge) needs to be interpreted and evaluated before you can use it, guidance helps give you the skill and wisdom you need in order to evaluate, interpret and act on the information. Spending a couple of hours learning the ropes or problem solving with an experienced player in your field, could help you turn looming failure into a successful pursuit. A seasoned manager can help you unravel what exactly particular information might mean to you. A mentor can save you years of frustration and put you on the fast track for promotion.

Support can be in many forms - encouragement, reassurance, sympathy and occasionally a good shove when you need it. Finding a good (informed) listener, who can resist the urge to "fix" things, means you'll have someone off whom you can bounce ideas and from whom you can get honest feedback. While family members may listen sympathetically, and have your best interests at heart, they're rarely objective. In some instances, your network may even provide financial support (although borrowing money through friends and acquaintances is always a risky proposition).

Most successful networking relationships are built around sharing in one or more of these four areas. Any one relationship doesn't have to do all four. Some of your relationships will be close with many facets, others will be more distant and focussed around specific goals.

People Never Needed Networking Before, Why Now?

Although the new global marketplace is tougher than ever, networking has been around pretty much as long as people have - it just wasn't called networking. Throughout human history there are examples of groups of individuals cooperating in a network-like fashion to promote the enrichment of those people with whom they had formal or informal relationships. Nepotism, the giving of favours and opportunities to relatives, is the most basic and oldest form of networking. But dealing only with relatives is pretty limiting and this "networking" soon expanded to extended family and unrelated individuals who had some other bond. Networking existed in the clans of Scotland, Italian Mafia, Indian tribes, and even ancient Rome. In Victorian England men's clubs actively formalized networking, perhaps originating the term "old boys' club." Amidst the gaming and social activities, schemes were hatched, business deals were signed, and marriages were arranged. While women were never allowed inside these clubs, the network of wives and mothers was every bit as powerful, if perhaps slightly less obvious.

As early as 1916, networking was identified, studied and quantified as people began to pay attention to the concept of "social capital." In his book *Bowling Alone*, Robert Putnam quotes an early social reformer L.J. Hanifan.

> *"...If he comes into contact with his neighbor, and they with other neighbors, there will be an accumulation of social capital, which may immediately satisfy his social needs and which may bear a social potentiality sufficient to the substantial improvement of living conditions in the whole community. The community as a whole will benefit by the cooperation of all its parts, while the individual will find in his associations the advantages of the help, the sympathy, and the fellowship of his neighbors."*

So, regardless of what you call it or where it happens, networking has been helping people to succeed for years.

The Magic of Networking

Still unconvinced? Can't picture what networking might do for you? Here's just one example from my own life.

Some years ago I met Meynen at a business meeting. We got to talking about our respective jobs (she was in insurance). I ended up agreeing to help her with some accent reduction, no charge. While I wasn't taking on any new language clients at the time, I admired her energy, warmth and enthusiasm, and we seemed to share many common ideas and ambitions. I suggested that if she was willing to come to the court where my son played basketball, we could work on her accent on Saturday mornings.

Now in retrospect, it doesn't seem like there would have been much networking value or opportunity here for me. Meynen was a recent immigrant who didn't have many contacts here, and I certainly didn't feel I needed any more insurance. After we'd been meeting for a couple of weeks she asked if I knew how her husband could get involved in coaching the kids' basketball. I introduced Daniel to the site coordinator, he completed all the required screening and two weeks later was coaching one of the other teams. A month later she referred her chiropractor to me for some personal presentation coaching. That summer I had an opportunity to bid on a large training contract for a new communications program in several East Asian countries. Without any Eastern experience or contacts, I needed help. I turned to Meynen for advice about the market, target audience and pricing. The following year Meynen decided she wanted to go back to university and get her MBA, choosing a prestigious business school where there were at least ten applicants for every one position. She had to send in two separate "personal statement" letters which would be central to the application process. She worked out some rough drafts and I used my communications expertise to help her improve her focus, marketability and language. After several e-mail versions flew back and forth between us, she sent them in and we waited, and then celebrated - she had been accepted.

Over the next year Meynen helped me develop two significant proposals for insurance companies and introduced me to two organizations that declared my recent conversation skills book as their "Book of the Month" choice. She successfully referred me as speaker to her business school - and Daniel now coaches my son's team and helps him with his basketball skills. I introduced Meynen to some well-placed management consultants for career advice and job leads, helped her with preparing for job interviews and networking receptions, and when she needed a summer internship, I made a few calls to help her get interviews. All in all, the relationship has exceeded my expectations (which were none) and has served us both exceedingly well.

Will every networking relationships work out this way? Not at all. Some may be even better, some may yield very little, but the example shows how well they <u>can</u> work, and how varied the benefits can be. If both parties are motivated, competent and proactive about giving and asking for help, the opportunities are theirs for the taking.

The Woman in the Red Dress

In the next ten chapters of this book you'll read about the specifics of how you can go about networking more effectively, finding out about some of the critical success factors. You'll meet the *Woman in the Red Dress* and learn about the importance of standing out above the noise. You'll find out how to maintain the balance of "favours" and how to ask for something when the time comes. You'll also learn how to:

> **The size and quality of your network affects the jobs you find, how much business you get, how quickly you are promoted, how well-known you become and how much money you earn**.

- Promote your value to others

- Add value to any networking relationship

- Stay visible and conspicuous in your network

- Ask those difficult "help me" questions

- Work a room at a networking reception

- Thank others effectively and productively
- Master the basics of good conversation
- Say goodbye while establishing an opening for follow-up
- Use business etiquette to your advantage

I'll deal with common questions like who pays for lunch, how to make follow-up phone calls and finally, with how to develop your own networking plan.

CHAPTER ONE SUMMARY

Networking can benefit anyone who is willing to put work into developing relationships and helping others.

Networking is a time-tested, proven means of increasing your business effectiveness and advancement opportunities.

Networking shouldn't be uncomfortable, embarrassing, exploitative or time-consuming.

The skills you need to be effective at networking can be identified, learned and refined.

Networking can be very enjoyable and become part of your daily routine.

You've gotta be original, because if you're like someone else, what do they need you for?

Bernadette Peters

Chapter 2

The Woman in the Red Dress
Stand Out Above the Noise

The World is Filled with "Noise"

These days the average person is exposed to hundreds of advertisements every day. Messages on billboards, T-shirts, coffee cups, commercials, junk mail, public address systems and even golf tees all vie for our attention. Telemarketers, spammers and door-to-door salespeople intrude on our lives. Twenty-four hour news radio and television, free urban daily newspapers and the Internet all bring us such an abundance of headlines, statistics, global and local happenings that even real "information" has become a form of clutter. In the workplace, the barrage continues. Sometimes it seems like we are slaves to our electronics - PC's, cell phones, fax machines, PDA's and pagers.

Study after study finds that we feel more "stretched" by multiple demands than any previous generation. So what do we do? We simply filter out and ignore most of this "noise," and go about our lives doing our best to focus on the things that absolutely <u>require</u> our attention. New information, interesting people, good employees and many great opportunities all get buried amidst this noise and clutter.

Why Is this Important to You?

How many times have you heard the comment *"He's a really great (or smart, nice, interesting...) person, once you get to know him."* Unless you work in a very closed environment, most of us meet and talk to between five to ten new people EVERY day (many more in some occupations). At an average business conference, participants meet upwards of forty or fifty new people. Over the course of a year we meet thousands of "good" people who go unnoticed, unrecognized, unrewarded because people never "get to know them" well enough to appreciate their value and unique qualities. Regardless of how smart, loyal, productive or valuable you are, in order to have anyone recognize your value or to find you interesting enough to want to get to know you further, first you have to get them to notice you.

> **Thousands of "good" people go unnoticed, unrecognized and unrewarded because people never get to know them well enough to appreciate their value and unique qualities.**

While you may believe that you provide better service, better value, better performance, or better whatever, most bosses, potential employers, colleagues, customers and new people whom you meet, at first may see little meaningful difference. These days it's tough to stand out above the crowd and so how do you get anyone to stop what they are doing long enough to notice you, listen to your pitch, read your book, look at your résumé, recognize your great work or just want to talk to you?

The Woman in the Red Dress

Some years ago I attended a "networking event" at a local club. Like many other such meetings it included an opportunity for a few members to take about five minutes each to introduce themselves to the group and to talk about their skills, occupation, background and business goals.

At this particular meeting, Li, a woman in her late twenties and a relatively recent immigrant from China, presented her intromercial, as they had become known. As she was introduced and walked to the front of the room, every jaw in the room dropped. She was wearing an absolutely gorgeous, neck to ankle, screaming red, silk, traditional Chinese dress in what had to be about a size 2. She looked stunning. I can't speak for the men in the audience but I don't believe there was a woman there who wasn't thinking about how unfair it was that anyone could fit into a dress that size. Every eye in the room was rivetted on her. In her five minutes she talked about her experience in international marketing, her heritage and how it had influenced her career and current line of work.

Afterwards, during the networking portion of the meeting, just about everyone went over to chat with Li, some to find out more about her business and others just meet her. Once you began to talk with her you found a charming, intelligent business woman with an innate social grace. Two years later, everyone attended that day still remembers Li and her presentation. Many of them still do business with her company.

In just five short minutes, she made a lasting impact on everyone in the room.

Reflecting back to Li and her red dress, I think about the

hundreds of these sorts of presentations I've seen over the years, at various events. Some were polished, many were rambling, some were informative and a few were really, really bad. The response to most of these intromercials is usually pretty predictable. People sit through the session with polite interest. Occasionally something connects with one or two people in the audience and they go over afterwards to talk with the speaker some more. A few of the really dedicated networkers make a point of stopping off to chat briefly with each of the speakers.

It's the same at sales presentations, conferences, workshops, university, work and even meetings - wherever we meet new people. The vast majority of these meetings and events never leave any real impression at all and are quickly forgotten, swept aside in the hustle of other business and personal priorities. Think about the last time you attended a conference. How many of the people whom you met do _you_ still remember?

In fact, of the thousands of people we meet throughout our lives, most are soon forgotten (and most forget us as well). So how do you "connect," as Li did, ensuring people have a chance to get to know you? Even if you never attend a single networking event, you still need to "connect" with the boss, the professor, the interviewer, the customer and anyone else you want to work with or get to know. Since we can't all wear size 2 traditional Chinese dress, how do we avoid being "soon forgotten?"

Stand Out Above the Noise

In order to "stand out above the noise" and grab attention in a positive way, we can use one, or some combination, of five basic approaches. Not all approaches are appropriate or effective in all situations - in fact sometimes a particular strategy might be quite unsuitable. Consider the situation, the environment, your strengths/assets, the person you want to meet, and choose from the following:

Link Yourself Through an Existing Connection

By far the fastest and easiest way to connect is through an "introduction" and yet most people fail to take advantage of this opportunity. Being introduced by a well-regarded colleague has much more impact than just walking up and introducing yourself.

With so many people competing for our time and money, many of us routinely evade cold calls of any kind, whether they be from salespeople, job applicants or someone just wanting an opinion on an idea. Most of the time we focus on how to get away or say no effectively rather than listening with an open mind. On the other hand, when you call up a colleague and say *"...Janice, would you take a few minutes and hear Bill's idea..."* and your relationship is sound, it becomes a considerable opening for Bill, and Janice is most likely to comply. By providing the introduction you are giving your tacit seal of approval, implying that you believe Bill has something of value to offer Janice, or that he's deserving of any information or support that she might provide.

So, once you've decided whom you want to meet, sit down and map out a strategy that will accomplish this. Sometimes it's easy and you can arrange the meeting quickly with just one phone call. Sometimes it may take a series of introductions with some time in-between to get acquainted. However you do it, be sure you do have something of value to offer, or that you genuinely need the other person's help. Any time you call in a favour frivolously you weaken your overall relationship.

Make a Visual Impact

In situations where there are many people, either all at once or sequentially, competing for interviews, sales, media recognition or any other "attention" goal, making a strong visual impact can get you the opening you need. Visual attention can be gained in many ways and the woman in the red dress is the most obvious example. In my line of work I end up being invited to judge many speech competitions and there always seems to be at least one contestant who dresses noticeably better than the others. Not excessively so, but just enough to stand out for those critical first few moments. Then there are always a couple of people who look conspicuously worse than everyone else. I've never understood why anyone would show up for a contest or interview in jeans or casual clothes, but people do it all the time (to their misfortune).

Mankind has been using visual attraction successfully as a marketing strategy for millennia, from war paint, to giving away dollar bills to having bikini clad models at trade shows. Your challenge is to find an approach that works for you as an individual. Whatever you choose, using your judgement as to what is appropriate is absolutely critical. Evaluate your audience carefully. How is their sense of humour? How much is too much? Will they make the connection or will it be tough to sell? What is the downside? One time I attended an all day strategic planning session where the lead presenter arrived in a clown suit. It made his point very effectively (something about the company not being taken seriously) but as the day wore on it became distracting and turned from an attractor into a detractor. He might have been better off changing into regular clothes at the first break.

If You Can...Be Noticeably "Better" in Some Meaningful Way

Something unique about you that is particularly attractive to the target audience - highest marks, best looking, unique style, best productivity, winning an award or an Olympic medal - will almost always get you in the door. Recruiters at business schools routinely at least talk to the top three or four students (sometimes more depending on how many they are hiring). Being an officer or participating in some other visible way in clubs and associations sets you apart from the regular membership. Winning some significant award in your company will get attention throughout the organization, sometimes all the way up to the CEO. Then, when you meet the CEO either at the awards ceremony or later at a company function, you can be sure to get at least a few minutes of his time (and it won't look bad on your performance appraisal either). Having your writing be made a "Book of the Month" choice will ensure a greater readership and perhaps make the difference in persuading a distributor or store representative to listen to why they should carry your book.

All of the above serve to benefit you immediately and directly, but more importantly they also help in setting you apart in future situations. They give you, and others, plenty of material for your introduction and add to the appeal of your résumé, cover letter or bio.

So sit down and analyse your strengths. Where do you want to go? Who do you want to meet? For what will they be looking? What unique assets do you have, which you can accentuate, to draw positive attention to yourself. How can you ensure that this information reaches the right person?

Although being first, or in some other way unique, is effective, it's probably one of the most difficult to pull off. There's only so much room at the top. While being the best is good and gets you the attention you need, being second, third or somewhere near the top, rarely has the same impact. In the words of car racing great Bobby Unser, *"No one ever remembers who finished second."* Remember those on-campus recruiters who routinely screen applicants using grades, interviewing the top three or four? It's great if you make the cut or win the award, but what about all the people who didn't? This doesn't mean that you shouldn't try, but rather that you should realistically assess your chances before focussing all of your efforts on this as your "attention-getting" strategy. A student in the middle of the mark range might do better to concentrate on meeting the right people through introductions, or focussing on his exceptional work history, rather than spending all his efforts on moving up a couple of places in the grade list.

Be Seen as Expert

Becoming an expert is more than being noticeably better, winning an award or finishing first. Being an "expert" means that you have special knowledge or skill in a particular subject, and are regarded as an authority on that subject. Most of us have heard comments such as *"Go ask Daphne, she knows everything about that project."*

Becoming and expert can be a particular challenge because not only must you <u>be</u> an expert, but you also must be <u>seen</u> as being the expert. If you have some unique knowledge or skill that is useful or appealing to others, learn even more about it and make sure that you really are, and stay, the expert. Then you need to "get the word out." This begins with self-promotion (not with bragging). You can read more about this in the next chapter "It's What You Show, Not What You Know." Publishing articles, speaking at special interest groups and any related media coverage can help you be seen as being the expert. Inside your company, you could offer to help others, present on the topic at Lunch 'n Learn, or write about it in the company newsletter.

Whatever subject you choose to be expert in, be sure that it is suitable <u>and that it will enhance your long term goals</u>. Many years ago I was consulting at a large corporation and met Mallory, the Director of their Medical Product Services Division. This was back when PowerPoint was still a bit of a novelty and many technically challenged executives (most of them actually) and their administrative assistants were still struggling to use it. Mallory was a quick learner, liked technical problems and seemed to grasp most things intuitively. She was well regarded and hoped to apply for a Vice President position shortly. In the course of her job she was frequently required to present to the Board of Directors and to the Senior Management team, usually in PowerPoint. She quickly became viewed as the company expert in PowerPoint, even more so than the people in computer services. It wasn't unusual for her boss, other directors, secretaries or even the CEO to call her up and ask for her help with PowerPoint, sometimes with little consideration for her own work. The trouble was that, while it was a valuable service and she was the expert, knowing PowerPoint wasn't seen as an executive level skill. In fact, most of the executives used to joke about their own technical ineptness. So Mallory's expertise in a valuable skill, which was commonly viewed a non-executive type function, actually diminished her stature in the organization. She was passed over for two successive promotions and eventually left the company.

Draw Attention to "Common Ground."

You run into someone from your high school, the first place you ever worked, or the faraway country where you were born and ...instant connection. A man sits near you in a waiting room reading a book by your favourite author, so you strike up a conversation. While at an obscure film festival, you run into a distant acquaintance from work and you wind up sitting together. Will you ever be able to just walk by him again at work? These are just a few of the examples of what happens when you discover common ground. You begin talking, even though you never really knew one another before. There's a warmth in your thoughts and it almost feels like you're old friends. If you talk again later, and then one of these people asked you to look over a proposal for them, could you say no? Not likely. So if you deliberately draw attention to this common ground in order to foster a connection, is it any less valid? Not really. The connection was already there. Anything you have in common with the boss, the interviewer, the client or the prospect is fair game.

Fraternities, special interest groups, clubs, favourite sports, ethnic connections and hobbies - any of these can make the difference between a warm lead and a cold call. The only real choice is how you go about drawing attention to this connection without seeming obvious. First, you need to research the person you want to meet. Check company reports, the Internet and newspaper articles. Talk to friends, colleagues and other people in your network. Find genuine common ground. Joining the CEO's hunting club when you have no interest in hunting counts as sucking up, not finding common ground, and your lack of real interest and knowledge will soon show through. Focus on areas where there is an honest shared interest. Then communicate your shared interests, hobbies or background as subtly as you can. This is a long-term approach so don't try to accomplish it in one meeting. Wear your fraternity or club pins with some regularity (assuming you're proud of them). Talk about your home town. Mention your interesting hobbies. Put your certificates on your office wall. These strategies are good even if you don't have a particular target in mind. They give you something to talk about in casual conversation. Remember, we like to do business with people we feel we know and you never know when you'll run into an "old friend."

Then Make Your Connections Count

Whatever strategy you use to stand out above the daily noise, make sure you take advantage of it immediately. There's no point in finally being introduced to that agent who could make you a star, then mumbling self-consciously and wasting the opportunity. While you don't want to rush in and immediately ask for the job, the audition, the sale or whatever other goal you're pursuing, you must capitalize on the opportunity and lay the ground work for follow-up. At the very least, you want to make enough of an impression and connection so that you'll be remembered (positively) if you telephone the next day.

Learn how to make conversation effectively (see Chapter 8 "The Big Deal About Small Talk"). Develop some self-introductions suitable for different situations. Don't be embarrassed to talk about your work and accomplishments. The initial common interest or introduction is just an opener, and your goal is to find some more shared interests to discuss. Then you need to communicate something about your background and goals, and to set the follow-up plan into motion. Following up may include anything from a request to meet later, a promise to send an invitation, a request for statistics/details, or an offer to deliver some information/work - anything that gives you the chance to continue the relationship.

CHAPTER TWO SUMMARY

Find a way to stand out above the noise by...

- Linking Yourself Through an Existing Connection
- Making a Visual Impact
- Being Noticeably Better or Unique
- Being Seen as an Expert
- Drawing Attention to "Common Ground."

Then, when you get their attention, take advantage of it before you lose it!

People make judgements, choose a course of action and begin relationships based on what they <u>believe to be true</u>, not necessarily on what <u>is true</u>.

Chapter 3

It's What You Show, Not What You Know
Learn to Promote Yourself and Your Value to Others

Most of us have been brought up to believe that boasting is impolite and socially unacceptable. Bragging is bad and humility is good, right? Well, in business networking, unless you can communicate your value to others, it doesn't matter who you are, what you've done or where you've been. Sure you might not want to run around boasting endlessly, but self-promotion, or the art of tactfully spreading the word about your accomplishments and connections, is a critical skill you just have to develop.

"You know you should talk to Alice about that proposal. I remember she was the leader on a research project with an oil company a while ago. She could really save your team a lot of time." That's how many networking conversations play out, assuming that the players have the information to make that recommendation. If people don't know about your strengths, skills

and other unique attributes, how can you network effectively? While some people in your network may eventually become close friends, whom you'll see often and who'll get to know you well, the majority won't - you just don't have that kind of time available. One way or another, you have to get the word out.

Unfortunately, talking about ourselves makes many of us extremely uncomfortable, especially with introverts. We feel it's alright to promote the company, its products or even someone else, but quite another to go on about our own accomplishments. Most of us have a lifetime of indoctrination to cast off.

But It's What's Inside that Really Counts - Right?

When you talk about business networking, what's inside counts... in the long-run. In the short run, it's what you show, not what you know. In today's hectic business and social world the reality is that, unless there's a relatively quick connection or some other motivation, most people don't hang around long enough to get to know what's inside. We've become used to making quick choices based on immediately available, obvious information and our perceptions and expectations. As Neil Postman points out in his book *Amusing Ourselves to Death*, the three hundred pound plus, twenty seventh United States President, Howard Taft could never aspire to be President nowadays. Today elections are won and lost in the visual medium of television, and since he wouldn't fit today's image of what a United States President should look like, the public would never get to hear about this knowledge, experience and leadership skill.

Depending on the exact situation and motivation, most people develop a pretty definite, but not necessarily very accurate, first impression within one to four minutes of meeting you. If you've finally managed to get that critical introduction you desperately needed, you have only a short while to make a positive impact and to start planning a follow-up. Bad first impressions can take months or even years to undo. Sometimes you never get a second chance. So if you can do something to make sure that your good reputation and accomplishments precede you, why not?

Think of yourself as a good book, and your self- promotion as the cover. Most of us choose a book based on the title, the look and feel of the cover, testimonials about the content, reputation of the author, the table of contents/summary and only occasionally by glancing through the actual writing. Based on all of these factors, we decide if the book will meet our reading goals (whether those goals be fun, entertainment, education, relaxation, information or whatever) and if we'll invest time in actually reading it. Yes, later, if the book doesn't deliver on its promises - if what's inside isn't any good - we're unlikely to finish it or to read any other books by the same author; however, the initial decision isn't based on what's inside.

Each of us has a responsibility to make sure that our "cover," including our appearance, reputation, accomplishments and connections, promote further "reading."

But My Good Work Speaks for Itself - Not!

The only thing a job well done says is that it was a job well done. It doesn't tell anyone about the knowledge, skill or experience that was required. It doesn't speak to the dedication, education or effort that was required. It doesn't mention who, on the team, contributed and who didn't. Once it's done, people move on and forget about it. This is especially true with work that consists of tangible outputs (e.g. reports, programming, typing, research), where there is no close and immediately obvious relationship between the final product and the person who did the work. Take a financial analyst for example. As long as he does his budgets in a competent and error-free way, gets his reports and analyses out accurately and on time, and answers his clients questions well, it's pretty much a non-event.

> *John is a computer programmer, a very good computer programmer. Usually, he spends his day programming and testing. His work is on time, well documented and error-free. John is also a very smart guy who spends a lot of time thinking about how things could run more smoothly, and about how the new development process could be more efficient...but never shares it because he's so busy doing a good job programming. If you got to know him you'd find he's also got a wonderful sense of humour and is great with people. He's applied for a few Team Leader positions at both his own company and others but is never quite the right "fit."*
>
> *Where do you suppose he'll be in ten years? Most likely ...programming.*

Come promotion or performance appraisal time, that past work is pretty silent. Study after study has shown that relationships, gut instincts and "impressions" can be far more influential in promotion decisions than a job well done and good performance appraisals.

Once you get outside of your workplace, what distinguishes you from any of the many other people that do jobs like yours? If all you do is say, "I'm a computer programmer," how would we know that you were recruited early out of your class at university and that you're a whiz at something in particular and might be just the person to help out on...? Job title and on the job performance tell us nothing about your personality, history, unique qualities and "networking value." Even if other people aren't consciously evaluating networking potential, they will immediately stereotype you based on any title you provide. It's not enough to be different or better, you have to be able to show it.

Maybe if I Say Nice Things About Others People...

If you say nice things about other people, will they do the same for you? Maybe, but most likely not. This misconception is right up there with your good work speaking for itself. While it's always a good idea to speak positively about others, and we generally don't like negative people, there's no guarantee that anyone will see the need to reciprocate your positive comments. Just as most bosses and colleagues frequently (usually?) forget to provide ongoing positive feedback, we just aren't in the habit of spending a lot of time building up other people. Most of us are far too busy worrying about our own lives to even notice all the good things around them, let alone to spread the word. Sure, if your name happens to come up and it happens to be relevant, you might get some compliments. But then, even if someone does say a few good things about you, will it be exactly the image or information that you want out there? Do you really want to leave it to chance?

But No One Wants to Listen to Me Brag

We all hate listening to people who go on and on about how wonderful they are, all the important people they know and how they can do anything better than almost anyone else. But I'm not talking about bragging here. Most of us could do a far better job of communicating our strengths and accomplishments and still do it within the accepted norms. Throughout our lives there are countless opportunities to share the promotional information about ourselves and our accomplishments without any "in your face" boasting and selling. This self-promotion includes how you look, how you explain your job, how you present your accomplishments and to some extent, how others talk about you.

Before You Say a Word

Appearance matters! While it might be nice to think that people care more about the inside than the outside, the outside is what they see first. By the time a conversation begins, we've subconsciously drawn all kinds of conclusions about the other person's education, socioeconomic status, job and intelligence. These conclusions affect how we feel about the person, our expectations and their credibility. Then, once the conversation does start, approximately fifty five percent of our interpersonal communication is based on body language and appearance. Over thirty five percent is speaking voice, including rate, tone and pitch, leaving less than ten percent for the words we say. So if you're trying to present yourself as a rising star in the banking world, you better be sure you look and sound like one. The same goes for just about any other career. Each of us carries around a cartload of prejudices about what we think people in specific jobs should look like. We might tolerate jeans and t-shirt on the CEO of a small Internet start-up company, but we're unlikely to do business with a bank where the manager and staff dress that way. Similarly, we don't expect the cashier at the grocery store or the gas station attendant to be wearing a designer suit.

At one of my conversation skills workshops I met a delightful gentleman who was a production line manager. He was hoping to move out of the production line area and into a department manager position within a year. The trouble was that when you met him, you didn't think department manager. Although bright, funny and knowledgeable, he'd always sit slouched in his chair, legs spread and stretched out, wearing jeans and a knit shirt. His language was colloquial and filled with slang. Based on that appearance, he'll probably have to work at least twice as hard to get the promotion as someone who looks the part. Think carefully about what is appropriate for the image you want to present and the goals you've set for yourself. Everything about you should reflect your desired image (which should be based on your real accomplishments and goals), including your clothes, business cards, résumé, language and gestures. For some more information on this subject, see also Chapter 9 "Mind Your Manners."

Learn to Articulate What You Do

Promoting yourself effectively continues with being able to

explain clearly what it is you do for a living. Rightly or wrongly, when you meet new people, *"...and so what do you do..."* is one of the first questions to come up in conversation. If you answer with a label (doctor, lawyer, teacher, salesman, cashier, student, etc.), you rob yourself of the opportunity to explain what you do and what sets you apart from all the others in similar jobs. As soon as you tell people *"I'm an accountant for..."* or *"I'm a teacher,"* a stereotype comes to mind, prejudiced by the characteristics of every accountant or teacher they've ever met or seen on television. Stereotypes rarely work in your favour, so try to use something descriptive such as *"I work with new immigrants to help them evaluate their skills and present themselves positively in their written job applications."* It says far more about you and your work than if you had said *"I write résumés."* Being descriptive and constructive is much more than just putting a positive spin on things. Your goal is to communicate exactly what you do, in terms and value to which the listener can relate. You can follow this with a brief example that fills in some details and helps them visualize your contribution more clearly. *"You know how people always struggle to write an eye-catching cover letter. I help them develop one that is relevant, appealing, and that does more than repeat what's in their résumé."*

Your first step in developing this self-introduction is to get a clear picture in your own mind of what is important in your work, and then to put it in terms of what need you fill and how your work affects others. In Appendix A you'll find a blank template to help you with this process.

You might want to develop at least three or four different self-introductions so that depending on the situation, you can refer to the one that's most relevant. How you introduce yourself in a formal meeting with people "in the business," is unlikely to be suitable when you meet other parents at your son's soccer game. You would need yet a different introduction when you are trying to sell to a new client. Once you've developed these introductions, use them with discretion. They should serve <u>as a foundation</u> for your conversation, not a mini speech into which you launch the moment you meet someone new. Whenever I go to receptions, I'm always surprised at the number of people who deliver apparently memorized intromercials without any customization. They make no effort to find out about my interests first. Obviously they use the same one over and over. Your introduction will be much more effective if you can take a few basic details about yourself and your work, and then give them some relevance based on what you know about the person to whom you're speaking.

Understand Your Strengths and the Value You Bring

Before you can develop that fascinating self-introduction, you do need to have a clear image of the value you bring to your work. Going back to that résumé writer, her statement of *"I work with new immigrants to help them document their skills and present themselves positively in their written job applications,"* clearly presents the *value* of her work, rather than the *task* (writing résumés). This assessment should include not only the value of the work itself, but also the unique strengths that you bring to that job. So, for example, we can look at the job of a corporate trainer. The value of the job might be that the trainer helps employees learn the additional skills they need to do their work more effectively. The unique strengths of the individual in the job might be that he is able to present the training in such an interesting and appealing way, that there is a waiting list for his classes. In conversation, there would be nothing wrong with him saying just that.

Sit down and evaluate your work. What value does the work have? What needs does it fill? Catalogue the unique strengths that you bring. If you have trouble with this part, and many people do, enlist the aid of a few close colleagues or friends who are familiar with your work.

Present Yourself with Conviction and Confidence

Even after understanding their needs, identifying individual strengths and writing a self-introduction, many people still have trouble saying the words. Those years of conditioning start getting in the way again. As with every other form of public speaking, presenting a self-introduction with conviction and confidence takes practice, practice and more practice. Begin with short pieces, adding gradually as you gain confidence and keeping in mind a few basic rules. Here are a few other suggestions to help.

Say it With Stories. Describe your accomplishments as they happened with some comments about relevance and impact. Not only is this more interesting than a laundry list of your assets, but it's accurate and informative. Don't present subjective conclusions about your own importance.

Context and Presentation Count. Bragging that your father owns a really big bank, with no context, is just that - bragging. When you're looking for a job in a financial area, talking about how you've spent every summer learning the business and working your way up through even the most basic of jobs at your father's bank, is absolutely appropriate and necessary.

Don't Exaggerate. Making up non-existent or fancy job titles, exaggerating your position or overstating your actual job duties, doesn't serve you well (and will eventually catch up with you). Sometimes it takes some digging and reflection, but most people can usually find at least a few significant accomplishments.

Inform, Don't Irritate. Your goal in presenting your skills and accomplishments with pride should be just that - to present your real skills and accomplishments with reasonable and appropriate pride. As soon as you start showing off at the expense of others, going on too long, or talking about things that have no relevance, you've crossed the line from informing into boasting.

When Others Are Speaking for You

Just as you can't count on others to promote your skills and to speak out on your behalf, you also can't count on them to say the right things if and when they do speak for you. It isn't that people deliberately sabotage or misrepresent, their perspectives and priorities are just different from yours. They don't necessarily know exactly how you want to be viewed or which characteristics you feel are most important.

A few years ago I was asked to present a workshop on e-mail communication. While I frequently talk on the subject of e-mail communication and e-mail etiquette, it's actually a very small portion of my business and mostly presented as a component of a larger communications program or workshop series. The host was usually very articulate and since I've worked with him many times, he apparently didn't feel it necessary to write down his introduction. Right before introducing me, something distracted him. He stumbled through the introduction and then gave up and said, *"Here's Renate - the e-mail expert."* That's certainly not the way I'd care to be remembered and not very good for any future business unrelated to e-mail. If I had provided my introducer with a pre-written introduction as I usually do, I could have avoided this.

When others are speaking out on your behalf, be sure that you do your best to see that they say what you need to be said. This means that when you are being presented as a speaker, you offer to write out your introduction. If someone else insists on writing it, at the very least, ask to preview the introduction. When you ask for a letter of reference or testimonial, don't be afraid to mention the key points you'd like included and always ask, in general terms, what else your reference provider plans to say. If he's unwilling to discuss this, perhaps he's not the best choice. Since testimonials are such a huge part of a speaker's credibility and press kit, I offer people sample testimonial letters. Most are happy to be saved the effort of creating the letter alone.

Similarly, any press releases, articles or reports about you or your business should never go out before you've reviewed and approved them. Once they're out there, if there's a problem, you can't fix it.

And Finally, Remember to Sell the Benefits

Whether you're promoting yourself, documenting your abilities for a résumé or cover letter, or asking others to endorse you, remember that presenting your skills and accomplishments abstractly won't advance your cause. You can't assume that just because you talk about how you worked your way up through the ranks, that your listener will automatically infer that you know the business inside out. Consider how your skills and abilities will benefit your audience and then make it clear. *"I practically grew up in the banking business. Working through all of those jobs has helped me be able to answer customer questions much more completely..."* Always present your skills (in this case, broad experience) in terms of their needs (happy and informed customers).

CHAPTER THREE SUMMARY

Unless you can communicate your value to others in your network and you can sell that value in terms of how it benefits them, it really doesn't matter who you are, what you've done, or how much you know.

Learn to promote yourself and your value to others through your appearance, self-introduction and the ways in which you have others endorse you.

---

*It is by spending oneself
that one becomes rich.*

Sarah Bernhardt

Chapter 4

Overdrawn at the Networking Bank
Add Value, All the Time

Our whole monetary system evolved because bartering only really worked when two individuals wanted to trade goods or services at a particular point in time. By developing currency, people could buy items from one person and sell to another, or buy something today and sell something at some later date. If networking only involved immediate direct exchange between two individuals, it would run into the same problems as bartering. What if you had nothing the other person wanted? What if you needed something later?

The joy of networking is that it works much like a very unstructured monetary system. The products and services being "sold" are information, influence, guidance and support. Because these exchanges don't always happen immediately, we have a "currency" of trust, respect and favours owed. In this networking economic system, value is only vaguely defined and usually measured in terms of the benefits to the recipient. Obligations are non-specific and can be transferred through the currency of credibility, trust and respect. Repayment is always at the service provider's discretion and "ability to pay," and the transactional nature of the whole process is always understood but rarely spoken. Because the system is so loose, we need to make sure that we always keep trust, respect and favours (owed to us) "on deposit" in our networking "accounts." The greater your accrued trust, respect, favours and your perceived value to others, the healthier your networking account.

You Can't Spend What You Haven't Earned

Throughout your business and personal life you need to continually and deliberately accrue "perceived value" (which is quite different from self-worth) for networking purposes. These deposits aren't just for your own accounts. You're making deposits on behalf of everyone else in your network, and they are doing the same for you. You'll want to keep many different accounts for different purposes. To help keep these accounts healthy and growing, there are some basic network "banking" guidelines that are useful to follow.

Give First

This doesn't mean that you have to go far out of your way for someone whom you just met, but it does have to start somewhere - and many people won't make the first move. Small things can go a long way in a new relationship - information about an upcoming lecture, a lead about a new job posting you just saw, e-mailing a helpful article you just ran across - every little bit helps.

Give Freely, Give Often

Every time you provide someone else with information, feedback, support, leads, influence or anything else of that nature, you're making an investment. The trouble is that you never know which account you're going to need to dip into, so you have to keep them all topped up. It may sound like a lot of work, but most of networking isn't about doing big favours. Sure, leads and referrals are much appreciated, but the regular exchange of information and support is just as helpful and necessary. (e.g. If you get a notice about an interesting new lecture series, it takes only moments to forward it to any people in your network who would benefit from it.) So, if you reasonably can help, then do.

Don't Let the Cheque Bounce

Offering to help out is like writing a cheque; once you've written it, it becomes a firm obligation and the other person has every right to cash it in. So be realistic about your capabilities and the strength of your network. If you promise (to make a referral call, or to put in a good word, or to send over some information) and then don't deliver, it's like a bounced cheque, and it costs you more than not making the promise in the first place. Sometimes when we really want to help, it's tempting to make an offer that we're not sure we can deliver. If this is the case, check into it first, and then make the offer. Don't overestimate your network, skills or capability. Don't try to be something you're not.

Don't Underestimate Your Ability to Add Value

But what do I have to offer someone like...? This common refrain is heard frequently from people new to networking, students and people who perceive themselves to be in "inferior" or "insignificant" jobs. The reality is that anyone can contribute to a networking relationship, providing they put in the required effort. You have a great deal to offer since "you" includes who you are; your history; where you work; your friends, relatives, neighbours; all your ideas, skills and education; even the books you read and television you watch. It's the scope and depth of your involvement that is more important than the status of your job. A secretary who knows everyone and everything that happens in the company can be a much greater networking asset than a manager or executive who knows only his own job and department.

Don't Get Overdrawn

As with your bank account, it isn't a good idea to be in networking debt too deep or for too long. We all have problems, times when we can't help out and situations that may temporarily overwhelm us. That's the whole point of making regular deposits and building up a healthy positive balance. So if you have to step back for some time or find that you have personal issues to deal with for a while - that's fine - in the short-run.

A few years ago, a university associate of mine ran into some problems when he had to work long hours because of a proposed faculty merger. He rarely returned phone calls, didn't answer e-mails and didn't show up at events he'd committed to attending. In the short term, everyone understood, but as weeks turned into months, his "disappearance" caused problems for others in his network. People stopped counting on him and then gave up calling him. I'd hear comments like *"You'd better have a backup plan, Savich isn't likely to show."* Eventually, people stopped talking about him altogether. While no one had expected him to keep up on everything, had he at least stayed in touch and kept a few key commitments, he would have maintained his "balance." By the time he reappeared on the scene, people had developed different linkages. Three years later people are still hesitant to count on him.

Don't Spread Yourself Too Thin

In networking, it's the quality of relationships that is important, not the quantity. Having a couple of dollars in the pocket of every pair of pants, with a few more in bank accounts all over the city, isn't good financial management. Sure, the money has value, but the way you have it organized, you don't have enough critical mass to do anything with it. Networking is like that. All networking connections don't have to be deep, close relationships. You'll want to spend more time and energy on some people, while keeping active but more distant relationship with others. Any time you find you're having trouble adding value for your contacts, when you aren't getting anything back, or when you're missing out on promises or commitments, then it's time to re-evaluate the quality of your relationships. Look at why you entered into them, what they cost you (in time and effort) and what you get out of them - then make a conscious choice about where to focus your attention.

Invest Wisely

After hearing that you need to give first and give often, it may seem strange to hear that you also should give cautiously, but you do need to be mindful of the value of your time. As with real money, the time and effort you have available to invest in networking is a scarce and valuable resource. Make conscious choices about where and how much you invest.

It may sound noble and altruistic to help as many people as you can, but it's not very realistic. Just as you need to be selective about where you make your charitable donations, you also need to be selective in networking, choosing the relationships you work on the most. This doesn't mean you never do anything without expecting a return, but rather that you look at the "big picture" and focus on where you can do the most good - for yourself and others. If you can combine your networking with other enjoyable business and social activities, it means you'll be able to accomplish more over all.

When you get the urge to help, ask yourself *"Is this a wise use of my time and resources?"* Are you adding real value or would anyone else do as well? You want to be respected for the <u>unique</u> value and <u>specific</u> skills that you can contribute, not be seen just as another pair of hands. There's an old adage that goes "familiarity breeds contempt." If you're always around, available for everything and anything, you won't be appreciated for any exceptional qualities and abilities.

Don't Burn Bridges - You Might Need Them Later

You've decided to review and refocus your networking plan, and this means you're going to be dropping out of some activities and potentially "dropping" some people. Maybe you've been downsized out of your job of ten years or you're moving across the country. Regardless of your current needs and feelings, don't be hasty and "burn your bridges". Tact, good manners and an eye to the future will stand you in good stead. Try to leave on a positive note. It costs you little and you never know when you'll meet again.

You Make Deposits to Your Networking Accounts When...

Networking deposits are easy to make if you focus on more than the big stuff (although you should do some of that as well). Pass on ideas, resources, leads and information; be there to talk over strategies, problems and concerns; say thank you whenever you can; show others that you care and are thinking about them; choose projects where you can demonstrate (not show off) your skills; establish your character, skills and stature through others (awards, articles and certificates); and publicly recognize the achievements and contributions of others. Many other activities can add value as well, and the only way you recognize these opportunities is through listening well and evaluating what your contacts need and want.

You Deplete Your Account When...

Any time you accept advice, information, favours or support you are using up your networking capital - but then that's what it's there for. Just be sure you are also making deposits. It's those unnecessary withdrawals you want to avoid. Behaving unethically, not respecting people's time, calling in favours when you don't need to do so, and failing to stay in touch, all deplete your networking value, and for no good cause.

Asking for something too soon in a networking relationship, or asking for something that is beyond the other person's ability to help, can hurt the relationship more than almost anything else. The situation quickly becomes awkward and it reflects poorly on your judgement. It puts the other person in the difficult position of either having to decline, admit they can't help, or to try to help beyond their normal reach - all of which are undesirable.

Taking is Good Too!

Finally, remember that networking is give <u>and take</u>. Most people like helping out, and like feeling as if they are contributing. Don't just focus on building up networking capital; sometimes you have to allow others to do things for you. What's the point of having money if you never use it? If you're in a relationship where you do all the (obvious) giving, and you value the relationship, be sure to allow the other person to "even things up."

CHAPTER FOUR SUMMARY

Keep a positive "balance" in all your networking accounts.

Follow the basic guidelines for good "investing."

Remember to give and take in any networking relationship.

---

*"...I know the game, you'll forget my name,
and I won't be here in another year
If I don't stay on the charts."*

*from The Entertainer
Billy Joel*

Chapter 5

Out of Sight is Out of Mind
Follow Up Relentlessly

"Out of Sight, Out of Mind"

That about sums it up. Try asking for a favour from someone with whom you haven't been in touch for a few years and you'll find out just how tough it can be once a relationship fades. You wouldn't expect to receive (or give) referrals, advice or support from strangers; and those people with whom we've allowed our relationship to fade are little more than strangers.

All that "noise" that you've struggled to stand out above doesn't go away after you've succeeded in making a connection; it stays there waiting to once again engulf you in the anonymity of the daily hustle and bustle. So once you've gone to all the trouble of getting someone's attention, making the connection and establishing your reputation, you have to nurture that relationship to keep it active, alive and productive. In networking, those high profile, conspicuous activities such as trading of referrals, leads and favours get most of the attention, but it's the little things, such as saying thank you and remembering to follow up, that secure a relationship over the long run. They have the biggest impact on our unconscious mind and how we feel about each other (versus what we think about each other).

Staying visible, following up effectively and remembering to say thank you don't have to be time-consuming activities. Once you get into a routine, they barely take any time at all.

The Job's Not Done Until You've Followed Up

Any time you give out referrals or leads of any kind, it's just good business to follow up. Your goal here is to protect your network.

Let's say you refer Scott (a project manager in a hospital), to your close associate Malcolm (a CEO of a major hospital) to talk about career advancement opportunities in healthcare, making the introduction and setting the stage for the meeting. You'll need to touch base with both Scott and Malcolm afterwards. If Scott doesn't let you know how it went automatically, after a suitable time period you'll want to find out if he actually followed through on the lead and on what happened. You might also suggest to him that next time you'd like to hear how it went. You need to contact Malcolm to thank him for seeing Scott, to ensure that the referral was appropriate, and to do any damage control if Scott either didn't follow through or made an unfavourable impression. If you heard back from Scott and you know that the meeting went really well, then a short thank you note to Malcolm might be sufficient in the short run, but at some point you do want to hear his view on how it went. For more on saying thank you, see below.

Saying Thank You is Critical

I remember reading an old Ann Landers column, many years ago, in which a reader was complaining about the general lack of manners and appreciation in the world. In her usual direct manner, Ann replied, "If you want gratitude, look in the dictionary." She went on to hammer home the message that you should always give thanks, but never expect it. In all the years since I read that column, her message has only become more relevant.

When you make a mistake at work, how long is it before you hear about it? How often does the boss (or a colleague or family member) compliment or thank you for a job well done? If you're like most of us, complaints come quickly and easily, while compliments are rare. Yet praise, encouragement and gratitude are among the cheapest and most effective recognition tools available, perhaps precisely because they are so rare. You would think that with all the basic networking books out there, people would get the message that sending a thank you note is important, but it just isn't true. Most people still don't go much further than a mumbled *"...thanks."* This gives you yet another opportunity to stand out in a positive way. Aside from the fact that it's just plain good manners, there are four main reasons to say *"thanks."*

- You really are grateful. Saying thanks makes you, and them, feel good.

- Lots of folks don't say thank you, so you get to look good.

- Saying thanks gives you another opportunity to reinforce key messages, promises and needs.

- Saying thanks is another chance to maintain visibility and continue the relationship.

So When is Saying Thanks Necessary?

When should you say thanks? Well, whenever someone does

something for you directly or indirectly, or for someone else at your request, you should acknowledge their efforts. "Something" is pretty much anything that requires some deliberate action or work including, but not limited to, activities such as providing influence, information, guidance or support. When in doubt, put yourself in the place of the person on the receiving end. (e.g. receiving several thank you cards from the same person over the space of a couple of months might be a bit too much, even if you have been repeatedly helpful.)

It's More than Just Saying "Thanks"

Regardless of how you eventually send your thank you messages, most of the time they should contain much more than a simple *"thanks."* Keeping in mind your short and long-term goals, and based on the following example, you can decide which components to include.

The thank you note below is from Freda, a brand manager for a major consumer products firm, who has just met with Anil, the managing partner from a well-known marketing consulting firm. Freda feels she is stagnating in her current job and wants to move into some type of consulting. She is looking for advice as to how to begin the process and how to make her experience more attractive to consulting firms. The meeting was set up by Delia, who belongs to the same karate club as Anil. Delia and Freda have been good friends for years. Freda's typed thank you letter to Anil might include something such as this:

"Thank you for taking the time out of your working day to meet with me and review the hiring and advancement process for consultants." (Freda explains for what specific actions she is thanking Anil.)

"I know you were very busy on Tuesday. I hope your board presentation in the afternoon went well and that your proposal was

accepted." (She shows she was listening to his opening comments and that she cares about Anil's success.)

"The overall approach we discussed will definitely add to my marketability and complement my strong work experience in international marketing." (Freda states her satisfaction with the information received and does some subtle self-promotion about her exceptional work history - which she has identified as her greatest asset.)

"Your ideas and suggestions will help me to develop a more focussed plan for moving into the consulting field." (Freda reinforces how Anil's information will help her.)

"I have already signed up for the course you recommended and the class begins in the Fall semester." (Freda shows that she is following up on Anil's suggestion.)

"I look forward to seeing the market sector statistics you said you would find and send to me at the end of the quarter. I've included my current mailing and e-mail addresses with this note." (Freda reminds Anil about his promise and also ensures that he has her contact information.)

"As promised, I've included the link to that great university marketing database that I mentioned. I hope you find it as helpful as I do." (Freda follows up on her promise and shows that she can add value to the relationship as well.)

"I look forward to seeing you at the Plastics and Polymers in Packaging Conference next month and I hope I'll have some successes to share with you by then." (Freda lays the foundation for a subsequent meeting and gives herself an excuse to talk to Anil again.)

"Thank you again for your time. You were just as helpful and knowledgeable as Delia said you would be." (Freda says a final

thank you and puts in an indirect good word for Delia.)

Freda's thank you letter is sincere, straightforward, not overly effusive and takes less than a page. You can see that she used the opportunity to cover a lot of ground without being obvious or fawning. Clearly you won't need to always send such a detailed letter. Sometimes just a couple of the elements are necessary and occasionally a simple thank you is all that is needed (see more on this below).

Will That Be Paper or ...?

Figuring out what and when to say thanks is usually pretty straightforward but often choosing how to say thank you is a challenge. Is a simple verbal *"thanks"* enough? When do you send a formal letter? Should you hand write or type a letter? When should you think about sending a gift?

While it may be mostly true that "It's the thought that counts," your choice of medium does matter and goes a long way to setting you apart from the crowd. In general, the more someone did for you, the more formal your thank you should be. Below is a list of the most obvious alternatives, along with some of the relevant considerations.

Always begin by saying thank you, in person, if that's possible. Usually you would do this over the departing handshake. *"Thank you for...I really appreciate....and look forward to..."* You don't want to go on for more than two or three sentences at this time. It's also gracious to occasionally say thank you in public at a later occasion. Not only does this convey your gratitude, but it builds up the recipient in the eyes of others. Something along the lines of *"Thank you so much for sending me those statistics Michael, it saved me a great deal of time and made our bid much more competitive,"* is suitable.

Telephone calls are appropriate if you share a relatively

informal relationship or if you frequently trade referrals and contacts. Freda would reasonably call up Delia to thank her and let her know how the meeting with Anil went. Telephone calls don't work well if the person is difficult to reach or if you need to convey detailed information.

A faxed thank you letter isn't a great choice because it usually ends up on the fax machine in the middle of the office and you really can't predict when or how it will eventually make its way to the target. It's a bit less personal than a mailed letter but may be suitable when you need the detail and formality of a letter but don't want it to arrive too long after the event.

Sending *an e-mail note* is quick, relatively informal and mostly (but not always) will be opened first-hand by the intended recipient. The biggest drawback about e-mail these days is the sheer quantity of both legitimate and unsolicited messages. It's easy to get lost in the overflowing electronic mail box and some people routinely don't open mail they're not expecting. Since e-mail has become the most common method to send a quick thank you note, it has also lost much of its impact. If Freda can't reach Delia by phone, she might want to send an e-mail before too much time passes.

A typed letter is preferable when you want to communicate your thanks in a detailed, professional and formal way. While you could go over some of the details by phone or e-mail, having a hard copy allows the recipient to refer back as necessary. This type of formal communication shouldn't be overused. If Freda sent off a letter after her meeting with Anil this week and then wants to add a second thank you note next week, when she receives the market sector report, another typed letter would be excessive. It would be reasonable to send a short follow up e-mail message letting Anil know it arrived and that she's using it. Whenever timeliness is important, a formal letter via "snail mail" isn't a good choice.

A *handwritten* thank you card can be an elegant and unique touch. Fewer and fewer people seem to be bothering so it helps you to stand out. There isn't room for much more than a brief note so it can't replace a formal thank you letter. If Freda later gets a new job based on some of Anil's suggestions, a thank you card, to let him know, would be an appropriate gesture.

Gifts are suitable when someone has been exceedingly helpful, gone substantially out of their way to assist you, or when their support has resulted in something of considerable value to you. If you get a valuable new contract, job or major customer as a result of someone expending major effort on making the referral, then a thank you gift is appropriate. If you aren't familiar with the recipient's tastes and hobbies, thank you gifts should be somewhat impersonal items such as gift baskets, flowers, desk accessories, business card holders or gift certificates, and also relatively inexpensive. When a contact is especially helpful and supportive on an ongoing basis, for example, by sending you frequent referrals, consider sending a seasonal gift basket at some point during the year. Christmas is the most obvious choice, however since your gift may be lost among the many gifts received at that time of the year, you might want to do something at Easter, Thanksgiving or some other occasion instead. Since most government offices and a few companies do have policies against accepting (or giving) gifts, it's worth checking before sending something the first time. Usually a quick call to their Human Resources department can resolve this question.

Just Thinking of You

If you're not seeing/calling a contact regularly, and sometimes even if you are, you want to be sure they know you value your relationship with them and that you're thinking of them. Hopefully, they too, will think of you. Some of the easiest ways to "stay in sight" and to demonstrate "thinking of you" are through sending of unsolicited but helpful information, by "clipping and sending," and by sending occasional cards.

In the course of our business and personal lives we encounter many useful sources, great leads, interesting jobs and intriguing facts, some of which may be of value to other people in your network. At the same time, many things that are directly relevant and helpful to each of us get lost in the noise and bustle of our lives and we'd never notice them without the help of others. Passing around this sort of information amounts to "looking out for each other." It takes only a few minutes to send a note or e-mail with the relevant piece of information. Something like *"Hi Angelina, I saw this great lecture series advertised and it seems right up your alley - I thought you might be interested."* is useful, non-intrusive and demonstrates your thoughtfulness.

When you're reading your daily or local newspaper, thumbing through a magazine or newsletter, and wading through junk mail or advertisements, now and then you run across items that are directly relevant to people in your network. Sometimes it may just be a column related to a project that a colleague is working on. Other times it may be an article about an associate or his business. Clip it and send it. Friends regularly send me business cards, advertisements, articles, and once I actually received an entire book. The other day someone even sent me some basketball tickets they'd won and didn't need (my son is a raving fan). Each article, gift or piece of information is much appreciated and valued because not only does it give me something I can use, but it means that someone knows me well enough to see the connection and cared enough to send it.

Occasional cards include any greeting cards designed for a specific "occasion" such as birthdays, milestones, seasonal and religious holidays, and significant events. They're a great way of keeping in touch provided they are used with appropriate thought and attention. Non-denominational "holiday greetings" sent at Christmas time are the most common and least personal. If you know the recipient well, you can send a more personalized and meaningful card. Cards congratulating friends or colleagues on promotions, business successes and other achievements let them know that you've been keeping up and that you wish them well. Birthday greetings are also popular. The possibilities are virtually endless if you're creative and pay attention to what's going on around you. One business associate sends me a "frost free" celebration card every year, to mark the safe planting day for gardeners, because he knows me (and my gardening hobby) well enough to know it's suitable and appreciated.

Good judgement is critical with any of these visibility strategies. Getting frequent newspaper articles from someone you don't know well on something you're only vaguely connected with, can be irritating. A birthday card to the CEO might be a bit much if you're several layers away in the organization. On the other hand, if you chatted briefly with the CEO at the company Christmas party and he mentioned how much he likes golf, then sending him an enjoyable newspaper clipping, which he might not have run across himself, that announces the "Study Proves Golfers Make Better CEO's," would be perfectly appropriate.

Don't Forget To Call

All of the above "staying in touch" suggestions can go a long way towards building a better relationship, but none take the place of an occasional telephone call (or visit). On the phone you get to exchange information, catch up, and find out about new plans. So get in the habit of calling once in a while. Get together for coffee or lunch. With some people this will be monthly; with others once a year is enough. Just don't leave it so long that it becomes awkward. If you need to, you can lay the groundwork for a phone call when you're sending a card or clipping.

Keep Them Up-to Date

All of these strategies are aimed at maintaining your visibility and strengthening your network, however, you also need to keep in mind the productivity of your network. Your network will be effective only if you, and those in it, are aware of what is happening with one another. If you change your business focus, get a new job, move, win an award, publish a book or do anything else notable, be sure that the people in your network, who should hear about it, do. Not only is it sound business practice, but it goes back to promoting yourself. If they don't know you just won an award, received a promotion or were named to a prestigious Board, how can it enhance your credibility?

This doesn't have to be a big deal. If you change jobs, update everyone in your e-mail networking contact group when you're sending out your new e-mail address. Whenever you're sending notes (thinking of you or thank you) or calling people, be sure to pass on your latest news, and to ask about theirs. When you get new business cards, send them out to your colleagues and friends, along with a short note and update.

CHAPTER FIVE SUMMARY

Out of sight is out of mind so stay visible by:
- Following up
- Saying thank you appropriately
- Keeping in touch
- Remembering to call
- Updating people on your circumstances

When you are surrounded by sameness, you get only variations on the same.

Kevin Sullivan
Apple Computers

Chapter 6

Variety is the Spice of Life
Diversify Your Network

We like to be around people who are like us. That's just human nature. It's easier to socialize with people in our own age group, who share our lifestyle, who work in the same type of business or who come from a similar educational background. But for successful and optimal networking, diversity is a must.

Many formal networking clubs are clustered around a common client base. Typically, these are groups of small business owners and self-employed individuals who are expected to refer business to each other. Usually membership is restricted to one person in each business category, so there would only be one chiropractor, one insurance salesperson, one decorator and so on. The groups are often also quite homogeneous in terms of age and socio-economic status. If you restrict yourself to people who are much like yourself, or who operate only in a similar client base, you're robbing yourself of great opportunities. To get the full range of opportunities networking can offer you, both in business and in your personal life, you need to mix with people who allow you access to information, contacts, resources and ideas outside of your normal business and social sphere. Leigh Thompson, in *Making the Team*, calls these people "boundary spanners."

"Boundary spanners" are important for general networking but are absolutely critical for you if you work in a large organization. Careful and productive linkages with people up and down, as well as across, the organization can solidify your position and make you more effective in your work. You'll have allies throughout the company, you're less likely to be caught unawares by new initiatives and restructuring, you'll know what projects other departments are working on, and your own productivity will be improved as you have access to other resources and information.

Networking across boundaries, both inside and outside of the organization, also allows you to maximize your own credibility and reputation. Remember the old saying *"No man is a prophet in his own land."* Regardless of your expertise in your field, people close to you may quickly begin to take your skills for granted and forget about your specialized knowledge, whereas outside of your regular circles, you may be recognized for the unique value and perspectives you offer. Most of us have run into this when we see consultants being brought in. You think *"I could have told them that!"* Sometimes it takes an outsider to make people listen and there's no reason you can't be that "expert" - somewhere else.

Take some time to evaluate your existing network. Catalogue your own characteristics in terms of age, gender, professional status, ethnic group, job type, educational level and background, skills, hobbies, departmental links and customer groups. Are you an introvert or extrovert? Do you work mostly in the public or private sector; with big companies or small ones? What about your political, social and religious perspectives? Now look at your network. How different from you are the people in your network?

Finding and networking with "boundary spanners" doesn't have to be tough or awkward. Nor does it mean you have to hang around people with whom you have nothing in common. It just takes a conscious effort, first to meet people who are different from you in some useful way, and then to develop networking relationships with them.

If you, for example, enjoy photography and join a camera club, chances are that very few people there will be from your normal business circle. There will also probably be huge diversity in age, ethnic group, profession and education. Since you start out with a common love of photography, you'll always have something to talk about. You can share outings, photos, techniques, stories of missed shots and many other similar experiences, all the time getting to know each other and developing a networking base.

As with most things, balance is critical. You won't want to join five different hobby clubs - that's taking diversity too far. Diversity can be anywhere you look for it - a sports club, the place where you take evening classes or at the hockey rink while you're watching your kids play. You can even find it right in your own organization by talking to people in different types of jobs and different levels in the organization. Try to invest your networking efforts over a few different areas where you either have to spend time anyway, or you really enjoy the other activities.

Here's a sample range of planned networking opportunities for one person. Angelina, whose background is in rehabilitation therapy, works in a large downtown teaching hospital as a Program Manager. She's taking business classes at night and hopes to start up her own community rehabilitation therapy clinic within the next couple of years.

Group	Purpose and Regular Time Commitment
Business Networking Group	Monthly meeting of hospital Program Managers to mix with others who share similar customer base. Trade ideas and discuss common issues.
Hospital Health and Safety Committee	Monthly meeting with others throughout the organization, strengthening cross-organizational linkages.
Daughters dance class	Spend two evenings a week at this class. Use time to meet and get to know other parents, diversifying network.
German Cultural Association	Monthly meetings to help plan cultural events for the German community.
Professional Association	To maintain professional standing, continue education, teach and learn from others. Meet other independent practitioners and learn about running an independent business.
Sports & Fitness Club	Daily visits to gym at work and occasional squash game with colleagues from work.
Community College	Small business courses. Learns business skills and meets other current and future entrepreneurs.

While each group has a formal purpose, Angelina meets a wide cross-section of people who allow her to further her current business goals and go outside of her usual organizational and professional boundaries. At each event she makes a particular effort to get to know the others participating. Each situation provides enough beginning common ground to support conversation as people find other shared interests. Depending on these other shared interests, she can follow up and develop some stronger and more personal networking relationships.

What's the right combination for you? You need to work out how much time you have available, considering your business and family commitments. Try to balance your time allocated to formal and ongoing group commitments to leave enough time for one-on-one networking and follow-up activities. Wherever possible, you want to blend networking into activities that already fit into your life and also meet other objectives. (e.g. Angelina is already spending two hours a week at her daughter's dance class, along with periodic out of town trips to recitals and contests, so it only makes sense for her to use that time for networking as well.) The most important thing to remember is that there isn't much point to spending all your time with people who are just like you.

CHAPTER SIX SUMMARY

Networking with people who are too similar to you isn't a good use of your networking time and effort.

Find and network with "boundary spanners" who allow you access to information, contacts and resources outside of your usual sphere.

Aim for a good balance of people of different age, gender, profession, education, socio-economic group, ethnic group etc.

Maximize your productivity in finding diverse contacts by combining networking with other routine activities such as hobbies, sports or your children's activities.

---

*Blessed are those who
expect nothing, for they
shall not be disappointed.*

Jonathan Swift

Chapter 7

"Being There" is Not Enough
Make the Party Worth Your Time

Michael is a mid-level director at a large regional hospital. He knows that if he wants to make the jump to senior management, either through promotion or by getting a job at a different hospital, he's got to get out more and establish stronger relationships with other executives in his own hospital and throughout the health care industry. According to Michael *"...at the senior level, everyone pretty much knows everyone else, in all the big hospitals and in the government. Even if you apply for a position at a different hospital, they've already talked to each other. Without support and connections in that group, it's really tough to break in."* Knowing that, Michael has made an effort to get on some regional and inter-hospital committees. Whenever there are opportunities to mingle with the "right" people, he says *"I drag myself out there."* Usually though, he says it's pretty much a wasted effort. *"I go in with the best of intentions, determined to talk to at least a few of the big names, but it just doesn't happen. I walk in and everyone there seems to know everyone else. They all look so comfortable with each other and are already talking in small groups. I feel really awkward and out of place. Sometimes I get up the courage to join a group but I always feel like an outsider. I never know what to talk about. We exchange a few pleasantries and then I bow out. I go and get myself something to eat, talk to a couple of people at my level and then, as soon as I think I can safely leave, I take off. The whole way home I think about what a waste of time it was."*

Does any of this sound familiar? If you're serious about building your network of business, "networking events" are an essential part of the process. Networking events include any gathering where the primary purpose is meeting others and developing or improving business contacts. The most common examples are receptions before and during conferences, lunch club meetings, networking group events and some parties and seasonal celebrations. While Michael in the story above may think he's alone in his discomfort, over seventy percent of people admit to feeling anxious when they go to these types of events. Even among those people who enjoy the social aspect, many find the results disappointing.

Ashok, a self-employed safety consultant, says *"I love going to any and all of these things. I could talk to people all night and I feel so buzzed at the end of the evening. I trade business cards with ten or so people and feel like I've really connected. But when I sit down the next day and look at all those business cards, I don't really have a reason to call. Once in a while something will come up and I might phone up someone I met, but mostly they just sit in my card file. I never hear back from anybody I meet, except of course from the ones who are trying to sell me something."*

Most of the concerns related to social anxiety can be minimized through regular practice and by improving conversation skill (see the chapter "The Big Deal About Small Talk"). But other very basic problems, such as a lack of clear purpose, unreasonable expectations and inadequate preparation, are more often the real issue behind perceived "failure" at these events. The function of these gatherings isn't to get leads, sell yourself, have a fun evening or to give out business cards. More realistic goals include to meet new and interesting people, to reconnect with past acquaintances and to establish a reason (and lay the groundwork) to follow up with them later. Nothing more or less. Given the time available in an average evening event, this is the most you can expect to do towards the beginning of a business or networking relationship. Good preparation and specific objectives can help you get the most out of these networking events.

Before the Networking Event

Be informed. You can't build relationships if you have nothing to talk about. Current events, movies, sports scores, business news and even the weather, all give us a place to begin where everyone is equal and has something to contribute. Take a few minutes now and check if you are informed enough for basic small talk. Turn to the Conversation Builder in Appendix B and see how much you can complete within five minutes. For more help in this topic, see "The Big Deal About Small Talk." If it's a company event, make sure you know what's happening in your department, the company as a whole and with your industry in general. If it's a conference or professional association meeting, brush up on those background details. Plan what you're willing to share about yourself as well.

Find out who will be there. This information is surprisingly easy to come by. Most conference organizers will at least tell you the company names of people who will be attending and often busy registration people will send you an entire pre-registration list. If you are a club member, organizers of networking club meetings will also provide this information. With company events, you can usually ask HR or other organizing department who is coming, or at least who has been invited. As long as you don't ask for confidential information, most people are quite willing to oblige. The point of this whole research is so that you know ahead of time who will be there and can plan for an effective meeting.

Decide whom you want to meet and do some background research on them. Begin by selecting four to six people whom you'd really like to meet or get to know better. Write down the names as well as what you already know about them. Do some investigation into their job, background, hobbies, education and colleagues/friends. Here your goal is to:

- See if you can identify a colleague, acquaintance or "friend of a friend" who could introduce you.

- Develop an approach to use if you can't get an introduction - something along the lines of... *"I'm really interested in that project you did with..."*

- To identify interests, hobbies, or any other area where you might find common ground once the conversation gets going.

This doesn't mean you'll rush up to someone and say *"Guess what? We went to the same university"* If he has teenage kids, you might want to talk about yours; if she is an outdoors enthusiast, perhaps you talk about your upcoming camping trip. Remember, you're looking for <u>shared</u> interests. You begin with four to six names because you won't find obvious common interests with everyone and you can't expect to "connect" with everyone.

Don't visibly "gear up." You've seen it - they arrive with cell phone, pager and PDA attached. At first opportunity they whip out the PDA, portable keyboard and/or business card scanner to show everyone what busy and successful professionals they are. It's ostentatious, annoying and won't win you any friends.

Establish a specific, measurable and reasonable goal that YOU have control over. How many people you'll approach and talk to. Who you want to meet. How many people you want to get to know well enough to arrange a follow-up get-together.

Don't forget the business cards. You won't be handing them out to every single person you meet, but you do want to be able to give out contact information when you do connect with someone.

During the Event

If you've arranged for an introduction to someone you wanted to meet, wait until the first rush is over and you're sure you'll have time to talk for a few minutes. When the time is right, go for it. Of course you should have done some background research so you can easily find something to discuss with them.

Look for groups of three people standing around talking. The probability of intruding on a private conversation is much greater with groups of two. If you strike up a conversation with someone standing alone and the conversation doesn't go well, it can be difficult to extricate yourself tactfully. If any group is huddled in with heads together that sends out a signal that they aren't really open to outsiders. As you walk around, listen for interesting conversation and hover openly on the periphery of the group. If people look up at you, just smile and look interested. A return smile or movement to let you into the group is usually a favourable signal for joining in. Wait a short while and then feel free to participate by offering up a comment. Then play it by ear.

Focus on LISTENING, not worrying about what you're going to say next. If you've done your homework about the event, any speakers and guests, and you pay attention to the conversation, openings for comments will come up. Don't spend a lot of time thinking about what's in the conversation for you, or how you can mention that great project you just finished. It's tempting to try to "sell" them on yourself, but you just can't do that in one evening.

*Don't hijack the conversation...*or give them your life history or try to get an interview. Your goal is to join in and "connect." Five to ten minutes in any one group is more than enough. If you connect, and find you're having a great discussion with someone, consider saying something along the lines of *"I'd really like to talk with you more about this. How about I give you a call and we get together later?"* You're aiming for any strategy that leaves an opening for continuing the conversation later. If it's someone whose opinion/help you really need you might try *."..how about I buy you lunch and you can tell me more..."* Mission accomplished.

Present your business card in an effective way when the time is right. Don't just deal them out like you're playing poker or hand them out the minute you meet - it's likely to end up filed (if you're lucky) or forgotten. Try to present your card individually once you have established some connection or common ground. This way the card has some tangible relevance. When you receive a business card, write a short note on it to help yourself recollect details, context and any promises. Since few other people actually remember to do this, when you hand out your card you could write down a few words (not an essay) to help jog the other person's memory. After all, it's in your interest that they remember you.

Don't hand out brochures, photocopied handouts, press kits... unless they ask. It's presumptuous, not a good use of your money and doesn't convey a professional image.

Stop in and say goodbye to anyone you connected with as you are getting ready to leave. Few people bother with this courtesy, so it's a memorable way to differentiate yourself. Just shake hands, say goodbye and say something like *."..I just wanted to say how* *great it was talking to you...I hope we can get together..I'll call you. .."* leaving the way open for your follow-up. Also remember to stop and thank anyone who helped you out with an introduction.

After the Event

If you said you'd call, send something, or you promised to do anything, make sure you do it, soon - before you forget and the opportunity slips away. If someone was especially helpful or made a referral, send a thank you card. Call people with whom you connected and give the first referral, lead, favour or whatever, and keep making deposits to that networking bank (see "Overdrawn at the Networking Bank"). Don't immediately put everyone you met on your mailing list for electronic newsletters, advertising or promotions. While it may have some short term benefit in visibility, it won't help in long-term relationship building. If you do have a newsletter you want to send out, ask if people would be interested in receiving it before you send it their way.

CHAPTER SEVEN SUMMARY

When attending a "networking event:"

- Establish specific goals over which you have control.
- Plan ahead by doing research on the event and people attending.
- Plan who you want to meet and arrange introductions where possible.
- Spend your time "connecting" and laying the groundwork for follow-up. Leave the sales pitch for later.

Conversation

What is it? A mystery! It's the art of never seeming bored, of touching everything with interest, of pleasing with trifles, of being fascinating with nothing at all. How do we define this lively darting about with words, of hitting them back and forth, this sort of brief smile of ideas which should be conversation?

Guy de Maupassant

Chapter 8

The Big Deal About Small Talk
Smooth Your Way with Good Conversation

Conversational skill, that is the ability to communicate with others verbally with ease and with confidence, is consistently a better predictor of business and personal success than any other factor. How far you go, in whatever career you choose, often has more to do with your conversational skill than with your intelligence, education, socio-economic background, diligence or how good you are at your job. So while good relationships are the foundation of networking success, it's conversation that makes these relationships possible. Regardless of how smart, loyal, diligent, kind, caring and thoughtful you are, if people don't know, it doesn't matter in the world of business advancement and career success. It all goes back to <u>what you show, not what you know</u>. Through conversation we get to know each other; assess character and attitudes; exchange ideas and opinions; find common ground;

build trust; and lay the foundation for future business relationships.

Small Talk vs. Conversation

Most dictionaries define conversation as something like "...the informal oral exchange of information or ideas." These days conversation is also a complex process of relationship-building through the exchange of words and visual signals. We typically don't really get into real "conversation" without indulging in some "small talk" first. Small talk is that superficial talking you do right when you first meet, something like warming up before you start the real exercise. Common subjects such as news, weather, sports are the foundation of small talk because they are safe, relatively risk free and don't require any in-depth knowledge.

Usually, by tiptoeing through some small talk, you find some common interests and then, if you want to do so, you move on into the deeper process of conversation and relationship building. Both conversation and small talk are skills in which we can make rapid improvement by focussing on the key areas discussed below. If you feel you need more help with conversation, refer to my previous book "Good Conversation is for Everyone."

Use and Provide Free Information

When most conversations falter, they do so not because the participants don't have anything in common to talk about, but because one or both participants aren't giving or using "free information." Free information is the cornerstone of all good conversation. Free information includes any unsolicited comments and information provided by the speaker, in addition to answering a specific question or following the main thread of conversation.

Consider the traditional *"Good morning. How are you?"* question, which John asks of Neetha as they both arrive at work at the same time on Friday morning. Neetha answers *"Hi John. I'm great! It looks like I'll finally be able to go camping this weekend."* Everything after *"I'm great!"* is free information, since it is provided in addition to the main answer. John can either continue on his way, ask a new question or follow up on the free information with something like *"I didn't know you were into camping. I love backpacking and trail camping. What kind of camping do you do?"* In addition to following up, John has added his own free information about backpacking.

Unfortunately, more often than not, we are so focussed on the ritual of saying good morning, worrying about what to say, or on accomplishing some other objective, that we don't really listen to the answers, and we often miss these invitations to explore. If both participants continue to provide these short snippets of information with each comment or answer, and both parties are listening well, then there's more than enough fuel to keep the conversation going.

Ask Open-Ended Questions

Ritual questions such as *"How are you?"* and closed questions such as *"Do you drive to work?"* don't promote conversation because they invite short, specific answers. Although you could include some free information with your answer, the way in which these questions are phrased doesn't encourage that. In most general conversations, the best questions are unstructured ones that allow indeterminate replies. These are called open or open-ended and include words such as "what", "how" and "tell me about." Ideally they should encourage thinking, require several words or phrases to answer, and also invite people to share and expand (e.g. If the conversation is about commuting to work, a question such as *"What's your trip to work like in the morning?"* is a much more effective opening than *"Do you drive to work?"*)

Listen, Really Listen...

There's a big difference between *listening* and *waiting for your turn to talk*. Often there's so much going on around us that it's very tempting to finish off the other person's sentences, interrupt, eavesdrop on a nearby conversation or to let your mind wander to other things you need to deal with. When this temptation strikes, resist!

Listening should be an active process that takes all of your attention. If you approach the conversation with an open and accepting mind, you'll find you hear much more and learn interesting new information. You'll never know what value the message has until you hear it. Even if you don't think you're interested in the topic or person, stop, wait and listen. Let the speaker finish, without assuming that you know where he is going with his words, even if he is taking a long time to get to the point or you disagree. Interrupting, for any reason, is rude and implies that you think what you have to say is more important than what the other person has to say or that you think you can say it better or faster.

Work at tuning out common distractions such as background noise and other conversations. If you actively listen to what's being said, not only will you get better information, but the speaker will also be able to tell that you're really interested. Try not to let your mind wander. Focus on the primary message and try to avoid thinking about your weekend, your vacation plans, the next conversation or anything that doesn't pertain to the immediate conversation. Don't doodle, look around, shuffle your papers, go through your bag...

It's not enough to listen when you're in conversation, you also have to be seen to be listening. If you've ever stood talking to someone and been confronted by either a blank expression or eyes that flit around the room, you'll know how distracting it is. Concentrate on showing your interest honestly by leaning in, nodding when you agree, asking for clarification, making supportive comments and smiling when appropriate.

...And Don't Forget to Share

Most of us have been brought up believing that the best way to be a good listener is to ask many questions and to let the other person do all the talking. Many of us have also been taught it's rude to talk about yourself too much. Yes, you should ask some open-ended questions, and yes, you should listen with genuine interest and respect, but any one-sided conversation eventually becomes boring, for both of you. One person is doing all the "giving" and one is just "taking." People may assume that you're snobbish or that you have nothing to offer. Even if you think that people aren't really interested in you or what you have to say (mostly this is an incorrect assumption anyway), you need to hold up your end of the conversation. Remember, it's an *exchange* of information and you can't find common ground if one of you isn't contributing.

If you are actively involved in hobbies or sports, are able to talk about your work in an interesting way and are genuinely interested in other people's opinions about the things you are involved in, you should have more than enough to say for your end of the conversation.

Be Interesting and Informed

Now and then I do run into someone who genuinely has little to talk about, more so than just being afraid to share. They're not involved in any activities outside of work. They don't seem to read the paper or keep up with the news. They don't offer an opinion on anything that's happening. In these instances it can be really tough for even the best conversationalist to keep the exchange of information going.

In most conversations, there are really only three possible topics of conversation - you, the other person and the rest of the world. In the above sections you've read about listening well (so you can talk about them) and being prepared to share (so you can talk about you), so all that's left is being able to talk about what's going on in the rest of the world. To be sure you can hold up your end of the conversation, you need to keep informed on what's happening in the world around you. Mostly this means keeping up with the news and current events - especially on those areas where you don't have a particular interest. So if you don't like sports, scan the sports headlines. If you aren't really interested in the business news, listen to the short business bulletins on an all news station. If you haven't already done so, try completing the Conversation Builder in Appendix B. It gives you a way of assessing the breadth of your general knowledge. If you find yourself consistently unfamiliar with a specific area, make a special effort to learn more.

Once you have the information, develop an opinion on current issues. You don't need to be controversial or argumentative, but if all you do is repeat news, people might as well read the paper. Your analysis and opinion is what makes the conversation interesting, and it allows people to learn more about you.

Words Aren't Everything

Remember from Chapter 2 that less than ten percent of our spoken conversation is through *what* we say. The rest is how we say it. Approximately fifty five percent is related to body language including facial expression, gestures, posture and other body movements. The rest is communicated through voice (including rate, pitch, volume).

Body language is important in order to show you are listening (by leaning in, nodding, smiling etc.) and also in reflecting your passion and enthusiasm for whatever you are talking about (energetic, sad, serious, angry). What's really important is that much of this non-verbal communication happens before we even begin talking, so the conversation could be in trouble before you say a word. If you're interested in talking to the other person, or enthusiastic about your subject, make sure that your body language and voice matches your feelings. Smile before you even start talking. Don't fidget and play with your hair or doodle. Don't be afraid to use emphatic gestures. When you're excited, sound excited. If you're interested in learning more about body language, try watching a television show or news report without the sound turned on. See how much you can infer just by watching.

Finally, one small note of caution - while it's a good idea to make sure your body is generally saying what you want it to say and that it's agreeing with what's coming out of your mouth, reaching firm conclusions and making judgements about other people based on their body language is risky. People show their feelings in many different ways and many other people are quite unaware of their body language - so in this instance, give them the benefit of the doubt.

CHAPTER EIGHT SUMMARY

Good conversational skill is essential for building relationships. Improve your conversations by:

- Providing and using "free information."
- Asking open-ended questions and listening actively.
- Being interesting & informed, and sharing information about yourself.
- Making sure your body language and voice agree with your words.

We cannot always oblige; but we can always speak obligingly.

Voltaire

Chapter 9

Mind Your Manners
Use Business Etiquette to Your Advantage

These days we don't often sit down to formal dinners. In some workplaces "Casual Fridays" have spread to become casual every day. Using first names is much more common than going with titles. Does etiquette really matter any more? Isn't etiquette an anachronism? If it does still matter, how is it relevant in networking?

Networking is all about building relationships to mutual advantage. Etiquette is all about showing respect for others and recognizing that "rules of conduct" make it easier for everyone to work together and get to know each other. Understanding conventions and norms of social and business behaviour can help you create and maintain a positive first impression - one of being intelligent, articulate, informed, gracious and self-assured. Your good manners will make others more comfortable around you.

Courtesy and respect might not actually get you the referral, the job, the information or the sale but they can help close the deal and make others more comfortable around you. Poor manners and sloppy behaviour will make sure you don't get anywhere but out the door or waiting by the phone. Appropriate behaviour is important in all relationships and the higher up you get in the business world, the more critical these "rules of conduct" can be to your success.

Not only do good manners make you look more respectful, authoritative and professional, but "knowing the rules" can make you feel more confident and actually improve your performance in stressful situations. Remember being invited out for dinner and not knowing when to stand up/sit down, what to do with the napkin, which bread plate was yours, which fork to use, or whether it was alright to order a drink or dessert? Etiquette basics can take these worries off your "plate" and leave you to pay attention to what's really important - building relationships.

More Choices, More Opportunities to Blunder

Today we do live in a far more relaxed environment than the one in which our parents and grandparents grew up. In both our business and social surroundings we have more choices available to us. Unfortunately all this openness and increased choice actually make life more difficult for us. As few as ten years ago, life was much simpler. Whether you were going to work, to a business lunch, a convention or a reception, there were no real decisions to make. In most cases you just wore a suit and referred to everyone by their title. Rules for dining and attending parties were equally straightforward. Executives mostly didn't mix with regular staff so you didn't really need to worry about how to relate to people outside your level. Today you always have to <u>decide</u>. Will that be business casual, formal suit or really casual? Since fast food and casual dining are the norm, most people aren't familiar with the multiple utensils and complexity of a formal dinner. How do you behave if you're having lunch with the CEO? Everywhere there are choices, decisions and questions.

Fortunately, good manners and proper etiquette usually make sense and so they aren't that difficult to learn or follow. Want to know when casual dress is really suitable? Who pays for what at the networking lunch? How do you introduce people correctly? Can I leave my cell phone on in a meeting? Will I offend her if I hold the door open? Which fork is the right one? This chapter includes general guidelines for behaviour in the areas where people today have the most choices and usually the most difficulty. It covers the basics of clothing, handshaking, eating out, introductions, language and using business cards. It will also help you identify any specific areas where you may need more detailed information and advice.

The Clothes Make the Man (or Woman)

Well, not really, but they might as well because the people you meet jump to a whole lot of conclusions about you based on how you're dressed. You can use this to your advantage by ensuring you always dress in a manner that's appropriate to the impression you want to leave behind - or send on ahead.

Regardless of the generally acceptable attire in your usual place of work or business circles, any man or woman serious about meeting people and networking should own and be comfortable in each of the following types of dress.

Traditional / Formal Business Dress: For men the traditional, formal business wear usually includes a dark coloured business suit and tie. This is coordinated with leather shoes and belt and dark coloured socks. Women wear business-type skirt or pants suit with traditional leather pumps. Some formal business environments still heavily favour women wearing skirts over pants.

General Business Wear: General business attire is still fairly formal but takes a more relaxed approach. For men, this usually means a blazer or sport coat over dress shirt and tailored dress pants. Here women are more free to wear pants suits as well as coordinated separates. As with men, the outfit should include some type of jacket, blazer or sport coat. Again, both men and women should wear coordinated hosiery, leather shoes and belt if necessary.

Business Casual: This is probably the toughest category to define and is very dependent on the industry you work in (not just your company). For men this most often includes khakis or other wrinkle resistant pants combined with a knit type collared shirt, coordinated socks and leather loafers. Women can wear a sweater instead of a jacket along with matching pants/skirt and shirt or blouse. Because this is probably the most confusing and discretionary category, and also in much demand, many stores have developed "business casual" sections and special product lines. While some very informal companies in information technology and arts allow jeans, T-shirts and athletic shoes, these don't really qualify as business casual - they're just plain casual.

Formal Evening Wear: While you don't need to rush out and buy a tuxedo or floor-length black evening dress, you do need to be able to dress suitably for more formal receptions and seasonal celebrations.

So what do you wear where? Your goal is to look classy and professional, whatever the situation. This means paying attention to the culture in your workplace, the trends in your industry and the norms among the people with whom you are mixing. It's just as bad to show up in a banker's suit when everyone else is in khakis as it is to show up in khakis when everyone else is all suited up. So check! Ask. Find out what the executives in that company usually wear. Do some Internet research. Phone up the HR department and ask (no one has to know who is calling). It's always worth a little advance scouting. For after-hours events, receptions, conferences and workshops, you can usually figure out what would be appropriate. If people are coming during or immediately after work hours, they probably won't change. If it's an evening affair where people have had time to go home to change, it will probably be more formal. At conferences and workshops away from the office, dress is usually more relaxed than at work but again, check. If you are not entirely sure, dress for the more formal probability. You can always take off the jacket.

The trouble with rules and guidelines is that there are always all kinds of exceptions. Clothing is a very industry-specific thing. Some groups are very casual, right down to jeans and T-shirts (but never for an interview!), some are more flamboyant and colourful and some really value individuality. Most often, changing once you get where you're going isn't an option, so ask, check, double check, and investigate.

Being prepared for the four basic style categories doesn't mean everyone has to look the same. Not at all! Within each category there is plenty of room for individual expression. If picking out clothes and matching accessories aren't your forte, consult with an expert. Most of the better clothing stores have knowledgeable staff who can help you plan and coordinate styles and colours that work for you, your budget and your networking or career goals.

Introductions

Introductions help oil the networking machinery, assisting all participants to develop relationships more quickly and easily. When you're the host, it's also the expected thing for you to do, and being able to introduce people correctly, with warmth and sincerity, will only reflect well on you.

While favouritism, organizational structure-based rank, "consequence" and perceived importance may be less visible in today's relaxed and casual environment, distinctions are still noteworthy in the process of making introductions. The "less important" person is introduced to the "more important" person. So the introduction usually begins something like..."Mr. More Important, I'd like you to meet my partner Mr. Less Important, who works in..." Perceived importance usually relates to seniority, fame, age, experience, popularity, relative success, political office or position in the company. Clients, visitors or guests usually (not always though) are viewed as being "more important." With introductions among peers, order is flexible, but it doesn't hurt to vary the order so there isn't any perceived bias or elevation in stature.

Along with the introductions by name, it's polite and helpful to include a few additional details that help people remember each other and establish relevance for future conversation. e.g. *"Mr. Armitage, I'd like you to meet Joe Smith. Joe is a real estate agent from Chicago who has just published a great book on home buying. Joe, this is Mr. Fred Armitage, the book agent who helped Marilyn increase her book sales last year."* Fred is considered more "important" than Joe because he is in a position to help Joe with his book distribution. Each of them now have sufficient information to continue the conversation if/when the introducer moves on but...it's much more polite for the host not to rush off immediately after the introduction.

If you are the guest and someone has failed to introduce you, do it yourself. The longer people stay near each other without an introduction, the more awkward it can become. *"Hello, I don't think we've met yet. I'm Janice Freedman, a friend of Michael's from the university..."* (See chapter 3, "It's What You Show, Not What You Know" for more on self-introductions.) Skip any fancy titles - just use your first and last name. Any interesting credentials are bound to come out later in the conversation and it only sounds pretentious to slide them in right at the beginning.

Handshaking 101

Greeting each other with a firm handshake is one of the rituals of meeting people in our Western business world. While it may be a formality that most of us go through without much thought, never underestimate its importance. A handshake is still widely believed to convey trust and sincerity, perhaps a carry-over from medieval days when you first had to put down your sword in order to shake. Whatever the history, current research supports the trust theory. The Incomm Center for Trade Show Research studied visitor responses with and without handshakes and found shaking hands resulted in *"higher degree of intimacy and trust within a matter of seconds"* and that when you shake hands on meeting someone new, they are twice as likely to remember you than if you didn't shake hands.

The handshake is part of that all-important first impression and people are sizing you up as you shake. As with just about every other aspect of networking, your goal is to appear confident, authoritative and capable without sending out any negative signals (sweaty palms, dead fish handshake, finger-only touch). If you aren't used to the process, practice on friends and relatives until it becomes second nature. First, make sure you're standing up. After discreetly ensuring your hand is warm and dry and while looking directly at the other person, extend your hand, thumb pointing upwards, and with a firm (but not bone-breaking) grip, clasp hands. Then pump two or three (max) times and release. That's it. No two handed grips, no power play, no hanging on to the other person's shoulder at the same time. The whole thing should only last two to three seconds, so don't keep the grip even if the introduction drags on. If you have cold hands and can't seem to warm them up, just make some suitable remark about the room temperature or having just come in from outside.

In most cases, the person hosting the meeting, reception, party or event initiates the handshake, but if it isn't forthcoming a few seconds into the greeting, feel free to extend your hand. Some men still wait for the woman to extend her hand first so if this seems to be happening, women should oblige by reaching out shortly after meeting or being introduced. Handshaking hasn't always been as common for women as it has been for men and so many women still find the process uncomfortable, especially when greeting other women. Today a handshake is usually expected, regardless of gender, and most business meetings and meals begin and end with a handshake.

What about hugs and kisses? While they may be acceptable in the art, entertainment or fashion world, hugs and kisses are inappropriate in business. Unless you know the other person really well and/or haven't seen him/her in a long time, avoid this practice. Even so, greeting one person with a hug/kiss and others with a handshake broadcasts all kinds of messages about inequity and familiarity. Best bet...if it's business, stick to handshakes.

Eating Out

Most networking involves getting to know people outside of your office, department and workplace and while you can begin relationships at conferences, workshops and other events, sooner or later you'll find yourself meeting to talk over coffee, drinks or a meal. At the same time, many employers now include a dinner or breakfast interview as part of the screening process for the short list of candidates. This section includes a few basic guidelines to help you through some of the most commonly confusing situations encountered while "eating out" for business. If you find yourself regularly dining out in formal settings for business, or if you often encounter multicultural dining situations, you might consider reading a more detailed manual on the subject.

He (she) who extends the invitation, usually picks up the tab. Considering that whenever you ask someone for information or assistance, they're giving you their time and knowledge, the price of coffee or a meal is not much to pay. *"I'd love to hear about how the whole consulting process works...perhaps I could buy you lunch and we could talk some more..."* is how the invitation often goes. Or sometimes it's just *"Perhaps we could continue the conversation over coffee."* Regardless of how you extended the invitation or organized the get-together, if you are the recipient of news, connections, influence or any other networking benefit, you should pay the bill. Sometimes students who are networking to explore the market find that their guest will offer to pay (either on their own, or from an expense account). While it may be tempting, after all he's employed and you're not, you pay the tab. Like everything else in networking, the situation affects how you are perceived. You want to behave with class, grace and dignity. That also means no bickering over the bill so make it clear up front.

Anything on the menu is fair game. Your guest should feel free to order anything on the menu, so invite your guest to a place where both/all of you will be comfortable and you know you can afford the bill. But conversely, when you're the guest, you should stick to a mid-price range. When you are the host at lunch or dinner, make sure you arrive a few minutes early so you can organize who gets the bill with the maitre d'. This is especially true for women since some unenlightened waiters still automatically give the bill to the man at the table.

Play it safe when ordering. Stay away from anything that is potentially messy, difficult to eat, pungent, or which might impede your conversation. Try to avoid anything which takes a lot longer to prepare than what others are having. Order the same number of courses as other people so you don't end up either playing with your utensils or eating alone. If you need to order the wine and aren't sure how/what, ask the waiter *"What do you recommend?"*

Pass the butter, bread and sauce before helping yourself. If the bread, butter or whatever, happens to be parked by your plate and you want to have some, it's polite to offer it to others first. Pick up the bread basket (plate, sauce etc.) and say "Would anyone like some bread?" Offer it to others or pass it around and get yours when it makes it back to you.

In most cases people take their cue about drinks and dessert from the host. If the host is ordering a drink or dessert, you may feel free to do the same. If the host or other guests are overindulging, you should NOT feel free to do the same.

Use cutlery and other items in the order they are presented. Since the napkin is there when you sit down, place it on your lap as soon as all the introductions are completed. When in doubt about the cutlery, work from the outside in. If there are multiple sets of utensils they will usually get cleared with each departing course. Bread and salad plates are usually placed on your left and glasses on your right. If you end up misusing an implement or don't know which to use, don't make a big deal out of it. Most people are too busy worrying about which fork to use themselves. When you're finished a course, rest any utensils together in the centre to centre right of your plate (like clock hands saying 4:20). If you're not done, keep the bottom ends of the utensils apart on either side of your plate (like a clock showing 4:40).

Don't start talking business the moment you sit down. For true "networking" meals out, your goal is to get to know one another as well as to exchange information. While older rules such as "no business until coffee arrives" aren't really observed any more, it's still a good idea to begin with the "getting to know each other" part and let the business slide in later. Even with short business lunches where there is a specific goal to be accomplished, try to spend at least a few minutes catching up and getting (re)acquainted.

If you don't know, think "polite" and do your best without making a big deal about it. Eating out involves a myriad of potential conflicts, problems and new experiences. You can't possibly prepare for them all even if you read up extensively or attend etiquette classes. So when you encounter a situation where your guidelines don't help, first consider what the polite action might be. How would you like to be treated? What would make the others at the table feel most comfortable? If that doesn't work, try following the lead of someone who seems to know what they are doing (although this is risky since may people don't know any more about it than you do). Whatever your choice, stay calm, do your best, be polite and respectful. Most of the time, no one will notice and even if they do, they'll forgive any faux pas in the wake of all your other good manners.

Cell Phone Etiquette

When in doubt, turn it off. Anytime you talk on the phone while you are meeting with others, you're sending the message "This call is more important to me than you are." So unless it really is very important, don't take calls while you're meeting with others. If you do have to leave your cell phone on, turn it on silent mode and excuse yourself if you need to take a call. Explain and apologize ahead of time if you are waiting for a call. Make it short and get back to your meeting.

Your Spoken Words

As with all the other components of etiquette, your language says volumes about you. An experienced listener can usually identify a speaker's geographic, educational and socio-economic background within minutes of beginning a conversation, usually regardless of the actual topic. Your voice and language not only affects how you are perceived but also whether people listen to you and find you believable.

Think polite, respectful and classy. This means no jargon, no slang, no foul language and no questionable jokes - even if others are indulging. You want to make yourself perfectly clear to everyone listening so avoiding colloquialisms is also a good idea. Interrupting is rude and immediately puts you in a negative light. For more on the spoken word, see the chapter on making conversation.

Business Cards

Business cards are a must for anyone serious about networking. Scribbling your contact information on a napkin, piece of paper or someone else's card is unprofessional and inappropriate - and virtually guarantees that it will get lost.

At minimum, your card should contain your name, phone number and e-mail address. Snail mail address and some indication of your line of work are also helpful. If you buy your own cards, as opposed to company mandated cards, spend some time thinking about the image you want to convey. Good cards are a small price to pay and can leave a lasting impression. Avoid overly pretentious, glitzy cards with fancy titles that don't really add value. In most cases, your business card is a supporting document that reinforces your face to face meeting. Your card should suit you, your image, and clearly support the impression you establish in person.

If you have trouble developing a good business card, do some additional research or get some professional help. It's worth the relatively small investment. Dirty, dog-eared, out of date cards or cards with handwritten corrections won't make you look very professional or credible. Plain business card cases can be picked up for a couple of dollars. Buy a few and make sure you always have plenty of current business card in every briefcase, purse, jacket and travel case.

Business Gifts

Occasionally you will want to give thank you gifts but keep these to the minimum. In recent years, especially in the public sector, gifts are frowned upon. Even when employees are allowed to accept gifts, many have to "declare" them to ensure no conflict of interest. If you're sure that a gift is needed and appropriate, stay with traditional items such as gift baskets. They might not be very exciting but it will keep you out of trouble - this is one area where it's better not to stand out. For more information on saying "thank you" see the chapter "Out of Sight is Out of Mind."

When You Don't Know the Rule

People have written tomes on etiquette. Others make a living at teaching etiquette. So it stands to reason that you're going to run into situations where you don't know the "right" behaviour, answer or rule. Your first choice is always to check and find out in advance. This is especially true in multicultural situations where you can't necessarily reason it out.

If you don't have time to check (as in you need an answer now), consider applying the Golden Rule - treat others the way you would like to be treated. If you make a social gaffe, don't make a big deal about it. Just apologize and move on.

CHAPTER NINE SUMMARY

Good manners and etiquette make it easier for everyone to work together.

Master the basics of etiquette so you can concentrate your energy on making connections instead of worrying about which fork to use.

When in doubt, apply the Golden Rule.

Ask and it shall be given you; seek and ye shall find; knock, and it shall be opened unto you.

Book of Matthew

Chapter 10

If You Could Read My Mind
When You Need Something, Ask!

You've been nurturing your network for what seems like an eternity. You've met lots of interesting people and made sure that you, in turn, are interesting and informed. You've even managed to help out a few other people along the way. Now, you need something - a referral, a place on a work team, a summer job for your daughter, career advice, a shot at the big proposal, or just some help with your résumé or cover letter.

First of all, not asking isn't a viable option; neither is hinting or dancing around the issue. You can't expect people to guess at your needs, even if they know you well. That would be much like having someone else in your family order your meal for you at a restaurant. If you're lucky, you may get something satisfactory, but you're unlikely to get exactly what you wanted at that particular meal. Sooner or later, <u>you will have to come right out and ask</u> for whatever it is that you need.

For many people, "asking" is the single toughest part of networking. If they say yes, great; but what if they say no? This is where you have to put yourself on the line and face the possibility of rejection. There are all kinds of psycho-social issues at play here. For some people it's just that possibility of rejection. Others feel as if they are "using" people. Many believe it's an imposition or that no one would want to help them out. Whatever the reason, there are some basic facts and guidelines that can help you overcome this hurdle.

People Really Don't Mind Helping.

<u>People don't mind!</u> Honest! No, it isn't an imposition and no, they won't think less of you for asking. But before you worry about other people, ask yourself how <u>you</u> feel about helping other people? Are you ready, willing to do whatever you can, regardless of whether there's any obvious benefit in it for you? If you aren't, work on this first. Networking requires a great deal of selfless giving. It's definitely worth it, but there is rarely an immediate return. Once you're sure that you can do your part, ask yourself, why wouldn't others do the same?

Over the years, I've had hundreds of people call me up and ask for help in many different ways. Referrals, advice, support, as long as they know what they want and a suitable direct or indirect relationship exists, no problem. In researching this book, I interviewed dozens of managers, executives and professionals, asking how they felt about being asked for help, information or favours. The answer was a resounding *"No, I don't mind at all."* A Vice-President at a brokerage firm said *"My job is so competitive and tough on relationships, it's actually nice to be able to help someone else along for a change."* A hospital CEO commented *"I welcome people coming to me for career advice...in fact I like helping."* These comments are from busy, successful and well known people - and aren't they the ones from whom you want to learn and get help?

Make Sure the Relationship is Ready

Most of the people in the above survey also added something like *"...as long as the request is reasonable and comes from someone I respect."* Asking for help too early in a networking relationship can ruin a good contact. How do you know if it's too early? This is something you need to judge for yourself but you can work it out logically.

The bigger the request in terms of inconvenience and personal risk for the individual being asked, the stronger the relationship needs to be in order to support the request. Think of your company CEO you've met once at a Christmas party. You found you went to the same university and have the same major in your MBA. He went on and got a second graduate degree elsewhere. You seemed to connect well. You talked for about five minutes regarding which degrees are best for certain jobs. Calling up that CEO to ask for a job, referral or a "good word" is presumptuous and probably won't get you very far. Asking that same CEO if you could buy him coffee and talk about what kinds of degrees would be best for you next, is quite OK. When in doubt, try mentally reversing roles. How would you feel about being asked? Consider also the time commitment involved. For many people, time is their most precious resource. Things such as making a quick phone call, asking a secretary to send out some statistics, or dictating a short letter of recommendation, don't take much time. Meeting for coffee or lunch may be low risk but a big demand in a busy schedule - so be flexible about when and where you meet.

Asking the Question

If you stumble into asking, mumbling and masking your

request with *"I hope you don't mind..."* and other such qualifiers, you'll make whomever you're asking uncomfortable. Often they really want to help but aren't sure exactly how, so make it easy for them. Before you pop the question, use the following four suggestions to work out what you are going to say.

Be sure they can help. Just because Lana did a project five years ago over at General Motors, doesn't mean that she can help get you an interview with their design department. The quality of other people's networking relationships will vary. Time passes. GM is a big company. Who knows how well Lana's project went. Do your homework <u>before</u> asking. That way you won't put anyone in the awkward position of having to decline your request because they can't do as you are asking.

Be specific about what you want them to do. If you need a lead, say so. If you want some career advice, ask. If you would like a written letter of introduction or endorsement, say so. Vague requests such as *"I know they'd be much more interested in interviewing me if they heard from someone else how good I was,"* doesn't do the job. Much more effective is *"John, you're friends with that recruiter over at Lyon's, aren't you? Would you talk to her and mention how well that project I organized for your company went?"* So whether you want a call, a letter, information, education, statistics or anything else, spell it out. In instances where you want a testimonial or written reference, you might even consider offering some sample letters. I do this all the time with testimonials. It saves them time and when a client is happy with my work, they're pleased to oblige.

Be concise and don't drag out the request. If you've laid the ground work well and you have a well established relationship, outline the situation and make your request. Spending too much time building up to the question only makes things awkward and makes you appear weak.

Ask the right question. Hopeful "can you help"type questions usually don't yield much. *"Do you know anyone who could help with my application to Lincoln Plus?"* is too vague, doesn't say what kind of help you need, and makes it too easy to answer *"well, not really..."* Much better is, *"Gary, whom do you know over at Lincoln Plus that I could call to ask a few questions about this Systems Analyst position?"* That request makes it clear what you need and is much harder to refuse.

Give enough notice and information. When giving help of any kind, most people like to know exactly what they are getting into, and possible consequences, and to have enough time to complete the task on their schedule. It's unreasonable to ask a colleague to make a call, write a letter, go through their files or anything else, today. The bigger the task, the more notice you should try to provide; just don't leave the request open-ended. Without getting into excessive details, provide all the necessary information about who, what, when, where and why. If there is a deadline, say so.

If You Still Can't Do It

You know it's alright to ask. You believe it's not a really big favour. You're positive he is able to do what you are asking. You know you've done stuff for him in the past. But...when it comes right down to it, you just can't make yourself pick up the phone and say the words or, when the opportunity comes up in the conversation, you just let it go by (kicking yourself when you get home or back to your office). All is not yet lost.

Consider a different environment. Some people are really good on the phone. Others are much more comfortable face-to-face where they can read body language. Many of us prefer informal, casual conversations while some prefer to ask in formal, office situations. Find your comfort zone. You can also do it in steps. First ask for a meeting. Then pop the question once you've introduced the subject. Just try not to make a really big deal of it.

Pick a Time. Make the Call.

One well known company president I've worked with hates calling anyone, to ask for anything. Even though she knows her fear is illogical, that she is well regarded, and that people usually go out of their way to help her, she still finds it virtually impossible to "pop the question." When I ask her, she admits that no one has ever actually said no. Although she really fears asking, she knows that she does have to do it if she needs support. Sometimes she needs to be assured of backing at a board meeting or in delicate negotiations.

Her solution is to schedule it like a meeting. She says she writes down what she wants to say (in case the words get away from her) and then books a time, say 11:07 a.m. Tuesday. She tries for a time she knows the other person is usually available. She won't schedule anything else really difficult that morning and tells herself that calling is the ONLY major task on her list. At 11:07 she picks up the phone and calls. The script keeps her on track and even if she gets voice mail, she leaves a message and moves on. *"That way I don't have to obsess about it for days. I know once I set a time, it's like a meeting. I have to be there."*

Borrow Some Courage and Support

If you're still nervous, consider bringing along some help. *"Fred and I were talking about what a great opportunity this project is. You know I'd love to be involved Peter."* Sometimes bringing a third person into the conversation (at least in spirit), can help soften the discomfort and shift the focus away from the request and onto a different aspect of the subject. Make sure you really do discuss it with Fred though and that you do get your question in there. But...don't fall into the common trap of trying to shift responsibility. Something like *"Fred suggested I talk to you about getting on the project"* just weakens your request and makes you look ineffectual and timid.

Accept that Sometimes People Will Say No

Despite all your hard work, research, planning, groundwork and relationship-building, sometimes people will say no. Good preparation can minimize the probability, but still, "no" happens. Sometimes your relationship isn't as good as you thought it was. Occasionally other people build themselves up beyond their real capability. Perhaps you don't have all the information about the cost of whatever you're asking. Regardless of the reason, as long as it's only happening infrequently, accept that it's a normal part of networking and move on. If you find that you're unsuccessful more often than not, it's time to re-examine your relationships. Do an honest analysis of your "networking capital." Have you been holding up your end of relationships? See if all your assumptions are correct. Talk it over with someone you respect and then try again.

CHAPTER TEN SUMMARY

In order to reap the benefits of your networking activities, you have to ask for help when you need it.

When you want to ask:

- Be sure they can help
- Be specific
- Be concise
- Give enough information and notice

---

*Give me a stock clerk with a goal
and I'll give you a man who will
make history.*

*Give me a man with no goals and
I'll give you a stock clerk.*

J. C. Penney

Chapter 11

Anywhere's Not a Better Place to Be
Make a Plan and Work the Plan

"One day Alice came to a fork in the road and saw a Cheshire cat in a tree. Which road do I take? she asked. Where do you want to go? was his response. I don't know, Alice answered."

"Then, said the cat, it doesn't matter." (Lewis Carroll)

Networking is fun! Absolutely! You meet really interesting people and learn many important lessons along the way. Many people do approach networking in this way. They go to receptions, lunches and conventions with some vague thought of "meeting people." Sometimes they connect, get a lead or learn something new, but in many cases it's all very serendipitous - helpful, fun, occasionally exciting and rewarding, but all quite accidental and passive.

If we were all like Alice in Wonderland, that might be enough, but "fun" isn't quite why people network nor, presumably, why you picked up this book. We all have goals for business, career and personal advancement and active networking is a vehicle to help us meet those goals. Networking without specific goals is like choosing a vacation destination by showing up at the airport and boarding whichever plane was leaving that day. It might get you somewhere really interesting and enjoyable, but most likely not. The best vacations usually are those in which we have a clear goal, a well thought out (but not necessarily rigid) plan and a realistic budget. So it is with networking. A well thought out networking plan makes it much more likely that you'll achieve your desired goals, and meet them more quickly. Along the way you'll still meet many interesting people, reap some unexpected rewards and help many others meet their goals.

Your Networking Plan

Most well developed "plans" have several common elements including specific goals, objectives, milestones, budget, resources, evaluation criteria and target dates. The main distinguishing feature of a good networking plan is that it is a long-term endeavour, or a work-in-progress, rather than a single use, time-limited document. Beginning your networking plan may take several days or weeks. Fortunately, you don't have to finish the plan before you start working on the implementation.

You can record and manage it all in a binder, on computer, on your palm organizer - whatever works for you as long as you include sections for your goals, objectives, resources, and budget analysis.

What Do You Want to Accomplish Through Networking?

Begin by evaluating where you are and what you want to accomplish. Most of us have a specific key "goal" that we hope to achieve in the long-run. It can be anything you like...becoming company president, starting up your own business, changing careers or getting elected to political office (e.g. Angelina, whom you met earlier in this book, works as a hospital Program Manager and wants to open up an independent rehabilitation therapy clinic). Michael is the department director who wants to move up into senior management. Just remember, this is your goal.

Don't let your goal or "vision" be constrained by lack of credentials, support or knowledge. Clearly you can't get a degree in a month or two, nor can you become a city council member in a short time, but if you're prepared to invest the time and effort, your plan can get you there. After all, you're networking to help fill in these gaps.

Once you've identified your key goal, list any specific objectives or "stepping stones" that you already know you'll have to achieve along the way. Again, these objectives can be anything, as long as they'll get you closer to realizing your goal. Over time you will refine, update and maybe even change your list.

What Else Will You Need to Accomplish These Goals?

Do a realistic assessment of what stands between you and your goals and objectives. Do you have a good idea of what you need to do or will you need help to develop a beginning plan? Will you need additional education, certification or accreditation. Pay particular attention to any activities that will take considerable time to accomplish (e.g. getting a part-time degree). You'll want to get started on those immediately, in some way (e.g. finding out about loans for mature students). Write down the broad tasks first and then break them down into smaller, more manageable activities.

Who Will You Need to Help You with the Above?

Here you want to list everyone you might need, by role, or name if you have it, without letting details, like the fact that you don't know any of these people, get in the way. Make a comprehensive list. Over time you'll add and remove names from this list. Who can help you establish your plan? Who can help you get the right information? Who has already accomplished what you'd like to achieve? Is there anyone doing the job whom you particularly admire? (e.g. If you want to run for provincial government office in the future, and you don't know anything about how to get there, you should speak to a member of parliament early on in the process.)

Who Do You Know Now?

List all of the people whom you know now. Don't qualify this list in any way other than these people should either know you or at least recognize your name if you reintroduced yourself. It's not just a list of people you know well, or from whom you could ask a favour today. Statistically speaking, the average person should be able to come up with a list of around 250 people. Some people will have more, some a few less. If you're having trouble coming even close to this number, take a structured approach. First list the family members on all sides. Now list all the people with whom you work at your current job, and then at past jobs. With whom did you go to school that you could still track down? What about church members, people at the gym, parents of your children's friends, Scout Leaders, neighbours, members of your community association? Don't forget clubs, professional associations, the cleaning staff at work and the waitress at the restaurant where you have lunch every Friday.

Once you have the list, write in what you know about these people. List any useful information about jobs, employers, educational background, relatives. This will take some time so when you're adding this information, don't start with all the people in one group such as all your university friends, or all your family. Just to make it more diverse, and immediately useful, work on "filling in the blanks" a few people at a time from each part of your life. You might also start with the people you know best, then pick up background information on others over time.

Who, on Your List, Can Help You?

Compare the lists of "whom you know" and "whom you need". Who can help you now? With whom will you need to get reacquainted first? Who can help you get to some of the people you'll need in the long run. Sometimes you'll have an ally right there waiting for you. Other times you will begin quite far from your target people and work towards them gradually. Focus your first networking conversations on the people you already know and add others gradually. Again, for diversity, spend some time getting to know a few people with whom you wouldn't normally associate.

Which Current Activities Support Networking?

Look at the activities, clubs, associations and organizations with which you are currently involved. Start with the ones that are "required" such as mandatory work committees, classes your children attend, any memberships you are required to maintain and activities you really enjoy. Evaluate these for networking potential. Now look at the "optional" activities - those where you "just belong" and don't really do much. Do they have any networking potential. Are they a good use of your time? Can they be replaced with better opportunities?

What's Your Time Budget?

In networking, the biggest expense is your time. If you can incorporate networking activities into your daily life, it doesn't have to be a great deal of "extra" time, but if you're new to networking or haven't maintained your relationships, you will need to make specific additional effort. How can you better use existing activities? How much additional time are you prepared to spend? What are specific time constraints? Are there ways around these time constraints?

Develop a Working Plan

If there are gaps in your lists and you need to meet some new and different people, list these in order of priority. Since you can't meet everyone and join every club immediately, you'll need to begin with the most important, urgent or helpful connections. Consider where you might meet these people. Are there any clubs, associations, committees you need to join or reevaluate? Remember Angelina's activity grid in the chapter on diversity. Work out a similar chart for yourself, ensuring it gets you to the people you want to meet and fits in with your time budget.

Prepare Yourself

Get yourself ready to network by developing a set of self-introductions. Remember what you read in "It's What You Show, Not What You Know," these are foundations to work from, not a line you toss out every time you meet a new person.

How will you "Stand Out Above the Noise" and distinguish yourself? Will you need help to do this? If so, add these names to your lists.

Start Working the Plan

Begin today with a list of people you need to call, reconnect with, or just touch base with. On the list, be clear about why you need to talk to them. Set yourself a goal of how many people you want to contact per day, week or month. Whether you decide on one person per day or one per week, begin making those calls today. Record how it went. Did you meet your goal for the call? What will you do differently next time?

Do the same for clubs and associations. Who do you want to meet there? Will you meet one new person per event or target a specific individual? Either is fine as long as it serves your purpose and moves you closer to your goal. Take a few minutes before any event and plan to whom you will talk, why and how you will evaluate success. Remember to do your homework before attending any networking events (as discussed in the Chapter ""Being There" is Not Enough.") After each event, jot down a few notes about what went well and what you want to do differently next time.

Make It <u>Your</u> Plan

Make it YOUR plan by adding as much or as little detail as you need in order to be comfortable with it. Some people like to record every call and thank you card. Others like to keep it more general with regular milestones. Whichever you choose, review it daily to begin with and once you're well on your way, review it at least weekly. Make sure you evaluate your activities for their effectiveness and value-added and keep...

...working the plan! Happy Networking!

CHAPTER ELEVEN SUMMARY

Good networking, like vacations, requires careful planning including goals, objectives, resources and target dates.

Evaluate your current contacts against your needed contacts and develop a working plan.

Your "Networking Plan" is a "work-in-progress" that needs frequent revision and re-evaluation. Make it work for you.

Begin working your plan TODAY!

Appendices

Appendix A:　　　Planning Your Self-Introduction

Here is a worksheet in which you can practice developing a self introduction. A sample introduction is included in the light grey.

What is the task that you do? This is for information only so that you can avoid using this to present yourself. *e.g. I help people write resumes and cover letters.*

What need do you fill? *e.g. Most people struggle to write compelling resumes and appealing cover letters, especially those who are new to the country.*

What is important in your work? *e.g. Many people can't articulate what they do for job applications and so miss out on good opportunities. I help them document their skills well in their resume and then develop a cover letter that is relevant, appealing, and does more than repeat what's in their resume.*

Unique strengths. *e.g. I've worked with agencies and HR departments for years. I understand what recruiters & employers are looking for in written applications. I'm also good at helping people identify relevant skills. I'm able to help people better show how their skills suit the needs of prospective employers.*

How does your work affect others? *e.g. I work with new immigrants to help them document their skills and present themselves positively in their written job applications.*

What is the value that you bring? Putting all of the above together to explain your value - this would be the example of what you might say to introduce yourself: *e.g. I work with new immigrants to help them document their skills and present themselves positively in their written job applications. You know how people always struggle to write an eye-catching cover letter? I help them develop one that is relevant, appealing, and that does more than repeat what's in their resume.*

Appendix B: The ConversationBuilder

Use this ConversationBuilder to track your awareness of current affairs topics. Make copies and use a new sheet every day.

Take five minutes each day (over lunch, coffee, on the bus or whenever you can make the time) and complete this chart. For items 1-9, see if you can list the top two items in each category. If you find that you're consistently leaving particular areas blank or have no new information, take the time to specifically look out for these topics in your daily news gathering.

There are also some categories called Family, Work, and Personal (items 10 - 12). Here you list one relevant topic that you'd be willing to talk about and which is suitable for discussion. Completing these sections helps ensure you have material when it's your turn to share information.

Finally, there are the miscellaneous categories (13-16) of entertaining and harmless trivia. These items are your back up when conversation gets stalled and or you need to lighten the mood. Word of the Day (WOTD) helps you increase your vocabulary; and "Duh!" is where you include arcane, silly or ridiculous information presented in the news.

*****

Be Prepared! - Daily Conversation Background Information

1. International Current Events	2. USA Current Events	3. National / Local Current Events	4. Community Events
5. Business Happenings stock market mergers lawsuits	6. Sports News (n.b. wins losses)	7. Movies (new, hot, flopped, star news)	8. Television
9. Weather	10. Family	11. Work	12. Personal
13. WOTD (Word of the Day)	14. Joke	15. Duh!	16. Trivia

Appendix C: Bibliography & Additional Reading

The following list of books related to networking and networking capital is intended to provide readers with additional information and should not be interpreted as an endorsement of any particular author or their opinions.

Crawford, Fred and Mathews, Ryan. (2001) *The Myth of Excellence: Why Great Companies Never Try to Be the Best at Everything.* New York, NY: Three Rivers Press.

Klaus, Peggy. (2003) *Brag: The Art of Tooting Your Horn Without Blowing It.* New York, NY: Warner Books.

Popyk, Bob. (2000) *Here's My Card: How to Network Using Your Business Card to Actually Create More Business.* Los Angeles, CA: Renaissance Books.

Postman, Neil. (1985) *Amusing Ourselves to Death: Public Discourse in the Age of Show Business.* New York, NY.

Penguin Books.

Post, Peggy and Peter. (1999) *The Etiquette Advantage in Business: Personal Skills for Business Success.* New York, NY: Harper Collins Books.

Putnam, Robert. (2000) *Bowling Alone: The Collapse and Revival of the American Community.* New York, NY: Simon & Schuster.

Thompson, Leigh. (2004) *Making the Team: A Guide for Managers.* Upper Saddle River, NJ: Prentice Hall.

The Incomm Center for Trade Show Research
http://www.tradeshowresearch.com

Index

Index

Also Available from Make Your Words Count:

Good Conversation is for Everyone:
Ten Steps To Better Conversations

Do you ever wonder what to say next? Do you live in awe of people who seem to have a natural "gift of the gab?"

Good Conversation is for Everyone who has ever

- felt at a loss for words in conversation
- stayed home from a party to avoid social conversation
- been afraid to "do lunch"
- felt a lack of conversation skill was holding them back in business
- or just needed a little help knowing what to say.

Popular speaker and award winning leader Renate Zorn shares practical tips, facts and a step-by-step approach to improving conversation skills. Written in an easy-to-read and conversational style, the book is filled with personal stories, motivational quotes, real life examples and easy to use suggestions.

Good Conversation is for Everyone includes ideas on:

- beginning, joining and ending a conversation
- finding something to talk about
- being ready for conversation
- understanding body language
- preparing for social events.

Also included are helpful worksheets and self-assessment quizzes. *Good Conversation is for Everyone* is now available at a bookstore near you.

Coming in 2005 from Renate Zorn

There's a Hole in My Bucket
Dissident Stories of Inspiration and Opportunity

Read about some of the faulty assumptions and widespread "system failure" in our social structure and stop letting popular beliefs and establishment thinking deprive you of satisfaction and happiness. This collection of inspirational stories includes:

The Facts of Life

Read along as Anastasia meets a homeless man who teaches her some of the real truths about corporate success, job interviews and trying to please others.

Goodby Old Friend

Bookstores carry *Getting to Yes*, *Turning No into Yes* and 183 other ways to get people to say yes. Well what's so bad about saying no? Find out how bringing "No!" back into the English language and into your vocabulary can make a difference in your life.

No Time for Heroes

Popular celebrity, sports and political heroes turn out to be murderers, rapists and philanderers. Where can you find the real heroes of the 21st century? Try looking in the mirror.

Reduce, Reuse, Recycle

Who are the real winners in mergers and downsizing? What happens to all the people we don't "need" any more? *Reduce, Reuse and Recycle* is a provocative look at what happens to us when the times change faster than we do.

For these and other timely stories including The Big Fix, Sometimes it Takes 47 Years and Graduation Day, watch for *There's a Hole in My Bucket.* Available in bookstores in 2005.

Get to Know the Author

Renate Zorn is a popular speaker and author who helps others live up to their potential and reach their goals. Her message is clear: *You are the only architect of change in your life.* By accepting the challenges you face, making a decision to change, and getting the right help, you can do and be anything you wish.

Renate holds undergraduate and graduate degrees from the University of Toronto with studies including business, communications and psychology. She has been an Educational Consultant at McMaster University for the last fifteen years, and also teaches public speaking, business communication and conversation skills at the Dufferin-Peel Catholic District School Board. She has travelled and studied Canada, U.S., Europe, Australia and throughout Africa and the Caribbean, exploring conversation & other communication skills.

Also published in magazines, newsletters and professional journals, Renate is known for her insight into self-development and communication as keys to personal and business success. Her first book *Good Conversation is for Everyone* received rave reviews in Canada and the U.S. and was featured on shows such as Canada AM & Breakfast Television. Her inspirational third book, *There's a Hole in My Bucket*, will be in bookstores in 2005.

A long time and award winning member of Toastmasters International, Renate is a Distinguished Toastmaster, the highest available award. She has served as trainer, club/district officer, coach, mentor & chief judge and has successfully competed in the Toastmasters International Speech Contest as well as Humorous Speech and Evaluation. Currently she is the coordinator of the Toastmasters District 60 Speakers Bureau.

Renate's home base is in Mississauga, Canada where she lives with her husband, two sons and family dog Remington. In her leisure time she runs, coaches little league soccer and studies Shotokan karate where she has earned her black belt.

To Book Renate for Your Organization

Warm up your audience for a conference, book a retreat workshop or listen to an inspiring keynote presentation. Renate's most popular workshops and keynote presentations include:

* Golf Was Never Just a Game
* No Time for Heroes
* Freedom, Anytime
* Before You Press "Send"
* Sometimes it Takes 47 Years
* What's the Big Deal About Small Talk?

To book Renate to speak to your group or business, contact Make Your Words Count at 905-567-8454 or e-mail to info@makeyourwordscount.com

Additional Copy Ordering Information

Name:	
Company Name:	
Street Address:	

City:	Province/State:
Postal/Zip Code:	Country:
Telephone (　　)	
E-mail Address:	

The Woman in the Red Dress Quantity Ordered @ Can $19.95	Sub-total:
Good Conversation is for Everyone Quantity Ordered @ Can $19.95	Sub-total
Taxes: Canadian residents please add 7% GST	
Shipping & Handling: add 15% for orders under $100.	
Total	

☐ Yes, please add my name to the subscriber list for your electronic Communications newsletter "In the Spotlight."

☐ Yes, please notify me of upcoming releases and new offers.

Mail your order with cheque or money order payable to:

Make Your Words Count!
A12-1250 Eglinton Ave. West. Suite 232
Mississauga, ON. L5V 1N3

Discounts available on large volume orders. Contact us at
info@makeyourwordscount.com

END